Spy Stories for Boys

General von Streimer was seated on the sand, sunbathing.

Spy Stories for Boys

ILLUSTRATED BY Reg Gray

HAMLYN
London · New York · Sydney · Toronto

The publishers wish to express their thanks to I.P.C. Magazines Ltd., for permission to include *Man-Hunt, Time is the Enemy, Spies Die at Dawn* and *Mountain Death* in this collection.

First published 1970
Sixth impression 1978 by
The Hamlyn Publishing Group Limited
LONDON · NEW YORK · SYDNEY · TORONTO
Astronaut House, Feltham, Middlesex, England

ISBN 0 601 08665 1
Printed in Great Britain by Butler & Tanner Ltd,
Frome and London

Contents

Time is the Enemy *by Lee Mayne* 9
Spy Dive *by Geoffrey Cowan* 27
Spies Die at Dawn *by Sean Gregory* 56
The Disappearing Lake *by Joyce Eley* 137
Man-Hunt *by Lee Mayne* 148
Mountain Death *by Howard Braddock* 170
Alpine Assignment 281
Contact Zodiac! *by Justin Long* 290
The Battle of Wits *by Tom Stirling* 314
Ghost Planes *by Lee Mayne* 340

The Hawk plummetted out of the tree.

List of Illustrations

General von Streimer was seated on
the sand, sunbathing. Frontispiece
The Hawk plummetted out of the tree. 6
Perrin tried feverishly to raise the radio operator. 8
Steve was pointing vigorously to one side. 36
His mouthpiece was wrenched free. 51
He came to rest on all fours. 66
Maturez strode over to him, seizing the arms
of the chair. 92
Below in the courtyard, the guards were racing about. 104
More and more pelicans began to descend. 145
The bunk was empty – Giulio had gone. 163
Sammy lay with his head against the polished wood. 195
He hurled Masters sideways and outwards. 225
Confronting them stood a policeman with a
levelled revolver. 246
A vast section of snow had broken loose. 274
'Try removing that jacket,' he suggested. 284
The cyclist scowled and rode on. 301
The tent collapsed in a tangle of heaving canvas. 310
Richard was lying in the long grass. 333
The bullet caught the big cat fair and square. 349

Perrin tried feverishly to raise the radio operator.

Time is the Enemy

by Lee Mayne

Footsteps halted outside the condemned cell of Fresnes Prison in Paris. Carlos Bianchi looked up slowly from the tattered magazine he was reading. A key rattled in the lock and the heavy steel door swung open. For a moment, the little Italian stared dully at the tall, slim man framed in the doorway. Then he sprang to his feet, sending the chair crashing over in his eager excitement.

'The Hawk!' he cried, hoarsely. Inspector Jean Collet, ace Interpol agent, came into the cell. His lean, aquiline face made him look like the fierce, courageous bird after which he was named. But Bianchi knew better. It was the merciless speed with which The Hawk pounced out of the blue that had earned him his name.

The little Italian stared at the visitor. 'You really came,' he said, unbelievingly.

'When a condemned man puts in a special request to see me,' said The Hawk, quietly, 'I'm naturally curious.'

Bianchi grabbed his sleeve. 'Inspector,' he pleaded, 'I need your help. I'm innocent – I swear it! You must believe me!'

'Me believe you?' The Hawk eyed him sternly. 'I've sent you to jail three times.'

'That's *why*,' Bianchi said, unexpectedly. 'Those three times you caught me,' the Italian went on. 'Did I plead innocent?'

The Hawk shook his head.

'Well, now I *am* saying it. I'm a crook – sure. You know my record. Robbery, forgery, fraud – yes. But never any rough stuff. Inspector, I've never committed a crime of violence in my life!'

'That's true,' The Hawk nodded thoughtfully. 'You've never been judged a killer . . . until now,' he added, grimly.

'I didn't do it!' Bianchi cried, intensely. 'I swear I'm innocent! You must believe me! Please, Inspector, help me!'

'Why haven't you asked me before?' The Hawk demanded.

'I didn't really believe an innocent man would be –' Bianchi swallowed '– executed. But now my last appeal has been turned down.'

The Hawk's eyes seemed to bore right through the Italian. It was a look that would make the most hardened criminal quail, but Bianchi did not flinch or try to avoid the gaze. After a few moments, The Hawk rose abruptly. Without another word to the condemned man, he went out. The steel door clanged shut behind him. Bianchi sat staring at the door. Even after he'd gone, The Hawk's dynamic personality still seemed to fill the bleak cell.

In the corridor outside, Duval, the Governor of Fresnes Prison, stood waiting.

'Well?' he asked, as he led the Interpol man back to his office. The Hawk shrugged, noncommittally. 'When is the execution?' he asked.

'Friday at dawn.'

The Hawk eyed him tensely. 'Friday? And it's Tuesday now! That means I've got less than three days.'

'To do what, Inspector?'

'To clear Bianchi.'

In The Hawk's office at Interpol, four men sat around his desk with thick dossiers before them. With The Hawk were his assistant, Paul Laval, Inspector Henri Gardot of the French Sûreté, and Maître Claude Balard, the lawyer who had defended Bianchi at his trial.

Laval closed the dossier he had been reading. 'You're wasting your time, chief,' he said with finality.

The Hawk grunted and turned to Inspector Gardot. 'You handled the case, Henri,' he said. 'What do you think?'

The Inspector shrugged. 'I've never seen a more straightforward case.'

The Hawk eyed him shrewdly. His keen insight sensed something in the Inspector's manner which was not obvious to the others. 'You mean you never had even the slightest shadow of doubt about Bianchi's guilt?'

Inspector Gardot got up, crossed to the window and stood staring out.

'Consider the facts,' he said slowly. 'Bianchi and Vanel, the murdered man, were partners in crime. They did a job together in Rome. Bianchi was caught and went to jail. Vanel got away scot-free.

'When Bianchi was released, he made straight for Vanel's home, here in Paris, presumably to get his cut of the proceeds of the Rome crime.' The Sûreté detective paused for a moment while he lit his pipe. He looked faintly ill at ease.

'The next day, Vanel was found dead, killed with a blow from a poker which had Bianchi's fingerprints on it. A drawer of Vanel's desk had been broken open and money was missing from it. We searched Bianchi's room and found notes which were positively identified as being in Vanel's possession the day before.'

'You see, chief,' Laval interjected, 'everything fits: fingerprints, stolen money, and a revenge motive.'

The Hawk was staring hard at the Sûreté man. 'You still

haven't given me your opinion, Henri,' he said quietly.

'I assembled the facts. The rest was up to the legal department. On that evidence, they *had* to accuse Bianchi.' The Inspector's tone was abrupt. 'They had no other choice.'

'And yet you aren't *certain*?'

The Inspector turned. 'Jean,' he said ruefully, 'there are times when I swear you can see through a brick wall.' He sighed heavily. 'You're right, of course,' he admitted. 'I'm not certain. Bianchi is a clever man, yet this was a clumsy crime. The murderer acted like a fool, but Bianchi is not a fool.'

'You can't ignore facts,' said Laval.

The lawyer now broke in.

'Gentlemen, as you know, I defended Bianchi. My opinion is that he was . . . guilty.' He paused to give his words effect.

'What was Bianchi's story? He said he called twice at the Vanel home. The first time was at 6 p.m. when he was let in by Madame Vanel. Bianchi waited in the library, and used the poker to stir the fire – that's how his fingerprints were found on it. He waited an hour, but Vanel didn't show up. So he went away again and returned at 9 p.m.

'This time, he claims, Madame Vanel told him her husband had been in, but had gone out again.' The lawyer smiled his disbelief. 'Next morning, Bianchi tells us, an unknown messenger arrived at his hotel with an envelope containing money which later proved to have come from Vanel's desk. A very thin story. And that's not all,' Maître Balard continued. 'We know that Vanel was killed at about 8 p.m. Where was Bianchi at that time?'

The telephone shrilled. The Hawk picked up the phone. 'Inspector Collet here.' He raised an eyebrow. 'Yes, sir, I *was* hoping to reopen the Bianchi case. I suppose the Prison Governor told you.' The Hawk's face suddenly turned grim.

'Very well sir, then I'll do so on my own responsibility . . .

Yes, I understand. If I'm wrong, I'll resign!' His eyes were like blue steel as he replaced the receiver.

Laval looked at him apprehensively. He had never seen his chief looking so angry, or so determined to have his way.

'The Préfecture suggest, very forcibly, that I am to leave the Bianchi case alone.'

His lips tightened. 'I refused.'

Inspector Gardot looked at him grimly. 'You're crazy, Jean!' he protested. 'Your whole future is at stake!'

'So is a man's life,' said The Hawk.

'Only in *your* opinion, Inspector Collet. *I* think you're making a big mistake.' The cold, precise tones of the lawyer, Maître Balard, cut like a knife. 'There's evidence in the Bianchi case that did not come out at the trial.' He paused. 'Evidence that proves, without doubt, that Bianchi *is* guilty,' he finished heavily.

The Hawk's brain raced. If the lawyer was right, then he'd just sacrificed his whole career for nothing.

The Hawk, Paul Laval and Inspector Gardot stared at Maître Balard intently.

'You see,' the lawyer told them, 'when I interviewed Bianchi just after his arrest, he said he had an alibi for the time of Vanel's murder. He claims he was sitting on a park bench with a priest.'

'A priest!' The Hawk frowned.

'And what a priest!' grinned the lawyer. 'A red-bearded giant with a broken nose who showed him card tricks.' He sneered. 'What a story!'

'But not impossible,' said The Hawk quietly.

'That's not all,' continued Balard. 'Bianchi also said the priest left for Austria that night – from the Gare d'Orléans!'

'That's not . . .' Laval broke in.

'Not the station for Austria – exactly,' the lawyer finished. 'We checked with the staff at the Gare d'Orléans, and no one had seen such a priest that night, or any other night. We also made thorough inquiries at the Gare de l'Est – the real terminus for trains for Austria. It was the same there; no one saw a priest answering Bianchi's description.'

There was a heavy silence as the three detectives let the information sink in.

'It was no alibi,' Maître Balard concluded, 'just a stupid, made-up story. I strongly advised Bianchi not to mention the matter any further.'

The Hawk watched in silence as the lawyer gathered his papers, put them in his briefcase and left with a polite bow. Laval looked gloomily at The Hawk.

'Well, that settles it,' he said.

'Exactly,' said The Hawk. 'What Maître Balard told us settles it absolutely.' Laval looked at him sharply. To his astonishment, The Hawk was smiling.

Laval shrugged. 'Well, maybe we can start up a private detective agency.'

'We?' asked The Hawk, quizzically.

'You don't think I want to stay on here after they throw you out?'

The Hawk patted his assistant's shoulder affectionately. 'Thanks, Paul,' he said. 'I won't forget – if I *am* thrown out!'

'But now we're certain that Bianchi is guilty . . .' Gardot began, hopelessly.

'You mean – now we're certain he's *innocent*!' The Hawk replied, calmly. The other two looked at him in amazement. 'Don't you see,' he continued, 'Bianchi may be a crook, but he's no fool – and not a killer, either. Only a complete idiot would make up an alibi like that if it weren't true. It's too complicated to be a lie. It's so unlikely that it must be true.'

The others looked at him with open mouths. Laval was the first to recover.

'Put that way, chief,' he said, 'it sounds as if you're right.'

Gardot nodded.

'I'd better be,' The Hawk observed, grimly, 'otherwise I won't have the opportunity to make any more mistakes – not as an Interpol agent, anyway. I shall have to move fast.'

'What's your first move?' asked Gardot.

'Vienna! Somewhere in Austria, there's a priest who can prove that Bianchi told his lawyer the truth. Fantastic as it may sound, that alibi is his only hope.'

'I'll book you a flight, chief,' said Laval, as he grabbed the 'phone.

'Thanks. Tell the Vienna police I'm on my way and I'd be grateful for their assistance. Give them the background to the case, too, and ask them to prepare a list of the monasteries or other places where our red-haired priest may be.'

Laval was through to the airline. Gardot looked at his watch.

'Five-twenty,' he said. 'It'll be late at night by the time you get to Vienna. You won't be able to do much until tomorrow.'

'That means you'll have just two days – *two days* – to try and prove Bianchi isn't guilty. Jean, don't you think you ought to call the Préfecture and – apologise? Perhaps they'd . . .'

The Hawk's eyes flashed.

'Let an innocent man die, just to save my job? No job is worth that price.' There was a rough edge to his voice.

Gardot looked shamefaced. 'Sorry, Jean – I should know better.'

The Hawk gave him a quick smile. 'Forget it, Henri.' He turned to Laval. 'I'll call from Vienna and let you know what progress I make.'

But twenty-four hours later, when he made the call, it was a gloomy story The Hawk had to tell his assistant. There was no trace of a priest like the one Bianchi had described, either in Vienna or anywhere near. The Austrian police were widening their search over the whole country. The Hawk's incisive voice gave no hint of the strain he was feeling after thirty-six hours with hardly any food or rest.

'I'm coming back on the next flight,' he concluded. 'The Austrians can carry on trying to find the priest. My staying here won't help. The next move is to see the murdered man's widow – Madame Vanel. Maybe she can give me a lead.

'He can't see Madame Vanel until tomorrow,' Laval said to himself as he hung up. 'That means he'll have just one day to save Bianchi – and himself.' He shook his head. It was impossible.

Next morning, The Hawk drove through the blinding rain, straight from the airport to Madame Vanel's home on the outskirts of Paris. The tremendous pressure at which he was working would have been too much for any other man, but only faint traces of fatigue were beginning to show in the creases around his eyes as he skilfully manoeuvred the car through the slippery, cobbled streets.

His knock at the door of the Vanel home was answered by a man.

'My name is Dr Lenoir,' said the man, when The Hawk introduced himself. 'I am Madame Vanel's medical adviser. I must warn you to be very careful, Inspector. She has not yet fully recovered from the shock of this terrible affair.'

Despite his desperate awareness of every precious minute that ticked away, The Hawk remained tactful and unhurried during the interview with Madame Vanel.

Gently, he got her story from her. She had found her husband's body after Bianchi had left – at about 6 p.m. She had fainted from shock. It was not until the next morning that she recovered consciousness and called the police.

Why had she not given evidence at the trial? Dr Lenoir answered that question: Madame Vanel had been ill, and the case was conclusive without her testimony.

Finally, Madame Vanel made a supreme effort to pull herself together. 'Why are you asking me these questions?' she demanded, in a firmer voice.

The Hawk looked at her, steadily. 'Because I believe Bianchi is innocent.' Madame Vanel's cheeks turned ashen. She would have fallen had not the doctor put out an arm to steady her. His expression was full of suppressed anger.

'I'm all right.' Madame Vanel whispered. She stared at The Hawk.

'Your theory that Bianchi is innocent is quite wrong,' she said.

'Forgive me, Madame, but may I ask why you are so sure?' The Hawk's manner was quietly courteous.

'You may well ask,' Madame Vanel retorted, her voice growing stronger. 'The answer is simple. *I actually saw Bianchi commit the murder!*'

Despite his instinctive faith in Bianchi's innocence, The Hawk was badly shaken by Madame Vanel's flat assertion that she had actually seen the murder committed. Back in his office, he went over the details of the case once more with Laval and Inspector Gardot. 'It still doesn't add up!' he said, as they finished their summing up. 'There's something wrong somewhere. Bianchi is *not* guilty – I'm convinced of it!'

Gardot looked at the clock on the wall. 'Eleven fifteen,' he said. 'You've got less than nineteen hours left to prove it.'

Laval, The Hawk's assistant, nodded. 'The execution is at six tomorrow morning.'

The Hawk's jaw jutted obstinately. 'Five minutes would be enough to save him.' He got up and started to pace, angrily. 'Somewhere there's one vital fact we've missed,' he said. If I could just put a finger on it!'

'Look, Jean,' Gardot coaxed him. 'You've been working

non-stop for nearly forty-eight hours. Why not relax for a while? Come out and have a cup of coffee. Forget the case for a quarter of an hour and you'll be able to refresh your mind.'

The Hawk shook his head, but Laval took his chief's hat and held it out, convinced he was doing the right thing.

'He's right, you know,' he said firmly. 'Why not try it?'

The Hawk stood up and looked from one to the other. 'Two to one,' he smiled, wearily. 'All right, you win.'

Fifty yards from the Interpol building there was a small café, its gaily covered tables sprawling out on to the pavement. But there was no gaiety amongst the three detectives as they sat silently, drinking their coffee. Despite his friends' advice, The Hawk could not dismiss the case from his mind.

'We've opened up one new angle, anyway,' he said, thoughtfully.

'What's that?' the others asked.

'Madame Vanel said she saw Bianchi kill her husband. If Bianchi is innocent – and I believe he is – then she must be lying. Why? For one reason only – because she's mixed up in the killing!'

Laval looked at him excitedly.

'Do you think there's a chance of getting the truth out of her?'

The Hawk shook his head. 'Not in the time. If we had a few weeks – even a few days – but we've only got a few hours.' His lips tightened at the thought, and he sprang to his feet. Without a word, he headed back to Interpol Headquarters. Exchanging a quick glance, the others followed him. The Hawk had gone only a few yards when he was stopped by two young English boys. They wore Scouts' uniforms and carried large rucksacks.

'Excuse me, sir,' one of them said politely, in his best French. 'Can you tell us how to get to the Gare d'Orléans, please?'

The Hawk stopped short as the strong English accent caught his ear. He smiled pleasantly, as he directed the boys.

'Off on holiday?' he asked, casually.

'Yes, sir,' said the second boy. 'We're going to Nice.'

'Nice?' The Hawk frowned. 'Then you're going to the wrong station,' he said. 'You want the Gare de Lyon.'

The Scout who had originally asked for directions looked puzzled. 'But that's what I said, sir,' he pointed out.

The Hawk stared at him, his eyes wide with sudden comprehension. He had found the vital fact he needed to save Bianchi.

'Quick!' he said to Laval. 'A pencil and paper!' His assistant produced his notebook and The Hawk quickly scribbled two names: Gare de Lyon and Gare d'Orléans. He turned to the two boys.

'This is very important,' he explained, carefully. 'I am Inspector Collet of Interpol' – the Scouts nodded – 'and I want you to help me. Please read out the two names I have written.'

The boys complied. Like most English people, they pronounced Orléans as 'Or-*lee*-ong', and not as it should be: 'Or-*lay*-ong'. Run together, the names Gare de Lyon and Gare d'Orléans sounded almost identical when said with an English accent.

'Boys,' The Hawk smiled at the two Scouts, 'you've certainly done your good deed today. You've helped me to save a man's life.' He turned and hustled his two companions towards his car parked outside the office, leaving the puzzled English Scouts scratching their heads.

The Hawk refused to give his colleagues any explanation as the Interpol car roared through the Paris streets towards the Fresnes Prison.

'No,' he said. 'If you didn't spot it, then I may be wrong. Wait until we see Bianchi.' As the car roared on, both Laval and Gardot racked their brains for an explanation. One thing was certain – The Hawk was on to something big. His eyes were bright with excitement, his whole body charged with renewed energy.

Once inside the condemned cell at Fresnes Prison, he wasted no words.

'Just answer my questions,' he told Bianchi. 'There's no time for explanations. Now, I'm checking your alibi for the time of Vanel's murder. You say you were talking to a priest, right?'

Bianchi nodded.

'What language did you use? Your own Italian?'

'No – he couldn't speak Italian and I was no good at his English or German, so we spoke in French.'

'Now think carefully about this. He said he was on his way to the station.' The Hawk paused. 'What station?'

'The Gare d'Orléans – I told you,' replied the mystified Italian.

The Hawk glanced briefly at his two colleagues. Then he turned to Bianchi. 'Did he say it like this?' He took a breath, then with a broad English accent, he said: 'Gare de Lyon.'

'That's right,' Bianchi confirmed. 'Gare d'Orléans.'

Laval and Gardot exchanged a significant look. Now they knew what The Hawk was on to. But he hadn't finished with Bianchi yet.

'One more question. Were the priest's exact words that he was going to *Austria*?'

Bianchi thought for nearly a full minute, his eyes screwed up in the effort of concentration.

'Yes, he did.' The Hawk looked disappointed, but he hid his expression from the Italian.

'Are you quite sure?'

'Wait a minute!' Bianchi exclaimed. 'No – he didn't say Austria. He said *Vienna*.'

'And how did he say Vienna?' asked the Hawk, with deceptive casualness.

'In the French way, or the Austrian way, for that matter – *Vienne.*'

The Hawk stood up. 'Thanks, Bianchi. That's all.'

Outside the cell he turned triumphantly to the others.

'You see! We were on the wrong track,' he grinned, 'in more ways than one. The priest did not say he was going to the Gare d'Orléans for a train to Austria. He said he was going to the Gare de Lyon for a train to Vienne.'

'What's the difference?' asked Gardot. 'The Gare de Lyon still isn't right.'

The Hawk smiled. 'Not for the Vienna – or Vienne – in Austria. But the Gare de Lyon is the right station for Vienne *in France*! That's where the priest went – to Vienne. It's a few miles outside Lyon.'

Gardot and Laval looked at him in unconcealed admiration. The Hawk glanced at his watch.

'Now my only hope is that I can get there in time!'

The express train roared through the night towards Lyon. The Hawk sat back in his seat, apparently dozing. But, although his eyes were closed, his brain was working furiously. Lyon was the nearest big town to Vienne, and he would complete his journey by a fast car supplied by the Lyon police. Inspector Gardot had arranged that – it would save precious minutes. The helpful Sûreté man had also asked for local inquiries to be started to find the priest who was so vital to Bianchi's alibi.

If The Hawk's reasoning was correct and the priest, when found, was able to confirm the condemned man's story, then a quick telephone call to Fresnes Prison would get the execution postponed. Laval, his assistant, had gone to the prison to warn them of the expected call. Only the Governor had the authority to stop the execution, and Laval would not leave his side until The Hawk telephoned.

'If I telephone,' The Hawk thought grimly.

He opened his eyes. The train was slowing down. 'Funny,' he thought, 'there's no scheduled stop until Lyon, an hour away.' The train continued to lose speed until it was barely crawling along. Impatiently, The Hawk rose from his seat and went to find an attendant. 'What's the delay?' he asked shortly.

'There have been landslides along the line, brought down by the heavy rain these past four days,' the attendant explained. 'We were warned before leaving Paris. We can't take a chance along this stretch.'

The Hawk looked at his watch. The train was due at Lyon at 2 a.m. At the rate they were going, it would not arrive before three o'clock. The race against time to save Bianchi was becoming more desperate.

His guess was accurate. It was 3.15 a.m. when the train pulled into Lyon station.

It was a dismal morning, with heavy rain beating down remorselessly. The passengers alighted, looking grey-faced and fatigued under the station lights. One or two of them glanced curiously at the tall man who strode energetically towards the exit, but there was littlc to show the tremendous strain of the past three days.

Inspector Joliet of the Lyon police was waiting for him in a police car. He was a man after The Hawk's own heart – a man who went straight to the point.

'We've tried all the local priests for twenty miles round Vienne, but none of them fits your description. The only place left is a monastery about six miles from Vienne – there are a number of foreign priests there. It's your best bet, now.' He frowned. 'In fact, it's your *only* bet!'

'How long will it take to get there?' The Hawk asked crisply.

'In normal conditions – an hour. But, with all this rain, the mountain roads are in a terrible state. Better count on two hours at least!'

'That means we'll arrive about five-thirty.' The Hawk's face was serious. 'Bianchi's execution is due at six.'

'It's cutting things very fine,' Joliet agreed, sombrely. 'If the priest isn't at the monastery, your last chance has gone.'

The car roared off through the torrential rain. At first, progress was good. Then, after half an hour, the road started to narrow and the car began to buck and slide over a crumbling road surface, made treacherous by mud brought down by the torrential rain. Worse was to come when they reached the mountains. Here, conditions became nightmarish. Great sections of roadway had fallen away from the side of the mountain, leaving just enough room for the car to creep along the mountain wall, with its wheels spinning madly in the loose earth on the edge of a sheer drop into black emptiness.

When they arrived at the great monastery gate, even The Hawk's steel nerves were stretched to breaking point. Again he looked at his watch – 5.25 a.m. Just thirty-five minutes left to save Bianchi!

Despite the early hour, The Hawk was quickly admitted to the Father Superior. He explained his mission briefly.

'Such a description can only fit one man,' the Father Superior smiled. 'Father Ignatius.' He led the way from his office and, a few moments later, The Hawk's search was over. He was shaking hands with a giant of a priest, a man with a broken nose and a great red beard – exactly as Bianchi had described him.

The Hawk slipped a photograph of Bianchi from his pocket. 'Father, have you ever seen this man?' he asked.

'Sure, and I have that,' came the reply in an Irish brogue.

'When and where?'

With no hesitation, the Irish priest told of his meeting with

Bianchi. He confirmed the little Italian's story exactly. The alibi was proved!

'And who would be doubting it?' boomed the huge Irishman, truculently. 'Bring them here, and I'll tell them meself!'

The Hawk grinned. 'You must admit a giant priest, with a red beard and a broken nose who plays card tricks, does sound far-fetched,' he said.

'I see what you mean. But me nose I got when I was a bit of an amateur boxer. 'Tis fine proof I had more energy than skill,' Father Ignatius twinkled. 'As for the card tricks, I learn them to amuse the children. Would you be after letting me show you?' he added, eagerly.

'Thank you, Father,' The Hawk said, 'but I've got to get to Vienne. I want a telephone – urgently!'

'Sure and you're wasting your time,' Father Ignatius told him. 'The road's blocked and the telephone wires have been down since Wednesday.' The Hawk's blood ran cold.

'Then where *is* the nearest 'phone?'

The priest stared at him. 'Lyon, I suppose,' he said at last.

'Lyon! It's just taken two hours to get from there!' The Hawk's face set grimly. 'I've got just fifteen minutes to save a man's life!' He paced up and down, thinking furiously. 'To be beaten by rain in the age of jet planes and electronics!' he said, bitterly.

'Electronics!' shouted Father Ignatius. 'You've got the answer!'

The Hawk grabbed his arm. 'Tell me!'

'There's a youngster named Jacquot Perrin who lives in a village a couple of miles from here,' said the priest excitedly. 'He's an amateur radio operator.'

'How do I get there?'

'By following me!' roared Father Ignatius, as he headed for the door. The Hawk drove the car to the village himself, with a recklessness and skill that had the others gasping, and his watch indicated nine minutes before six as he hammered on the door of the young radio enthusiast's home.

Meanwhile, in Fresnes Prison, Laval was pacing the Governor's office. 'I don't understand it,' he said, for the hundredth time. 'Inspector Collet would have telephoned by now – even with bad news.'

The Governor shook his head helplessly.

'I'm sorry, Laval, but I can't hold up the execution without some definite word. I can wait just five minutes – no more. After that . . .' He broke off with a shrug.

Laval stared desperately at the 'phone.

At that moment, The Hawk was equally desperate as he watched Jacquot Perrin feverishly trying to raise the Interpol radio operator on his home-made set. At last, the boy tensed. He looked up in triumph.

'Got them!' he yelled. The Hawk almost snatched the microphone from him.

'This is Inspector Collet,' he rapped out. 'Telephone Fresnes Prison. Bianchi's alibi has been established – tell them to stop the execution. Repeat – stop execution!'

'Four minutes to six,' said the Prison Governor. He moved to the door. 'Are you coming, Laval?'

'No,' he said, wearily, 'I'll wait here.'

The Governor shrugged, then went off.

The detective sat staring at the clock.

Suddenly, the telephone bell shrilled. Laval literally threw himself across the desk.

'Laval here,' he said, eagerly. He listened to the brief message, then, dropping the receiver like a red-hot coal, plunged for the door. The hands of the clock hovered at 6 a.m.

Three hundred miles away, The Hawk sat by Jacquot's radio.

From his impassive face, none of the others could guess that his nerves were as taut as harp strings. Without warning, a voice broke through the crackle of static.

'Calling Inspector Collet – calling Inspector Collet . . .'

The Hawk grabbed the microphone. 'Collet answering – over.'

The metallic voice of the Interpol operator held more than a hint of excitement as he relayed his message.

'Your message received. Bianchi execution stopped. Congratulations, Laval!'

The boy Jacquot, who had played a vital part in saving the prisoner's life, gave a broad grin. Father Ignatius and Inspector Joliet slapped The Hawk on the back.

'It's astonishing what you can do when everyone works together and co-operates,' said The Hawk, softly.

'So Interpol has taught us,' replied Joliet, with a smile.

But his compliment fell on deaf ears. The Hawk was fast asleep.

Spy Dive

by Geoffrey Cowan

A bullet ricochetted off the surface of the low stone wall, sending fragments flying. Agent 779 dived, face down, behind the wall. Next moment, the rattle of machine-gun fire sent a series of staccato cracks close over his head. Beside him, the elderly diplomat he had been sent to rescue lay still, his hands pressing hard against his ears.

Both men were trapped – and they knew it!

Any moment now, the agent told himself, as he imagined the sound of running feet and rapid gunfire . . . Any moment now and *they* would charge . . .

He had to retaliate, prove he was not a failure. With catlike movements he edged above the low balustrade, his Luger levelling . . .

'Where are we?' The voice sounded close to Chip's right ear, breaking his concentration. '*Where are we?*' Again the voice demanded.

Chip blinked hard, drawing his gaze from the spy thriller he had been reading. He looked blankly towards the source of the penetrating voice.

'Chip, if you would only read the map with as much concentration as you read that book we'd know where we were!'

Thoughts of Agent 779 vanished instantly. Closing the

paper-back, one page dog-eared, Chip reached down for the map, which had slipped off his knees on to the floor. He glanced at his elder brother.

'Sorry, Steve. I . . . er . . . got a bit carried away.'

'We'll both be, if you don't stop reading that wretched book and work out where we are! I thought you were supposed to be the tops at map-reading.'

Steve's voice sounded resentful, even worried, as he glanced momentarily from the narrow road to his younger brother.

Holding the map inches from his face, Chip followed a meandering course with a jerky finger.

'Can't you drive this thing without making it feel as though it's on square wheels? It would help, you know,' he said, trying to retrieve his place.

Steve gazed ahead, his hands fixed firmly on the Volkswagen's driving wheel. He could see little through the haze of squally rain that shrouded the windscreen.

'My guess is we're way off course. This is more like a track than a 'B' road, which the map says it ought to be . . .'

It was evening and already what little light they had was fading quickly with the gathering stormclouds.

'If only there were a signpost or something,' Chip said, knowing full well there would be more chance of seeing a flying saucer on the track than that. 'Whatever made the Club Sec. pick Scotland, Steve? It's nothing but hills and – hey! *What's that?*'

Chip's arm darted out.

Steve swung the wheel viciously right and then corrected.

'Chip, if you get up to any more tricks like that, we'll be lost all right – for good!'

'But, Steve, over there! Off the coast . . .' With one hand on the wheel, the elder brother rubbed with the other hand against the side window to clear the condensation.

'A light flashing! See it?'

Chip's voice had risen. A quick glance told Steve his brother was right.

They were driving along a highland coast road. Beyond it, perhaps half-a-mile out to sea, a yellow light blinked.

'Must be pretty powerful for us to see it in this weather,' Steve said non-commitally.

But his brother was more emphatic.

'It's sending messages – to somewhere along the coast. Bet it's a spy ship!'

Steve laughed. Yes, they had had a puncture. Yes, they were probably lost. But a spy ship – that was one thing he was not prepared to accept.

'Chip, one of these days your imagination is going to earn you a lot of money. Ever thought of being a writer . . .?'

But Chip was not amused.

'Very funny – I don't think!' Chip gazed sternly ahead.

'Just like your spy theory,' his brother added.

A brief silence followed as Steve held the Volkswagen's course along the narrow road, which now turned slightly inland again.

Chip cast one long look at the flickering offshore light, before it was obscured by a promontory.

'Reckon we're in for quite a storm,' Steve announced long minutes later. 'This rain is only a foretaste. Seems our trip is carrying its own personal jinx with it, at the moment . . .' The windscreen wipers were working now.

'Well, it wasn't *my* fault we had the puncture,' Chip said thumbing through his paper-back again. But, this time, Steve was not prepared to let his brother relax.

'Chip! Here we are in the middle of nowhere with night coming on, and all you can do is turn to that book. The map would be a better idea . . .'

Clicking his tongue despondently, the younger brother

resumed his arduous task of trying to discover just where they were. It was hard to see in the failing light.

A sudden blinding light, followed shortly by a thunderous crash, helped him with his task.

Both Chip and Steve watched the snaking finger of lightning point earthwards. Glistening water reflected its outline.

'Over there, Chip! That must be the loch, surely!'

'Blow the loch,' Chip said, retrieving the map from near his feet. 'Another bang like that and I'll be in no state to go paddling – let alone diving!'

'Don't tell me you're getting cold feet – even before we hit the water . . .' Steve said, following home his advantage. He was grinning now. He'd thought the approaching storm was just more of the bad luck that had been travelling with them. But, strangely, the lightning seemed to be leading them to their objective.

'We'll draw up beside the loch and have some supper. All this driving's given me an appetite. We should see the others shortly.'

Before Chip could add a sarcastic reply about his brother always being hungry, a second thunderous boom roared overhead.

Chip started, banging his knee on the door handle.

'Don't get out yet, Chip. I know you're eager, but it would be better for me to stop first,' his brother teased.

Chip's eyes blazed for a moment as he struggled to stifle a groan.

Wet tyres hissed as they swerved on even wetter ground. Securing the hand-brake, Steve turned off the ignition and sighed with relief.

'Pheewww! Well, we made it! Now – I wonder where the others are?'

Edging forward on his seat, he glanced about the heavily

wooded, shadow-lined shores of the loch, expecting to see other vehicles dotted around. But he could see no other signs of life. Steve was disappointed, but didn't want to show it.

'Reckon we must have beaten the rest here – thanks to my short cut!' Chip said proudly.

'That's right. And I suppose you even arranged for the lightning to illuminate the loch. Easier than looking for a signpost we might have missed . . .'

'Something like that,' the younger brother remarked, folding the map. He grinned impishly. 'Now, I think it's *your* turn to be useful – like fixing some grub. I think I've earned mine.' Soon Steve was busying himself over the Volkswagen's self-contained cooker. Chip watched both light and rain fading outside.

'I'll just take a quick stroll round the loch while you play at cooking, Steve. The storm's dying out.'

Distant thunder rumbled as Chip jumped down on to the damp ground. The loch surface appeared oily-black and uninviting beneath the darkening sky. A keen breeze caused faint ripples to slap shorewards.

His feet only inches from the edge, Chip gazed thoughtfully across the huge expanse of water which served to remind him of the vessel he had sighted earlier.

And those signals . . . What could they have meant? It seemed unlikely there would be a shipping base on such a barren section of coast. Chip's mind revolved around his original theory of a spy ship. Perhaps . . .

Suddenly, Chip sprang back with a start. Cold water was seeping into his chuck boots. The ripples on the loch had suddenly become waves.

Regaining his balance, he studied the surface of the water. Something had disturbed it – something must be moving out there!

A chill ran swiftly up Chip's back, causing the nape of his neck to tingle. There was no boat on the loch – he could see that, despite the evening shadows.

Narrowing his eyes, he focused harder on the loch. Then a slow realisation numbed him. He blinked several times before looking again. No, he had not been mistaken. A foaming wake splayed out in a 'V' shape behind something moving swiftly just under the surface of the water.

Chip was left with a vague impression of a long, tubular object slicing across the loch, before it disappeared. Only a heavy shoreward rippling remained as proof that he had not been dreaming.

'Grub up!' Steve's voice echoed hearteningly, followed by a resounding clanging noise. Chip stirred, turning towards the warm glow coming from the interior of the motorised caravan.

'All right, I'm coming,' he heard himself reply. 'There's no need to keep bashing that tin plate. This isn't the Wild West, you know . . .'

Not until he was mounting the single step into the large camping vehicle, did Chip turn to look back at the now smooth loch waters.

Settling comfortably on one of the built-in bunks, he absent-mindedly savoured the bacon and eggs, his thoughts lingering on stories of the Loch Ness Monster.

First, the offshore signalling, and now this! If things kept up at this rate, Chip told himself, maybe he might even take up his brother's suggestion about writing, and with no strain on his imagination!

'Good?'

'Mm?' Chip looked suddenly at the plate of food before him and then at Steve.

'The food, I mean . . .'

'Oh . . . er . . . you bet!' Chip said, waking from his daydream. He didn't want to tell his brother of the loch incident – not after his sceptical reaction to his spy ship theory.

'I was just overwhelmed by the luscious odour for a moment. It looks and smells almost too good to eat!' the younger brother added, watching the effect registering on Steve's face.

'Flattery won't get you out of the washing up,' Steve grinned. 'So you'd better eat it and build up your energy.'

Hunger overcame conversation for the next few minutes as they emptied their plates without pausing. It had been a long day – even longer for Chip – and only now did he realise his appetite had been neglected.

Three-quarters of an hour later, the two boys were bedded down for the night. There was a faint click and the Volkswagen was engulfed in darkness. Withdrawing his hand from the battery-operated light-switch, Steve pulled the bunk's covers around himself and nestled down. He was more tired than he had thought.

'I expect the others will arrive in cavalcade tomorrow. We might even manage a dive before them, if they're late.'

'That's providing I don't sleep through the rest of the holiday,' Chip said, gazing at the roof and waiting for his eyes to grow accustomed to the dark. But his reply was wasted. Steve was already drifting into the unconsciousness of sleep.

Though his limbs longed for rest, Chip lay uneasily for what seemed hours. Again and again he asked himself the same questions. Many times he glanced out of the window towards the icy black waters of the loch. There *had* been movement beneath the loch's surface. He was sure of it. Besides, there had been the heavy swell – even his brother couldn't have discounted that. But why . . . ?

Of course. Chip came to the sudden realisation that tomorrow he might find the answer. He shivered, uncertain whether it was due to more than the crisp night air.

In the morning they would dive into the water – just as the moving object had done!

His mind at rest, Chip was finally able to sleep.

Mist hung in low clouds, moving slowly above the loch. It was early. Rubbing his eyes, Chip noticed, for the first time, the densely forested slopes leading down to the water's edge. But wisps of fog writhed between the trees, making visibility poor.

A long droning sound made him turn. Steve was kneeling over his diving equipment, his face contorted in a yawn.

'I know you've a pretty good built-in fog-horn, Steve, but we're not even *on* the water, you know.'

'We'll be in it, as soon as you wake your ideas up, Chip. Come on, we'll check over the gear before we dive . . .'

As the two of them busied themselves among a selection of cylinders, rubber suits and face masks, Chip recalled the rippling movement on the water the previous night. He was glad that Steve had woken him early, to disturb unpleasant dreams.

Chip fingered his diver's watch pensively. He had intended to tell his brother what he had seen. But now, in the reassuring daylight, the idea seemed rather absurd.

'Flippers always make me feel like a frog out of water,' said Steve, grinning to himself as he edged awkwardly up to the edge of the loch, a short while later.

Chip inspected his brother's appearance with some amusement. Both were wearing their black 'wet' suits and full face masks, which incorporated the mouth-piece.

'They match your looks,' he mumbled, securing his own single, compressed-air cylinder on his back. A brief glance confirmed that the dagger was fixed firmly in its sheath, strapped to his leg.

'Anyone would think we were going shark-hunting with these!' he said, tapping the knife.

'All part of the standard equipment – I'll remind you next time you're caught up in weed, with your air running low. Come on – you first! I'll follow you . . .'

'That's right,' Chip replied, passing his brother in the water. 'Want me to test it first, in case it's too cold? You should have brought a hot waterbottle!'

A brief cascading shower marked Chip's disappearance beneath the surface. Dipping his mask in the water, to prevent condensation during the dive, Steve cast a final glance about the shore.

Perhaps it was the slight movement that had attracted him to do so. Emerging from a derelict crofter's cottage was a figure, watching him. Steve replaced his mask slowly, noting the observer was using binoculars.

Come to think of it, he told himself, he hadn't even spotted the low-lying building until now. Anyway, it was probably just a bird-spotter using the ruin. He shrugged. After all, it would be an ideal site.

Concentric circles rippled shorewards, following Steve's dive. The water was far from clear, after the previous night's rainstorm.

Steve drew at his oxygen mouth-piece, and kicked down towards the hazy outline of his brother. Conditions were hardly good for the dive and Steve had already decided they would not make it a long one.

A vertical trail of bubbles marked the spot where Chip waited for his brother to join him. Next moment, they flipped their legs and continued deeper. Steve pointed to his diver's watch and then indicated the number ten with his fingers. Chip nodded. Ten minutes wouldn't exactly make this the longest dive on record but he, too, realised the water was anything but ideal. Besides, he thought, they could at least brag about being broken in before the other club members arrived. He swam on downwards.

Steve was pointing vigorously to one side.

The water was cold. Chip could tell that, despite his rubber suit. Noticing the mild wake from his brother's flippers, a memory stirred suddenly. But even as he recalled the rippling movement from the previous evening, he felt something clamp tightly on to his arm.

Startled, Chip twisted in a flurry of bubbles. He relaxed again, grinning, as he saw it was only Steve. His brother had caught up faster than he had expected.

Mustn't let Steve think I've got the jitters, he told himself. But his relief was short-lived. The mixed expression of anxiety and amazement on his brother's face brought all his own doubts racing back.

Steve was pointing vigorously to one side and just a little below them. In doing so, his hand pierced a glowing beam of light. The beam moved fully on to him, as Steve kicked out to clear it. He closed his eyes, momentarily dazzled by its brilliance. In that split-second, Chip followed the light to its source. What he saw made him snatch a shallow breath. Steve, too, now gazed fixedly in the same direction.

At first, each tried to reason with himself – to convince himself that the massive, vaguely circular outline was nothing more than a phenomenon caused by the disturbed silt. But that wouldn't account for the light . . .

Chip's stomach tightened. Somehow the huge bubble was linked with the rippling on the surface. But how? Before he had time to doubt himself, he brushed his brother's sleeve and dived. Steve hesitated before following, and again the slowly moving, broad beam of light lit him up before passing on.

A cold smoothness registered against the palm of Chip's hand as he touched the surface of the immense globe. He turned to Steve, who was indicating that they should split up and swim round it in opposite directions.

Chip raised his thumb in agreement. But almost instantly he

wished he hadn't. There was something eerie and ominous about the silent, floating globe – something that signalled a red danger light in his mind.

Cautiously, Chip began to swim around the bubble's circumference. Above, he could still see the light-beam hovering in an arc. It was being emitted from the bubble – but why?

Edging down the underside of the massive globe, he saw what appeared to be a cylinder attached to the base. An approaching line of rising bubbles told him Steve had also noticed it, though he could not yet actually see his brother.

A deep, grating sound halted Chip in mid-stroke. Every nerve in his body told him something was about to happen.

It did.

Darkness closed on the water about him.

The beam of light – Chip thought quickly. He was right; a brief glance upwards proved that. It was no longer there. Someone – or something – had turned it off!

A sudden, powerful current pulled at him; a distant whirring sounded in his ears. Next moment, a secondary upsurge threw him head over heels.

Don't panic . . . Chip forced the thought into his mind. Suddenly, the water erupted in a series of gushing bubbles. Sucking hard at his mouthpiece he swam hard to clear the current. He could do little; his body was being tossed about like a sweet paper in a gale. But he must not pass out.

Slowly the sensation passed. Chip felt his breathing return to normal. His eyes began to focus again on the turbulent water. What of the bubble-like structure? And Steve? *Where was Steve . . . ?*

He collected his thoughts, spilled like loose leaves of paper dropped from a folder. He peered hard into the muddy water about him. He could see little – but enough to make a horrifying realisation rock his body.

Both the bubble – and Steve – had vanished!

For long seconds Chip remained mentally numbed and motionless. Then, slowly, he began to swim for the surface. There was just a slim chance that Steve had been hurled upwards and carried clear. If he were *not* beside the loch – Chip hesitated at the prospect – then there would be little hope. But, nevertheless, he would take the Volkswagen and search for help.

A weariness he had never before experienced overcame him as he waded towards the shore. Ripping his mask off, he closed his eyes and drew in the keen, fresh air. When he opened them again he noticed the water slapping against his legs. He covered the last few yards, slowly and slumped to the ground.

Steve was nowhere to be seen.

It was the slamming of a car door that roused him again. Chip sat up, recalling their own vehicle parked nearby. He turned, but it was strange how the trees concealed it and it took him a minute or two before he noticed the early sunlight reflected off the bumper.

Throwing clear his heavy cylinder, he ran forward. Steve . . . He could see his outline through the trees. Yes, there was no doubt. His black suit glistened with droplets of water. Then he *had* made it . . .

Chip burst into the small clearing, towards the crouching figure.

'You old son of a gun, Steve! I thought . . . the bubble . . .'

'What bubble?' A deep, menacing voice accompanied the similarly unfriendly face that turned towards him.

For the second time that morning, Chip's frayed nerves received a severe shock. It was not Steve, but a man Chip had never seen before in his life.

Instinctively Chip turned to run. But a steel grip closed on his wrist.

'You're wanted *here*!' his captor grinned, revealing well

formed teeth. 'You'd better start talking . . .'

For a moment Chip muttered incoherently. He gazed up at the square face beneath cropped blond hair. He had no idea what was going on. But of one thing he was certain – both he and Steve had somehow got caught up in a web of circumstances from which there was little hope of escape!

'My brother . . . we were diving,' Chip began, but paused, a picture re-forming of Steve's disappearance.

'We're from Naval Security – investigating reports of strange disturbances in the loch. We could help – more than you realise . . .' the second man said, easing his grip on Chip's wrist.

Chip gazed at the cold blue eyes fixed on him. He noticed now that both men wore frogmen's suits.

A faint prickling registered like a sixth sense, confirming the uncertainty he felt. Something told Chip he could not trust the men but, if there were the slightest chance of saving Steve, he knew he *had* to.

Chip talked.

He explained hastily about the bubble structure before telling them about Steve's mysterious disappearance. Then he waited to see the effect on the two men.

They exchanged a brief glance. One nodded and the other turned to address Chip.

'That underwater turbulence that threw you clear; it caught us, too. A fault developed in our sea-scooter. We had to surface to repair it. Then Gustav, here,' the man hesitated to indicate his companion, 'spotted your vehicle!'

Two words reacted upon Chip like a time-bomb.

'*Sea-scooter!*'

'Yes. There is just room for the three of us. We will dive again now, and look for your friend. Follow me . . .'

Again Chip was momentarily unsure. There was something icy and detached about the two men. As they turned towards the loch, he noticed how one walked close behind him. But, then, the whole set-up was like a dream sequence, he told himself firmly. And, whatever happened, he must gamble everything to save Steve . . .

'Wow!' Chip exclaimed at the torpedo shaped, motorised scooter that was suddenly revealed from beneath overhanging trees nearby.

'Originally, the slight fault developed last night. The impact of the rushing water weakened it again. But it's all in order now . . .'

So that was it!

Finally, Chip had grasped one piece of the huge puzzle. The rippling on the water the previous evening had obviously been caused by the sea-scooter. But there were other questions that badly needed answers . . . What was the bubble? Where was Steve? *What was going on?*

A barely audible humming told Chip they were underway. He was seated in the middle seat of the scooter, sandwiched between the two men. It was a squeeze, all right, but there was no time to think of discomfort. As the water closed over his head he drew in deeply from his cylinder of compressed air.

He had no idea if there was any hope at all for Steve. But the same sixth sense that had reacted a few minutes ago was working overtime.

Chip was convinced that Steve was alive!

The sea-scooter nosed steeply downwards, its small but powerful propeller thrusting them through the water.

Visibility was a little better now. Chip could even see two fish drift past, darting off at an angle at their approach.

He wondered how the two men would detect the area in which the bubble had appeared. The loch was immense and undoubtedly very deep. But he noticed that the men appeared to be in no doubt as to the exact direction they were taking.

The sea-scooter was levelling now.

Chip estimated their depth at around fifty feet. He gazed desperately from behind his mask. At every shadow and each vague movement of an underwater current he felt himself growing tense. Steve must be down here somewhere; he had to be . . .

It occurred to him only slowly at first; the water was becoming darker. A faint click, followed by a penetrating beam appearing from the nose of the scooter, confirmed his gradual realisation.

Chip turned to the man behind him, his expression suddenly changing. But the unflinching gaze that met his questioning look brought back the feeling of mistrust which he had felt before the three of them had dived.

Next moment, a rocky ceiling closed overhead. Uneven walls passed on either side. Immediately, Chip knew why the water was blacker. They were entering a subterranean tunnel!

In one swift movement, he sprang from his seat, his hands clawing at the water. But as his legs kicked, a sharp blow on his head made him reel. He felt a stabbing pain, and noticed too late the shadowy shape of a rock projecting from the craggy wall beside him. His limbs went limp, and then there was nothing . . .

'I haven't the foggiest idea what you're talking about!' Steve heard himself say for what must have been the twentieth time.

Once more, he wearily eyed the strange dome-like roof. Then a voice made him glance directly ahead. A tall man, wearing a blue uniform, stood motionless. Only his lips moved. Steve wished they wouldn't. The interrogation had lasted for so long, he could barely control what he was saying.

'We picked you up in the light-beam. Our surface man spotted you entering the loch. What were you doing?'

'Either you've a rotten memory or you just like stories. How many more times do I have to tell you? I just like diving – strange though this may seem to you. And there's a whole club full of others that do, too. They'll probably be near the loch now, if they're not already having a dive . . .'

'I doubt that,' the lips twitched again. So, too, did the man's cheek muscles. He was coming to the end of his patience. 'There's an invisible radio beam encircling the whole area. It would pick up any infiltrators. Immediately, our agent would send a message to us – and to concealed security forces nearby. But, somehow, you got through. How . . . ?'

Steve was still puzzling with another question. He knew radio waves would not travel through water. But then, there was that man with the binoculars he had seen. He must have contacted the 'blue-boys' down here with some ultra-new equipment. One way or another, Steve told himself, since he had been dragged into the air-lock an inconceivably long time ago, he had hit upon something big.

But he wished he hadn't!

'It must have been the storm – a breakdown in the circuits or something due to the lightning. How should I know? I only wanted a swim.'

Steve gripped the padded arm of the chair tightly. He was tired and hungry, but his chief concern was for Chip. Had he got clear? If so, where was he? Would he have gone for help . . . ?

'Intelligence have informed us someone is leaking information out about out presence here. The consequences could be disastrous. It would put your power in the lead – a lead we could not afford at any cost!'

'*My* power!' Steve spat the words out angrily. 'Just what do you think my aqua-lung club would want with your outsize bubble?'

Steve checked himself. He was about to demand his release, and to mention his brother. But, so far, no one had talked of Chip. Steve recalled only he, himself, had been caught in the beam of the search-light. Perhaps it would be better if his brother stayed out of it . . .

Had Steve known it, his efforts to keep his younger brother out of trouble were wasted.

Chip's head throbbed violently. He opened his eyes and blinked hard. His hand touched the smooth metal of the sea-scooter's side. Water was disappearing beneath it. Only now did Chip realise he was no longer wearing his mask.

There was a resounding clang as metal hit metal, while Chip watched steel doors close. Then, slowly, he turned.

An artificial light beamed down on him, illuminating the box-room enclosure he was in.

A movement brought back a montage of jumbled thoughts and memories: the two men were clambering out of the scooter. One was already climbing metal steps towards a hatch in the ceiling.

'Get up! *Move!*'

The words echoed painfully in his throbbing head as a hand gave Chip a forceful shove.

Final minute eddies of water vanished through the narrowing crack before the floor was sealed shut.

Chip was led up the steps and along a passage. He noticed port-holes and white-capped waves beyond. The sea . . . he was on a boat. Even as he made his way towards a metal doorway, he remembered the tunnel from the loch.

A firm push from behind sent his thoughts scattering again. Chip hit the floor and rolled over. He felt rope bite into his ankles.

'Free, you're dangerous – whoever you are! Your interference could have destroyed months of careful research and planning.'

'Always reckoned to be a bit of a bungler!' Chip grinned. But his words held no humour. The cold metal floor rubbed his wrists together.

The door banged shut. There was the sound of a bolt sliding and faint words echoed.

'He'll give no more trouble. But his partner could be in the bubble . . .'

'Too bad!' A new voice replied. Chip bit his lip and listened; he could only just hear what was being said.

'We have all the information required,' continued the voice. 'I have received instructions. We depart tonight. But first you and Gustav will destroy the bubble craft – you will leave just after sunset!'

There was the faintest trace of an accent in the voice. Chip thought hard, but could determine nothing more than that the speaker was probably central European. But the man had not finished.

Chip rolled across the floor, missing vital words. But now he could hear more clearly, as he lay beside the door.

'You two will take the scooter. It will bc a simple matter to place limpet mines . . . You will have ten minutes to get clear . . .'

Chip could not understand the brief reply each man uttered, though he imagined it to be some sort of acknowledgement.

In the silence that followed, Chip inspected the room thoughtfully. If the ship sailed, he knew he would go with it. There could be no telling what they would do with him. But, more important, what had happened to Steve? Chip had felt all along that his brother was alive, and now he was certain he must be inside the huge bubble, just as one of his captors had said.

What the bubble actually was, Chip still had no idea. For that matter he did not care. All he knew was that to save Steve he had to stop the plan he had overheard.

Chip halted his continual straining against his bonds. The corded rope bit hard on his flesh, numbing his hands. But that would not go on for much longer: Chip had seen his one chance to escape.

'Craaack!'

Glass splintered and Chip withdrew his heel. He was glad Gustav or the other man had not removed his 'wet' suit. Carefully, he rolled over, so that his fingers touched one sharp fragment from the smashed glass of the mask he had spotted by the wall.

Other equipment lay in disorderly fashion close by. It had been *their* mistake to lock him in a store-room, he grinned to himself.

The first step was to cut through the rope; the next . . . he hesitated, pondering on what he would do. But already a rough plan was forming in his mind.

With one final effort, Chip parted the last remaining strand of the rope around his wrists.

Wiping perspiration from his forehead, he continued to untie his ankles. Then he edged to the door and listened.

A brief shuffling of restless feet told him all that he needed to know. The room was being guarded. Moving silently across to the single porthole, Chip looked out across the expanse of choppy water. As he focused on the cliffs in the distance he noticed a trailing line up their side. He realised all at once what that represented. Only the previous day he had been reading a spy thriller as Steve had driven the Volkswagen along that winding road.

Now Chip was on the very vessel which he had seen sending the mysterious signals. He scratched his chin thoughtfully. Steve would not laugh now. Beyond doubt, it *was* a spy ship!

A crimson sun settled on the water as Chip glanced through the porthole several hours later.

Everything was ready; he nodded to himself. His fingers closed more tightly on the two disc shapes in his hands. The room was in shadow now, but he could still see the various pieces of diving equipment silhouetted against the wall in the corner. The weight-belt he had found would certainly carry someone down – but faster than they might ever imagine!

Chip's stomach gave a hungry rumble. The tension he felt probably caused it to protest a little more violently than it would otherwise have done.

Food: the thought wavered across his mind. But it also served to remind him it was nearly time for action – it must be, if his plan were to succeed. He knew that shortly the sea-scooter would return to the loch. Somehow, he had to be on it!

Chip's one gamble was that his captors would bring him something to eat. He had had nothing since boarding the ship. Otherwise, he would have to think of something else . . .

A well-greased bolt was withdrawn. Chip looked up with a start; he had scarcely noticed the quiet footsteps preceding the sudden sound.

Now a throat was cleared, and the metal door between himself and freedom swung open.

Even as the guard entered, Chip hurled one of the small but heavy lead weights straight at the port-hole. Glass shattered with a resounding crash. The heavily built man swung round, both gaze and pistol turned towards the direction from which the noise had come.

At that moment, Chip acted. He had positioned himself behind the door, and now he brought his hand, which held the second weight, down before the guard could even guess what was happening.

There was a dull thud as the man hit the floor. Chip breathed a long, relieved sigh. Then, grabbing an air cylinder, flippers and another mask, he cautiously peered round the doorway.

The long, grey-painted corridor was empty. As he secured the cylinder to his back, he hesitated; a strong but pleasant odour drifted towards him.

Chip's mouth creased in a nervous smile. The guard lay motionless where he had fallen. Inches from his outstretched hand, a tin plate had loosed its contents across the floor.

What a waste! That's what Steve would have said – in any circumstances other than these. Gravy spread in an ever-expanding pool. Chip noticed it was already seeping round a small metal object.

Of course! The pistol. He had better take that. He'd never fired a gun in his life. But he had watched Steve use an air-rifle. Besides, even the report might halt eager pursuers.

The corridor seemed endless as Chip walked quickly towards the far end. Behind him, the door from his own temporary cell was once again locked, housing the unconscious guard.

Chip guessed the sea-scooter had entered the hull of the ship through a submarine air-lock. That was where he must head for.

But one question worried him more than any other. When would the man named Gustav and his partner leave for the loch?

The vaguest suggestion of a creak made Chip throw himself behind a fire-locker. A door was opened and a voice gave him the answer.

'You will leave now. Everything is ready.'

For the second time that day, Chip heard the same indistinguishable reply and the two men he had first seen at the loch walked past him and down the iron steps.

Chip waited a moment or two, and then followed.

He glanced about him, but there was no time now to consider the risk. Luck had been with him so far. It just had to remain a little longer.

At the bottom of the steps, the two men paused. Chip halted uncertainly behind – and slightly above them.

'See you in the air-lock, Gustav. I'll just pull on my suit and cylinders. The explosives are packed . . .'

The other man nodded briefly and continued down a secondary corridor. Gustav turned towards a door, opened it, and disappeared from sight.

From now on, Chip's plan held no detail. He knew he had to replace one of the agents on the sea-scooter. Gripping the pistol firmly he pulled the goggles up over his face and walked down the side corridor.

It would be touch and go. But this was his one chance – while the two men were separated.

'Ah, Gustav – I said the air-lock. I'll just strap this on . . .'

A cold chill ran up Chip's spine as he watched the man clasp the steel diver's knife. So far, he had not been recognised by the other's fleeting glance. But he could not afford a longer one . . .

It was as the man bent down to secure the holster that Chip moved. His own swiftness startled him as the pistol butt rose and came down again.

The man did not rise again.

It took only seconds for Chip to reach the hatch into the air-lock, through which he had ascended earlier. He felt slightly more confident now, knowing he had not been instantly recognised. The dagger, too, added to his reassurance, clipped in its sheath on his calf.

Nevertheless, he climbed down into the air-lock, every nerve tuned like a bow-string. Yes, Gustav was there all right. He was seated in the front of the sea-scooter.

Chip appeared to readjust his goggles as the man acknowledged him. Then he sat astride the rear seat and water closed over his mask.

It had worked.

The underwater journey through the tunnel and into the loch was one which Chip would never forget. He thanked his lucky stars that Gustav was steering the scooter. Now he hoped he would stay lucky!

There was no light from the evening sky and visibility was poor – though now Chip did not mind. Slowly, however, the massive circular outline loomed before them. Chip's thoughts turned from Steve to the small but powerful magnetic mines that were loaded aboard the scooter. He had once read a spy story which included the use of limpet mines. They were fixed to the hull of the vessel intended to be destroyed. Then a timing device would be set . . .

The vibration caused by their engine suddenly ceased and the scooter glided gracefully to a halt. The man called Gustav slipped from his seat and turned towards the net bag containing the mines, gesturing to Chip to bring them. Chip did so, ensuring he kept his face away from the other's gaze.

While he swam behind the agent towards the huge bubble, Chip was thinking harder than he had ever done in his life.

Handing over the four explosives, he returned swiftly to the scooter while Gustav secured the mines to the side of the bubble and set timing devices. The slightest glimmer of an idea had occurred to him.

Chip had watched the man working the controls of the scooter. Now he pressed a button and clung on as the small craft plunged forward. He did not stop it, but aimed its nose directly towards the bubble.

Gustav spun round, his face twisting in a combination of amazement and anger. As Chip closed in, the agent realised his mistake.

There was a booming clang as the scooter struck home. Chip gripped the controls savagely. If there were anyone within the globe-like structure the sound would immediately alert them.

His mouthpiece was wrenched free.

It was a long shot, but his next move was not.

Momentarily stunned, Gustav reeled over at the mercy of the scooter's undercurrent. Chip calculated he had just enough time to do what he had to do.

Drawing the dagger from its sheath attached to his leg, he slipped the blade under the first mine, where it clung to the wall of the bubble. But it was stuck hard.

Chip strained every muscle as he levered at the knife. As the mine separated he was thrown suddenly backwards. It took only a few seconds to place it in the net bag he carried.

Now Chip worked feverishly to detach the three other magnetic explosives. And Gustav . . . how long would he remain dazed?

Steel fingers closing round his throat gave him the answer. Then, his mouthpiece was wrenched free . . .

Chip was never quite sure what happened after that. But the grip went limp; air once more returned to his lungs. Opening his eyes, he watched a frogman leave him and swim to the last remaining mine attached to the bubble.

Chip checked his diver's watch, blinking hard. He knew the mines had been set for a ten-minute clearance. At least five of those precious minutes had gone.

Now he noticed other frogmen in the water nearby. The darker suit revealed Gustav's limp form being dragged away by other men.

Chip swam to join the frogman who struggled with the last attached explosive. The horror on the man's face told him all he needed to know: obviously, the time-device could not be altered.

But Chip did not hesitate. He was determined to carry out the plan he had begun when Gustav had attacked him. Taking the four mines, he turned and swam powerfully to the floating sea-scooter, so far forgotten.

He indicated to the other frogmen to stay clear. The four explosives were soon stuck firmly to the scooter's torpedo-shaped hull. Then Chip started the engine for the second time, and climbed aboard.

He would return the 'eggs' to the nest!

Seconds ticked by faster than he imagined, as he checked his watch. Three minutes . . . But, already, on looking again, it was down to two and a half . . .

There was the tunnel. Chip dived clear.

His arms and legs ached with the effort – but he swam back without halting. Any moment, he expected the water to erupt about him.

Finally, his hand touched the bubble. Strong arms dragged him up through the cylindrical air-lock at its base.

Next moment, the circular craft rocked violently. Chip felt something hit his head and his mind raced to greet unconsciousness.

Words penetrated Chip's brain in a blur of fleeting impressions. A calm voice encouraged him to open his eyes.

'He's O.K.,' he heard someone say. Then a face peered down at him.

'Chip, you've not only saved the day; you've saved our lives into the bargain! Though you had to go and knock yourself out on that ledge!'

Slowly, painfully, memories became more distinct. Chip recalled the 'honeycombed' round roof he had noted before . . . nothing.

'*Steve!*' The name parted from Chip's mouth before full impact had registered.

'That's right!' his brother responded, a broad grin spreading across his face. 'Thanks to you. There's a lot I want to hear . . .'

'That goes for all of us,' a new voice interrupted. Chip turned to focus on the tall man beside Steve. 'Tell us all about it!'

'"Industrial espionage on an international level"; that's what the Naval Commander said, didn't he?' Steve looked at his brother.

'Watch where you're driving – or the Volkswagen will be taking a dive into the loch with us!' Chip interrupted. His brother turned again to the road ahead. Beyond it, they could already see several other vehicles parked beside a large expanse of water. They were glad to be there, at last.

'It was the storm which led us to think we were at the right loch,' the elder brother continued.

'And which somehow got us through the radio defence beam. I really would like to take another look at that bubble!' Chip said. He fanned the pages of a book with his fingers.

'All the Commander said was that it was undergoing pressure tests before use in the Pacific . . . and then something about it housing experts and the equipment to mine the sea-bed at tremendous depths for precious minerals. He shut up like a clam after that, so the whole thing must be very hush-hush. Still, he certainly made it worth our while not to be curious.'

'And more!' Chip agreed, glancing over his shoulder at the brand new ultra-sophisticated diving gear in the back of the Volkswagen. 'Just wait till the others see it, and hear our story!'

'I bet they'll wish they could have seen those Naval destroyers round up your spy ship, eh?'

Chip grinned reminiscently. It had been exciting.

'It seems my captors thought it well worth the risks they took, spying on the bubble, to get a headstart on mining all those billions of pounds' worth of minerals lying untouched on the sea-bed!'

'Talking of risk, Chip, you took a few yourself. But those

men from the Navy who took me into the bubble would never have believed my story, but for you turning up . . . They thought I was an enemy agent.'

'That's hardly surprising, with your pug-ugly mug and aggressive nature,' Chip added, before lowering his head. Steve was about to reply when he noticed his brother had returned to the dog-eared page in his spy-thriller. But this time he had no intention of disturbing him!

Spies Die at Dawn

by Sean Gregory

The First Shot is Fired

TOP SECRET (DE-CYPHERED)
TO: OFFICE OF SPECIAL SERVICES,
WASHINGTON, D.C.
COPY TO: DEPARTMENT OF STATE, FOREIGN
OFFICE (DEPT. XNO).
FROM: CHECKMATE, LONDON
DATE AS CYPHERED.

THE MAN YOU WANT IS KNOWN AS TOLEDO STEELE AND IS AT PRESENT ON HOLIDAY IN SAN FRANCISCO. HE HAS OFTEN BEEN EMPLOYED BY THIS DEPARTMENT AND CAN BE HIGHLY RECOMMENDED. HE STILL OCCASIONALLY WORKS FOR THIS DEPARTMENT ON SPECIAL ASSIGNMENTS ALTHOUGH OFFICIALLY HIS CONNECTION HAS BEEN TERMINATED. HE SPEAKS FLUENT SPANISH AND SPENT SIX MONTHS IN THE STATE OF URSULINO IN 1957. HIS ADDRESS IN SAN FRANCISCO FOLLOWS BY SEPARATE CYPHER.

(ENDS)

MEMO FROM O.S.S. (DEPT. SA) TO O.S.S. (DEPT.

FRISCO): TOP SECRET. DATE AS CYPHERED. ATTACHED WILL INFORM YOU ABOUT TOLEDO STEELE. SET HIM ON KEPERLA BUSINESS AND GIVE HIM REASONABLY FREE HAND.

(ENDS)

The shot echoed through the dark alley like a thunderclap crashing over cloudbanks. It woke the buildings to life and its sound bounced with jangling discord off a dustbin close against the wall. It was an angry sound, as though the person squeezing the trigger had forced a lifetime of hatred into the bullet before it surged from the pistol muzzle.

Toledo Steele heard the bee-like whine of the bullet in the same instant as his perfectly-trained reflexes threw him to the dust of the alley. He rolled over, squeezing himself against the wall, as far behind the dustbin as possible. He stayed there, not moving, a figure turned to stone. The rough paving was cool against his shoulder as he pressed close to the ground; the smell of the garbage wrinkled his nostrils.

After the shot came silence. The silence dropped on the alley like a warm blanket falling on a June night. Nothing stirred between the buildings.

Toledo Steele waited, hardly breathing. The fingers of his left hand explored the paving cautiously, feeling through the dark for the comforting touch of the silver-topped cane which had fallen from his hand when he thrust for cover. His fingers explored without noise, drifting across the paving like spiders, casting this way and that through the litter of paper and rubbish.

Then, at the end of the alley where it turned into the Via Pamplona, there was a rustle of movement. It was no more than the faintest twitch of a movement, the dying echo of a step in the dark, but to Toledo Steele's ears, super-tuned for the slightest indication of the gunman's presence, it sounded like an explosion. His eyes strained through the darkness, trying to catch sight of the person who shared the alley with him; ten minutes earlier and the lights from the Via Pamplona would easily have silhouetted him, but now the street lighting was darkened and the few remaining advertising signs were too far away to be of use.

The movement came again. Toledo recognised it this time as a light footfall, the sound made by someone walking on tip-toe, cautious step by cautious step. At the same time, his seeking fingers brushed across the head of his cane, and he drew it gently towards him. There was no other sound as he twisted the silver knob which formed the cane, and the cane that was more than just a cane, became, swiftly and silently, the deadly blade of a swordstick.

Toledo waited. The footsteps came again, a little more sure this time, as though the gunman was convinced he had dealt effectively with his victim. But whoever it was still trod on the tips of his toes, for there was no echoing crunch of a heel. Step by step, the would-be killer drew nearer and Toledo tensed his muscles for a sudden, slashing leap that would carry him alongside the gunman, ready to thrust the rapier into unsuspecting flesh.

He moved. He came up from behind the dustbin like a rocket, jumping to where sound told him the man now stood. His left hand whipped round the other's body and fell, as though drawn by invisible magnets, on to a wrist. It was, to his surprise, a slim wrist round which his strong fingers gripped easily. And – another surprise – the hand held no gun.

His reflexes carried the rapier to within fractional inches of the other's throat as he whispered, 'Move, you jackal, and you are food for the dogs.'

Into that whisper he managed to put a ferocity which stopped his captive dead. He also held the wrist so tightly that the prisoner gave a yelp of pain which was followed immediately by a startled query in a voice pitched too high to belong to a man.

'Qué es?' The question was asked in an accent which was decidedly not native South American. Toledo's fingers let go of the wrist, which was undoubtedly a woman's. And the owner said, 'Take your hands off me!'

She said it in English, too, with an American accent. Toledo stepped back, bringing the rapier up so that its point rested delicately at the curve of the woman's throat. 'You're a lousy marksman,' he said, 'but I'm a very good swordsman, and I have no scruples about killing women who try to kill me.'

'I should most certainly like to kill you, if you gave me a chance,' the woman said savagely. She sounded like an angry leopardess, waiting her chance to leap, and once again she had relapsed into her bad Spanish.

Toledo replied in the same language: 'Be sure, then, that I shall not give you that chance, Señorita.' In English he added, 'Turn around.'

The beam of a pencil flashlight sprang suddenly across the woman. She recoiled as the light illuminated her features. Toledo saw a girl of about twenty-five, a honey-blonde with large eyes that were dark with fear. At her ears were jade drops that twinkled like emerald fire in the light.

'Turn around and walk ahead of me,' Toledo said.

The girl's upper lip curled. 'Satisfied, Señor?' She was back in Spanish once more.

'Just turn around and let's go on talking in English. You're better in that language.' He watched the colour mount in her throat as she whirled on her heel. 'The door immediately facing you,' he told her. 'Just push it and walk up the stairs.'

She moved easily, Toledo thought, as she walked ahead of him. He watched her as he slid the bolts home on the street door. He thought about the bolts, and realised he was doing this for some queer reason that lurked at the back of his mind. But he could not say what it was.

She had the look of a woman who was accustomed to expensive living, to escorts who treated her courteously, rather than urging her at sword-point.

He sighed and snapped on the electric light. Sheathing the rapier as quickly as he had brought it into action only a few moments ago, he took the girl's arm, led her up a flight of stairs, and then nodded towards a door on the first landing.

'I live here,' he said.

She gave him a glance of curiosity as he steered her into the small, badly furnished room with its iron bedstead, one chair, and chest of drawers. She was obviously comparing the room with his immaculate grey gaberdine suit, his cream nylon shirt, and his carefully knotted silk tie.

Toledo closed the door behind him and reached out with his cane to draw the tattered curtains across the single window. From the window could be seen the harbour, and beyond the harbour, on a long promontory jutting out to sea, the black walls of the Castellado. Toledo thought about the Castellado at that moment and remembered why he was here in São Vittorio, seaport capital of Ursulino. He wondered if the girl had anything to do with his reason for being there.

He caught her mood of curiosity. 'Yes, I really live here,' he said.

He pointed to the bed. 'You can sit over there. I'll take the chair.' He spun the chair round in a swift movement and dropped on it with his arms resting on the back.

'You speak English very well,' said the girl. She looked as though she was very frightened but was determined not to show it.

He corrected her. 'I speak English perfectly. Now,' he said pleasantly, 'perhaps you'll tell me why you tried to shoot me just now. I think you owe me an explanation, at least!'

The angry look returned to her dark eyes. 'I didn't shoot at you. I didn't even have a gun.'

'You could have got rid of it somewhere,' Toledo pointed out. 'Someone shot at me, and you were the only other person in the alley.'

'I don't know about being the only person in the alley, but I didn't shoot at you.' Her voice was a strong denial. 'I was as scared as you were.'

Toledo looked at her through narrowed eyes, saying, 'Well, you've no pockets to conceal a hairpin, let along a gun. So if you didn't shoot at me, you must have got rid of the gun.'

'I tell you, I didn't!' Her cheeks were dark with sudden colour. 'Anyway, Mr Toledo Steele, do you usually do this when people call on you – I mean, force perfect strangers up to your room at the point of a dagger?'

'It's a rapier,' Toledo corrected mildly. Then he added, quickly, 'How do you know my name?'

She started to say something, checked herself and said, 'I was – told.'

'Let's not play around,' said Toledo. 'Someone told you – who?' He picked up the rapier and patted her arm with it.

The girl looked annoyed. 'You needn't think you can force me to tell you. But I don't see that it matters, anyway. Colonel Maturez told me.'

'Maturez? You mean El Presidente's right-hand man? Then I take it you work for him,' said Toledo.

'I don't work for anybody. My name is Lynn Keperla. I'm in São Vittorio to visit my husband's grave. He died of fever here about six months ago.'

Toledo sat bolt upright. 'You're Gene Keperla's wife?'

'Widow,' she said quietly.

'All right. So you went to see Maturez about getting permission to trek into the mountains to see where your husband is buried – am I right in thinking that is what happened?'

She nodded. 'And Maturez sent me to see you. He said you had known my husband and that you could take me into the mountains.'

'So . . .' Toledo drawled out the word through pursed lips. Maturez had sent Lynn Keperla to see him. Only Maturez had never met him and, by rights, should not even know of his existence. Furthermore, Maturez had invented a flimsy story to persuade the girl to do this. Toledo had never met Gene Keperla and certainly did not know where in the mountains he was supposed to be buried.

He produced his wallet and held up a photograph in front of the girl. 'Do you know this man?' he asked.

Lynn Keperla's eyes lit up. 'Why – that's my husband. That's Gene! Then you did know him?'

'I've never seen him in my life,' replied Toledo. 'That's what makes all this so very interesting. You know, I believe you now. You didn't shoot at me. Somebody else did the shooting, and they were aiming at you!'

'At me? But why should anyone want to kill me?'

The Escape that Failed

'Because you've turned up out of the blue and want to go hunting for Gene Keperla's grave,' he said with conviction.

'I honestly don't understand,' she said with a puzzled expression. 'Who would be shooting at me, and why?'

'The exact person I can't name,' replied Toledo. 'But I do know this – he would be employed by Colonel Maturez.'

'Oh, come now!' she laughed. 'People like Colonel Maturez don't go around hiring other people to shoot complete strangers. You're joking.'

'I'm most certainly not,' said Toledo. 'Look – you'll have to trust me. I know more about this than you do. When Maturez sent you here tonight, he sent you into a trap. He doesn't want you, for some reason of his own, to visit your husband's grave – wherever it is. So he decided to get rid of you – a shot in the dark, an arrest, immediate imprisonment for someone. And you know who that someone would have been?' He touched his chest. 'Me!'

'Now you're saying Colonel Maturez doesn't like you, either!'

Toledo nodded. 'That's right. He's never met me, but he knows – or guesses – why I'm here. Maturez is plotting for power – the President is an old man, and Maturez wants to be certain he succeeds, whether by fair means or foul. Until you came along, I thought he hadn't a notion I was even in São Vittorio . . . which just shows how wrong you can be. But now he does know I'm here, he also knows I can upset his apple cart.'

He stood up and pulled aside the curtains. 'Over there is the Castellado. Everyone thinks it's just an old castle now, full of historic relics and used as a barracks for the police and the Presidential Guards. You know what's underneath? The old dungeons, which Maturez has brought back into use.'

The girl shook her head. 'I'm afraid I don't understand. I still think you're making all this up.'

'I'll put it in a nutshell,' Toledo said, 'Maturez doesn't want you around. He doesn't want me around, either. So he sends you here, has a gunman follow you, shoot at you, and then springs a trap with police all around the block. The police arrest me for killing you, and down I go into the Castellado – and that's the last anyone ever sees of me. I wondered why a local gendarme didn't come around when the shot was fired,' he added. 'Now I know!'

Lynn Keperla sat up straight, one hand at her throat. 'But why should Maturez – ?' She paused, her eyes wide with amazement.

'Some day,' said Toledo Steele, 'when I have more time, I'll explain the politics of this interesting little state of Ursulino. I'll also give you the facts of life as they concern Colonel Maturez. I might even tell you why I'm living in one room on the waterfront like a tramp.' He listened again. 'But right now,' he added quickly, 'you're getting out of here, and you're going fast!'

There was noise suddenly from the alley – the tramp of feet, the barking of orders, the clatter of automatic rifles. Then someone began beating against the street door, and Toledo grinned.

'What did I tell you?' There was a cynical twist to his mouth. 'Here come the local flatfeet, all ready to arrest me and knock you off in the same breath!'

She stood up, colour draining from her face. 'But where can I go? If they're in the alley –'

'I had the forethought to bolt the front door,' said Toledo coolly. 'That should give us about two minutes. You're going over the roof.' He slid to the window, thrusting back the curtains and opening it wide in a movement that looked as if it had been rehearsed a score of times. Outside lay a flat roof from which an iron staircase led upwards and across to the next building. Toledo grasped the girl's wrist.

He pointed. 'Up the staircase – across the next roof – through the skylight – down the stairs – knock on the door of number 15 – there's a back way to the main street. They know about letting people through – why d'you think I chose this place?' His smile was an invitation to danger and recklessness and trouble and laughter, all rolled into one. 'I'll try to help you – later,' he said. 'Now get going – and meet me in the Café Horan tomorrow morning at eleven!'

She didn't answer, but her smile in return was enough. Then she was gone, and on to the flat roof, and racing up the narrow iron steps. Toledo left the window open and turned back to the door. At the foot of the stairs there was a crash as the bolts to the street door gave way and police poured into the building. Again moving as though to a prearranged plan – which, in fact, it was, for Toledo Steele had lived this long only by taking what he considered were well-calculated risks – he swept the chair into place under the handle of the door and snapped the old-fashioned lock. He swung himself on to the flat roof and waited, poised delicately to the left of the open window. And, once again, the silver-topped cane was in his hand, and bared to its sinister length.

He did not have long to wait. The door banged open in a matter of seconds under the shoulders of the police, and men thronged into the room. For a few seconds there was confusion, with much shouting in Spanish. 'The window – he has gone that way!' they called.

A head poked through the curtains, its owner sniffing the night air, tainted with the smells of the harbour.

Toledo said, 'Boo!' and neatly scratched the policeman's left ear. Instantly the head withdrew to the accompaniment of a yell, and again there was considerable noise and shouting from the room.

Next came a fusillade of shots, directed straight out of the window and doing no more damage than clipping a portion of the balustrade. Toledo gave vent to a loud groan, on the principle that he should encourage this waste of ammunition. There was a cry of triumph from within the room, and another head popped out of the window, this time preceded by a hand holding a heavy service-pattern revolver.

It was time to go, Toledo Steele thought. He had given the girl a chance to get clear; now it was his turn to make a getaway. His sword-arm flicked neatly, and the back of the policeman's wrist was suddenly bloodstained, and he let go the revolver with a yelp of pain. Toledo sheathed the swordstick like a conjurer

He came to rest on all fours.

getting rid of his nightly pack of cards, reversed it, and brought the top down on the unfortunate policeman's head. The policeman said something like 'Ugh', and draped himself half in and half out of the window, effectively blocking the way for his colleagues.

Toledo whipped round, leaping the low balustrade to the left of the window and dropping like a cat on the sloping eaves of the adjoining roof. Again it looked like a carefully rehearsed movement, and again it was just that. He came to rest on all fours, the slim swordstick gripped, pirate-fashion, between his teeth; in fact, he looked for all the world like one of the old-time pirates who had once swarmed the southern seas, and he was certainly equally as dangerous.

Cautiously he let himself slide down the tiles until his feet came to rest against a guttering. He swung over, using the guttering as a pivot to launch his body to the ground, ten feet below. He fell in the centre of a mass of rubble, but a centre that was magically clear of all obstructions. The magic was again concerned with Toledo Steele, who for the past three days had made certain that there was a cleared space just ready for him.

Above, on the flat roof, the confusion was growing worse, and the shouting was even louder. Toledo Steele paused to light a cigarette, then tucked the silver-topped cane under his left arm with the air of a dandy and strolled out of the yard.

He was not prepared for the sharp muzzle of the gun that poked into his ribs, nor the soft voice which, close to his ear, said in Spanish, 'Señor Steele! You will oblige me by raising your hands!'

Toledo said, 'Why goodness me – of course.' He said it with a mildness of tone which would have made those who knew him worry, for Toledo Steele was very mild when he was very dangerous. But the man who held the gun in his ribs did not know him and, in fact, had never met him before.

The man with the gun snapped an order. 'Guards! Come quickly!' The sound of running feet followed the command in a flash, and four or five burly soldiers loomed out of the darkness. A light clicked on, momentarily blinding Toledo, and a hand took away his precious swordstick. Other hands spun him round to face the man with the gun.

Dimly, through the haze of torches, Toledo saw his captor. The man was taller than himself, and probably weighed another fifteen or twenty pounds. He wore the blue uniform of the Presidential Guard, with its double-breasted high-collared tunic and riding breeches tucked into mirror-polished boots. His peaked cap gave him the appearance of a wartime Nazi general.

'Good evening, Señor Steele,' he said. 'My name is Colonel Maturez.' This time he spoke in English.

Toledo flipped a mock salute from his forehead. 'You have a natty taste in uniforms,' he murmured. 'But maybe that's habit. As I remember, wasn't your name once Baldur Fleischmann, and weren't you a major in the Gestapo?'

Maturez bowed slightly. 'Very clever, Señor Steele. As it happens, you are quite correct – and that only increases my suspicions about you. The American Office of Special Services chooses a clever man to do its business in our little country.'

Toledo grinned at him. 'O.S.S.? You think I work for them? Brother, are you off beam!'

The Colonel shrugged. 'Do not bother to deny it. Naturally, you do not have an American accent, but my information is that you came here from San Francisco and that you have dollars to spend. There is other information, too.'

'Quite a little spy-ring, aren't you?' commented Toledo. 'Well – where do we go from here?'

'I think we shall go to the Castellado,' replied Maturez pleasantly. 'You are a dangerous man, Señor Steele, but the

Castellado will keep you safe until I am ready to make a decision about you!'

'You chill my blood,' Toledo grinned. 'But let's go, Baldur, my nasty old Nazi. The inside of your best prison is something to which I have been looking forward for a considerable time!'

Break-out!

It was a dark, dirty, and miserable cell. It was also located so many feet below ground that Toledo Steele felt it was beneath the level of the harbour bottom. The consequence was that the cell was not just damp – it was practically a miniature swimming pool.

The Castellado prison of São Vittorio was ostensibly a show-place for tourists. Built on the tip of a promontory that jutted into the South Atlantic like a pointing finger, it towered some two hundred feet above ground with the majesty of a mediaeval castle. Exactly how far below ground it extended, no one outside Ursulino really knew, but by now Toledo Steele had a good idea. He also considered that the Castellado the tourists knew – the intricate maze of above-ground staircases and vast halls – was only a very small part of the enormous structure. Originally built with slave labour by one of the pirate chieftains who had settled on this part of the coast, it was now apparently disused and served as a museum and a monument to the past.

At least, thought Toledo, that's what the guide-books said and what the tourists were told. He looked round the dripping walls of his cell and added a rider to his thoughts: *Brother, they should be with me now!*

Only a tiny corner of light, from the flickering lantern of the guard in the passage, penetrated into the cell through the twelve-inch square iron grating in the door. By standing on his toes, Toledo could just see through the grating to where the guard stood propped against the wall, chewing reflectively on a slice of beef. This group of cells was arranged in a rough semi-circle facing the guard, with the passage leading off at a tangent. Whether there was anyone in the other cells, Toledo could not see; that was a matter which could wait, anyway. For the moment he had achieved his object – to get inside the Castellado – though his original intention had not been to achieve that object as a prisoner himself.

The guards, hustling him down the rocky passages into the depths of the prison, had not bothered to carry out more than a perfunctory search of his pockets. It was presumed that those confined in the depths of the Castellado were confined for good and all; the use of a hidden file or a hacksaw blade would have been like trying to break into Fort Knox with a tin-opener. Accordingly, Toledo removed his left shoe and sock and produced pieces of green paper that rustled invitingly; he also felt his ankle where the razor blade in its chamois sheath was taped neatly to his flesh, and the inside of his thigh, where a light-weight ·32 was a constant reassurance.

He thought about Colonel Maturez and was instantly glad that the Colonel had immediately handed him over to the guards, postponing temporarily the inevitable talk with his prisoner. Colonel Maturez, hc felt, would not have missed such points; his search would have been very thorough indeed.

Toledo rustled the slip of green paper at the grating. He spoke in Spanish. 'Señor Capitan! Señor Capitan! I would speak with you!'

The guard ambled towards the cell, grumbling to himself. His keys jingled invitingly at the leather belt on his hip. Then his eyes caught sight of the ten-dollar bill of good American currency, and his hand reached out to take it. Toledo made a pretence of snatching it back, but was just not quick enough to keep the guard's fingers off the bill.

'Do not think,' said the guard, pocketing the bill with a furtive look over his shoulder, 'that you can bribe me to let you free. Even if I were to be persuaded to unlock your cell door and permit you a chance of escape, you would not get past the other guards on the levels above.' He chuckled. 'Rest easy, man. You will leave here only in a box.'

'Those are words without comfort,' Toledo said, making his voice sound dismal. 'But I had not expected to receive more than a little information from the tendering of this money.'

'Information?' The guard sounded puzzled. 'What information can be of value to you here? You are not concerned with the weather nor with anything of what happens outside this pest-hole. What good can it do you?'

'The information I seek,' said Toledo confidentially, 'concerns matters within the Castellado. Satisfy my curiosity, I pray you. For instance, is there perhaps another American imprisoned here?' He lowered his voice. 'If there is, I am prepared to pay well for a message delivered to him.'

'You have more of – this?' The guard's tone was incredulous. For answer, Toledo stepped back from the door and rustled the rest of his money. The guard added: 'Most certainly there is an American here. He inhabits a cell on the level above this. For a consideration' – his voice dropped to a coaxing purr, or as near to that state as it would ever get – 'I can deliver your message to him.'

'Excellent! You are a clever man, Señor Capitan.' Toledo rustled the money again. 'Pray open the door and join me for a moment so that I may write by the light of your lantern. Otherwise I cannot see to write my note.'

'You take me for a fool?' The guard was instantly on the defensive. 'Were I to enter your cell, you might attack me.'

Toledo laughed. 'Attack you? Señor Capitan, how is that possible? You are armed, and I am not.' He waved the dollar bills carelessly across the grating. 'Come – let us discuss this like friends.'

Greed overcame the guard's fears in a rush. 'Very well. But the slightest trick and I shall shoot.' He unhooked the lantern and began fumbling with the lock on the cell door. Toledo stood back, waiting. This was a moment when he could not fail, for if he did, he would not get a second chance.

Muttering to himself, the guard pushed open the door and stepped inside. He carried the lantern in one hand, his keys and his pistol in the other. He was a big man, big and fierce. He was also, Toledo thought, rather stupid.

'Where is the money?' he queried, closing the cell door behind him.

'Here.' Balanced on one leg, Toledo pretended to fumble in his shoe. 'I am finding it for you.' The effort of balance was too much for him. He stumbled, falling forward and clutching for support. The fall brought him, with the carefully calculated precision of a circus clown's tumble, into contact with the guard's pistol-hand. He grabbed and twisted, yanking the guard off balance. The pair of them fell headlong into a pool of water, the guard losing his keys and his gun at the same instant. He also intended to let out a yell which would awaken every guard in the Castellado, but Toledo was at least five jumps ahead of him on this. Five fingers that felt like a steel trap closed over the back of the guard's neck and banged his head hard on to the stone floor of the cell. The guard lost interest.

Toledo stood up, breathing heavily. It had been over more quickly than he had hoped. The lantern, falling into the swimming pool of the cell's floor, had gone out, and there was nothing around but inky blackness. Curiously, there was no sound from the other cells, which led Toledo to suppose that he had been deliberately placed alone in this lowest level of the vast prison.

There was no time to speculate, however. As best he could in the darkness, Toledo trussed the guard with his own braces and stuffed the man's dirty handkerchief in his mouth as a gag. With luck, it would give him enough time to get clear. He had a final thought, and retrieved the ten-dollar bill which had first tempted the guard. Experience, considered Toledo Steele, must be bought.

Then, picking up the man's revolver – which had luckily fallen on a dry patch of floor – he left the cell, locking the door behind him and dropping the keys through the grating in the door of another cell. Definitely these other cells were empty; he now realised there had not been a murmur from any one of them.

His eyes were growing more accustomed to the dark. Carefully, letting his left hand brush the wall, he moved along the passage. A flight of stone steps about twenty paces along the passage led upwards to a chamber where another lantern was burning. This presumably was the next level where the American, of whom the guard had spoken, was confined. Heavy footsteps pounding the stone flags also spoke of a further guard.

Toledo went up the steps in a cat-like rush, three at a time, soundlessly. There was a little smile playing at the corners of his mouth; he was in a beautiful, a wonderful jam, and he was enjoying every second of it.

He came upon the guard like a Red Indian on his prey. The man was standing full in the centre of the semi-circular chamber, watching the cell doors. He felt very safe and very sure.

And then Toledo's arm was around his throat, and the revolver was pressing hard against his lower ribs, and a smoothly wicked voice was saying in excellent Spanish, 'Quiet, Señor Guardia, unless you wish to die before your time.'

The guard wanted to live his full span of years; he stayed quiet. But there was sudden movement from the cells; voices began asking questions, begging, pleading. Toledo answered them: 'I am the opener of prison gates. Stay quiet and you will be free.' To the guard he added, 'In which cell is the American?'

The prisoner nodded towards the nearest of the half-dozen doors. Even had he dared, it was doubtful if he could have spoken, for his teeth were chattering with fright.

'You answer well,' Toledo told him. Swiftly he reversed the revolver and brought it down at just the right point on the guard's skull to lay him out without doing any permanent injury. Toledo was in a reasonably merciful mood and he had no quarrel with the guards themselves; they were merely doing their duty. He let the man crumple to the floor and immediately began removing the bunch of keys from his belt.

At the same time a voice came from the nearest cell. 'Who's there? What's going on?' The voice spoke English with a strong Middle West intonation, and Toledo knew he had found his man.

He tried various keys in the lock until one of them swung the door open. He spoke to the prisoner. 'Take it easy, pal. Just pretend I'm from American Express.'

The man was about his own age, but shorter in stature and running to fat. He wore a crumpled tan gaberdine suit and soiled suede shoes. His nylon shirt looked as if it had not been washed for a month and his necktie was loose and tattered. He came out of the cell in a stumbling run, thrusting out his hand in greeting.

'I don't know who you are – but thanks! Man, am I glad to see you!' His plump fingers grasped Toledo's hand. 'I'm Gene Keperla, by the way.'

'We can save the Dr-Livingstone-I-presume stuff for later,' said Toledo. 'My name's Steele. Now – let's get out of here!' He pointed to the unconscious guard. 'Help me get him into the cell.'

Together they hauled the man into the cell which Keperla

had just vacated, and Toledo locked the door. Then he unlocked the door of the adjoining cell and tossed the bunch of keys inside.

'That ought to start something,' he commented, and was immediately proved right. There was a wild shout from inside the cell and a tattered, ragged creature burst into the open, waving the keys around his head. Without taking any notice of either Toledo or the American, he began unlocking the other doors.

'You use a gun?' As the American nodded in reply, Toledo thrust the heavy service revolver into Keperla's hand. He unfastened the little ·32 strapped to his thigh, weighing it gently in the palm. He would have preferred the deadly swordstick, but that was now presumably a trophy of Colonel Maturez and therefore could be considered lost.

Temporarily lost, Toledo reminded himself. He wanted the return of his swordstick.

They set off up the next flight of steps. This was a circular staircase, apparently to somewhere just below ground level. The room in which they found themselves had a grating in the roof through which daylight filtered; better still, it was unoccupied. It seemed, from the weapons stacked around the walls, to be a guard-room, but like everything else about the Castellado, it was run in a fairly slap-happy fashion.

One exit from the guard-room, Toledo found by opening the door and peering out, led up stone steps to the main courtyard of the prison. As an escape route, it was something of a dead end, for groups of guards were obviously drilling in the courtyard.

There was, however, another door. This gave on to an interior corridor which terminated in another circular staircase. Probably it eventually found its way into the above-ground parts of the Castellado.

Toledo pointed to this door. 'Here's our exit.'

The American immediately protested. 'But the other door

leads to the courtyard. This way, we're only going back into the building.'

'How long,' asked Toledo grimly, 'do you think we'd last out there?' He glanced at the guard-room clock. 'Fifteen minutes to ten,' he commented. 'I've an appointment at eleven, and I want to keep it.'

He went into the corridor, running lightly to the foot of the stairs. Still no one was about. With Keperla at his heels, he took the stairs which brought him out in another corridor, this time at ground level. The corridor gave on to a series of rooms, all with locked doors, but at one end was an arch leading to a fresh part of the prison.

Toledo jerked a thumb towards the arch. 'We go that-a-way!' He raced along the corridor, flattening himself against the wall as he turned the corner – and instantly was in trouble.

They were in a large kitchen in which were a cook, a man who was apparently the under-cook, and a brace of guards engaged in obtaining rations. And, from below ground, Toledo could hear the noise of escaping prisoners pounding after them.

The cook, the under-cook, and the two guards faced them, open-mouthed. Then one of the guards decided to be brave. He reached for the revolver he wore at his waist.

Toledo's bullet scored neatly across his wrist and shattered a glass jar on the table behind him. In Spanish, Toledo said: 'The wise man moves cautiously at all times. Let there be no heroics, please, or you will regret it – I can assure you.'

There was no time to immobilise the four men; in a matter of seconds, the escape of the prisoners would have resounded all over the Castellado. But behind the cook stood a four-foot-high cauldron which was used for soup.

Toledo waved his automatic. 'Against the cauldron, Señores.' The men backed up, watching him for a false move. 'Seat yourselves on the edge,' he ordered.

When they were precariously balanced on the cauldron's lip, he took a sudden step forward, lifting his pistol menacingly. The first man threw up his arms to ward off an expected blow and fell backwards into the cauldron. Toledo flipped the heels of the next guard before quickly pushing the two cooks in the chest. That put four of the opposition literally in the pot, he thought, and banged down the heavy iron lid.

At that moment the door out of the kitchen opened, disclosing a view of cars and lorries beyond, and a fresh guard burst into the room, saying: 'The noise – what is all the noise?'

'Just a visitation,' replied Toledo mildly, and hurled a can of flour at him.

He followed the can with a running leap that took him into the guard's midriff. As he did so, Keperla flashed by him and levelled the revolver with obvious menace.

'No killing, you fool!' snarled Toledo. He thrust a fist into the guard's jaw, watching him crash backwards into a table loaded with crockery. Then he grabbed Keperla's shoulder. 'Cars out there – let's get one!'

They dashed into the next part of the prison, which was the garage. There were about five men visible here, two of them engaged in washing down a car, the other three chatting in a corner.

Toledo picked the car that was being washed – a big Lancia with a convertible body. He barked an order. 'Get the engine going – I'll hold them off and then join you!'

Keperla leapt at the car, pushing over one of the carwashers and dealing the other a blow with his revolver. Instantly the group of three began moving forward. Toledo snapped a bullet into the ground at their feet; they sprang to cover behind vehicles while he gave them another two shots for good measure.

Behind him, the Lancia's engine woke to life and he felt,

rather than actually heard, it moving away. He whirled as Keperla let in the clutch with a bang and the car jerked forward.

'You fool!' Toledo shouted. He jumped for the car, tumbling over into the back seat. He added, half in and half out of the car, 'You weren't going to wait for me!'

'A mistake!' Keperla panted. He swung the big car round and out of the garage, heading down the slope to the main gates of the Castellado. Beyond the gates stretched the main road back to São Vittorio – and freedom.

'I didn't mean to get the car going as quick as that,' Keperla explained. He changed gear neatly, setting the car at the gates.

Toledo rolled on to the rear seat. There wasn't time to hold an inquest. Behind them, guards were tumbling out of the garage, some of them with rifles. He shot a glance ahead. Already the main gates had started to close.

'Keep your foot down, pal – or we'll be minced meat between those gates,' he muttered.

Keperla didn't reply. He was hunched over the wheel, hurling the powerful car at the ever-narrowing gap between the gates. There were beads of sweat on his forehead, but he was handling the car like a master.

The walls loomed up, suddenly seeming very large and ugly in the morning sunshine. Somewhere a guard loosed off a shot that came near them, and Toledo ducked his head. Then there was a moment when everything seemed to be toppling in on them, and the great granite pillars on either side looked like monstrous mountains about to crush them. And then they were through, and the gates were grinding together just behind the car's tail-lights.

Toledo sank back on the cushions. 'Best jail-break I ever took part in,' he remarked conversationally, adding, 'This is an adventure I'm beginning to enjoy.'

Enter – a Tramp

The Café Horan was São Vittorio's main public eating place. It was also the capital of Ursulino's morning coffee-house, aperitif centre, night club, and a gossip exchange. Yasis, the Greek who owned the place, had lived in São Vittorio for more than twenty years – that is to say, through three revolutions, one minor earthquake, and a border war with its northern neighbour that had resolved precisely nothing for either side. Yasis, in fact, had seen Ursulino through most of its phases, including a monarchy and two republics. At the moment he lived under the protection of a fairly benevolent republic and he was growing fat and complacent. He tended towards a state of mind in which there was nothing left to surprise him.

In that he was wrong.

The morning after Toledo Steele's arrest by Colonel Maturez' police force there appeared in the Café Horan, at eleven a.m. precisely, a figure whose appearance, even by local standards, was decidedly villainous. It wore soiled trousers, a T-shirt which would never again see its original colour of light blue, and faded sandals. It looked as if it had not washed in several years, and certainly its hair could not have been combed for a considerable number of months. Furthermore, the growth of beard on its chin coupled with the festooning of mud that hung about is face and hair, added one hundred per cent to its tramp-like appearance.

Yasis was mildly disturbed. He rose from his normal position behind the cash desk and moved his four chins and three stomachs ponderously towards the tramp. His whole being seemed to say that the newcomer couldn't do that there here.

'Your pardon, sir, but –' he started to say.

'Shut up, Yasis, and don't be a fool,' replied Toledo Steele's voice from behind the dirt. 'Do you think I *like* looking this way?'

'Strewth!' said Yasis with feeling. It was the only English oath he knew and he considered it highly suitable for the occasion. He also thought Toledo's smell more than should be encouraged. He wrinkled his nose.

Toledo said, spotting the sign of distaste, 'Throw me out if you like, but get the English girl who sits in the corner by the juke-box to meet me behind your kitchens. You'll be paid well as usual.' He broke off and whined something in Spanish. Then he added, 'Now – throw me out!'

Yasis snapped his fingers and two of his waiters appeared to escort the tramp to the door. 'See this person goes to the kitchen and is given food,' said Yasis imperiously. 'Charity towards the unfortunate ones is ever a virtue in the sight of Heaven.'

Ten minutes later Toledo Steele, huddled on the kitchen doorstep with a bowl of soup between his hands, looked up to see Lynn Keperla approaching.

Any connection between the dirty, evil-smelling tramp and Toledo Steele obviously did not occur to her. She stood near the kitchen door and looked around for the man she had seen the previous night.

'Looking for me?' Toledo asked.

The girl jumped aside as though she had stepped barefoot on to a hot stone. She said sharply, 'What on earth – ?'

Toledo interrupted her. 'Keep your voice down and pretend you don't notice me. Just listen to what I have to say. I'm dressed like this because it's the only way I could get into town past the noses of Maturez' guards. Last night, after you got away, Maturez himself picked me up, and I spent most of the night in the Castellado.'

Lynn took a couple of steps away, then back, as though moving about while she waited for someone. 'I thought you said it was practically escape-proof,' she said.

Toledo took a spoonful of soup noisily. 'That's all you know, beautiful. The Castellado is still a very efficient prison underground.' He chuckled. 'But it would have to be a very efficient prison indeed to hold me. Now, will you do something for me?'

Cautiously, the girl answered, 'It depends.'

'Still don't trust me, do you? All I want you to do is to send a cable for me. The address is: "Steele, Poste Restante, San Francisco," and the message says, "Deal concluded." There isn't any signature.'

Lynn nodded. 'I have it. Do you mind telling me what it means?'

'Meet me on the north road out of town at ten tonight and I'll explain,' said Toledo. 'Just take a walk along the road and I'll pick you up. And by the way, don't on any account send that cable until the latest possible moment.'

'All right.' The girl still seemed doubtful. 'I owe you something for getting me away last night.'

'We are all in debt to one another,' Toledo said with a grin. He returned to his soup, watching Lynn as she walked away. Presently, he rose, handed the empty bowl through the kitchen window, and gave profuse thanks in Spanish to the plump and pleasant female who served as cook. Then he shuffled out of the yard and into the streets of São Vittorio.

He took his time about moving through the town, noticing how the local police seemed well in evidence and how more members of Maturez' Presidential Guard than usual seemed to be strolling through the streets. Walking with the effortless shuffle of the permanent tramp, he made his way towards the Central Square, where workmen were busy erecting a grandstand of sorts, facing a dais that was already in place by the fountain in the middle of the square. He rested for many minutes in the shade by the grandstand, apparently dozing, but actually making careful mental notes of the building of the grandstand

and the positioning of the temporary buildings.

Then he arose and wandered leisurely down the back streets until he came to a shop that sold second-hand clothing of all descriptions.

The proprietor, who bustled out from the back parlour to greet his customer, seemed at first inclined – as Yasis had been – to throw the tramp back into the street.

'I may look like the wrath of Heaven, Juanero, but I assure you that I am Señor Steele,' Toledo whispered.

Anton Juanero threw up his hands in horror. 'Señor Steele! to come here when the police are searching for you! They have already paid me one visit this morning.'

'They have?' Toledo was immediately interested. 'Doesn't it seem strange to you, Anton, that the police should connect me with you so suddenly?'

Juanero, a small man with a heavy moustache and large soulful eyes, made a gesture of dismissal. 'It may be nothing. They searched many houses, I understand. Naturally, they did not tell me for whom they were looking, but I learn certain matters.'

Toledo made his way into the parlour at the back of the shop, where cool shades kept the heat of the day from entering and an electric fan disturbed the air. 'Possibly,' he nodded. 'Yet someone betrayed me to the police last night, and Colonel Maturez' men came looking for me. I escaped from the Castellado by great good fortune. I also took with me an American called Gene Keperla,' he added.

Juanero was astonished. 'Señor Steele! If you took Keperla with you, you took a corpse. You know yourself that Keperla is dead. I have many of his belongings with me here, from the time when he lodged with me.'

Toledo stared hard at the man. 'That, also, was in my mind.'

'There is the possibility of an impostor,' said Juanero.

'Why should a man in prison pose as a dead man?' Toledo threw the question at him. He paused for a moment. 'But we shall find out these things in good time. Meanwhile, Keperla is resting in a clearing in the bush, some six miles from town, and I am here.' He had a sudden thought and asked, 'What is your opinion of Yasis?'

The second-hand dealer shrugged. 'I have never known him to be disloyal. You have suspicions, Señor Steele?'

'I have suspicions.' Toledo dropped into a chair. 'I shall rest here during the afternoon. I shall wash, shave, change my clothes and sleep. I should also like to see again the rock samples which Señor Keperla left with you.'

'I will bring them,' Juanero replied. There was a look of fear in his eyes. 'But the police – suppose they come again?'

'The police will not search again until nightfall – it is too hot. And by then I shall be away – and you, dear Anton, will be driving me in your car.'

Juanero mouthed an oath, but he did not continue to argue. And Toledo permitted himself a quiet smile of triumph. He had spent more than a month preparing for this eventuality – the friendship cultivated with Yasis and Juanero, the stacking of money and clothes with the second-hand dealer, the careful spying-out of the ground, the rehearsals for sudden escapes. He thought that his belief in taking calculated risks only was more than paying off.

So, during the long afternoon, Toledo rested and relaxed. He thought about Keperla and about the man who called himself Gene Keperla. He thought about Colonel Maturez, and about the old, lonely man who was the President of Ursulino and how he stood between Maturez and power.

He talked with Juanero on this subject. Juanero explained what he believed. 'In two days' time is the Festival of the Republic, five years to the day from the peaceful founding of the present Republic. That is why the grandstands are being erected in the Central Square – there will be a public holiday and much rejoicing.' He shook his head sadly. 'But from the interest Colonel Maturez has shown in you, I fear the Festival may never take place. Certain of the Presidential Guard are not too loyal to El Presidente himself – they would prefer Maturez, who is a man of action rather than a man of peace. Also Captain Rodriguez, who is Chief of Police in São Vittorio, is a man for Maturez. There are signs. Nothing outward, but small signs.'

'You think, then, there might be revolution?'

'A most discreet revolution,' explained Juanero. 'If El Presidente were to die suddenly . . .'

'Friend Maturez would take over, of course,' said Toledo. He held up one of the rock samples. It glinted brassily in the dull light of the parlour. 'Gene Keperla was a prospector for oil, of course. He worked alone. Now, El Presidente had granted him a prospector's licence – to search for oil – and he went into the mountains. Alone?'

Juanero shrugged. 'So far as I know. Indians who live in the mountains reported the finding of his grave. They said he had died of fever.'

'They might have killed him,' Toledo said.

'For what reason? He had little money, and our Indians are not as uncivilised as people would make out.'

'Yet he died, and another man was imprisoned in his name,' Toledo mused. 'I find that interesting – particularly when I examine these small pieces of rock.' He studied them again.

Juanero started up. He peered through the curtains into the shop and, beyond the shop, into the street. 'There is a policeman on patrol outside,' he said sharply.

Toledo pulled aside the curtains. 'He patrols the other side of the street.' He looked at Juanero. 'Now that is really interesting. Here is what you must do, Anton . . .'

With nightfall, Anton Juanero brought his somewhat battered but serviceable Chevrolet up to the front door of his shop. Patrolling on the other side of the street was a gloomy member of the police, who considered that all these extra duties for the sake of finding one foreigner were highly unnecessary. He would much rather have been enjoying himself with a glass of tequila in a bar somewhere, but Captain Mendoza had ordered him to watch the second-hand clothes store of Anton Juanero, and watch it he must.

There was, however, nothing suspicious about Juanero having a quick drink with his girl-friend and, an hour later when Juanero opened the door of his shop and stepped on to the dusty pavement, he seemed contented with life – and, as the policeman saw it, why should he not be? The young lady followed him out of the shop, the hood of her cloak held high, and together they got into the car and drove away. In the shadows on the opposite side of the street, the policeman smiled benevolently.

Toledo Steele threw back the cloak and stretched himself luxuriously in the car as Juanero took a corner on two wheels. He looked at his watch. The time was ten p.m.

'You must thank your girl-friend for me,' he said. 'It was most obliging of her to lend me this cloak.'

Juanero pulled a face. 'I wish I could share your coolness, Señor Steele. But this is a dangerous game you play, and I have no desire to be stood against a wall.'

Toledo Steele patted him on the shoulder. 'If Colonel Maturez wins, you will have no choice. You will be stood against a wall and shot.' He pointed. 'The lady I wish to meet should be walking along the north road. After that you can drive us six miles out of town.'

Juanero huddled over the wheel. 'At a time like this – you go to keep an assignation!'

'You are too down-to-earth, my friend,' said Toledo. He looked at the grandstand and the dais as they passed through the Central Square. 'So the President's going to declare the Festival open from up there in two days. I wonder . . .'

The Chevrolet turned another bend and headed northwards. Juanero drove as though he had taken lessons from Graham Hill, except that he had not mastered the finer points of cornering. He changed up with a protesting scrape from the clutch and thrust the accelerator down to the floorboards.

Toledo peered down the lane of light produced by the head-lamps. He jerked a thumb forward. 'Better tread on those brakes, friend. The lady's up ahead.'

The car stopped suddenly with the same sense of determination as characterised all of Juanero's driving. Toledo Steele thrust hard against the window for support before opening the door and leaning out to greet Lynn Keperla.

'I told you we'd be here,' he remarked, as though it were the most normal thing in the world to meet a girl on a lonely road in a South American republic, with most of the police force of that republic on his heels. 'Come aboard and we'll go driving.'

Thc girl climbed in beside him. Juanero let in the clutch with a bang and the car hurled itself forward. 'Well, at least you're looking more normal now,' Lynn decided. 'But where are we going?'

'Out of São Vittorio,' Toledo explained calmly. 'There are too many police looking for me in the town, and I have a counter-revolution to arrange. Did you send my cable?'

The girl let out an exasperated 'Ohhh! Of course I sent your cable,' she said with irritation, 'just before the office closed, as you told me. But you really are the most maddening person. All this talk of plots and revolutions . . .'

Toledo interrupted her. 'Counter-revolution, I said. There's a difference. Colonel Maturez, I think, is planning the revolution – I'm planning the counter-revolution.'

She shook her head, mystified. 'It's too involved for me. I wish you'd tell me who you are and what you're really doing. In fact, I honestly don't know why I trust you.'

'I'm a private citizen who likes freedom,' he announced.

'Look, Mr Steele – you're just being evasive. What are you really doing in São Vittorio?'

Toledo smiled in the half-dark of the car. Suddenly his lean face looked surprisingly sinister. 'Exactly the same as you, young lady . . . trying to get Gene Keperla out of the Castellado.'

The girl recoiled as though he had slapped her face. She stared at him, saying nothing. Juanero, driving, took no notice of the conversation, which was in English, anyway. His attention was focused on keeping the big car firmly on the dusty road.

Toledo went on. 'You say you're Mrs Gene Keperla, but so far I've not had any proof of it. I came to Ursulino because I understood that Keperla was still alive and held prisoner in the Castellado. I think you came for a similar reason.'

The girl lowered her head. 'Something like that. After the report of Gene's death, I had a letter from him. I couldn't be sure it really came from Gene, so I thought I would come to find out for myself; and that's why I'm here. I had to know.'

'That adds up. Let's tell this story from the beginning: Gene Keperla, a geologist-cum-prospector, comes to Ursulino to look for oil. He disappears, and it's officially announced that he died of fever and was buried in the mountains. Then there are whispers that maybe Kerperla isn't dead at all, but a prisoner in the Castellado. So the U.S. State Department looks around for someone who knows Ursulino, and it just happens I'm in San Francisco and my Government mentions it to Washington . . . and here I am.'

He leaned back in his seat and blew smoke at the windscreen. Toledo was enjoying himself. 'My job is to get inside the Castellado and find Keperla, without causing any kind of an international incident. By good luck, you and that stray pistol shooting did the trick for me last night.' He asked, 'What do you think happened to your husband?'

Lynn Keperla looked down at the floor. 'I think he was – murdered.'

'Why?'

'Because he had found something – oil, perhaps.'

'That doesn't fit in,' said Toledo. 'The President granted him a concession to prospect for oil. A big oil strike down here would please El Presidente mightily – it would mean prosperity for his country.' Toledo shook his head. 'Maybe your husband found something . . . but it wasn't oil.'

'It doesn't seem to make sense, somehow.' Lynn touched Toledo's arm. 'You were in the Castellado last night – did you find out anything about my husband?'

The car stopped with a squeal of brakes. Juanero opened the door and pointed. 'This is where you told me to stop, Señor Steele.'

Toledo did not answer the girl directly. 'Out you go,' he said. 'I want you to meet someone.' He turned to Juanero as he stepped on to the road. 'Go back home and wait for me, Anton. And thank you for your help tonight!'

The second-hand clothes dealer crossed himself. 'May the saints watch over you . . . and me, too!' He swung the big car round and was away, obviously only too glad to be returning to town.

Toledo pointed up the track. 'Follow me. It's only a short walk.' He parted the bushes and set out along the rough lane, picking his way with the ease of a gun-dog. The girl stumbled after him, her high heels making it difficult for her to avoid losing her balance in the roughest parts.

Soon they came to a clearing where a man was squatting beside a small fire. Half hidden under a mountain of bush and scrub stood a big car. The man, a gun in his hand, rose to his feet as they entered the clearing. Toledo took three quick steps across the open space and kicked the fire to ashes. He whirled angrily on the man.

'I told you not to light a fire! Or do you want to go back to that pest-hole?'

'I was cold,' the man scowled. 'I didn't think it would be seen.' He looked at the girl. 'Who's she?'

Toledo finished stamping on the remains of the fire. There was a little smile playing on his lips. 'This lady?' he said, his eyebrows raised. 'Why – this is Mrs Lynn Keperla – your wife?'

There was a cry of surprise from the girl. 'That's not Gene!'

Almost simultaneously the man Toledo knew as Gene Keperla let out a similar exclamation of alarm. 'That's not my wife! I'm Gene Keperla, all right, but she isn't my wife!'

'Well! In fact, well, well!' Toledo grinned. He folded his arms and regarded the pair. 'Now this is all most interesting. You say you're Gene Keperla, and she says she's the wife of your bosom . . . yet you don't know one another. It seems to me that one of you is lying – but which one? And how am I going to discover the truth?'

'I've told the truth!' the girl burst out. 'Now I'm going back to town!' She turned on her heel and began to run.

Keperla started to move. 'I'm going, too!' His plump face was beaded with sweat, although the night was cold.

Toledo moved just a little faster than either of them. His foot shot out and the girl tripped and fell headlong; with the same reflex movement his fist crashed down on Keperla's wrist and the American dropped his gun with a cry of pain.

The little ·32 was suddenly in evidence in Toledo's other

hand. He shook his head sadly. 'No one's leaving just yet. If either of you returned to town, you'd be picked up in a matter of minutes by Maturez' men.'

Clutching his wrist, the American turned to glare at him. 'You're going to keep us here by force?'

On the ground, Lynn struggled to a sitting position.

'By force, if you want it that way.' Toledo waved the pistol at the girl. 'There are some rugs in the car, beautiful.'

She spat her answer at him. 'Get them yourself!'

Toledo laughed. 'You really like making things hard for yourself, don't you?' He reached down, caught her wrist, and pulled her gently upright. Then he pushed her towards the car. 'Just get the rugs.'

This time she obeyed, while Toledo kept the gun trained on Keperla. Or the man who called himself Keperla. The answer to that question Toledo didn't know himself yet, although he had some ideas on the subject. Meanwhile, he would continue to think of the American as Gene Keperla.

'The rugs will keep you warm,' Toledo told his prisoners as Lynn returned to the clearing, bearing three heavy car blankets. 'But just so you don't have any ideas about going anywhere, take off your shoes and socks, Keperla. And you, Lynn – off with those pretty shoes and stockings.'

When they had done as they were told, Toledo picked up the bundle. Selecting a shoe carefully, he hurled it with all his might far into the bush. He did the same with the other three shoes, and pocketed the socks and stockings. Finally he lifted the bonnet of the car, removed the distributor head, and pocketed it also.

'If I ladder your nylons, I'll buy you a new pair, Lynn,' he said. He looked at them standing before him in their bare feet. 'It's pretty rugged, either in the bush or on the road, without shoes. I'd certainly not try it, if I were you.'

The girl made a movement. 'But where are you going?

You're not going to leave me here alone with – him!'

Toledo, picking up the gun which Keperla had dropped, said, 'Lynn, if you go back to town, you'll be picked up by Maturez' men. I know you don't believe me, but that's the truth.' He put the gun into her hands. 'If this man is your husband, you needn't worry about spending the night with him. If he isn't, this gun ought to keep you safe.' He paused. 'I don't like doing this, but it's the only way I know of keeping both of you out of Maturez' hands for a little while longer.'

He swung on his heel, then stopped at the edge of the clearing. 'Personally, I have a date to keep with Colonel Maturez. He forgot to return my cane.'

He was gone, thrusting silently and swiftly down the path to the main road, and the plump man in the dirty gaberdine suit and slim girl with honey-coloured hair were left staring at each other.

The Fate of Anton Juanero

Colonel Enrico Maturez, the former Baldur Fleischmann, stopped pacing the thick-piled carpet that covered every inch of the floor of his massive office. He pointed an accusing finger at the man who sat hunched up in a chair before the Colonel's ornate mahogany desk, looking distinctly unhappy.

'You had him in the Castellado,' he snapped, 'and he got free. He stole my car – and you don't know where it is. He even had the audacity to return to town last night and persuade that girl to send a cable for him – and still you couldn't find him!' He threw up his hands above his head in a gesture of despair. 'And even the censors let his cable go through!'

Captain Juan Rodriguez, Chief of Police of São Vittorio, squirmed. He was having a bad time, and he didn't like it. He was a heavy, stolid man, who had risen to his present position

Maturez strode over to him, seizing the arms of the chair.

largely through influence and the ability to pick the right side at the right time. As a Chief of Police he was about as much use as a trained St Bernard, but in Ursulino that was normally in his favour, since crime waves, as such, rarely came his way, and his duties consisted mostly of collecting the highest bribes possible for evasion of taxes and smuggling. Furthermore, he did not like this German upstart who had come to Ursulino ten years before, become El Presidente's adviser, and risen to power.

He sighed. 'Colonel – my men cannot find ghosts. Since this Señor Steele escaped from the Castellado, taking with him the American, there has not been the slightest trace of them anywhere. We have searched, but there is nothing.' He shrugged his shoulders heavily. 'But absolutely nothing.'

Maturez strode over to him, seizing the arms of Rodriguez' chair to peer into his eyes. 'You are sometimes an idiot, Juan. Since Steele came here four weeks ago, I have had him watched closely. He's a very clever man, and he is an agent of the American Government – I am sure of that! The fact that he knew me made me certain he is a spy. Now he escapes from a prison that is said to be escape-proof, and you cannot find him.' He threw out a question. 'The guard who let him free – what does he say?'

'He keeps to his story,' The Chief of Police replied. 'We have tried several methods of persuasion, but I do not believe he was an accomplice – at least, not willingly.' He paused, and his small eyes lit up. 'But there is another possibility. A second-hand clothes dealer, Anton Juanero, was stopped on returning to town earlier this evening. He is being questioned now.'

'What makes you think he might know something?'

Rodriguez spread out his hands, palms uppermost. 'He is known to be sympathetic towards the regime – that is one point. Furthermore, Steele is known to have visited him several times in the past weeks – your excellent records showed me that,

Colonel. And the original Keperla, the true Keperla, lodged with Juanero before he went into the mountains.'

'At least, then, you have learned something,' Maturez said. He stood up. 'But you must work faster. El Presidente is old, very old. The Festival of the Republic is less than two days away, and I am convinced that El Presidente will die before it takes place.' Colonel Maturez smiled, and there was a moment of evil behind his smile. 'In fact, I am convinced that El Presidente will die almost immediately before the Festival, in which case it will be necessary to appoint his successor without delay.'

Rodriguez stretched himself lazily. 'You have suggested as much before. Naturally, I and my men will follow El Presidente's chosen successor without hesitation. At a time like this, it is necessary for the police and the Presidential Guards to obey orders.' He passed a hand across his mouth. 'Free elections, of course, can come later.'

Maturez brought his hand down on the other's shoulder. 'Of course. I should not wish there to be any lack of democracy in the arrangements. You can trust all your men?'

'Implicitly.' Rodriguez stood up. 'And now, with your permission, Colonel, I will be going.'

Before Maturez could answer, the telephone on his desk shrilled. He picked it up, listened, then turned to the Chief of Police. 'No, wait here, Juan. I have to go to El Presidente – he wishes to see me urgently.'

Rodriguez subsided again into the chair as the Colonel closed the door behind him. He was beginning to feel better. No doubt the man Steele would be caught before morning, and all would be well again. There was, of course, the matter of the American prisoner, and also of the girl, but these things could be arranged. He smiled to himself. Even though he did not like him, he had to recognise that Maturez had chosen a highly convenient time, when the one man who represented the Consular interests of half a dozen countries, including Britain and the United States, was up-country on a hunting expedition. If everything went well, there would be no fuss at all.

The cold ring of the gun that touched lightly on the back of his neck brought him back to reality. In Captain Juan Rodriguez' ear a voice said gently, 'It will be best if you relax, Captain. To kill you would make a shocking mess on the carpet.'

Captain Rodriguez relaxed. He felt quite sick. The voice continued. 'I doubt if you would know me, but you certainly know of me. My name is Señor Toledo Steele, and I am the terror of police-chiefs.' The voice paused, then added, 'You may shiver now if you wish.'

Captain Rodriguez did not shiver. He stayed perfectly still and wished the muzzle of the gun – it was Toledo's pet ·32, but to Rodriguez it felt like an atomic cannon – would go away from the back of his neck.

'I have been listening to your conversation with Colonel Maturez,' said Toledo Steele, and moved around in front of the chair to face the Chief of Police. To Rodriguez it was like being forced to gaze on his executioner before the axe fell; he had an uncomfortable twisting sensation in the pit of his stomach.

'You did not know it, Captain, but I was hidden behind the curtains all the time,' Toledo told him softly. 'The Presidential Palace, I fear, is all too easy to break into – I can assure you I had no trouble at all.' His voice hardened, but surprisingly, a little smile touched his lips. 'Captain Rodriguez, you mentioned something about one Anton Juanero, who is at the moment being questioned. Where is he?'

The face of the Chief of Police went blank. He gulped, but no words came forth. Toledo dug the pistol in the pit of the man's stomach to emphasise his question.

Rodriguez said, 'It would be more than my life is worth –'

'Undoubtedly,' said Toledo Steele. 'It would also be more

than your worthless life not to tell me. So speak up, Captain.'

'He is held in the Castellado,' Rodriguez mumbled. He began to shake.

'The Castellado,' remarked Toledo, with the same hard smile at his lips, 'is a big place. You also have a large stomach. Do you wish to locate the exact whereabouts of this Anton Juanero or shall I use this pistol to trace a pattern of the Castellado on your stomach?'

'The third level,' Rodriguez stammered quickly. 'You will find the room of questioning.'

'Excellent,' said Toledo smoothly. 'I trust you do not lie.' He tried another question. 'There is the matter of the American whom I rescued from the Castellado. He tried to pose to me as Keperla, but, of course, that is not so. No doubt you know who he is?'

Rodriguez' eyes swept the room wildly, seeking a way of escape from the relentless questioning. Toledo put the muzzle of the gun against the man's chin and moved it from left to right persuasively.

Finally the Chief of Police spoke. 'His real name is Crandell. He went with Keperla into the mountains, though that fact was not known to anyone here in São Vittorio.'

Toledo returned to English. 'Dear boy,' he said mildly, and snapped the fat man's head back with a slick left to the point. Captain Rodriguez' eyes glazed and he subsided lower in the chair.

Toledo stood beside him and gave the problem thought. The capture of Anton Juanero had introduced a new factor which changed his plans. Originally he had intended merely to find out more of Colonel Maturez' plans for revolution and then enjoy himself by harassing the Colonel and possibly delaying those plans considerably. But if Anton were in the Castellado and, moreover, in the room of questioning . . . the most important thing was to get him out. But how? To break into the prison openly was out of the question, for every guard in São Vittorio would be on the watch for Toledo Steele.

Therefore . . . Toledo eyed the telephone with a new interest.

He picked it up and listened to the voice of the operator. Then, in as good an imitation of the Chief of Police's tones as he could muster, he demanded, 'This is Captain Rodriguez. Connect me with the Castellado immediately; I wish to speak to the guard-room.'

He waited, wondering whether his imitation was successful. But there was the usual clicking of telephone cords, and then the voice of the Corporal of the Guard answering.

'This is Captain Rodriguez,' Toledo repeated. 'You have a prisoner there in the room of questioning – a man by the name of Anton Juanero. Release him immediately and bring him to the Presidential Palace.'

There was some muttering at the other end. Then the Corporal said. 'But your Excellency . . . a message has just come from the room of questioning for you.. The man Anton Juanero died five minutes ago, during the interrogation.'

A Visit to the President

Toledo took a deep breath. Anton Juanero, the kindly, harmless little clothes-dealer, a man who wanted nothing out of life but a pleasant existence and a peaceful country in which to live . . .

'Presumably he talked before he died?' Toledo rasped.

There was again much muttering off the 'phone. Finally the Corporal replied. 'I regret, your Excellency, but he died without speaking. I regret exceedingly, your Excellency . . .'

'Fool!' Toledo snapped, and crashed the 'phone back on its hook. So Juanero had remained true to himself, even up to the last. Toledo Steele looked at the unconscious body of the gross

Chief of Police and for a moment his finger itched on the trigger of the little ·32. Then he controlled himself, and the wave of anger was past. Once again he was his cool, clear-thinking self.

He walked to the door and peered into the corridor. Two Presidential Guards stood on duty at either end of the long passage, ceremonially watching the great staircases. Toledo thought his best way out of the Palace would be the way he had entered it – by means of a drainpipe at the darkened rear of the building and a precarious hand-over-hand climb around the ledges to Maturez' room. On the other hand, he did wish to leave as yet. He had a yearning to accomplish one other deed inside the Palace.

What he had overheard while concealed behind the curtain had convinced him that the President was in danger. Toledo Steele had never met the President and had no great feelings either way about him; but he did not like Colonel Maturez and he was quite determined that the Colonel should not be allowed to go around upsetting the present seat of Government in Ursulino. That his instructions from the State Department made no mention of interfering in revolutions was a matter which Toledo Steele conveniently overlooked at this juncture. He was an expert at playing things off the cuff, as a certain man sitting in an office in Shaftesbury Avenue knew only too well. But the State Department, in 'borrowing' him from the net-work of counter espionage agents controlled by the single man in the Shaftesbury Avenue office, did not know this fact about Toledo Steele . . .

The instructions from the State Department official were firmly fixed in Toledo's mind. 'You are a private citizen, Mr Steele. But if you care to visit São Vittorio, and if you care to bring about a prison break which will free Mr Gene Keperla – whom we believe to be in the Castellado, but whom we also cannot *prove* to be there – we shall be more than grateful.

Naturally, we cannot help you in any way . . .'

Toledo shrugged. The official had not said anything about not interfering in revolutions, and anyway, the man he had freed from the Castellado was not Gene Keperla. If the State Department had wanted him to avoid all interference in Ursulino's forthcoming revolution, they should have said so.

He picked up the 'phone again. 'This is Captain Rodriguez,' he announced. 'Is Colonel Maturez still with El Presidente?' When the operator confirmed that this was so, he added, 'When he leaves, would you see that he is told I have gone home? Good.'

Toledo then went to work on the still unconscious Chief of Police. First he gagged the man with his own handkerchief, then used shoelaces and braces to tie his hands and feet. Finally he lugged the Captain into a corner of the room by the vast window, arranging the curtains to cover his body.

He returned to the centre of the room and considered the next move. While he was standing there, his eyes rested on something which Colonel Maturez had laid carelessly aside on the great desk. It was his swordstick, obviously destined to be a trophy for the Colonel's collection. Toledo picked it up, testing it lovingly. The point was sharp. He felt better already.

He went to the door again. This time he threw it wide open and walked boldly into the corridor. Instantly the two guards were on the alert, their eyes goggling at the sight of this stranger, in faultless grey gaberdine, making signs at them. Then he jumped back inside the room and waited.

There was not long to wait. In a matter of seconds the guards were thundering after him into the room; they might not have understood the full implication of the signs, but they realised a stranger should not be in this part of the Palace. Toledo stepped aside politely to let them enter, then menaced them calmly with the ·32 in his left hand and the drawn rapier in his other.

'Softly, my good friends,' he said. 'It is essential that you remain quiet.'

The taller of the two, a gloomy-looking man with a drooping moustache, was the only one who spoke. 'Who are you?' he asked.

'The upsetter of thrones,' said Toledo. 'Now turn around and remain silent.'

As they obeyed, he stepped swiftly up to them and delivered a rabbit punch with the side of his hand to each one's neck. The guards tottered at the knees before crumpling to the floor.

'So far,' Toledo Steele thought, 'it's been like taking candy from babies.' He regarded the bodies sadly. 'Perhaps I am getting old.'

He slid into the corridor, closing the door gently behind him. The key which had been on the inside of the door he transferred to the outside, snapped the lock over, and then dropped the key into a nearby spittoon. He sauntered along the corridor towards the Presidential apartments, the location of which was fixed in his memory by much study of the official guide book to the Palace.

At an imposing door another Presidential Guard was on duty. He eyed Toledo glumly, apparently bored with his task. Toledo, one hand resting on the ·32 in his jacket pocket, tapped the guard on the chest with the silver-topped knob of his cane.

'You will let me pass,' he informed the man. 'My name is Lloyd George and El Presidente is awaiting me.'

It was sheer, unadulterated nerve, but it was perfect. The guard's instant reasoning was that if this well-dressed stranger had come thus far in the Palace, he must be a person of some importance. To delay him now might result in considerable trouble later on. The stranger's name was unusual, but what did that matter? Accordingly he slapped the butt of his automatic rifle hard and stood aside while Toledo passed into the room and closed the door behind him.

He was in a large, plainly furnished room. To his right a wood fire burned brightly in an open grate; to the left a curtained doorway apparently gave on to other rooms, possibly the Presidential bedchamber. A great refectory table stood in the centre of the room, with at one end of it a heavy mahogany chair. The room, with its simple furnishings, reflected the taste of the man who occupied it, and Toledo suddenly felt cheered at the knowledge that El Presidente was as good and kindly a man as Anton Juanero had claimed.

Two men were in the room beside himself. One of them was Colonel Maturez. The other was a small, grave-faced man of considerable age. He wore a dark blue suit which seemed too large for his shrunken figure, and on his feet were soft carpet slippers. He had a small goatee beard, and his thinning hair was as white as sun-bleached stone. But there was intense, forceful life in his blue eyes as he turned to stare at the intruder.

Toledo found himself immediately impressed by the man's eyes. It was said that he was a man of courage and determination, of great integrity and complete lack of self-interest. Toledo found himself liking El Presidente on sight.

But he did not let his interest in the President of Ursulino detract his attention from Colonel Maturez. Toledo's hand flashed into the open with the ·32 pointed squarely at the Colonel's middle.

Maturez froze, his mouth half open. 'Don't shout for the guard, Colonel,' Toledo murmured. 'You would not wish to die with a bullet in your stomach, would you?' Suddenly switching to German, he added, 'But all the same, I should like to kill you that way, you fatherless son of a bitch!' He saw Maturez' eyes flash with rage. To the President, Toledo continued: 'I apologise for this intrusion, Señor Presidente, but I wished to give you fair warning in the presence of this man.'

The President peered at him. 'Are you the man Steele, for whom my police are even now searching?'

Toledo made him a bow. 'Correct, Señor Presidente.'

'And what is the warning of which you speak?'

Toledo took a step forward and dug the ferrule of his cane into Maturez' chest. 'This man is not loyal to you, Señor Presidente. He plots revolution and he means to kill you before the Festival of the Republic takes place. I have heard him talking with your Chief of Police, Captain Rodriguez, and I swear it is so.'

'You lie!' Maturez snapped. He swung on the President. 'I tell you he lies, Señor Presidente!'

The little man nodded. 'No doubt. But it is a big lie and therefore worth hearing.' He stared at Toledo. 'Do you have proof of what you say?'

'No proof,' replied Toledo, 'but my own word. It is possible that you will not believe that word, but now I have told you, it is equally possible that you will watch yourself more carefully.' He thought a moment before going on to say, 'Señor Presidente, certain things are done in Ursulino which I feel are without your knowledge. Do you, for instance, know that a certain Anton Juanero, a second-hand clothes dealer of this town, was tortured to death in the Castellado tonight because he refused to reveal my hiding-place?'

The President's eyes darkened. 'You say that? It is not possible.'

'Again he lies,' said Maturez confidently. He swung away, looking out of the window.

'I do not lie,' Toledo said. 'If you seek the truth, Señor Presidente, look for yourself tonight in the dungeons of the Castellado.'

'This I might do,' agreed the little man calmly. 'But first you will give yourself up to me, and we shall discuss this matter sensibly. Come.' He held out his hand for Toledo's gun.

Toledo laughed. 'Another time, Señor Presidente.' He took a backward leap to the door. 'Tonight I have work to do.' He saluted with the cane, and the smile at his lips this time was genuine. 'Good-night, Señor Presidente.'

Then he was gone, the door slamming behind him, and the surprised guard in the corridor suddenly found himself on the floor with his automatic rifle twisted between his knees. And Toledo was racing down the corridor towards Maturez' room again.

Behind him there were cries of 'After him!' and 'Guard the exits!' as he slid into the big office and closed the door gently. He knew what would happen. They would expect him to head for the stairs. Maturez' room would be the last place in which they would look for him.

The two guards were still unconscious on the floor. Captain Rodriguez had come to, behind the curtains, and was making ineffectual noises and wriggling; but he was safe.

Toledo crossed to the window, swinging on to the balustrade as though a perilous exit from a Presidential Palace, with armed guards ready to shoot him on sight, was something he did every day of his life. He put the silver-headed cane between his teeth and climbed on to the narrow ledge which ran around most of the Palace. Then, with a sheer drop of sixty feet below him, he began to inch his way along the ledge.

It had been enough of a nightmare on the earlier journey; now, with a miniature army on his trail, it was a trip of horror. Or, for anyone less conscious of immediate danger than Toledo Steele, it might have been. At moments like these he had the supreme knack of ignoring the non-essential dangers and concentrating only on the actual danger in front of him – which was the risk of falling. And that risk, he considered, was one of his calculated ones, with the odds on his side.

Far below, in the courtyard, the Presidential Guards were

Below in the courtyard, the guards were racing about.

racing about in high confusion as they searched for him. Toledo Steele thought they were welcome to their job; he did not think they were likely to bother him up here.

With the kind of concentration that would have enabled him to have solved simultaneous equations in the middle of a boiler factory, Toledo made his way steadily along the ledge. Once his foot skidded and he was forced to clutch at a cornice for support while he stayed motionless for a full two minutes, regaining his balance. Once a piece of the wall broke away under his grasp, tumbling with what seemed like the clatter of a thousand iron pails to the ground below. And again Toledo Steele froze, awaiting the probing finger of a searchlight, followed by the sharp rapping of rifle bolts as soldiers and police stood ready to blast him out of existence. But nothing happened.

He was within a matter of feet of the ending of his trip when a noise from the courtyard broke in on his concentration. For a split second he could not guess what it was that had cut across his mind; then he realised it was a girl's voice.

What was more, he recognised it as being Lynn's voice.

He stopped, twisting round to look into the section of the courtyard immediately below him. A car had driven through the Palace gates, a sleek staff car crammed with soldiers. The lights of the Palace fell full upon the shiny vehicle and its passengers.

In the rear seat were Lynn Keperla and the man whom Toledo now knew as Crandell. Soldiers stood over them with rifles at the ready.

As the car stopped, an officer stepped down and saluted another officer who came from the Palace.

The officer from the car said, 'Captain – we have the two prisoners. They were in the clearing as we were told.' He barked an order, and Lynn and Crandell limped from the car into the courtyard.

Toledo swore softly. The officer's words – 'They were in the clearing as we were told' – meant only one thing; either Anton Juanero had talked, or something else had gone seriously wrong. And Toledo had a sound idea, at that moment, about the something else.

Edge of Doom

Toledo Steele pressed his back hard against the wall at the rear of the Presidential Palace. He was on firm ground again and he was standing in the shadows, but soldiers were still thronging the courtyard and any minute one of them might start a search of the rear of the Palace. Nevertheless, Toledo stayed motionless and considered the next move.

He had speeded up the works by confronting El Presidente in the presence of Maturez with the knowledge that Maturez was about to turn traitor. Whether El Presidente fully believed him was another matter; what did matter was that Maturez had been there when the President had been told and would therefore try to carry out his scheme more quickly. That was as Toledo intended it.

Toledo Steele leaned casually against the wall and summed up what he had . . . and didn't have:

1. A geologist named Gene Keperla had come to Ursulino six months ago to look for oil.
2. Keperla had died of fever, according to the official account, but unofficially was believed to have been arrested and held secretly in the Castellado.
3. He, Toledo Steele, had rescued from the Castellado a man who claimed to be Gene Keperla, but who most certainly wasn't.
4. Maturez was organising a revolutionary bid in which all he had to do was wait patiently and power would drop into his lap

with the eventual death of the President.

Toledo Steele shook his head.

Somehow, Toledo felt there was a connection between Keperla and Colonel Maturez' revolution.

And the more he thought about this, the more he realised that to discover the connection – and stop the revolution – he would have to be inside the Palace. He sighed. It was a long, hard climb up the drainpipe and around the ledge to Maturez' room.

Footsteps sounding on the cobbled paving froze him in the shadows. The soldiers had at last decided to look behind the Palace. Silently, Toledo unsheathed the swordstick; at moments like this, the value of a swift, noiseless weapon was measureless.

A figure turned the corner of the building and strode towards him. The man, silhouetted against the lights of the main courtyard, was an easy target for Toledo; at the same time, he was partially blinded by moving suddenly from light into darkness. He stopped, peering into the shadows.

With the skill and precision of a tiger, Toledo jumped.

He landed within inches of the man's toes. His own eyes, accustomed to the dark by now, instantly recognised the figure as a lieutenant of the Presidential Guard. The deadly rapier flicked upwards and touched in sinister fashion the lieutenant's throat.

'Do not cry out, lieutenant, or you will join your ancestors.'

Unfortunately – for him – the lieutenant was a brave young man. He was also an alert one. He yelled at the top of his voice and launched himself at Toledo.

Toledo threw his arms wide and brought his knee up in the same movement. The lieutenant literally crashed on to the knee with his tomach to the front and the full weight of his run behind it. He hurled Toledo backwards at the same time as he winded himself. They went to the ground together.

Toledo was up first, while the lieutenant was still trying to get his breath back and making very painful noises about it. Then, round the corner, came what looked like a full troop of guards, their automatic rifles at the ready.

There was only one thing to be done. Toledo grabbed the lieutenant and hauled him to his feet, the rapier held in front of the man's body and touching his windpipe.

'If you shoot, your lieutenant will die first,' Toledo said, and wondered whether the guards would take the chance.

But they stopped, open-mouthed. The lieutenant got some of his breath back and mumbled an order, but still none of his men moved. Behind them the tall figure of Colonel Maturez came into view.

'For the moment, Colonel, it's checkmate, I think,' Toledo murmured.

Maturez stepped forward. He spoke, as Toledo had done, in English. 'I am quite prepared to sacrifice a lieutenant for you, Steele. But that will not be necessary. You see, I have already placed El Presidente under preventive custody in his room, and unless you give up immediately I shall have him shot.'

Toledo let go of the officer, who staggered against the wall, still breathing heavily. He sheathed the swordstick, extended it, silver top first, towards the Colonel, and said, 'In that case . . .'

Maturez barked an order and the guards closed in. Rough hands grabbed Toledo by the arms and shoulders and he was hustled towards the main courtyard.

Ten minutes later Toledo was again in Colonel Maturez' office in the Palace. This time he sat in the chair that Captain Rodriguez had occupied. The Captain, rubbing his wrists and looking as though he might at any moment cut Toledo's throat, stood behind Maturez' desk, while Maturez himself reclined in his own chair, idly toying with the silver-topped cane.

Toledo looked at his wrists and ankles. This time, he thought, Maturez did not intend to give him the slightest chance of escape. Heavy manacles on his wrists were linked by a strong chain to leg-irons that would prevent him from moving more than a few inches at a time. A stout strap around his waist held him securely against the back of the chair.

Maturez picked up his thought. 'As you can see, Señor Steele, I regard you as a most dangerous criminal. I do not think you will free yourself, do you?'

'It seems most unlikely,' Toledo conceded. The guards had taken his gun, but they had again overlooked the razorblade attached to his left ankle; true it would be of no use against the chains, but it was better than nothing. 'Could I have a cigarette?' he asked.

'Of course.' Maturez leaned across the desk and put a cigarette between Toledo's lips, lighting it with a spirit lamp which burned all the time. 'For a man who will die in the morning, one cannot refuse such a request.'

'So, I'm already condemned?' Toledo enquired, drawing slowly on the cigarette with apparently relaxed enjoyment.

Maturez nodded. 'Naturally. I cannot allow you to go free. And this time I shall not entrust you to the Castellado for your last night on earth. You will remain here, as you are now.'

'It's a comforting thought,' Toledo said. 'What about El Presidente? I suppose you're still going to knock him off?'

'Correct. Of course, he will die peacefully, in his bed, and a state of emergency will be declared in the morning so that I can assume power.' The Colonel shrugged gracefully. 'In these matters, certain persons must always be eliminated.'

'How true,' agreed Toledo sagely. He looked at Captain Rodriguez. This time he spoke in Spanish. 'Undoubtedly the worthy Chief of Police will be the next one to be purged?'

Rodriguez started in alarm. He had not understood the earlier part of the conversation, but he caught the import of Toledo's question well enough.

Maturez swung on him, letting loose a stream of words. 'Pay no attention to him, Juan! You understand that he is only trying to save his own skin!'

Rodriguez shifted uncomfortably. The same thought that Toledo had voiced had occurred to him often in the past. But he also knew he was not strong enough to challenge Maturez. He had taken a tiger by the tail and now there was nothing to do but let it pull him where it willed.

He spoke slowly. 'It might be better if he died now.' His hand rested ominously on the butt of his revolver.

'Calm yourself, Juan. He will die tomorrow as a public spectacle.' Maturez stared fixedly at Toledo. 'You are a spy and therefore will not be recognised by your own country. So far as this country is concerned, you will die as a native of Ursulino, under a name which will ensure there are no inquiries.' He pointed the cane towards the ceiling. 'Something like Pedro Hernandez, I fancy – a would-be assassin who broke into the Palace and so terrified El Presidente that he collapsed of a heart-attack. An excellent idea, don't you agree?'

'Oh, terrific,' said Toledo. He was beginning to be tired of the conversation. 'What about Crandell and the girl?'

Maturez chuckled. 'I have arrangements for both of them.' He stood up. 'Come, Juan. We must go now, Steele, for we have much to do before morning.' He paused. 'One more thing. The key to your chains is in the bottom drawer of my desk . . . but somehow I do not think you can get to it.'

'Stay with it, Baldur,' Toledo said. 'You're doing fine.' Again, in Spanish, he added to Rodriguez, 'If you trust him, Señor Capitan, you will find yourself at the end of a rope.'

Maturez came around the desk and slashed Toledo across the mouth with the back of his hand. 'Keep that tongue of yours quiet, or I will have it cut out before you die!'

Rodriguez said nothing. He was still thinking. The thought

process moved steadily, but slowly, inside his brain, and what was likely to come out of it, not even Rodriguez himself knew.

An hour passed for Toledo. He tested the strength of the manacles, but quickly realised that more than force would be needed to break them. The strap securing him to the chair was buckled at the back, well out of his reach, and the chair itself was far too heavy to lift, so he was helpless. He sat there, thinking about the morning, and knowing that unless the near impossible happened, he would die in a few hours' time.

The Vanishing President

It had happened before, of course. Perhaps, if he was extraordinarily lucky, it might be allowed to happen again.

There had been the time in a Gestapo prison at Hamburg, where only an air-raid – which blew the prison apart in the process of flattening most of the city – had saved him. On that occasion, he remembered, he had been ready to die the next day. In fact, the R.A.F. bombs which crumpled Hamburg had almost killed him in freeing him from the cell.

But one could not expect an air-raid out of the blue to wreck the Presidential Palace, kill Maturez and his aides and free him at the same time. In any case, there were still these confounded chains . . .

The door opened softly behind him. Maturez or Rodriguez returning to torment him some more, no doubt. Toledo closed his eyes, hoping they might consider him asleep.

'Wake up! For heavens' sake, wake up!' said the voice of Lynn Keperla.

Toledo blinked at her. 'How on earth did you get here?'

'I'm in a room two doors along,' Lynn answered. 'I knew you were here, and it was easy to slip along when the guard's back was turned.'

'You took a big risk,' said Toledo slowly.

'Maturez didn't bother to have me guarded,' the girl said. 'I think he has a somewhat feudal view about women – he doesn't believe they're capable of much beyond the kitchen.'

'He'll learn. You believe me now about Maturez and his intentions?'

Lynn nodded. 'After you left us together in the clearing, the man you rescued from the Castellado did some talking. I think he wanted to boast a little.' Her voice shook. 'He told me how he met Gene in the mountains and suggested they went prospecting together. Then he killed my husband and returned to São Vittorio, intended to pose as him. He went to Maturez with the idea, and Maturez let him think he would agree to it, and then he suddenly shut him up in the Castellado and left him there.'

'That's our Colonel all over,' agreed Toledo. 'He listens to Crandell, picks his brains, and then throws him into jug until he tells everything he knows. Do you know what your husband found?'

'Gold. But none of it will do any of us any good now, just as it didn't do poor Gene any good.' She stretched out a hand and felt the heavy chain at Toledo's wrists. 'If there was only some way of getting you free.'

'Take it easy. There is.' He jerked his head towards the desk. 'Maturez was kind enough to explain that the key to these handcuffs is in the bottom drawer of his desk – because he knew I couldn't get to it.'

The girl was around the desk in a flash. She fumbled in the drawer and emerged holding a key. 'This looks like it.' Another few moments of struggling with the locks on the manacles, and Toledo's wrists were free. He began unlocking the chains on his ankles while Lynn freed the strap at his waist.

'Where's Crandell?' he asked.

'Maturez locked him up with the President,' replied Lynn.

'They're in the Presidential Suite, as far as I can make out.'

'He'll keep,' said Toledo, and added, 'You know that finding Crandell posing as your husband means –'

'That my husband is really dead?' The girl's pick-up of his sentence was steady. 'Yes, I know that.'

'You'd have had to face it, sooner or later. Better now, when you can't think about it.' He touched her shoulders. 'But – well, I'd like to say I'm sorry.'

He got to his feet, moving silently to the door. Two guards still stood on sentry duty in the corridor. They were different men from the ones he had laid out earlier in the night. In addition, a third sentry, apparently newly come on duty, was patrolling the corridor itself, his back turned as Toledo peered through the crack in the door.

He shook his head. 'You're not going back to your room that way. The only way is along the ledge.' Toledo pointed to the window.

The girl shuddered. 'I've no head for heights.' She walked to the window and looked out. Meanwhile Toledo was casting around the room, looking into cupboards and opening drawers.

He let out a soft cry of interest as he opened one door. Inside, resting on hangers, was a collection of five or six of Maturez' uniforms. Toledo pulled one out, studied it thoughtfully, and said, 'Turn round and spare your blushes. I'm going to change my clothes.'

When he again gave her the word to look, it was a totally different Toledo Steele who stood there. The uniform cast him in an entirely fresh mould, gave him an air of sinister raffishness that turned him into a living replica of a Ruritanian operatic star. He finished buckling on the sword, pulled Maturez' peaked cap jauntily over one eye, and saluted her gravely.

'A trifle too long in the leg, but we mustn't quibble at trifles. Now, Mrs Lynn Keperla, I think we'll try our luck with the sentries.'

This time Toledo opened the door with a flourish. Taking the girl firmly by the arm, he marched into the corridor, turning sharp right and walking boldly towards the President's suite. The ruse worked as sweetly as a clockwork motor with the patrolling sentry, who slapped the butt of his automatic rifle smartly to salute Toledo. Gravely, Toledo Steele returned the salute with the military precision of Wellington Barracks, and they pressed on.

But here was a different story. The guard on the door took one look at Toledo and readied his rifle for instant action.

Toledo said gaily, 'But lo! we are discovered!' and thrust Lynn ahead of him past the soldier. 'Keep going,' he told her.

The sentry, realising his potential enemies were splitting up, barked, 'Stand still!'

'Certainly,' agreed Toledo, and stayed where he was, while the girl continued walking steadily down the corridor.

For a moment the guard wavered, not knowing whether to cover Toledo or the girl, and in that instant Toledo Steele had him. His strong fingers came down over the man's automatic rifle, twisting it forward at the floor, as the guard squeezed the trigger and a burst of shots thudded into the carpet. The noise in the corridor was tremendous, as though a dozen cans were being hammered at once. Lynn gave a little cry and pressed against the wall, while the sentry let out a yell which could have been heard in Mexico – whether for aid or from surprise at hearing his own rifle firing, Toledo did not know.

Then Toledo had the gun between his hands, and he was bringing it round in a scythe-like sweep which caught the soldier's side and sent him sprawling across the corridor to subside against the far wall.

'Come on!' Toledo shouted, and thrust the door open, leaping commando-fashion into the room with the rifle tucked under his arm. The girl followed, banging the door shut.

And they stayed there, almost suspended on the tips of their toes.

The room was empty. The big table was in its accustomed place, the fire still burned cheerfully in the grate, but the room was devoid of anyone but themselves.

Feet thudded along the corridor. Reacting automatically, Toledo turned the lock in the heavy door and cast about for something with which to barricade it. The table was the most suitable piece of furniture in the room. As fists crashed against the woodwork, he was already hauling it into place.

'Get away from the door – they'll start shooting in a minute!' he ordered.

The girl obeyed, following at his heels as he charged into the room he had previously marked as the President's bedroom. Like the first room, it was empty. So, too, was the adjoining dressing-room and the bathroom.

At that moment the first fusillade of shots crashed through the door.

Lynn turned to him, clutching his arm.

'They couldn't have got out,' he said. 'The sentry must have been there all the time. And there wouldn't be a sentry at the door if Maturez had taken them away.'

He jumped to the window in the main room; it was shut and barred. Just as quickly he dropped to the floor, rolling over out of the line of fire as another burst of shooting echoed through the room. He landed up against Lynn, who was on one knee just inside the bedroom. She was examining a portion of the wall where the wallpaper appeared to have been newly torn.

'What about a secret passage?' she suggested.

Toledo sat up and threw his arms around her. 'I associate with a genius! Of course – no sensible president in a republic like this would ever live in a palace that didn't have secret passages!'

The girl was already running her fingers along the tear in the wallpaper. Obviously the door was normally kept papered over, but recent use had split the paper, though the door was now shut tight again. Quickly she peeled back the tear, showing where the edges of a steel door, three feet by three feet, were plainly visible in the brick wall. But it was closed as firmly as a safe, and the lock had no key.

In the corridor, the guards were attacking the door with axes now. Lynn sank against the steel getaway, pressing her face against the cool metal. 'That beats us,' she sighed.

'Not yet.' said Toledo Steele. 'Get away from the door – well away.'

As the girl obeyed, he raised the rifle, aiming it at the lock. There was a crescendo of noise as a stream of bullets hurtled into the door, drowning the crashing of the axes from the corridor. Then, suddenly, the metal seemed to buckle and sag crazily, and the door swung back on well-oiled hinges.

'In you go!' snapped Toledo, giving the girl a gentle push. She squeezed her way feet first through the narrow opening. Her voice came hollowly from inside. 'There's a ladder here.'

Swiftly, Toledo followed her into the secret tunnel. The automatic rifle was empty, but he still had the ceremonial sword. He clambered hand over hand down the steel rungs of the ladder into pitch darkness, his footfalls resounding like hammer blows on an anvil.

Soon he was beside the girl at the foot of the ladder, with a low passage stretching away before them. They could feel the passage from the wave of cool air that came to meet them, but in the darkness they could see nothing. Voices sounded above their heads.

'That's the guards,' said Toledo. 'They'll be after us in a minute.'

He seized her arm and hurried her into the passage, feeling the breeze against his face. The only way they could move was to stretch their hands in front of them and grope, as quickly as possible, along the passage, which seemed to be carved out of the solid rock. It curved and wound like a snake, so that within a matter of seconds neither Toledo nor the girl had the slightest idea in which direction they were facing. But they kept going, forcing their way into the dark at risk of bumped heads and barked shins.

Suddenly, there was the faintest gleam of light ahead of them, the merest twinkle of a light and the sound of something swishing.

Toledo peered into the tunnel. 'Hear that? It's the sea.' He forged ahead, the girl by his side.

The light grew stronger, and Toledo realised it came from the stars and that the tunnel came out in the cliffs close to the promontory on which the Castellado was built. Doubtless the secret passage had been cut out of the rock in the same period as the underground network of the Castellado itself, and later joined to the more modern Presidential Palace.

He broke into the open, breathing the cool clean air of the night as one who, less than an hour before, had thought he was doomed to die before morning.

And at that moment there was a grinding, clashing noise, and the girl screamed and went to her knees, whimpering.

'What the –?' Toledo cried. He went down after her, feeling her shoulders under his fingers.

She said, 'Trap. My leg.' Then she fainted.

Toledo let his hands explore the ground at the entrance to the tunnel. Something glinted in the starlight, and he saw what had made the girl scream. Her left leg, just below the calf, was held securely in the jaws of a heavy man-trap that cut into her flesh like blunted knives.

'Hell. Oh, hell!' Toledo breathed.

And then something slashed through the night at his head, and the stars spun round in a giant catherine wheel, and the world went black as he dropped to the ground and lost consciousness.

A Kind of Justice

Colonel Maturez lit a cigarette. He perched himself on the edge of his desk and blew smoke into the air.

Outside the room, dawn was breaking over the Palace courtyard. Wisps of cool morning air drifted through the partly open windows, stirring the papers on Maturez' desk.

He spoke. 'You, Mrs Keperla, are going to be the bait in the trap.'

Facing him, in the chair which Toledo Steele had occupied only a few hours before, was Lynn Keperla. Her face was dirty and her hair ruffled. The white blouse she wore was no longer white, and was torn at her left shoulder. Her leg, where the man-trap had seized it, was black and angry with an ugly bruise.

'I've already been in one trap tonight. That's enough, I feel,' she responded.

Maturez laughed. 'You were lucky to escape with nothing more than bruises – I've known men have their legs broken in those traps.'

'Thanks for nothing,' said Lynn smoothly. She did not feel very smooth, and she was very frightened, but she did not want to let Maturez notice.

They were alone in the room. Earlier, Captain Rodriguez had been there, but after a muttered conversation with Maturez he had left, apparently to carry out certain orders.

'As I have said, you will be the bait in this new trap. Apparently Steele thought it better to leave you to your fate, once he realised you were caught. It is my guess that he joined up with El

Presidente and the man called Crandell, and that they are hiding out together somewhere.'

He waved the cigarette. 'Now, as you must see, I need the President. Alive, he could be a serious embarrassment to my plans. Therefore I intend to bargain with Steele for El Presidente . . . and I think both Steele and El Presidente himself will walk into the trap.'

'And you think Steele will give himself up for me? Aren't you forgetting that he abandoned me just now?' The girl's voice was bitter. To come out of her faint with soldiers around her, and to hear them say that Toledo Steele had got away was a blow. Yet, somehow, she could not blame him completely. To have stayed with her would have meant sacrificing himself unnecessarily. Alive and free, he might still be able to help, she thought. Like most people who associated with Toledo Steele, however briefly, Lynn Keperla had gained immense faith in his ability to do almost anything.

'I think,' said Maturez slowly, 'that even Steele will come to terms when he learns what I propose to do with you.' His eyes travelled over her, coolly appraising her worth.

'The experiment should be – interesting.' The girl's voice shook a little as she answered him.

'I trust it will not be necessary,' returned Maturez. He strode to the door and summoned a guard. 'See that this woman is cared for,' he ordered. 'She is not to be harmed in any way, but she is to be guarded at all times. You understand?' The guard came to attention and nodded. Maturez said, 'Good day to you, Mrs Keperla. I would suggest you get some rest.'

Lynn Keperla limped to the door. 'If I were you, Colonel, I'd get some rest, too,' she said as she went out. 'I have a feeling you may need a lot of it shortly.'

Something whirled around at tremendous speed inside

Toledo Steele's head and went '*ping!*' He woke up and felt sick. There was a bright light above him, burning his eyes. All around were shrill, chirruping noises like thousands of miniature buzz-saws.

He tried it again and this time managed to get his eyes open without retching. Struggling into an upright position, he found he was in the same clearing in which he had previously left Lynn and Crandell. The sun was climbing high in the sky and all around him birds and insects were playing a high-pitched chorus. He rubbed the back of his head, feeling the bump gingerly.

A voice beside him spoke in liquid Spanish. 'You are recovered, Señor Steele? I trust the bump is not too painful?'

Toledo moved his head carefully and saw the President squatting nearby. The little man was as cool-headed out here in the bush as he had been in his Palace. A friendly smile played about his lips.

'So you're here too,' he remarked. He decided that that was too obvious an opening gambit, and added, 'Was it you who hit me?'

El Presidente shook his head. 'Not I. It was the other one. He thought you were one of the guards.'

'The other one?' Toledo's head was clearing. 'Oh – you mean the one they imprisoned with you – Keperla, or Crandell, as he's really called. A plump man with an American accent?'

'That is he,' agreed the President. 'I showed him the secret door and we left together. Then, when you followed and he struck you down, he took your sword and forced me to help him carry you.'

'But how did you get here? This is miles from the city.'

'By automobile, of course,' the little man returned. 'For some weeks now I have had a small car hidden in a cave on the beach, which is firm for driving, and from which a road leads to the town. You see, I also have had my suspicions of Colonel Maturez.' He pointed casually. A few feet beyond the clearing stood a small Fiat.

Toledo nodded approvingly. 'You're well organised. What about the girl who was with me?'

The President looked grave. 'The American would not let me stay to free her from the man-trap.' He sighed. 'I had arranged for it to be placed there to prevent pursuit from the Guards – there was no intention in my mind of harming anyone else. The lady – who is she, and why was she also escaping along the secret tunnel?'

'That kind of explanation can wait,' said Toledo. 'The point is – she's Maturez' prisoner and that isn't funny. I take it you now believe what I had to say about our friend, the Colonel?'

'You were undoubtedly correct,' nodded the President. There was a crackling noise from the little Fiat and the President's head turned towards it.

Toledo started up. The President said, 'Very high frequency radio. It is tuned to the Palace frequency. I think Maturez will guess that I shall listen to this frequency and he will try to send some message. That is why I have left the radio on.'

Now that he was on his feet, Toledo Steele felt better. He looked around the clearing. 'Why don't you take the car and go? I don't see Crandell anywhere.'

The President sighed. 'Unfortunately he is nearby. And he now has the revolver I kept in the automobile. I have tried to escape once without success, as you can see.' He stretched out his leg, showing a thin streak of blood on the cloth above his knee. 'It is a mere scratch and hardly painful, but it does not allow me to move very far.'

As the President spoke, the bushes parted and Crandell strode into the clearing. He saw Toledo standing upright, and his hand flew to his pocket.

'You've come round, then.' A heavy ·38 menaced them. 'Reckon you should thank me this time for rescuing you.'

'And leaving the girl?' said Toledo.

Crandell shrugged. 'There wasn't time to bother with her. If Maturez wants her let him have her.'

'Maturez wants El Presidente,' said Toledo Steele. 'While El Presidente is free and alive, he can't have a successful revolution.'

'Revolutions don't concern me,' the American replied. 'I'm interested in more important things –'

The radio crackled again, breaking in on his words. Then sounding strangely loud in the clearing, Colonel Maturez' voice came through the loudspeaker. He spoke in German. 'This is Fleischmann. I am calling Toledo Steele. I speak in German so that he and I may understand one another. If you hear me, Steele, reply at once.'

Crandell's revolver jerked. 'Stand still, chum. You're not doing any bargaining.'

Toledo Steele stared down the muzzle of the ·38, and beyond it, at Crandell. Behind the American, Maturez' voice boomed out of the radio again.

'I believe you are listening somewhere, Steele, because I am certain you are with our mutual friend, who will be sure to have a radio wherever he is.'

'Very clever,' thought Toledo, 'you think of everything.'

Maturez continued. 'I tell you this, Steele. I have with me an unusual prisoner for the more cruel of my soldiers. You must return at once, bringing with you our mutual friend. Otherwise I shall deal with Mrs Keperla. You have until nightfall to decide.'

The radio crackled again and went silent. 'That sounded like the voice of Colonel Maturez,' the President commented. 'What did he say?'

Toledo translated, adding, 'You understand what he means

about returning the "mutual friend". You, Señor Presidente, are the "mutual friend".'

Crandell lost his mood of tension. 'Well, if that's all he has to say, we can relax. Our friend, the President, is my trump card, and I'm certainly not playing him for the girl.'

Toledo nodded. 'I thought that would be your reaction. You think you can play off the President to Maturez against the gold you killed Keperla for – right?'

'You guessed dead right,' replied Crandell. 'Though how you knew it was gold beats me. Sure I killed Keperla – there's the biggest strike since the Yukon up there in the hills, and I wasn't cutting him in on it. And as long as I have our friend, the President, I've got something to bargain with Maturez for in getting the mining concession – or don't I make myself clear?'

Toledo leaned lazily against the trunk of a tree. 'Very clear indeed. Correct me if I'm wrong, but the President knows you are not Keperla, doesn't he? And he knows that Keperla discovered gold – right? So he wasn't willing to deal with you at any time because he suspected you had killed Keperla. But Maturez didn't suspect about Keperla's death – he knew. And he didn't have the President's scruples either, so long as he was cut in for a large percentage of the profits. So he locked you up in the Castellado and threatened to expose you as the fake Keperla unless you made him a partner.'

'You're a good guesser,' Crandell rasped. 'That's about what happened. Keperla hired me in the mountains to help him with the mules and such-like. He was after oil – a gold-strike didn't interest him much. He was ready to stake out the gold claim and push on for the oil he said is in the valleys. That's when we quarrelled.'

Toledo looked very lazy indeed. He stared dreamily over Crandell's shoulder. 'So you killed once, and you're ready to sacrifice the girl this time to keep your miserable goldfield.'

‘A million dollars in gold and you call it miserable?’

Crandell’s face was a study in amazement. ‘For that kind of strike I’d sell out to the devil himself!’

‘You already have, Crandell,’ Toledo told him. ‘Yes, you already – look behind you!’

The American didn’t move. He shook his head. ‘Can’t catch me on that old trick, Steele. I’ve been around –’ He stopped suddenly and looked down at his left ankle. Then he screamed.

If he had kept still, in all probability the rattler would have glided away. But rattlers are bad-tempered snakes, and they are particularly upset by sudden movements and sudden cries.

The rattlesnake struck once with a vicious, chattering dive at Crandell’s leg. He swung round, blazing away with the revolver, but it was too late. The snake, its evil head blown away, wriggled a few times and died, but by then Crandell was staring at his trouser-leg, torn just above the ankle, and the tiny pinpricks of blood that showed on his skin.

He dropped the gun and took a pace backwards. Toledo Steele shook his head sadly. ‘You can’t complain I didn’t warn you.’

‘My God! I’ll die . . .’ Crandell cried.

‘You most surely will,’ said Toledo in complete agreement. ‘And there is nothing I can do to save you.’

Later, as Toledo Steele drove the little Fiat on to the main highway with the President sitting beside him, he said, ‘I think that he deserved to die.’ He sighed. ‘Sometimes there seems to be a kind of justice in the heavens.’

A Trap is Laid

They drove into São Vittorio without hindrance. As Toledo had guessed, Maturez did not intend to publicise his revolution until later in the day. Furthermore, the Colonel wanted as little outward fuss and bother as possible in his search for Steele and the

President. Therefore there were no road blocks and no particular evidence of more soldiers and police. In the Central Square the grandstand and the dais were completed, and various citizens were engaged in draping them with bunting and hanging out as many flags of various nationalities as possible. But no one took any notice of a little grey Fiat containing two men, one of them huddled asleep in the passenger seat with his hat over his eyes, the other immaculate in the uniform of an officer of the Presidential Guard.

Toledo brought the little car decorously up to the side entrance of the Café Horan, swung the wheel hard over, and disappeared into the kitchen yard. It was still early enough for the café to be only partly awake. Yasis himself stood in the yard, yawning ponderously as he thought about the day's work. His yawn was cut off sharply as the Fiat slid to a standstill in front of him and Toledo Steele's face looked out.

Toledo smiled. 'You're going to hide me, Yasis.'

The Greek went white as he stammered, 'But I cannot – there is – it is impossible –'

'Nothing ' said Toledo Steele, 'is impossible,' and reinforced the suggestion with the sight of a revolver at the edge of the car door.

'No doubt something . . .' The Greek's voice trailed off. He was having a decidedly unhappy time.

'Undoubtedly,' agreed Toledo getting out of the car. The President got out too, and limped around the front of the car to join him. Yasis' three chins quivered.

'El Presidente!' he gasped.

'Well,' said Toledo 'he's certainly not Miss World!' He waved the revolver. 'A nice quiet room, Yasis, where the three of us can be undisturbed. And – take us by the back stairs, please.'

A few minutes later they were settled in a back room of the Café Horan, with the blinds drawn. Yasis stood near the door, anxious to leave.

Toledo motioned with the revolver. 'Sit down, Yasis. We're all going to have a heart-to-heart chat.'

Yasis sat on the bed. The President and Toledo occupied the only two chairs in the room. Toledo lit a cigarette.

'Yasis,' he said, 'you sold us out. You gave Anton Juanero into the hands of Rodriguez and his butchers. And because of that, Juanero is dead.'

'No! Oh, no! Señor Steele, I swear –'

'Do by all means,' said Toledo. 'But you were the only one who knew I had a link with Juanero . . . and the very day I reappear in town after escaping from the Castellado, Juanero's home is searched. That same evening there is a policeman carelessly patrolling outside, and later, Juanero is picked up in his car for no good reason and taken to the Castellado.' He shook his head sadly. 'Yasis, my fat Judas, you sold out . . . I should have guessed earlier, after the police staged that shooting incident down by the waterfront, but I thought you were with me.'

Yasis said something suddenly in Greek. Then, to the President, he added in Spanish, 'Naturally I am on the side of Maturez. Under a regime like this one, what opportunities are there for making money?' He spat contemptuously. 'Maturez will find you both, and then you will die!'

'But perhaps I shall kill you first,' said Toledo gently. He pressed the revolver against Yasis' ample stomach. 'Therefore you will do certain things for me, or I shall surely shoot you – here – and you will die with much pain.' He prodded with the gun a little harder. 'Now, what do you say?'

A little after two o'clock that afternoon, Colonel Maturez put down the 'phone and turned to his Chief of Police. The Colonel looked pleasant for the first time in many hours, although he had not slept through the night and the strain was beginning to show on him.

'Juan – that was the café-proprietor, Yasis,' he told Rodriguez. 'He has just heard from Steele. The pair of them – Steele and El Presidente – are going to the Café Horan at eight this evening. Yasis has said that if an officer and half a dozen men watch the place, they can capture them without difficulty!'

Rodriguez started his thought processes churning. There was an almost visible effort in his brain. 'An officer and six men,' he commented slowly. 'It does not seem much. I would suggest –'

'Normally, so should I,' agreed Maturez with surprising cheerfulness. 'But Steele will be on the alert. And Yasis has confirmed that Steele will enter the café by the back way and has no suspicions that anything will be wrong. Therefore, in the circumstances –'

'In the circumstances,' repeated Rodriguez, 'I agree entirely. I will arrange matters myself.'

Maturez looked as though he wished that thought had not occurred to his Chief of Police, but he did not comment. Instead he said, 'Tonight, I think, we may celebrate. You have the girl safe?'

'Locked in her room with a sentry at the door,' replied the Chief of Police.

Maturez nodded. 'It might be intriguing, I feel, for her to dine with me tonight . . . before I have Steele shot!'

At the Café Horan, Yasis also replaced the telephone and leaned weakly against the wall. His fat face was red and there was stark terror in his eyes. He looked helplessly at the gun which Toledo Steele had pressed firmly against his middle.

'You played that scene well,' he told Yasis. 'They won't dare to come before dark, otherwise they will think we might see them. So, when they finally arrive after eight, we shall have been here for several minutes. It's a good story, don't you agree?'

Yasis nodded, still staring fascinated at the revolver. Toledo continued. 'Now, my fat Judas, we'll go upstairs to your room, where you will send a message that you're ill and don't want to be disturbed all day. And after that we'll take it easy until dark.'

End of the Road

There was no apparent change in the town of São Vittorio with the coming of dusk that day. Preparations for the Festival of the Republic next day had gone on as normally. The townsfolk were looking forward to a public holiday, coupled with the added attraction of extra business, for farmers and ranchers from the surrounding country were already flocking into the streets.

No word of any change of government had come from the Presidential Palace. So far as the people of Ursulino knew, their President was alive and well and in his Palace; tomorrow there would be rejoicing, large quantities of firecrackers set off in the streets, and a certain amount of rollicking drunkenness by nightfall. It was a good country in which to live, and the people were happy. Innocent of Maturez' revolution, they would be completely off guard.

Toledo Steele remarked as much to El Presidente as they sat in Yasis' room. The Greek himself lay on his bed, a gag in his mouth and his hands tied behind him. The time was five minutes to eight.

'Happy people are often like sheep,' El Presidente replied. He shook his head. 'Suppose I had died as Maturez wished – suppose I still die tonight – what happens? Colonel Maturez assumes power, a state of emergency is declared, free elections are promised but never happen and before one realises it, this is a police state in which the individual is powerless. The curious thing is that Maturez' revolution has already taken place – yet who knows of it? If we fail tonight, tomorrow there may be scattered riots when Maturez announces the change in power, but such futile challenges can be met without any difficulty.'

'You make it sound too easy,' said Toledo. He held up a hand. 'That sounds like a police truck.' Quickly he got to his feet and pulled aside the curtains. A blue-painted police van was already in the kitchen yard, its tailboard down and backed against the door.

Toledo pulled the gag from Yasis' mouth and untied his wrists. 'You understand what to do?' he asked. The Greek nodded. 'And remember, I shall be behind you with this gun.'

They went downstairs. The President remained behind in Yasis' room, nursing on his knee a large and somewhat antique Colt which Toledo had found among the Greek's possessions.

They reached the kitchen 'No lights,' warned Toledo in a whisper as Yasis moved to open the door. He stood aside, out of sight of the men in the yard.

A lieutenant of the Presidential Guard stood outside. Yasis put his fingers to his lips for silence. 'Yourself and one other to take them,' he hissed. 'Post the remainder of your men outside.'

The lieutenant nodded and made a signal. He stepped into the darkened kitchen, followed by a private soldier. Yasis closed the door.

'They are in my room. Follow me – and make as little noise as possible.'

The two men turned after him, and in that instant Toledo Steele acted. He reversed the gun and brought it down with club-like force on the lieutenant's head, reasoning that of the two, the ordinary soldier might be the easier to terrify. As the lieutenant groaned and dropped to the floor, Toledo jammed the gun in the soldier's back.

'Too loud a breath, and you are dead,' he said. 'Pick up the officer, or I'll kill the pair of you.'

Yasis stood fidgeting.

The guard came to life. Toledo had reasoned correctly. There would be no heroics from this soldier, who merely wanted to remain alive. He bent down and picked up the lieutenant's feet, while Yasis took his shoulders. Toledo could have laughed with relief; it was going easily, much too easily.

El Presidente moved back from the door as Yasis and the guard bore the unconscious body of the lieutenant into the room.

'Pillow-cases!' snapped Toledo, and the President produced them from the pile that had previously been laid aside. While the President covered Yasis and the soldier, Toledo tied the lieutenant's wrists behind his back and gagged him. Then he threw a jug of water in the man's face.

The lieutenant woke up, spluttering, to find Toledo's face a few inches from his own, and the revolver tickling his throat.

'You are my prisoner,' Toledo told him 'Behave and you will live. Make one wrong move, and I'll shoot you dead.'

The lieutenant understood. So did the soldier. Toledo compared the size of the President with that of the soldier, and then said, 'It'll be a loose fit for you, but never mind.' To the soldier he said, 'Take off your clothes.'

The President was already stripping off his jacket and trousers. In a few moments they had changed clothes and Toledo was tying the soldier and gagging him as he had done the officer. Then he slipped pillowcases over the heads of both men.

'We're ready,' he announced. 'Take their guns and watch out in case the rest of the troops notice anything wrong.'

Toledo armed himself with the lieutenant's revolver in addition to the ·38 he had taken from Crandell. The President tucked the soldier's automatic rifle under his arm.

'What about me?' Yasis demanded, and received a prod from Toledo's gun in reply. He took the hint and walked out of the room.

They moved down the stairs in single file – Yasis, Toledo Steele, the two prisoners, and the President. Toledo could feel the back of his neck prickling. To capture a couple of unsuspecting Presidential Guards was one thing, but to bluff a way through the remaining five soldiers, all armed to the teeth, was quite a different story.

Yet, typically, his lips parted in a little smile, and his step assumed a more jaunty tread. This was adventure as he liked it, the kind of daredevil piracy in which he revelled. Unless you risked all, his smile seemed to say, there was no fun in living. Or dying, for that matter.

He glanced at his watch. Ten minutes past eight. There were twenty minutes in which to storm the Palace, launch a one-man counter-revolution, and – he almost laughed aloud as he thought of the cliché – save the Princess.

The night was bright with stars. Yasis halted on the doorstep and was prodded forward.

'Into the truck, Señor Yasis,' said Toledo Steele politely. He grabbed the prisoners and thrust them forward at the tailboard, so that they fell into the body of the truck after Yasis. Beside him a corporal came to attention in the half dark. Toledo kept his face away from him as he barked an order, 'There are more of them inside. Take your men and search the building!'

'Very good sir!' the corporal answered. Then he thought of something, changed his mind, and peered into Toledo's face. 'You are not Lieutenant Bernales!'

Toledo murmured, 'Never 'eard of 'im, mate!' and swung a terrific left hook to the man. The corporal grunted and folded up. At the same instant one of the soldiers approached, saw what was happening, and raised his rifle.

There were more soldiers running now. 'Señor Presidente – get aboard!' Toledo said, and gave the little man a push that carried him into the truck on top of the struggling lieutenant. He ran round to the driver's seat. The soldier behind the wheel suddenly found himself hauled into space by a pair of hands that seemed to have come from nowhere, while the laughter of demons sounded in his ear. After that he knew nothing, for the ground rose violently and struck the back of his head.

Toledo Steele started the motor and the truck lurched out of the yard. Someone opened fire with an automatic rifle, and he heard a scream. As the truck swung right he saw Yasis toppling slowly into the road, to sprawl there like a fat puppet with the strings removed, pathetically helpless and still.

'Señor Presidente – are you all right?' he called.

The little man's voice reassured him, and Toledo swept the truck through the gears and headed up the hill towards the Palace.

The main gates were open. Toledo did not hesitate. He roared the truck between the gates as though he were going over a grand prix finishing line and heaved on the wheel to bring it in a screeching half-circle to a standstill before the Palace entrance.

Toledo sprang out. The President was already climbing from the back of the truck. Two sentries began running down the steps, their rifles at the ready.

'This, Señor Presidente, is where you do your stuff,' remarked Toledo, and crossed his fingers.

The little man stood his ground. As the two Guards approached, he removed his soldier's helmet and waited. 'I am your President,' he said. 'Do you know me?'

The nearer of the guards stopped running. 'Señor Presidente! We were told you were ill and confined to your room!'

His companion joined in. 'We were given orders not to speak of your illness . . . but you are not ill.'

El Presidente took it calmly. Toledo thought he was magnificent. The little man said, 'Obviously I am not ill and you were misinformed. You will obey my orders and my orders alone.

Is that understood?'

Both soldiers snapped to attention and the President continued. 'In the truck you will find a lieutenant and a soldier of the Presidential Guard. They are to be kept under close arrest.'

He ran lightly up the steps of the Palace, Toledo following.

'I think I know where to find Maturez,' the President said grimly. Together he and Toledo passed into the main hall of the Palace and began climbing the great staircase. Toledo, looking around, thought it looked like an enlarged cinema theatre, decorated in bad taste. It was the first chance he had had of studying the over-ornate architecture of the building.

But he did not have more than a few seconds to waste on architecture. Captain Rodriguez, at the head of a dozen or so guards, rushed out of an ante-room at the foot of the stairs. The Chief of Police, probably for the first time in his life, acted swiftly.

'On the stairs – lie flat!' Toledo cried. He hurled himself at the balustrade, cuddling behind it for a quick shot at Rodriguez.

The Chief of Police sent a bullet whistling over the staircase and then dropped for cover. Simultaneously his men dispersed themselves around the main hall.

Toledo found the President beside him, squinting down the sights of his rifle. 'It may surprise you, but I have done this sort of thing before,' the President said to Toledo.

Another shot crashed over the stairs. Toledo saw a head appear and aimed for it. The man sagged to the carpet.

Rodriguez' voice sounded from the hall. 'Surrender, and I guarantee you fair treatment.'

'It's not my night for surrendering,' muttered Toledo. He decided to continue his study of the architecture. For a few seconds, until Rodriguez and his men summoned up enough courage to rush them, they were safe.

Toledo looked at the walls. Electric lights, held in giant

bronze fists, protruded at various points. From the centre of the high, vaulted ceiling hung a magnificent chandelier, designed at one time for candle-light and later converted to electricity. By the appearance of the fittings, the conversion had been carried out about the turn of the century. In fact, electric conduits disguised as ornamental pipes ran up the walls to the bronze fists.

And away in a corner of the hall, perched above a doorway, was a junction box, complete with master-switch and fuses.

Toledo grinned. 'I doubt if your electrical fittings would pass the country's fire regulations, Señor Presidente. And I think you're going to need new ones.'

He swung round, taking the automatic rifle from the President. With careful aim, he loosed off a blast at the junction box.

The effect was like a huge fair on a fireworks night. There was a crash from the junction box, then a splutter, and then a host of sparks and flame. Simultaneously all the lights in the hall went out.

'Come on!' shouted Toledo. He raced up the stairs, bent double, with the President panting behind. A fusillade of shots echoed wildly across the stairs.

At the head of the stairs Toledo gave the President a friendly push to one side. He ducked behind a pillar, waiting. The corridor was in darkness. Somewhere, far along it, a voice was barking orders.

'Maturez!' whispered Toledo.

Feet pounded on the staircase. Toledo took one smart step out from behind the pillar and sprayed the stairs carefully and scientifically with the rifle. He heard Rodriguez cry out first, and then guards who were still on their feet were tumbling backwards to the hall.

A figure approached and a voice in the darkness said, 'Señor Presidente?' It was one of the guards who had met them at the entrance. 'I entered through the rear of the Palace after I heard the firing. There are twenty guards loyal to you in the corridor.'

'You are promoted to Sergeant!' Toledo said immediately. He heard the President's chuckle beside him. 'Form a bodyguard for El Presidente and obey his commands,' he ordered.

He padded along the corridor in the direction of the Presidential Suite. There was a guard at the turn of the passage. He sprang forward as Toledo approached and levelled his rifle. Toledo backed hastily into the shelter of a doorway.

'What's happening? What is all the shooting about?' queried the guard.

Toledo took a coin from his pocket and tossed it lightly against the wall on the other side of the corridor. There was a burst of flame from the automatic rifle as the guard blasted at his unseen enemy. Toledo aimed and heard the guard's sudden cry.

He saw Maturez.

The Colonel had obtained candles and was standing in the doorway of the President's suite of rooms, holding one aloft. Behind him, other candles guttered eerily in the light breeze.

'Fleischmann!' Toledo called.

The man started, searching for the voice. There was a gun in his hand now. He banged a shot into the wall.

And then a pair of hands came out of the darkness and fell upon his gun wrist. Colonel Maturez cried out as he lost his pistol. He was pushed back into the room and the door was closed.

He saw Toledo Steele, who said, 'I have come for you, Fleischmann. Where is Lynn Keperla?'

The girl's cry came from the other side of the room. She was back against the wall, her hands behind her. As she ran forward, Toledo saw that her wrists were bound.

Colonel Maturez set the candle down on the table, then backed against it. 'Apparently I have lost,' he said. 'Well, others have lost before me.'

Toledo looked at the girl. Her hair was disarranged and she looked scared.

'You have lost, Fleischmann. And you will be tried and executed,' Toledo told him. 'Your little game is over.'

Colonel Maturez shook his head. He took two steps round the table. 'No. No. I shall not be tried, Steele.'

He did something quickly with his fingers. There was a crunch of glass between his teeth, and suddenly the smell of bitter almonds drifted across the room. Maturez clutched the table. His mouth twisted sharply. He turned his head to look into the fire. 'I cheat you . . .'

Then his knees sagged under him and he sank slowly to the floor, his hands tight across his stomach.

The girl came across the room to Toledo and into his arms, while he loosened the cords at her wrists. She was crying now.

Toledo tilted her head back and looked into her dark eyes. 'We've just had a counter-revolution. But tomorrow, after the Festival of the Republic, I'll take you driving into the hills and show you a gold-mine that's going to make you a millionairess.'

There was a little smile at his lips. He looked at her honey-coloured hair in the firelight, and he thought that showing Lynn Keperla a gold mine in the hills would be very pleasant indeed.

The Disappearing Lake

by Joyce Eley

Sally and Dick propped their bicycles against the eucalyptus and strolled down to the edge of the lake.

'Golly, it's the largest lake I've ever seen,' said Sally.

'Don't you have any big lakes in England?' Dick asked.

'Well, maybe we do, but not where I live. I say, Dick, what are these things sticking out above the water? They look like a fence.'

'That's just what they are. You see, this lake disappears.'

'Disappears?' echoed Sally.

'Yes. Sometimes it covers acres of land, but then it begins to shrink, and boundary fences that have been covered for years, gradually appear again. They say that people who go out on the lake disappear, too, and are never seen again,' he added with a grin.

'I must say you Aussies love telling creepy stories,' remarked Sally. 'I vote we have some lunch.'

While they were eating, Sally, who had been sent away from the German blitz on London to relatives in Australia, pondered once more over the strangeness of her safe new homeland.

After lunch they walked along the sandy shores to where a small gully ran through the trees down to the lake, and there, securely fastened to a stout post, was a little rowing boat.

'How about going for a row?' said Dick quite suddenly.

'We can't do that. We don't know who the boat belongs to,' Sally objected.

Dick bent over the boat. 'Hasn't been used for ages,' he declared. 'After all, we're only going to borrow it. Coming? Or are you afraid of disappearing?'

'Course not!' laughed Sally.

Dick quickly untied the boat, and a few moments later he was rowing steadily out into the lake. Sally sat back contentedly and let her hand trail in the cool water. She still found it difficult to get used to the temperatures well up in the eighties.

'There are some people paddling over there,' Sally suddenly exclaimed.

Dick laughed. 'There probably aren't any people for miles. Those are black-backed pelicans.'

'What huge birds!' Sally cried in amazement.

Soon a little wooded island came into view. Dick glanced over his shoulder. 'It's about a couple of miles on. Shall we try and land there, and do a bit of exploring?'

'Oh, yes!' said Sally. 'Let me have a turn at rowing. I can row, you know, even if I do catch a few crabs.' So Sally took the oars and pulled steadily until the island drew closer and they could see a small, sandy bay where it was possible to land. They tied the boat to a tree trunk and wandered into the scrub.

'Why, look, there's quite a track. People have been here before,' Sally said in surprise.

'Picnickers like ourselves, probably,' said Dick. 'Australians are great picnickers. If we keep to the track, we shan't get lost.'

'What's that sharp smell?'

'Gum trees,' Dick told her. 'Smell this.' And he crushed one of the slender, grey-green leaves of a eucalyptus.

'It smells healthy,' grinned Sally, sniffing deeply.

Quite suddenly the track widened. The trees were more widely spaced, as if the undergrowth had been cleared away, and there right in front of them was a large homestead, apparently in ruins.

Sally and Dick approached it, cautiously, but it seemed deserted. The front door, which opened on to the long wooden veranda, swung crazily on its hinges, and leaves and things were still piled up on the floor where the wind had blown them. They went from room to room trying to imagine what it must have been like when it was first built. Then quite unexpectedly, they came to a door that was obviously new and led, it appeared, to a small section built on at the back.

'Do you think we ought to go any farther?' Sally asked doubtfully. 'We're trespassing, you know.'

'Well, we may as well take a peep. A new door in this old ramshackle house! It's very odd.' He pushed the new door open as he spoke, and they stared in amazement into a room fitted up as a complete, miniature transmitting station. Neither of them heard the heavy footsteps crossing the room. Only when a man spoke did they realize that they were not alone.

'So,' he said. 'This is what comes of leaving Heinrich in charge. He forgets to lock up. What are you two doing here?'

Dick and Sally swung round to face a man wearing a black mackintosh.

'I am sorry, sir. We thought the house was empty and were just having a look round,' said Dick. 'We didn't mean any harm.'

'That remains to be seen,' said the man. 'Now you're here, you can stay put.'

'You can't keep us here,' Dick protested.

'We haven't done any damage,' added Sally.

'Better let them go. They're only kids,' said another voice from the doorway, and a second man came in. He had a round, jolly face and looked at the children with some amusement.

'Did no one ever tell you the legend of the lake?'

'You mean about people disappearing?' asked Dick.

'That's it, and that's what will happen to you if you don't give us your solemn promise not to tell anyone you ever saw this place.'

'That's no good,' the first man cut in. 'I'm not taking any risks tonight. All this stuff will be moved out by tomorrow, and then we can let them go.'

'Oh, very well,' said the man with a jolly face, and before Dick and Sally could attempt to resist, they were hustled through the transmitting room into a smaller room behind it. There was the click of the lock, and then all was silent. They found themselves in a small, windowless room with a skylight in the roof. The only furniture consisted of a table and three chairs.

Sally was the first to find her voice. 'They can't keep us here, can they?'

Dick frowned. 'I shouldn't have thought so. But we don't know who they are.'

'What do you mean?'

'Well, they don't seem to be here *lawfully*, do they? If they are, why have they locked us up?'

'They're afraid we'll tell someone what they're doing.'

'Exactly. And what *are* they doing?'

Dick sat at the table thoughtfully, his elbows on the surface, his head resting in his hands. 'That transmitting equipment means *something*, but what? There aren't any military bases around here, at least, not that I know of, so they're probably not spies. But they could be sending out propaganda for the Germans or the Japs.'

'In which case,' said Sally decisively, 'they're just as bad as spies.'

'They must be traitors of some kind,' agreed Dick. 'Why else set up a station in such an isolated spot like this.'

'It fits in with the legend – people disappear when they go out on the lake.'

'A legend which makes people either too frightened to come looking, or "explains" the disappearance of those who don't come back.'

'I wouldn't be satisfied with such an explanation,' said Sally.

Dick grinned. 'Ah, but you're not as simple-minded as some.'

'Thanks for the compliment. But how are we going to escape?'

Dick frowned again. 'That man's voice puzzles me – the man with the jolly face. I've heard him before. But where . . .?'

They examined the room carefully, but there appeared to be no way of getting out of it. Sally suggested piling the three chairs on the table and trying to reach the skylight, but the wobbly edifice was not high enough. Gradually the daylight faded. Then, abruptly, an electric light was switched on from somewhere outside. It was better than sitting in the dark, but the time dragged heavily. Sally fought hard to keep the tears out of her eyes.

'Do you really think they will let us go tomorrow?' she asked.

'I don't know, Sally, but don't worry,' said Dick, trying to reassure her. 'Mum and Dad will have expected us home long before this, and they'll have the police out searching for us.'

'But we didn't tell them where we were going,' said Sally, unable to keep a tremulous note out of her voice.

Dick did not answer, but started wandering round the room. He suddenly stopped by the door. 'This is made of quite thin wood,' he said.

'What's the good of that?' said Sally. 'It only leads into the transmitting room, even if we could break it down.'

'I know, but if I put my ear against it, I can hear what the men are saying. Come and listen.'

Sally pressed her ear against the door. 'It sounds like a foreign language.'

'One of them spoke in English just now. He said something about a launch.'

Then they both heard a voice say distinctly, 'What do we do with the kids?'

'Take them with us, of course,' came the reply. 'We don't want them poking about while we're gone. Have you got those two big lights? Right, let's go.'

They just had time to jump back from the door as it was flung open, and a tall man wearing a peaked white cap entered.

'So,' he said with a strong German accent, 'if you do exactly as you are told, no one is going to hurt you.'

'Do as they say,' Dick whispered. 'We may get the chance of making a break.'

They followed their captors outside to a small wooden jetty where a smart motor launch was anchored.

'Into this cabin,' ordered the man with the peaked cap as they walked up the gangway. Another man wearing some sort of uniform motioned them down a steep iron ladder, through a cramped room, and into a tiny cabin, the door of which he shut on them. Presently they could hear the throb of the engines, and by the rocking of the boat they knew that they had left the island and were afloat on the lake.

'Does the lake link up with the sea?' Sally asked as they sat disconsolately on the bunk.

'Not that I know of, but it's not far from the coast. I wish I knew what the men were up to.'

They could hear them laughing and talking in the other cabin, and there was the clink of glasses, but they were speaking in such low tones that the two prisoners could hardly hear anything. Then someone raised his voice and said quite clearly, 'Let's drink the health of good old Matilda. May she rest in peace.'

'Good heavens, I hope they're not going to bury someone!' said Sally.

'I do wish I could remember where I heard that voice before,' said Dick in perplexity.

Soon the boat began to rock vigorously. 'Wind's getting up,' said Dick. 'It does sometimes, and we have quite a squall.'

The party in the cabin became noisier and noisier. Suddenly the launch gave a great lurch, and there was a tearing sound. They could hear the men staggering to their feet and scrambling up the iron ladder. The boat gave another lurch, and Sally and Dick were flung to the floor.

'Come on Sally, the boat has struck something,' Dick gasped. He was able to force open the door, and they hurried through the outer cabin. The floor sloped at an alarming angle, and a litter of broken glass had been swept into a corner. As they climbed up the ladder, the wind nearly knocked them back again.

'Hold on tight!' Dick shouted. Through the dark, scurrying clouds they could see the glimmer of the moon momentarily lighting up a dark shape that moved jerkily over the water.

'There they are!' pointed Sally. 'They've taken the dinghy and left us to drown.'

'We shan't drown,' said Dick calmly. 'The launch has struck one of the fences. The water must have been lower than they thought. The boat seems to be firmly wedged, and the worst of the squall is over. Let's get out of this wind.'

'Well, I never thought I'd be shipwrecked on a lake,' said Sally. 'What's that you've got?'

'Food,' said Dick, grinning up at her from the bottom of the ladder. 'Come and get it.'

Gradually the wind died down, and they slept until it was just beginning to get light. It looked like a nice day.

'Let's get up on deck and see if we can find out where we are,' said Dick, but it was still too dark to see for any distance. As they reached the deck they heard the low throb of an aeroplane engine, and presently they caught sight of the aircraft's green and red flashing lights.

'It's a helicopter,' Dick exclaimed. 'I wonder if it's looking for us or if it's going to pick up those men somewhere.'

The helicopter hovered for a moment against the brightness of the morning sky before disappearing.

'Where's it gone?' asked Sally.

'It's landed behind that hill over there. The men must have arranged to meet it.'

'Dick!' Sally exclaimed, remembering. 'Didn't they say something about coming back?'

'Then we'd better get going. Right?'

They could now see the fence upon which the launch was securely jammed, and the shore did not seem too far away. 'I'm not sure I can swim all that distance,' Sally said uncertainly.

'It's not so far,' said Dick; 'we don't even need to swim. We can just haul ourselves along the fence. Are you game to try?

'I'm ready,' nodded Sally.

Hand over hand, they hauled themselves along the fence towards the shore. Not far away a black speck was bobbing.

'It's the dinghy coming back,' Sally gasped, clinging with aching arms to one of the posts. 'They're sure to see us when they get nearer.' Dick made no reply, for his gaze was fixed upon the sky. Flying low, in wedge-like formation, came the pelicans, their heads bent back and their great wings outstretched. In a few seconds they had surrounded the boy and girl, swooping down into the water and coming up with silvery fish struggling in their powerful beaks. More and more pelicans began to descend on the partly submerged fence.

'Here's our camouflage,' Dick laughed. 'They won't be able to distinguish us from the pelicans. Remember how you mistook them for people? Come on, now, we're nearly there. Let's swim!' So they swam between the bobbing files of pelicans that were continually landing on the water. At last, wet and

More and more pelicans began to descend.

exhausted, they struggled ashore and made their way to the road that skirted the lake. As they reached it, they saw a large, shining black car driving towards them.

'Is it some of the spies?' Sally muttered in dismay, preparing to dash into the bush.

'No, it's a police car.' Dick sighed with relief, waving his arms vigorously.

The car ground to a halt. 'Are you Richard Moore and Sally Sheraton?' asked a police officer.

The youngsters nodded.

'What's been going on? We've been out all night scouring the countryside for you. We found your bikes, and were just thinking of dragging the lake.'

Breathlessly Dick and Sally poured out their story.

'Here, hold on a minute! Is that the launch out there that you're talking about? Transmitting station on an island! This sounds interesting. We've been searching for that station for months.'

'Are they spies?' Dick queried.

'Spies? You could call them that. They run a station that broadcasts propaganda – Radio Waltzing Matilda, they call themselves.'

'Of course!' exclaimed Dick. 'Radio Matilda put on some jolly good programmes. I used to listen to it, though I turned it off whenever they got on to politics. No wonder I knew the announcer's voice.'

Dick told the police about the helicopter.

'Here, hop in,' said one of the men. 'There are a couple of blankets in the back. Wrap yourselves up while I put a call through to headquarters. They'll have someone over to the island in no time. Then we'll go and see if we can find out where the helicopter landed.'

'This must be the spot,' said the officer a few minutes later.

'The grass is trodden down all over the place.'

'Would this be anything?' asked Sally, picking up something black and shiny from the grass.

'I wouldn't be surprised,' said the policeman. 'It's a roll of film. We may be on to something. I'd better get you two home, though, now.'

Two days later Sally sat up in bed nursing a slight cold. Mrs Moore came in with a loaded breakfast tray, followed by Dick with an armful of newspapers.

'Have a look at these, Sal,' said Dick with his broad grin. 'We're famous!'

Sally read the headlines: 'Intrepid youngsters discover secret radio station.' 'Children solve mystery of Disappearing Lake.' 'Waltzing Matilda propaganda broadcasts have stopped for good.'

'Don't forget another reporter is coming this afternoon,' said Mrs Moore.

'What will you say if they ask you what you think of Australia? You can't say, the way people do about England, "I think your policemen are wonderful". Ours were a bit slow, if you ask me,' smiled Dick.

'Now, let me think,' said Sally solemnly. 'I shall say that your lakes are beauts. That's good Aussie, isn't it? And that I think your pelicans are wonderful!'

Man-Hunt

by Lee Mayne

With infinite care, Giulio Ascola slid the blade of his knife into the crack in the wall panelling. Gently, but firmly, he started to exert leverage on the handle until, with a slight splintering noise, a section of the panelling sprang open.

The little man flicked the button of his torch and allowed the tiny pencil-beam to wander over the wall safe he had just uncovered. Satisfied, he switched off and grinned to himself in the darkness.

'A push-over!' he thought. He started to rub the tips of his sensitive fingers on the sleeve of his jacket. Idly, he wondered why an important man like Senator Keeble should use such an old-fashioned model. 'Worse than a kid's piggy bank,' he shrugged. 'A babe-in-arms could open it.'

With practised ease, he adjusted a stethoscope to his ears and pressed the cup against the safe door just above the dial. Then, taking a deep breath, he started the task of breaking down the combination.

Suddenly he froze. Somewhere in the house a bell was shrilling insistently. Giulio cursed softly under his breath – he hadn't reckoned on the Senator having callers at three o'clock in the morning. Swiftly, he stuffed the stethoscope into his pocket and forced the wall panel shut. Shuffling footsteps sounded in the passage. Tense and uncertain, he hesitated – the way to the back of the house was cut off. The murmur of approaching voices spurred the little man into precipitate action. With desperate speed, he dived behind the heavy, velvet window-curtains.

The door opened, a switch clicked on and the room was flooded with light. Giulio, peeping through a tiny gap in the curtains, just managed to smother an involuntary gasp. A tousle-haired man in a dressing-gown was being hustled into the room, menaced by the automatics of two swarthy-faced gun-men.

'This is an absolute outrage!' he spluttered angrily.

'On the contrary Senator. Just a little business call.' A third man entered the room behind the two hoodlums. Dressed in immaculate evening dress, his iron-grey hair smoothly slicked back, the newcomer gave an immediate impression of being both wealthy and distinguished.

'I don't do business with racketeers!' snarled the Senator.

The other man smiled easily. 'I think you should listen to the deal,' he said. He gave a slight nod and, without a word, one of the gunmen grabbed the old man and slammed him down hard into a chair.

'It's quite simple,' said the tall man. 'Next week, in Washington, you will withdraw your support for the Undesirable Aliens Bill . . .'

'You blackmailing . . . *aaaah*!' Senator Keeble's angry protest ended in a groan as one of the silent hoodlums slapped him hard across the mouth.

'Also,' continued the other, 'you will deposit with me the sum of $10,000 as a guarantee of good faith.' He paused to light a cigarette. 'In return, we can offer you complete protection.'

'Protection!' The old man's eyes blazed. 'When that Bill goes through, nobody's going to need protection! We're going to clear scum like you right out of America – for good!'

The tall man studied the end of his cigarette. 'Meaning you are not interested in my little proposition?' he said casually.

'Meaning just that!' snapped the Senator, curtly.

The other shrugged. 'O.K.,' he said, carelessly. 'If that's how you feel . . .' Again he gave a brief nod to the gunmen.

'No . . .!' The old man started to claw his way out of the chair as he saw one of the stony-faced killers pick up a cushion and muffle his gun with it.

The shots came as three dull thuds. Senator Keeble slowly toppled forward and fell sprawling on to the floor.

The switch was snapped off, the door clicked softly shut and Giulio was again left in the darkened room – this time with a dead man for company!

But it was not that which sent waves of fear coursing through the little crook. Giulio Ascola knew something else. He knew that his own life was forfeit from that moment on. He had witnessed a Mafia killing!

Inspector Jean Collet wore a slight frown of concentration as he flicked through the dossier in front of him. He seemed unaware of the keen scrutiny he was undergoing from the broad-shouldered, pleasant-faced Irishman seated on the other side of his desk.

Captain Mike O'Connor, of the United States Treasury Department, was a shrewd judge of men. He eyed the preoccupied figure opposite him, taking in the striking aquiline features and the lithe strength of Interpol's ace detective.

'So you're The Hawk,' he thought. He nodded to himself. 'Well, one thing is certain, me boyo – I'd rather have you with me than against me!'

The Hawk looked up. 'Well,' he said, with a quick smile, 'now let me have the *real* story.'

'Huh?' The Treasury man looked blank.

'Giulio Ascola,' said The Hawk, tapping the dossier. 'A

third-rate safe-breaker with nothing bigger on his record than a $2,000 haul. Suddenly, the United States want him so badly that they send their top-flight Treasury agent to Paris to ask for Interpol co-operation in finding him. What's he done – cleaned out Fort Knox?'

'He's hotter than that,' said Captain O'Connor grimly. 'He's the only eye-witness to a Mafia killing!'

The Hawk listened quietly while the other told him about Senator Keeble's murder.

'The little guy Giulio must have panicked completely when the killers left,' O'Connor continued. 'He left his finger-prints all over the place. Naturally, the local cops thought he'd shot the old man himself.' He grunted, angrily. 'They started a hue and cry – the Press got hold of the story, and now the whole population of America knows about Giulio Ascola!'

'Surely that should have helped?' said The Hawk.

'It drove him to Europe.' The Treasury agent stood up. 'Once the headlines gave his identity, Giulio knew he was as good as dead if he stayed in America. The Mafia would get him for sure!'

The Mafia!

The Hawk let his mind dwell on the vicious organisation that struck terror into the hearts of men and women all over the United States. Starting in a small way among the Sicilian immigrants, its growth during the past fifty years had reached fantastic proportions. The proceeds from every form of crime, violence and extortion had brought wealth and power to the Mafia leaders. Now, many of them occupied positions of importance and trust, and were able to exert their evil influence in every sphere of American life. Hoboes or high financiers, from sheep-herders to Senators, all suffered from the extortion and protection rackets operated by these cold-blooded men who ordered killings as easily as they ordered their own meals.

'We've just got to find him!' O'Connor's voice cut across the

Interpol man's thoughts. 'If I can get him back to the States as a Federal witness, we can really hit the Mafia where it hurts!' He leaned over the desk. 'I believe Ascola's testimony will put the finger on one of their top men!'

The Hawk looked at him sharply. 'Why d'you think that?'

'Because, to put the screw on a guy as big as Senator Keeble, they'd *have* to send a big shot!' said O'Connor, emphatically.

Quickly, The Hawk reached for the intercom on his desk. 'We'll have to move really fast,' he said tersely. 'If Giulio Ascola is that dangerous to the Mafia, they'll stop at nothing to get him before we do!'

It was late that night before the two dishevelled, shirt-sleeved men finished sifting through the immediate reports that had come back to Interpol in response to The Hawk's priority message to all European countries.

O'Connor leaned back, wearily. 'So, what have we got?' he said, gloomily. '*One* report that tells us the little guy landed in Hamburg – and then disappeared!' He brushed the pile of messages aside irritably. 'We're no better off than we were eight hours ago!'

The Hawk rose and moved to stare out of the window.

'If you were Giulio – an Italian-American crook – and you wanted to disappear in Europe,' he said, thoughtfully, 'where would *you* go?' He turned to look at the Treasury agent.

O'Connor shrugged. 'I guess – some place where I could easily fade into the background,' he said. 'Somewhere I'd look like everyone else . . .' His eyes brightened as an idea hit him. 'Why, sure – Italy!'

'Not Italy,' The Hawk shook his head. 'Don't forget that the Mafia operate there as well as in the States, though to a lesser degree.' He reached for his jacket. 'No,' he said. 'My bet is a great cosmopolitan city where every sort of foreigner can mix without exciting attention, where every language is spoken daily, where there is a criminal underworld with friends who will help him.'

O'Connor raised a quizzical eyebrow. 'And where is this fugitive's paradise?'

The Hawk smiled. 'Soho – London – England!' he said. 'And that's just where I'm going on the first available plane!'

He took O'Connor's arm. 'Come on – I'll buy you a coffee.'

Five minutes later, the two men were walking through the lamp-lit Paris streets, enjoying the freshness of the night air as they headed towards The Hawk's favourite café.

'There's nothing goes on in the States that the Mafia don't know about,' O'Connor was saying. 'Those guys even know what the President is going to have tomorrow for breakfast!'

Without warning, The Hawk suddenly tripped the Treasury man and threw him heavily to the ground! A split second later, the Interpol ace was beside him, flattening himself to the pavement!

Brrrrrrrrrp! With a sound like tearing calico, a sub-machine gun ripped off a long burst. For a second, the twinkling muzzle flashes showed from the rearside window of the big closed car that swept past and roared away up the street.

Slowly, The Hawk got to his feet. He stared at the row of pock marks where the bullets had sprayed the wall only inches above their prostrate bodies. 'The Mafia know something else too,' he said, grimly. 'They know about us!'

Superintendent Bill Downs leant back in his chair and eyed The Hawk from under his thick bushy eyebrows. 'Trouble,' he growled, 'I can feel it in my bones.'

The Hawk returned his gaze with a look of surprised innocence.

'Trouble, Bill?' he said, in a wondering tone. 'I don't know what you mean. I simply want to know if a man named Giulio

Ascola is hiding in London. Its routine work, that's all. Why should there be trouble?'

The Superintendent took his pipe out of his mouth. 'Because,' he said, with great deliberation, 'every time Inspector Jean Collet of Interpol, Paris, comes anywhere within fifty miles of New Scotland Yard, London, there always *is* trouble.'

'It's just an ordinary inquiry,' The Hawk grinned at his old friend.

'Huh!' The Superintendent gave a cynical grunt. 'Jean,' he said, 'if you walked in here and "just inquired" what time it was, I'll bet half a year's pay I'd have a full-scale gang war on my hands inside an hour!' His eyes twinkled as he leant forward and jabbed his pipe stem at The Hawk. 'Come on – let's have it! What's the catch?'

The Hawk cocked a quizzical eyebrow. 'Bill,' he said, 'it's funny you should have mentioned gang warfare . . .'

Bill Downs groaned, theatrically, 'This is going to be worse than I thought.'

The Hawk's voice became deceptively casual. 'Ever heard of the Mafia?'

The laughter left the Yard man's face, and his eyes became hard and shrewd. 'I'm listening,' he said tersely.

In crisp, concise sentences, The Hawk sketched in details of the case, finishing up with the attempt to kill Mike O'Connor and himself in Paris.

The Superintendent pursed his lips. 'Sub-machine guns, eh?' he said, grimly. 'They're playing for keeps.'

'The Mafia always do,' replied The Hawk quietly. 'Bill – here in Europe we don't realise how big and ruthless their organisation has become.' He paused significantly. 'But just ask an American!'

'The Mafia,' Bill Downs said thoughtfully. 'They started years ago – bandits or something, in Sicily, weren't they?'

'They started as partisan fighters,' corrected The Hawk. 'That was a couple of hundred years ago. They only became bandits after Sicily was freed – they found it easier than going back to work on their farms. Later on, when a lot of them emigrated to America, they took the movement with them. Today, they're big business!' He stared at the Superintendent. 'Remember Murder Incorporated?'

The Yard man nodded. 'The gang of killers in the States during the thirties.'

'It's hard to believe, Bill,' said The Hawk, 'but I've been checking – in ten years, that gang committed over one thousand murders!' He paused. 'And the Mafia was behind the whole thing.'

Bill Downs whistled. 'One thousand!' He frowned. 'What kind of people were their victims? Other racketeers?'

'Anyone named and paid for! Other racketeers, policemen, politicians – they even planned to kill Thomas E. Dewey!' The Hawk's jaw set grimly. 'That was because he wanted an investigation!'

'But that was years ago – and they were all caught, anyway.'

'The *killers* were caught,' replied the Interpol man. 'But the Mafia organisation still went on.'

Bill Downs grimaced. 'Well – just let 'em keep out of *my* parish, that's all.'

'That's just it, Bill,' The Hawk said quietly. 'If they think Giulio Ascola is in London, they'll be around double quick. They want him dead, before the U.S. Treasury Department grab him as a Federal witness.'

For just two seconds, the Superintendent stared at The Hawk. Then he leant forward and flicked the switch of the intercom on his desk. Within minutes, the smooth, efficient organisation of Scotland Yard was moving into action in an all-out drive to find Giulio Ascola.

The Hawk picked up his top-coat and moved towards the door.

'Where are you going now?' asked the Yard man.

'I thought I'd do a little sightseeing around Soho on my own account,' smiled The Hawk.

The Superintendent looked dubious. 'O.K.,' he said. 'But watch yourself.'

'I will.' The Hawk gave him a quick wave from the doorway and was gone.

Bill Downs stared after him thoughfully. 'And so will I,' he muttered. Once again he flicked the intercom switch . . .

Giulio Ascola hastily dragged on the rough, seaman's sweater. The small safe-breaker's hands were trembling as he hurriedly grabbed the little heap of money from the tumbled bed and stuffed it in his trouser pocket. The sound of a door opening behind him made him turn like a startled rabbit. He let out a sharp breath of relief when he saw the old man who had entered the room.

'Got 'em?' he asked, tensely.

The old man nodded. 'I've got good friends down in the docks,' he said. He handed Giulio a passport and a seaman's ticket. 'Now, you remember where to go and what to do?'

'Yeah – yeah . . .' Giulio stared nervously out of the window at the teeming Soho street below. 'See anybody – any strangers hanging about?'

The old man shrugged. 'Here in Soho there are always strangers,' he said.

Giulio took a deep breath. 'O.K., Pop, I'm on my way.' He started for the door, then paused with his hand on the door handle. 'And thanks for your help.'

Again the old man shrugged. 'My own sister's boy. It is for *her* I do it – not you!'

Out in the street, Giulio slouched along, a nondescript figure mixing with the crowds on the narrow pavements. He turned into Berwick Market and began pushing his way through the chattering, noisy throng that surrounded the stalls.

'Going some place, Ascola?' Giulio's heart missed a beat as the hard voice sounded in his ear. He turned his head sharply and saw the swarthy face, the killer's eyes. With a yell of fear, he lashed out with his foot, felt the sharp jolt as his toecap met the other man's shin, then turned and ran for his life.

Cursing, the swarthy man started to limp after his intended victim. Then he stopped – there were quicker ways of finding out where his quarry was heading for than by following him. He turned away and started to walk back to the little café from which he had seen Giulio leave only a few minutes before.

The Hawk strolled slowly along Dean Street, his keen eyes missing nothing as he unobtrusively scanned the faces around him. Habitual loungers, hurrying office-girls, tradesmen, businessmen – his keen brain mentally pigeon-holed them all. Suddenly, he felt something thrust into his hand. He turned sharply, but whoever had come up behind him was now lost in the crowd. He looked at the note he had been given – it was a typewritten copy of a cablegram. 'Information from U.S. Ascola has uncle in London. Suggest you visit. Signed – O'Connor.' And written in pencil across the bottom was a hurried note from Superintendent Downs: 'Try Giuseppe's Café – off Soho Square.' The Hawk grinned – Bill Downs was certainly on the ball!

Outside Giuseppe's Café, The Hawk paused. 'Funny,' he thought, staring at the 'CLOSED' sign on the door. He glanced at his watch – 2.30 p.m. He'd never heard of a Soho café that stopped serving at that time.

With sudden decision, he turned away from the door and headed into the narrow alleyway that ran beside the café. His guess was right – there was a side door let into the wall that served as an entrance to the rear of the building. He pushed it gently – it gave to his touch. Every nerve in The Hawk's body tingled as his sixth sense warned him of danger ahead. Suddenly, from somewhere above, came a muffled groan. Throwing caution to the winds, The Hawk leapt up the stairs two at a time. On the upper landing, he paused – two doors faced him, and they were both closed. Once again he heard the sound of a man groaning with pain – this time he pinpointed the direction. With two quick strides, he was across the intervening space and had burst in through the farther door. Inside the room, he stopped – his face set grimly as he stared down at the figure of an old man lying face down on the floor. He could see that this was a victim of torture!

Suddenly, The Hawk froze! Something hard jabbed him in the small of the back!

'O.K., punk!' grated a harsh voice. 'Come on in and join the party!'

Few men like being jabbed in the back with a gun.

The Hawk was an exception!

An expert at unarmed combat, he knew how easy it was to disarm a gunman – if he came in close enough. He grinned to himself as he felt the gun grind against his spine – this one was certainly close!

With startling speed, The Hawk spun round, pivoting on the ball of his left foot. The gunman fired – but he was too late! The split-second delay between his brain's reaction to The Hawk's sudden movement and squeezing the trigger gave the Interpol man the time he needed. By twisting to the left, he had turned his body away from the gun barrel, which now pointed across his back instead of into it. As the bullet buried itself harmlessly in the wall behind him, The Hawk's lightning action was completed. His left arm slid over and under the other man's right fore-arm, forcing upward against the elbow joint, his upper arm clamping hard against his own body to trap the killer's gun hand under his arm-pit. At the same time, The Hawk's right hand flashed over in a deadly judo chop to the side of his assailant's neck. The man went down like a log!

A few moments later, when Superintendent Bill Downs burst into the room. The Hawk was already giving first aid to the old Italian café owner on the floor.

'You all right, Jean?' panted the man from Scotland Yard.

'Sure, Bill.' The Hawk straightened up. 'But that's more than I can say for poor old Giuseppe here. You'll be wanting an ambulance right away.'

The Superintendent jerked his head to one of the Flying Squad men who had followed him into the room. The man went off at the double.

'We heard the shot as we . . .' Bill Downs broke off as he saw the old man's injuries for the first time.

'He hasn't been shot, Bill,' said The Hawk, grimly. 'This is just the Mafia's way of getting information.'

The Superintendent's eyes were blazing with anger as he turned on the swarthy-faced gunman. His fierce expression made the man cower back against the two Squad men who had just yanked him to his feet.

'Just what did you try and torture out of him?' gritted Downs.

'I don't know what you mean,' shrugged the gunman. 'I found him like this.'

The Superintendent controlled himself with an obvious effort. 'Take him away!' he said, contemptuously.

'What am I being charged with?' The man was rapidly recovering his nerve, and now he faced Bill Downs with an insolent grin on his face.

'Assault . . . grievous bodily harm . . .' Downs snapped.

'You can't prove I laid a finger on him,' sneered the other.

'Attempted murder!' The Hawk's cold voice cut in like a knife. Bending down, he slipped a pencil from his pocket and hooked it through the trigger guard of the fallen revolver. 'Here's the gun, complete with fingerprints. The bullet is in the wall.' He turned slightly and indicated a dark patch on his jacket. 'And here's the powder burn to complete the evidence.'

'Proof enough,' nodded the Superintendent. He turned on the gunman. 'British courts don't like armed thugs,' he said. 'Particularly when they try to kill policemen!' He jerked his head to the Squad men. 'Take him away!'

'You don't scare me – copper!' spat the gunman viciously.

'And the Mafia don't scare us,' answered The Hawk, quietly. 'Your friends are going to find that out.'

It was forty-eight hours later when the doctors finally gave permission for old Giuseppe to be questioned. In the interim, Scotland Yard officers had subjected the gunman to intensive questioning but, true to the Mafia tradition of silence, he had maintained a tight-lipped indifference.

Now, as he sat quietly with Superintendent Downs at the old man's bed-side, The Hawk had an instinctive feeling that there was much more depending on the answers they were about to get than the hitherto straightforward man-hunt for Giulio Ascola.

Gently, but expertly, Bill Downs gradually drew the facts from the injured man. Yes – Giulio was his nephew. Yes – he had provided Giulio with a hiding place. What man could do less for his sister's son, when he came in fear of his life? Yes – he had given Giulio clothes and money. He had arranged for him to get out of the country – one must help one's family.

'Where has he gone, Giuseppe?' asked the Superintendent, casually.

The old man's eyes narrowed cautiously. 'I don't tell that

hoodlum no matter what he do to me,' he said, with an effort. 'Maybe I don't tell you, either.'

The Hawk leant forward. 'Giuseppe,' he said, 'we're trying to help your nephew, too. We know the Mafia are after him.' He paused to let his words sink in. 'Giulio has just *one* chance of staying alive – if we get to him before they do!'

For a moment, the old Italian's eyes searched The Hawk's face. Then he sank back on his pillows. 'I think you are a good man,' he muttered wearily. He closed his eyes. 'He went on the *Parana* to Amsterdam.'

Captain Koetzee of the Amsterdam Police gave a great bellow of welcome as he saw the tall figure come into the 'Arrivals' lounge at the airport.

'Jean!' he boomed. 'Ach! It's good to see you, man!'

The Hawk winced as a hand the size of a small ham slapped him on the back. He turned to exchange a warm greeting with the huge Dutchman, wondering, as he did so, just how many criminals had been fooled by this great beaming, moon-like face – behind which lay one of the shrewdest police brains in Europe.

'Any luck?' queried The Hawk, as soon as the two men were seated in the Dutch police car.

'*Ja* – the fishing is good in Amsterdam.' Koetzee's great shoulders shook with laughter. 'Any time you want to catch a little minnow, just ask old Piet.'

'Giulio Ascola is about the most important minnow you'll ever catch, Piet,' said The Hawk, seriously. 'He's the bait that's going to net us a school of sharks.' For some reason, the Interpol man was feeling as jumpy as a kitten – his instinct was warning him against something. For a moment he couldn't figure out what it was; then, suddenly, he knew! The big Dutch policeman's mood was too complacent – far too confident!

'Where is Ascola now?' The Hawk, asked, quickly.

'Sleeping peacefully on his bunk,' beamed Koetzee. 'Like *we* should be at this time of night.'

'In a cell?' queried The Hawk, urgently.

'No,' answered the other happily. 'In the seaman's hostel, where he's pretending to be a merchant sailor. We only located him half an hour ago, so I thought we'd wait and give *you* the pleasure of waking him up.'

The Hawk's face became grim and set. 'Tell your driver to step on it!' he jerked. 'We've got to get there – fast!'

Koetzee gave the order, then glanced at The Hawk, curiously. 'What's worrying you, Jean?' he asked quietly.

'The Mafia!' The Hawk's voice was tense. 'If your police were able to find Ascola – so can they!'

Koetzee chuckled. 'Forget it,' he said, confidently. 'Two of my best men are in the hostel with him – in beds either side of him!' He broke into a great gale of hearty laughter. 'They pretend to be sailors, too!'

The Hawk's face remained unsmiling. 'He won't be safe until we get him under lock and key,' he said.

'You don't know my men,' grinned Koetzee confidently.

'And *you* don't know the Mafia, Piet!' snapped back The Hawk.

Four minutes later, the little group of policemen burst into the dormitory of the seaman's hostel. Startled grunts and growls came from all sides as the sleeping men were awakened by the lights flooding on. All seemed to be thoroughly aroused – except two!

In four quick strides, The Hawk had crossed the room and ripped the blankets off the two recumbent figures. The men were dead!

There was no laughter now in Koetzee's face as he stared at the knife handles protruding from the bodies of his two detectives. He felt The Hawk's hand on his arm and sensed the quick

The bunk was empty – Giulio had gone.

pressure of sympathy. His eyes were hard and implacable as he glanced at the Interpol ace, but The Hawk did not notice. He was staring at the bunk beween the two dead men. It was empty – Giulio had gone!

Captain Piet Koetzee stared at the rumpled blanket on the empty bunk – then at his two dead men.

He turned to The Hawk. 'It couldn't have been the Mafia.' He strove hard to keep his voice steady. 'They were after Ascola – his body would be in the middle bunk here.'

The Hawk gave him a sympathetic look – he knew how the big Dutchman must be feeling. 'I'm sorry, Piet,' he said, quietly, 'but you're wrong.' He bent down and picked up the pillow that lay on the floor beside the empty bunk. 'Ascola used the old schoolboy trick – a pillow in the bed to make it look as if he was still there.' He showed Koetzee a sharp-edged slit in the fabric. 'They tried to knife him all right, but he fooled them – *and* your men!'

The Dutchman's round moon of a face was set and hard – an implacable light gleamed in his eyes. 'If it's the last thing I do,' he said, softly, 'I'm going to get those killers!'

He turned on his police driver. 'Radio Headquarters!' he barked. 'Tell 'em I want the whole dock area sealed off – top priority! Mobilise every available man for a house-to-house search!' As the man hurried off, Koetzee turned to The Hawk. 'They haven't had time to leave the area,' he growled. 'We'll find them!'

The Hawk pulled a long face. He realised that the death of the two Dutch detectives was affecting their Chief's normally brilliant judgment. 'Piet,' he said, quietly. '*How* are you going to find them – when you have no description of the men you're looking for?'

'We'll pull in everybody who can't give a proper account of their movements,' snapped the big Dutchman. 'There must have been two of them, probably three – that should make it easier.'

'There's a better way,' said The Hawk, evenly. 'Giulio Ascola. We know *his* description. Find him – and the Mafia thugs won't be far away.'

'To blazes with Ascola!' raged Koetzee. 'If it hadn't been for him . . .'

'Piet!' The Hawk's voice was sharp. 'Our job is police work – not revenge!'

Koetzee stared at him uncertainly for a moment, then, as the Interpol man's words took effect, the anger drained from him and his face cleared. Within seconds, he was his normal shrewd, calculating self.

'Sorry, Jean,' he said, apologetically. He looked at the two prone figures. 'I'd forgotten – we policemen aren't supposed to have feelings.'

'Let's say – we're not supposed to let them affect us,' said The Hawk. He gave a wry smile. 'Sometimes I think that's the toughest part of our job.'

An hour later, the intensive search for Ascola and the Mafia thugs was well under way. At Police Headquarters, Captain Koetzee stood in front of a large-scale map of the Amsterdam dock area. He grunted with satisfaction as he watched his men pin-pointing the patrol movements from the stream of reports that constantly flowed in.

'Good,' he growled, 'the net is closing! Soon we will have our fish . . .'

The Hawk was speaking on a telephone. Now he slammed down the receiver and turned to Koetzee. 'Piet,' he said, urgently. 'Your men *must* concentrate on Giulio Ascola. Tell them to find him . . .' he hesitated '. . . and guard him with their very lives!'

Koetzee eyed him, shrewdly. 'What did you just get from

Interpol, Jean?'

'Confirmation,' answered The Hawk, abruptly. He looked hard-eyed at the Dutch policeman. 'The Mafia are planning to operate in Europe on a big scale!'

Koetzee reacted sharply. '*What?*' he gasped out.

The Hawk explained. 'I suspected it after they tried to gun down the U.S. Treasury agent and myself in Paris,' he said. 'The attempt was too well organised to have been a rush job. That meant they had co-operation from some local gang. It was the same in London,' he went on. 'The gunman we caught belonged to a Soho gang – but he couldn't have traced Ascola so quickly on his own. He must have had a dozen pairs of eyes and ears to help him.'

Koetzee nodded. 'It certainly sounds as if there's a big brain at work.'

'But just *how* big – that's what I wanted to find out,' said The Hawk. 'I sent out a priority circular to all European countries before I left London.' He nodded towards the 'phone. 'Interpol have just analysed the replies . . .' Jean paused. 'Every major city reports the same thing – definite evidence that a new organising influence is at work amongst the gangs!'

The Hawk began to pace up and down. 'The man behind it *must* be one of the big Mafia leaders in the States; nobody else would have the experience or the ability.' He stopped and faced Koetzee. 'And I'm convinced it's the man responsible for the murder of Senator Keeble – the man Giulio Ascola can identify!'

The big Dutchman frowned. 'Why?' he asked.

'Because he's the one the F.B.I. and the U.S. Treasury Department are turning the heat on,' answered The Hawk. 'He's the one Senator Keeble was after when he started pushing his amendment to the Undesirable Aliens Bill. When he had the Senator killed, he went too far – and he knows it!' The Hawk was warming to his theory. 'So what does this smart man do?

He looks for a new field of operations, so that he can get out of the States.' Collet paused, significantly. 'And the whole of Europe is wide open for him!'

Koetzee shrugged despondently. 'If you're right, it looks as if he's already got a firm foothold. It's going to take some stamping out.'

'Not if we get Ascola,' said The Hawk challengingly. 'Through him, we can get the big man before he moves in.' He slapped Koetzee encouragingly on the shoulder. 'There's only one way to kill an octopus, Piet. Go for the head! Once we've dealt with that, the rest of the tentacles will die by themselves.'

Before Koetzee could reply, a police orderly hurriedly interrupted.

'They think they've located Ascola, sir!' he said, breathlessly.

As one man, the Captain and The Hawk dived for the door.

Five minutes later, they were moving swiftly through the shadowy alleys that honeycomb the buildings along the Amsterdam dock-side. Koetzee stopped suddenly, as one of his men materialised from the darkness of a doorway.

'He went down there, sir.' The words came softly, as the detective pointed ahead to a narrow passage.

'Sure it's Ascola?' The Hawk queried.

'Yes, sir – I caught a clear glimpse of his face in the light from a café further back.' The detective's tone was confident.

'Then why the blazes didn't you grab him?' growled Koetzee.

The man looked shamefaced. 'He was too quick for me,' he admitted. Then he brightened. 'But he can't get away – that passage only leads to the loading wharf.'

'Stay here and cover the entrance,' ordered Koetzee. Then, together, he and The Hawk melted into the black passage.

Stealthily, the two men emerged on to the water-front. For a moment they stood, immobile, as they listened intently. Then The Hawk's keen ears caught the faint chink of a foot that had stubbed against a mooring ring.

'There!' he breathed, pointing away to the right.

Crack! Crack! The darkness in front of them was suddenly split by two orange flashes. Away to the right, bullets ricochetted off the stone flags.

Like the avenging bird that gave him its name, The Hawk swooped! Koetzee gave a bull-like bellow and followed hard on his heels.

The two Mafia gunmen never knew what hit them!

The Hawk's victim was the luckier; two lightning judo cuts and he was out for the count. Koetzee, however, had a score to settle. The last thing The Hawk saw as he sprinted along the wharf after Ascola, was the second unfortunate thug held high in the big Dutchman's merciless grip. Seconds later, a resounding splash told him that the man had been thrown into the water.

Suddenly, The Hawk stopped dead in his tracks. Silhouetted against the night sky was the figure of a man edging his way painfully along the jib arm of one of the loading cranes. Terrified, Ascola was trying to climb to safety.

The Hawk went up the steel ladder like a monkey. Reaching the base of the jib arm, he started to edge his way, inch by inch, along the narrow girder. Suddenly, Ascola saw him.

'Get away from me!' he screamed. Giulio made a frantic effort to reach the hanging cable – missed his footing – clawed for a second at empty air and then, with a wail like a banshee, plummeted down into the dark waters below.

The Hawk did not hesitate. He poised himself for a second on the narrow girder, and then, quite deliberately, dived off the crane arm after Ascola . . .

It was just four days later when Billy Vedicci, the wealthy New York nightclub owner looked up from his special table in the 'Diamond Slipper'. He stood up to face the two men who had moved in to stand beside his chair. Dressed in immaculate evening dress, his iron grey hair smoothly slicked back, he presented a wealthy, distinguished-looking figure.

'Gentlemen?' He bowed slightly.

Captain Mike O'Connor smiled happily. 'I've been waiting a long time for this, Billy,' he said.

Vedicci raised his eyebrows. 'I don't know what you mean,' he said. He signalled a passing waiter and ordered a bottle of champagne. 'I'm leaving for Europe tomorrow – celebrating a little. Would you care to join me?'

'No thanks, Billy,' grinned O'Connor. 'This time *you* are joining *us*!' He glanced at The Hawk who stood, tall and impeccably dressed, beside him.

'That's right, Vedicci,' said The Hawk, softly. 'We've brought you a going-away present all the way from Amsterdam – Giulio Ascola. He's alive – and talking!'

Vedicci paled. 'A – a going-away present . . .?' he gulped.

The Hawk nodded. 'That's right, Vedicci.' His voice became as hard as steel. 'You're going away – *for good*!'

Mountain Death

by Howard Braddock

The Kidnapping

It was an ordinary south-west London street on an afternoon in July, with the breeze spinning little whirls of dust and paper along the gutters while a pungent smell of new-laid tar hung on the warm air.

The black saloon car that moved idly past rows of nondescript shops seemed ordinary, too – quite as ordinary as the people who straggled in wilting groups towards any available shade, whining to each other about the heat. Children ran around squealing, clutching ice-creams from the café across the way. Gravel-voiced barrow-boys stood beside highpiled trays of emerald, crimson and gold, shouting till the sweat ran down their faces.

'Fair steamer today, ain't it?' said Sammy, pounding scorched shoe leather along the pavement. 'I could do with a drink.'

Terry Shand grinned. 'Where's this café? How much farther? My feet are tired.'

'I don't mean tea,' said Sammy hurriedly.

Shand narrowed his eyes against the glare, searching shop-signs at the distant end of the street. 'This time of the afternoon you'll have tea – and like it.' He looked lean, tall, and cool in a suit of light worsted, with a quiet tie. Sammy's short, stocky frame ran with perspiration beneath a dark alpaca jacket.

'Not far,' said Sammy. 'See that black car near the pillarbox?

It's just there.' He blew out fat, moist cheeks doubtfully. 'Think he'll be there?'

Shand grunted again. 'He'd better be.'

'Corranzi's scared all right.'

'I'd be scared, too, if I knew what he says he knows.'

Sammy considered this. 'I'm scared myself now and again, but I don't act like a cops-and-robbers fairy story – won't say where he lives or even what he looks like. Only talks over the 'phone.' Grumpily he quoted: '"Meet me at Sylvia's Pantry, four-thirty. Take the end table along the far wall." What's he think we are? Come to that, what does the boss think we are – sending us on a goose-chase like this?'

Thoughtfully Shand said, 'Sometimes I wonder.'

They came at last to Sylvia's Pantry. The drab little café didn't live up to the whimsy of its title. Wedged between a drapery store and a bookshop, it boasted double-fronted windows, hung with beaded screens. Vaguely visible beyond, like goggle-eyed, oval fish in some bizarre aquarium, customers bent over their food. Cards announced the availability for patrons of 'Meat pies; Plaice and Chips; Fancy Cakes; Biscuits'. There were also 'Tea, Coffee, Ices, Minerals'. Whiffs of stale fat filtered through a basement grating.

The entrance yawned in cool dimness between the double windows. Four men emerged in a close-knit group. Nervously they shaded their eyes against the sudden impact of light. One of them threw a quick appraising glance at Shand and Sammy. They hustled between them an elderly, bare-headed man whose close-cropped grey hair glistened in the brassy sunlight.

The group burst unexpectedly into chatter, and made their way across the pavement towards the black car, occasionally breaking into gruff guffaws of laughter.

Yet there was something forced and artificial about their jocularity – as though the men deliberately tried to act naturally, but made a bad job of it. Alone among them the grey-haired, elderly man did not smile.

One man climbed into the car and started the engine.

'Ain't we going in?' asked Sammy, one foot on the low step.

Shand's fingers clamped like a steel-spring on Sammy's forearm. For a second that might have been eternity he stood rigid, gazing into hot, dark eyes; eyes piteous with a dreadful fear – eyes beneath thick, black brows that contrasted oddly with the grey moustache and grey hair. Bloodless lips opened, as though to speak, but no sound came.

Understanding smashed upon him in one great, dazzling flash. For a moment he felt breathless and petrified, as though unexpectedly kicked in the midriff. Then he snapped into action.

'Why, hello!' he smiled, simulating pleased surprise. 'Don't say you're going already?'

With hand outstretched, he took two steps towards the little group. Snarling, one of the two remaining men swung across to intercept.

'Keep out of this!' said the man. 'Mind your own business, and you won't get hurt.'

Shand grabbed his wrist with the speed of a striking cobra and hurled him to the pavement. Then he saw a fist coming towards his face – a hard, brown fist decorated with something that shone wickedly lemon-yellow in the harsh light. Half-dodging the blow, he stumbled over the man he had brought down. Something also smacked into the back of his skull, bringing him to his hands and knees. The pavement felt hot and rough to his palms as he waited there a second, trying to shake off the dizziness that followed the blow.

People were shouting. Somewhere a woman screamed.

The car engine roared. Shand raised his splitting head. He saw something that made his skin crawl. Those eyes were staring into his own again – eyes glazed by a horrible fear – from a rear window of the vehicle.

Then someone inside jerked the man away from the glass. Next instant the car moved off.

Shand picked himself up. All around were people – looking, waiting. Over the basement grille, Sammy also staggered groggily to his feet.

'Get a taxi – commandeer a car – anything!' croaked Shand. The top of his head seemed to keep raising itself, then clanging down again.

'Right.' Sammy spoke from cracked, swelling lips. He didn't waste words, but he had to know just one thing. 'Was it him?'

Shand nodded, then wished he hadn't. His watch registered 4.25. He tottered into the café. Nobody tried to stop him. 'A 'phone! Where's the 'phone?'

The girl behind the cake-counter gaped and turned her vacuous gaze towards a recess on the left.

Everything moved too slowly. The stifling street outside might have been stricken by some strange paralysis into a still, bright image beyond the beaded curtains. Shand impatiently watched the punched wheel as it swung back to zero each time while he dialled the code number. He must hurry. The police would soon be there.

They wasted no valuable seconds at the other end, though. 'Give your name,' said a voice, with crisp efficiency. 'Which department are you calling?'

Shand told them about Corranzi, the café, and the car. He gave descriptions of the men. He told them the licence number.

'Police radio networks?' suggested the voice.

'Either that,' said Shand bitterly, 'or telepathy. Which do you recommend? Put me through to the boss.' He dabbed at his bruised face with a handkerchief, and waited.

Another voice, timid and mouse-like, came on the line.

‘Trensham here. What have you to tell me?’

Shand again recounted – more briefly – what had happened.

‘Oh dear!’ said Trensham. ‘You’re quite certain who it was?’ He always spoke with deceptive mildness. Shand could easily picture the neat figure with the tired eyes, sitting behind the shabby desk that hid unmentionable secrets. Early and late Trensham was there – watching, calculating, directing. He held in his slender fingers the threads of many situations – situations that were constantly changing, sometimes from minute to minute – like a master playing chess on a dozen boards at once.

‘The description fits the man they told me had been sitting at the end table in the café for the last ten minutes. He got there early – too early.’

‘Hm,’ said Trensham. ‘Maybe we ought to have taken him more seriously.’

Nice of him, thought Shand. Nice of Trensham to say ‘we’ instead of ‘you’. Apparently he wasn’t to be blamed.

‘A pity,’ said Trensham.

‘That’s right – a pity.’

‘I’ll see what I can do at this end. Keep in touch.’

Shand left the telephone and stared through the beaded screens. He felt sick. Glare made him screw up his eyes after the gloom of the telephone cubby-hole. He looked at the spot where the black car had rested, seeing again in imagination the piteous face staring, with mute, despairing appeal, straight into his own.

Two policemen had joined the crowd. Shand made himself scarce along a passage that led to the kitchens and thence to a walled-in yard. He walked along an alleyway until it joined the wider thoroughfare. He turned left. Nobody took any notice of him.

Back at his apartment, Shand drew the curtains, fell on to his bed, laid his aching head gently on the pillow, and lit a cigarette. He touched the raw place scored across his cheek by the knuckle-duster and winced. He cursed. A few seconds later he was fast asleep.

The ringing of the 'phone woke him instantly. He reached automatically for the receiver. 'Yes?'

It was Sammy. 'They've found that car – abandoned. I'm at Greek Street police-station. Thought you might be at the office. I tried to ring you there first and they gave me the news. I followed it up.'

'And Corranzi?' He knew the answer quite well.

'Not a sign. Nor the so-and-so's who snatched him.'

Shand remembered how the black saloon had dwindled before his eyes into the distance. He wondered what any one of the people in that street might have said if they knew it could have been driving away with nearly eight million pounds in gold. Men in pursuit of that sort of money wouldn't bother much about a spot of kidnapping.

'Finger-prints?'

'Not a sign. Or anyway, none that's any good.'

'Oh?'

'Car's in the station yard. Stolen early this afternoon. They're going over it now. Not much hope, though. These boys knew their job.'

Shand wished he could say the same of himself. 'I might as well come along. See you in ten minutes.'

The estimate proved fairly accurate. His taxi swung into the grimy, red brick courtyard after little more than nine minutes had elapsed, yet during this short interval news of a further development had arrived. Late-evening sunshine stretched his shadow as he crossed to the little group huddled round the well-remembered black car.

'They switched,' said Sammy. 'Somebody saw 'em shifting into a fairly new, racing green job at the far end of the Edgware Road. One of 'em drove this crate back to the district and left it parked. Patrol cars've been given the word.'

There didn't seem to be much else to say. Shand looked at his watch. 'Nearly half-past seven. Let's eat.'

The next item of news arrived with the steak. Sammy had just picked up his knife and fork when the waiter came back to say there was a 'phone call for them.

'Oh, no!' pleaded Sammy. 'Not for the next ten minutes.'

Shand returned from the 'phone to find him sitting in front of an empty plate. 'You think too much of your stomach,' he grumbled.

'I wasn't going to waste it,' said Sammy, indignantly.

'You could have eaten mine, too,' said Shand. 'I haven't got time.' He threw some money on to the table. 'Come on – we're moving to the other side of Barnet.'

In the taxi, Shand explained. 'That green car stopped outside a house in a quiet street there. Some nosy neighbour, peeping over the aspidistra, saw four men go into the house. Two of 'em came out later and drove away.'

'Police find anything?'

Shand shrugged. 'What could they find? They'd got no good reason for a search warrant. A magistrate would have laughed in their faces. Besides, it's our pigeon. They're watching the place. Doesn't seem as though anybody's at home now.'

The street-lamps had already come on as they neared the house, but the windows of every dwelling still gaped wide in the hope of evening breezes that might dispel the day's dusty heat.

The driver slid back the plate-glass barrier and spoke over his shoulder. 'Much farther, guv'nor?'

Shand wondered. Then he said, 'This'll do.' He had seen, against the shadows, the outline of a parked police car. 'You needn't wait!'

A plain-clothes man met them. 'Along this side road – about a couple of hundred yards. House is empty – marked up as being for sale.'

Sammy grunted. 'Needn't have wondered about getting a warrant.'

The detective said, 'Not you, maybe. Folks like us have to keep our noses clean. The place is locked up. Can't go breaking and entering.'

'Did you just wait,' asked Shand, 'or do anything at all?'

'I sent a uniformed man to look round on the pretext that tramps might be using the house to sleep in. He saw nobody.'

Shand looked at him shrewdly. 'Four men went in, two came out. Think they're hiding?'

The detective shrugged. 'Maybe. Or they could have scampered the back way before we got here.'

'We'll soon find out,' said Shand.

In the last glow of twilight they saw the house looming darkly against the skyline. It was a large dwelling standing some thirty yards from the road in a quarter-acre of ground where shrubs sprawled unattended and mossy patches disfigured the approach drive. Great weeds tangled themselves across long-neglected flower-beds. Once, the headlights of some distant car, reflected blankly from uncurtained windows, made it seem as though the building was crouching in its dismal surroundings and watching their approach.

All three outside doors and a set of french windows leading into the house were locked. A pencil-thin beam of light from Shand's torch revealed no sign of their having been forced.

The windows were likewise intact. Sammy, following fifteen paces in the rear, came up close when they finished the circuit.

'Inside?' His whispered words were scarcely audible against the far-off hum of traffic.

'You've got a steak under your belt,' said Shand. 'I've got nothing. I don't feel like climbing through fanlights. Get busy on the front door.'

Sammy slid noiselessly into deeper darkness. There was a pause, then a slight metallic click. Shand joined him and together they moved into what looked and felt like the entrance to a tomb. In the hall they stood listening, feeling the stale, shut-in air cold and clammy on their faces. The house remained silent.

That tiny beam of light materialised once more, travelling slowly, painstakingly, across mouldy panelling and bare, dusty floorboards. It revealed a large curved staircase, chipped plaster, and solid, old-fashioned doorways. They located a dining-room with serving hatch leading to the kitchen. A rat scrabbled in a corner, turning for a moment so that its red eyes showed like two tiny, evil lamps. The men watched it. They weren't the sort to jump or catch their breath because of rats.

The big kitchen possessed a sink, a rusting giant of a cooking-range, and a stone floor. Smeared tracks showed where feet had scuffed the inevitable layer of accumulated dust.

Sammy produced his much-loved automatic – a huge ·45 with a kick like a sledge-hammer – and pulled back the well-oiled slide with a soft click. Shand touched his arm restrainingly.

Tracks led to the far end, beyond the sink. Here the dust spread in confusion, as though it had recently been disturbed, and Shand imagined some of it still hung in the air, tickling his nostrils. He yanked open the pantry door, then whistled softly. For there was somebody propped up inside, and even in the feeble light of the torch it was obvious that he was dead.

Return from the Dead

Shand walked with Sammy back along the dark drive to where the plain-clothes man still waited in the shadows between two street-lamps. 'That constable of yours was right – not a living soul anywhere around.' Sammy smiled grimly to himself. Here was stark truth with a vengeance. 'Somebody's been inside, though. You can see their footmarks in the dust.'

'Did they break in?'

Shand nipped this train of thought smartly in the bud; he didn't want police poking their noses into that house for the next few hours. 'Couldn't find a thing.' As an afterthought, he said, 'Might have been genuine – a prospective buyer being shown round.' He yawned. 'I'll see the agents tomorrow. Can't do anything about searching the grounds till daylight.'

'Suppose we'll have to,' grumbled Sammy. 'Goose-chase, that's what it is.'

They paused, giving time for the bait to be thoroughly swallowed.

'Well,' said Shand to the plain-clothes man, 'I'm off to bed. You staying on?'

'Not unless you want us. The inspector's left it to my discretion.'

Shand sighed with quiet relief. 'That's all right, then. We'll let you get some sleep, too. I can hardly keep my eyes open this weather.'

'Can we give you a lift?'

'Thanks, but we'll find a taxi. So long.'

They walked without haste towards the main thoroughfare. As soon as the police car had passed, Shand said, 'Go back and watch the house, Sammy. I'll ring up the boss.'

From a nearby petrol-station's call-box he told Trensham, 'We located him. He'd been – interrogated. He wasn't very pleasant to look at. Stone dead. I'm afraid.' No name was mentioned.

'Hm,' said Trensham. He didn't seem particularly surprised. 'This development's got to be kept hush-hush. We can't afford all the publicity of a wide-open murder hunt. You'll need help with him. I'll arrange that at this end. Have your assistant wait till the squad arrives. Did you find an address, by the way?'

Corranzi's pockets had undoubtedly been searched by the men who took him away, but who could tell what his assassins had found? A pocket diary? A wallet? A notebook? At all events he and Sammy had found nothing.

'No,' replied Shand. 'It's awkward not knowing where he lived.' Could the omnipotent Trensham 'arrange' this, too? 'I hope he'd got enough sense to leave confidential papers behind.'

'Any pointers? Any clue at all?'

'Not to a definite address. But there's this business of the fourth man.'

Down the 'phone he heard Trensham catch his breath. 'So you noticed that, too.'

Who could help it? Three men had hustled Corranzi from the café. One had driven the stolen black car to where the police located it later – yet there had been three again (not counting Corranzi) whom the neighbour had seen entering that deserted house.

'Two of them were recognisable from the descriptions,' said Shand. 'Hazy but recognisable. No doubt at all about you-know-who – but there was another man. About five-foot-six, burly, wearing a grey suit and hat.'

'Nothing more definite?'

'No. He must have joined the others about the time they switched cars. If only we could get a line on the district.'

'I'll see what I can do. Get some sleep now.'

If I can, thought Shand. How many men were there in London who stood about five-foot-six and wore grey suits? Come to that, how many in the country? Or Europe? Or the world?

Shand opened one eye. There was Sammy, standing at the end of the bed, regarding him with mute reproach. Shand swung his long legs from beneath the single sheet which had served as covering through the warm, stuffy night and sat on the edge of the bed. He hooked fingers into his thick, black hair and rubbed slowly. Then he glanced up. 'Well?'

'Dropped right into our lap.'

'What did?'

'Corranzi's address.'

Shand heaved himself to his feet. The other eye came open fast. 'You know it?'

Sammy nodded. 'Tell you in a moment – when we won't be overheard. I ordered some coffee on the way up. Ought to be here any time. I had a devil of a job to wake you.'

Shand yawned. 'All right. Carry on gloating. I can wait.' He walked into the bathroom and started the shower.

By the time he had flung a robe round himself and returned to the living-room, Sammy was busy pouring hot black coffee. He held out a cup.

'Enjoyed your little moment? All right, now tell me.'

'No particular credit due,' admitted Sammy. 'It just happened. Corranzi's niece got worried when the old man didn't go home last night. So what did she do? She told the police.'

Shand raised his eyebrows over the rim of the cup. 'Just like that?'

'When the report reached the clearing department at the Yard the name rang a bell with somebody, and they told Trensham. He'd heard about it just before I 'phoned to tell him the squad got the body away safely, so he said to drag you out of bed and get busy. So let's get a move on!'

Shand sipped reflectively. 'Is he having an eye kept on this niece meanwhile?'

'There's time to finish your coffee, I imagine.'

'The boss must have been wild at having Corranzi's name bandied about in common police-stations. Every syllable in the word's equal to a ton of high explosive.'

'I've got a nasty feeling we're sitting right on top of it, too.' Sammy shifted his stocky body uneasily. 'Anyway, he's fixing it.' He looked up into Shand's sardonic countenance. 'Is there anything he can't fix?'

'I doubt it – except an increase in my salary. What's his scheme?'

'Simple. Somebody's gone to the station to tell 'em it was all a mad mistake and that Corranzi's been staying the night with friends the niece didn't know about.'

'Hm. Not bad – unless they get stuffy and want to see Corranzi personally.'

'If they did,' said Sammy shortly, 'they'd know he hadn't been treated in a very friendly way.'

Shand looked down for a moment at his bare foot, wiggling his toes thoughtfully. 'What's the time?'

'Nearly nine.'

'What's this niece look like?'

'Not too bad, I believe. Still, you're the judge of women – not me.' He stared meaningfully at Shand's lean brown jaw. 'I think I'd shave, if that's what you're getting at.'

'What's the weather like?'

'Going to be hot again. Anything else I can tell you?'

Keeping a straight face, Shand said, 'No, I don't think so.'

Fifteen minutes later they were in a taxi heading towards Croydon, staring through glass at the bright morning and the early traffic. Sammy lowered the cab window on his side and sniffed deeply. 'That's a real breath of summer – smelt and enjoyed before the ever-present petrol fumes ruin it.'

He glanced at Shand for approval, only to find him brooding. 'I'd like it better if I hadn't got to tell this girl what's happened to her uncle.'

Leaving the taxi at a safe distance, they walked round the corner into a long rather dreary road of large, square buildings that had once enjoyed distinction as a residential section.

A man sat in the cool hallway of the house at the address they sought, his eyes missing nothing over the top of his newspaper.

Sammy went across and started talking to the man while Shand glanced along the list of tenants on an information board.

'Apartment seven,' said Sammy. 'Martin – the chap over there – says she's been in the flat ever since he arrived. Got the day off from work, apparently, on account of her uncle.'

They climbed to the second floor and knocked, eyeing each other while they waited. Shand pressed his ear to the door.

Hesitating footsteps approached on the other side. A girl's voice said, 'Who's there? Who is it?' She sounded rather frightened.

'Miss Corranzi? My name's Shand. Could I see you for a moment?' He spoke persuasively, smoothly.

'No – please go away.'

'There's news of your uncle – don't you want to hear it?'

A pause, during which the girl debated with herself. Then a lock clicked, a guard-chain rattled. A girl appeared. Tremulously she said, 'You know where he is?' She caught sight of Sammy and thrust her hand to her mouth in quick alarm.

'My assistant,' said Shand smoothly. 'May we come in?'

She was of striking appearance. She had the most beautiful black hair and a wonderfully clear, white complexion with just a touch of colour in the cheeks. Her eyes were violet blue. But a look of fear broke through her beauty.

Yet nothing was more clear than that Margo Corranzi was terrified; determined to resist her fear, though. Shand realised this from the defiant tilt of her chin as she closed the door and faced them once more. She made a little gesture of mingled invitation and embarrassment. 'Won't you sit down?'

There was one big armchair. Shand imagined it must have been Corranzi's. The living-room had been furnished frugally, yet with taste. Even a couple of cheap prints on the wall looked attractive. The carpet was worn but well-brushed. The room was pleasant enough – yet hardly the home for a man who hugged to himself the secret of nearly eight million pounds in gold.

'I'll sit over here,' he said, keeping the fixed, tight smile. 'You take this chair.'

She sat up straight, looking tense and anxious.

'You said you knew something about my uncle.'

Shand nodded. 'I'd arranged to meet him yesterday afternoon. He didn't turn up. Did he mention the matter at all?'

Distrust and fear still froze the girl's expression. Wordlessly she shook her head.

He produced the credential card, with photograph, issued by his department. 'I'm working for the British Treasury. Does that give you any idea why your uncle might want to see us? Or why we'd like to see him?'

Again she shook her head, looking at him from the corner of her eye. She was obviously holding something back. Sammy, leaning unobtrusively against a sideboard, wondered how long she might hold out.

'You've got to tell us,' said Shand harshly. 'It's essential – vital.'

Margo Corranzi gripped the chair-arms. He could see her fingers quivering. 'I won't . . . I won't . . .' Then her self-control broke down completely. 'Where's Uncle Carlo?' she pleaded. 'Where is he?'

'He had enemies,' said Shand sombrely. 'He had powerful enemies. Didn't he? Men from Europe – from Italy.'

She looked wildly about her. 'I – I don't know.'

'He must have told you about them,' Shand pursued. 'You must have suspected something. Who were these enemies of his?'

Slowly she bowed her head forward until it rested in her hands. Shand walked into the spotless little kitchen and drew a glass of water. He handed it to her. It wasn't turning out a very pleasant morning.

After a time she said, 'He – he's dead, isn't he?'

'Yes,' said Shand gruffly. 'I'm afraid so.'

She looked up. 'These men who did it – they won't escape?'

'What men?' He snapped the question involuntarily, then caught Sammy's eye. 'Ease up,' said the eye. 'The fish is hooked. Play it gently now.'

Shand said, more easily, 'We won't be able to find them unless you help us.'

For a few moments more Margo hesitated. Then she drew a deep breath and said, 'Poor Uncle Carlo! After eight years.' She glanced up at Shand. 'He – he wasn't hurt – too much?'

Shand had told lies before, so another wouldn't matter very much. And there was no need to distress her unnecessarily.

'No,' he replied. 'Not much.'

She leaned forward and placed her glass on the table. She seemed relieved.

Shand continued, 'Everything began back in Italy, I take it. Your uncle was Italian, of course.'

'Not since 1945, soon after we got to England. We both became naturalised. He was my guardian. He took care of me as a little girl – after my mother died and the Fascists killed my father.' She looked round the room. 'We were luckier in those days. There was a villa in the Alps, about ten miles from Monte Ragazzo.'

The story had begun. Shand didn't interrupt. Monte Ragazzo – here was the first open mention of an almost inaccessible snow-clad spike of a mountain that was currently causing jitters in the Chancelleries.

'So we lived there happily in Rossanata, with cypresses and

grape-vines and fountains in the courtyard and the little red-roofed houses scattered across the foothills. I had an English governess.'

Sammy slid quietly into the kitchen. Shand guessed he had gone to make some tea and blessed him for the bright idea.

'Afterwards Uncle Carlo took care of me. The war came, and times were even worse. There were the Germans – and the air raids – and then –'

Shand could easily imagine life for ordinary Italian people during the closing stages of the war. Apart from the actual fighting, there would be deserters from the German army plundering and looting, and partisans chasing after escaping Fascists. Then there would have been dreadful shortages of food and clothing. It couldn't have been very pleasant.

'So we reached England,' Margo continued, 'and because of what he'd done against the Germans the British Government gave Uncle Carlo naturalisation without waiting the usual five years. He was so proud to be an Englishman.' Her face grew sad again. 'Poor Uncle. All the time he wondered where the gold might be hidden. It gave him no rest.'

The gold! Did the stuff really exist – or was it merely legend? Or had some unknown seeker already found and spent this fabulous hoard? In their post-war poverty governments were hungry for gold. Evil men were hungry for gold, too. In such a situation individual lives would count for little.

'Everybody knew how Ricardo Masseratti tried to get the gold into Switzerland for Mussolini. The partisans' spies said the convoy had started. There was an ambush waiting in the pass towards Monte Ragazzo. But the gold cars never arrived. No one saw them again. Lots of people made expeditions to the mountains – the only route cars could have taken. They found nothing. Many suffered frostbite, and several died. Others were swindled by men from Rossanata pretending to know caves where the gold might be hidden.'

Sammy came in with the tea.

'Oh, thanks,' said Margo. She smiled. 'You see, I'm English enough to like tea.'

'But your uncle had a genuine hint about where this loot was hidden?' asked Shand. 'I mean, he was quite sure it existed?'

She looked at him over the edge of the cup and nodded. 'It was really Uncle Zorrio.'

'Another uncle?'

'They're both my father's brothers. Uncle Zorrio was rather mysterious. He used to know all sorts of peculiar people, and often went away for weeks at a time.'

Shand cut in. 'Was? Where's Zorrio now?'

Her face clouded again. 'We think he's – dead.' She set down the cup. 'Uncle Carlo sent him all the money we could spare – and some we couldn't spare.' She made a pathetic gesture that took in the frugal room. 'I gave him what I could from my wages – I work as a sales girl in a department store. All the time he said Uncle Zorrio must have money – for inquiries, for bribes – and that one day we would be rich again.'

Shand was puzzled. Was he, perhaps, a little touched in the head – this man Corranzi? With his peculiar telephone calls and his cloak-and-dagger approach? Yet they'd killed him, hadn't they? Killed him – rather unpleasantly. And who were 'they'?

Shand took a turn or two up and down the room. Then he turned to Margo. 'Two days ago your uncle telephoned our department. He wouldn't tell us the full story, but we'd heard before about the treasure of Monte Ragazzo. He thought the British Treasury would be interested in eight million pounds' worth of gold.'

'He didn't know where else to turn for help. He'd been – well, depressed, just lately – depressed and frightened. Men had been following him.'

Shand nodded. 'He was right about us being interested.' He refrained from repeating what Trensham had told him at the briefing – that the gold was English sovereigns, that it came under a claim for wartime loot, that even if the hoard were located there might be diplomatic wrangling between the governments of three or four different countries. But while possession might not actually be nine points of the law in this case, it certainly provided moral, if not genuinely legal, advantages to the nation whose agents first laid eyes on the booty.

'These men,' said Shand. 'Did Carlo know who they were?'

The girl shook her head. 'But they've broken in here twice.' She made a little gesture of uneasiness at the recollection. 'In the night. They could have killed both of us then, I suppose, if they'd wanted to.'

Shand's head went up in sudden alertness. 'What was it they wanted? Why did they break in?'

'I don't know.'

'Did they take anything? Papers, maybe?'

She dropped her arms in a movement of helplessness. 'They searched everywhere. The place isn't very neat just now, I'm afraid. I've been trying to tidy up. But after they'd been here – well a whirlwind could have blown through the room. And they did it so quietly. We heard nothing. But in the morning . . . well, it was terrible . . . just terrible.'

'Both times they came at night – while you were here?'

She nodded.

An uneasy hush fell upon the room. Even sounds of traffic in the street seemed suspiciously muted.

'So,' said Margo, in a small appealing voice, 'what do we do now?'

The question was solved for them in a dramatic way. A quick double tap on the door made all three jump. Instantly Sammy moved sideways and, although his hand travelled no more than six inches, that huge automatic reappeared in his grasp.

'Some day,' hissed Shand, 'that damned thing's going to overbalance you! Put it away!'

Wearing a hurt expression, Sammy obeyed.

Shand opened the door to find an elderly man standing there, a black hat in his hand.

The visitor paid him no attention. He looked across Shand's shoulder to where Margo stood beside her chair, gripping the wooden arm for support.

'Margo!' he said hoarsely. 'At last I find you!'

The girl started. Then into her eyes came an expression of dim recognition.

The man held out his hands. 'Don't you recognise your Uncle Zorrio again?'

She gave a little cry and ran forward, resting her head on his shoulder, with her arms flung about his neck.

'Uncle Zorrio!' she wept. 'Thank God you're alive!'

The Gold Talisman

Zorrio held the girl for a moment before pushing her gently away at arm's length. He looked into her face. 'My little Margo!' His light-brown eyes switched to Shand and Sammy. 'These gentlemen – who are they?' His chin went up half-aggressively, half-suspiciously.

Margo's violet eyes, now filled with tears of relief and thankfulness, looked across to Shand and Sammy. 'They're investigators,' she explained, 'from the British Government.'

Zorrio possessed eyes of a peculiarly light brown, but the balding grey hair and close-clipped moustache were modelled on those of his brother. The sallow, swarthy complexion could have been identical. He raised the grey, bushy eyebrows in a sudden expression of alertness. 'But Carlo – where is he?'

Shand stepped across, holding out his credential card. 'They caught him – he's dead.'

'Ah, so,' said Zorrio, softly. 'Dead.'

Shand looked at him curiously. 'You don't seem very surprised.'

Zorrio shrugged his shoulders. 'He was lucky, poor Carlo – lucky they did not kill him years ago.' The ghost of a sardonic smile flickered across his face. Those eyes reminded Shand of something, but he couldn't quite place it.

'Do not think,' said Zorrio, 'I condone his murder. He was my own brother – and this poor child's uncle, also. The guilty ones shall suffer. I shall hunt them out. I shall be revenged.'

Sometimes a fat little man standing on his dignity could be funny. Looking at Zorrio – and into his strange eyes – Shand had never felt less like laughing. 'All right – take it easy,' he said, 'Let's sit down and thrash matters out.'

The story had to be told again – Carlo hugging to himself the secret of hidden gold; the years of scraping together funds for Zorrio's activities in Italy; the continual haunting fear of discovery.

'Yes, yes,' said Zorrio. He cast a quick, almost furtive glance round the room. 'The money was useful – very useful. Rest assured it was not wasted. I did not know it had meant' – his gesture took in the meagre furnishing – 'this.' He paused reassuringly. 'But soon there will be the reward.'

He turned again to Shand. 'Does no mention come into this case of a man – a German – named Von Grinling?'

Sammy, still standing at the sideboard, jumped so violently that he bit his tongue.

'Von Grinling!'

Margo looked up at them from the chair. Her glance moved blankly from one to the other and back again. 'Who's Von Grinling?'

'I didn't know he came into the picture at all,' admitted Shand. 'If so, this is an even bigger job than we believed.'

Zorrio threw up his hands. 'A big job? Is it not big enough – even without Von Grinling?'

'We thought he was dead,' said Shand. 'He was supposed to have committed suicide with some of the other Nazi bigshots at Kemmelburg, in Bavaria, when the war ended.'

'But I have seen him!' declared Zorrio. 'He was not dead two weeks ago.'

'Seen him? Where?'

'In the mountains, near Rossanata.'

Two weeks, thought Shand, furiously. Where might he be now – that tall, thin, evil man with a nose like a vulture's beak, at whose door lay the deaths of nearly a thousand hostages in the secret wartime prison of Schloss Karlstein? Bavaria wasn't really so far from Northern Italy. Maybe Von Grinling had lain low all this time in the mountains or in neighbouring Switzerland. And now he, too, sought the treasure of Monte Ragazzo.

'Didn't you tell the authorities? After what his crowd did to some of the partisans, the Italians want to get their hands on him just as badly as the rest of us.'

Zorrio shook his head. 'There was no chance.' The half-smile flashed again. 'Certain people were embarrassing me at the time.' As an afterthought, he moved across and locked the door. 'To be frank,' he added disarmingly, 'they do so still.' He turned to the girl. 'Come, little Margo. Pack whatever is needed. You will leave this poor place with its sad memories.'

Shand, feeling the situation slipping from his grasp, said loudly, 'Not just yet.'

Zorrio's bushy eyebrows went up again. 'No? She is to stay here where gangsters may find her?'

'Not till we know what those men wanted who broke into this flat. They were looking for something they thought Carlo had. Any idea what it might be?'

Zorrio nodded. 'Undoubtedly.'

'Well?' rasped Shand.

Zorrio smiled. 'Let us sit down again, Signor Shand – Signor British Treasury agent. This gold – this treasure – belongs to whom?'

'Definitely to the British Government.'

'But the finder – whoever he is – will be rewarded, yes? A big reward – enough to make a man rich for the rest of his life.'

'Get this straight,' said Shand loudly. 'We were called in by Carlo. We've a perfect right to come in on the proposition. In any case, I don't intend to start bargaining with you.'

'What's it matter?' sighed Margo, wearily. 'What does anything matter, except poor Uncle Carlo?'

Zorrio took her hand. 'Three years' work matters, little Margo. Three years of patient piecing together of clues when everyone else had given up the treasure as lost.'

'Everyone?' asked Shand. 'How about those men who searched this flat?'

'Three years of self-denial by Carlo and yourself,' Zorrio continued. 'Now, when we can really begin to hope, you say, "What does it matter?"'

'You think so? Really?' asked Margo.

'But of course.' Zorrio's voice was confident and determined.

Shand's eyes were cool and watchful.

'What was it that Carlo held, *carissima*?' Zorrio's voice crooned persuasively. 'You do not know? Then I will tell you what it was.' He glanced round, almost mockingly. 'I will tell these gentlemen, too! Somewhere – well-hidden, I trust – he had a little talisman. Most suitably, it is of gold; most probably it provides one of the keys to our treasure house. You tell me, little Margo, where poor Carlo hid this emblem from the Children of the Dolomites.'

Shand took a turn at eyebrow-raising. 'Who the devil are they?'

'*Partigiani,*' announced Zorrio crisply. 'A brotherhood of mountaineers scattered across the wilder parts of Monte Ragazzo.' He shook his head. 'Tough, stubborn. They will not talk freely to outsiders.'

Sammy spoke for the first time. 'In that case, why didn't they grab the treasure for themselves?'

'Because, my friend, they do not know the full story. Their information is useful – perhaps vital – yet it provides only one piece in the puzzle.'

Shand came to a sudden decision. 'We're wasting time. Let's start looking for this gadget and take Miss Corranzi somewhere safer.'

'Yes, yes,' said Zorrio. 'That we will do.'

As soon as he got a chance, Shand whispered in Sammy's ear, 'You look after these two for a few moments. I'm going out to 'phone the boss and arrange a place where they can stay.'

Zorrio looked up sharply from where he was groping quickly and methodically through the contents of a small writing-bureau. Shand explained truthfully where he was going, to be rewarded with vigorous nods of approval. 'That is good. Both I and my niece thank you. She will begin to pack her belongings now. Perhaps by the time you return, your friend and I will have been lucky in our search.'

'I hope so,' said Shand briefly. He jerked his head in farewell and went down the stairs.

In the vestibule the man named Martin still read his paper.

'Sammy's up there,' Shand told him. 'The girl's all right. The Italian seems O.K., too. But don't let anybody into the flat. Nobody at all.'

'Right,' said Martin, and Shand left him.

In the privacy of a 'phone booth about a hundred yards along the street he told Trensham, 'Carlo's brother turned up. He says Von Grinling's still alive and trying to shove his nose into this affair.'

Trensham was obviously disturbed. Shand could tell by the way he said, 'Oh, dear!'

Shand waited.

'Usually,' said Trensham reflectively, 'people are glad to hear of someone returning from the dead. This time I'm not so sure.' There was another pause.

'If it's all right with you,' said Shand, 'I'll get Zorrio and the girl fixed up at a hide-out apartment. Carlo's address seems to be an open secret.'

'Do that,' said Trensham, and rang off.

Shand went back to the block of flats. 'All quiet?' he asked Martin.

'Whatever it is they're doing, they ain't making a sound. Nobody's been past this way.'

Shand's long legs took the stairs two at a time. He tapped perfunctorily on the door of apartment seven and turned the handle. The door was locked.

Sharply, he rapped knuckles on the wood again. No sound came from inside.

'It's me – Shand! Open up!'

He felt a sudden alarm.

The door gave to his shoulder at the second attempt. He stumbled into the room that he now knew so well. It was empty.

At least, he thought at first sight that it was empty. Then he noticed a pair of legs extending from beneath the table. They belonged to Sammy.

Shand stepped quickly into the small kitchen, then into the two bedrooms. Everywhere drawers had been hurriedly and carelessly pulled out. Their contents – clothes, trinkets, and domestic oddments – were strewn around in heaps like raw

Sammy lay with his head against the polished wood.

material for a jumble sale.

He returned to the living-room. Sammy lay with his head close against the polished wood, breathing hoarsely through his open mouth. He was out – colder than a frozen fish.

Surprise Identity

Shand grabbed the legs and hauled Sammy clear of the table. He filled a glass with water, splashed it over Sammy's head, and put in a few seconds' vigorous face-slapping. Sammy opened his eyes. They still looked glazed, and with good reason.

'What happened?' snapped Shand.

Sammy touched a lump on the back of his head and winced. 'Zorrio and the girl were rooting in the bureau. I bent down to look in the table drawer, and the roof fell on me.'

Shand said, 'Zorrio's gone. The girl too.'

Sammy did not seem surprised. 'I expect they got out the back way.'

'Martin's still down in the vestibule. They couldn't have passed him without his knowing it. I'll settle for Zorrio hustling her out through the back-yard. Martin can't be in two places at once.'

'She could have yelled, couldn't she?' Sammy asked. 'Women can yell loud enough when they want to. At least, that's my experience.'

Shand shrugged. He said, 'If you're fit to walk again, start off after 'em while the scent's warm.'

Sammy, now fanning himself with his hat, said, 'Everywhere's warming up. Going to be a rotten hot day again.'

'Get moving!' growled Shand. 'Nobody could help noticing Zorrio and that girl. Try the neighbours – the shops – the taxi-drivers. I'm going to break the sad news to Trensham.' He wasn't looking forward to the job. Through an open door he could see the disordered bedroom. 'I'll bet Zorrio found that talisman, too!'

'You mean this?' asked Sammy. Between finger and thumb he dangled a little gold trinket at the end of a fine chain. 'I thought we might hang on to it for ourselves.'

Shand placed the tiny object in the palm of his hand. It twinkled in the sunlight. The flat medallion – no larger than a sixpenny piece – portrayed a shield bearing an heraldic design of flags and floral emblems. He raised his eyes to Sammy's round face. 'Where did you find it?'

'When I went to make the tea. It was in the caddy.' He wrinkled his brow. 'Seemed funny, somehow, so I kept it. Either Carlo or the girl must have known it was there. Obviously it's gold, so if they've been hard-up because of sending money to Zorrio, why didn't they pawn it? I guessed it might be important. Then, when Zorrio got here, we heard that stuff about the Children of the Dolomites.'

'Don't let's hold an inquest right now,' said Shand. 'Get busy tracing those two.'

At that moment a bleary-eyed, unshaven individual entered the room. ''Oo broke this ruddy door?' he demanded. ''Ooever broke it'll ruddy well pay for it.'

Shand brushed past him.

'Martin!' he bellowed into the stair-well. 'Come up here!' He turned to the other man. 'You'll be paid for your door. Did you kick up as much row when the burglars broke it?'

'Wot d'you mean?'

Shand waved him aside. Apparently Carlo Corranzi had sought to hush up the breaking and entering activities of his enemies. 'Scrub round it, then. Did you see Miss Corranzi leave here with a man a few minutes ago?'

'Didn't know she'd got back from the police-station. Anyway, 'oo are you?'

Martin came in the doorway just then. 'He's all right, Henry. He's the boss.'

Henry's prominent Adam's apple bobbed. 'Oh,' he said more reasonably. 'That's all right, then. But 'e didn't 'ave no right breakin' doors. I'm responsible to the landlords.' He caught sight of the chaos in the bedroom. ''Ere, what's been going' on?'

'You know Mr Corranzi's disappeared?'

'Oh, yes, I knew that. Why, it was me first rang the coppers up for Miss Corranzi when she told me 'e 'adn't come 'ome. Cheaper 'n ringin' round all the casualty 'ospitals yourself. I told 'er so. "Let the rozzers do it", I said.'

'You must have been a great comfort to her,' said Shand.

'Took it brave, mark you, but I could see she'd been cryin' 'er little brown eyes out.'

'You colour-blind or something?'

'Well, you know – that sort o' greeny-brown. Wot do they call it? Hazel – that's it.'

Shand gestured irritably. 'I mean Margo Corranzi, who lived here with her uncle. Fairly tall girl – very black hair – sort of violet-coloured eyes.'

The man named Henry slowly began to shake his head. 'Ain't seen no woman like that round 'ere. Miss Corranzi's got light-brown 'air an' sort o' greenish eyes.'

Shand snarled at Martin. 'What's this? Didn't you tell me the Corranzi girl was in this flat, having a day off from work?'

Martin gulped. 'I came up here, just as you said, Mr Shand. She wouldn't open the door, but asked who it was. I said I'd been sent by the police to keep an eye on matters temporarily, but that if she was all right I wouldn't disturb her.'

Shand glowered for one long feverish moment. 'You fool! That girl wasn't Margo Corranzi! She was in there searching the flat for the same thing that made them murder Carlo!'

'She did it very prettily,' Shand told Trensham over the telephone. 'Any girl engaged in a job like that might have been excused jumping right out of her skin with fright when Martin tapped on the door.'

Trensham grunted. 'Suppose we try to earn a little admiration for ourselves,' he said. 'You've put a police call out, I take it?'

'For both of them. It's quite obvious that the man isn't Zorrio, either.'

There was a moment's pause at the other end. Then Trensham said softly, 'I missed that. Of course, he couldn't be.'

'As I see it,' Shand continued, 'this girl was sent to search the flat – for papers, the fancy medallion, or what have you. They must have been watching the place for quite a long time.'

'Then where's the real Margo Corranzi?'

'She went out quite early. She called at Greek Street police-station and was told there wasn't any news. Your polite little fiction about her uncle staying with friends hadn't percolated through the police channels. Nobody's seen her since, but more than likely she'll be back at the flat before long.'

Trensham thought for a moment.

'You were saying something about this violet-eyed Jezebel.'

'They're very thorough. I imagine she'd been primed with this story – just in case of awkwardness – and probably there was an arrangement whereby if she wasn't out of the place by a certain time the fake Zorrio would appear. When . . .'

'But didn't he charge straight in, announcing he was her uncle? Suppose there'd been someone around who knew the real Margo Corranzi?'

'He could have been mistaken, couldn't he? She'd have given him a cue – most likely that she was a long-lost cousin or some such rubbish.'

'The real point about her touching rigmarole,' said Trensham, 'is that it's probably true. It doesn't give away anything we wouldn't have found out fairly quickly for ourselves. It also persuaded you to help them search the apartment.'

'Had you heard this nonsense about the Children of the Dolomites?' asked Shand.

'I know about them,' said Trensham. He didn't intend to be sidetracked. 'The real trouble is that they're aware we're operating.'

'We couldn't have kept it quiet forever. It's certainly shaken them badly, though, because this pair decided to get out smartly. That's why they smacked Sammy and departed.'

'Did they get what they were looking for?'

'I don't know. Judging by the state of the bedrooms that girl had turned them over quite thoroughly. But at least, they didn't get the medallion.'

'Hm,' said Trensham. There was another pause. At last he trotted out the familiar formula. 'I'll see what I can do at this end. Meantime, I want you to go round to Central Records and check up on an old friend of ours – Lorne Masters.'

'Masters? He's not mixed up in this?'

'It's the kind of job he'd like, don't you think? In fact, he might even be our fourth man. He's about five-foot-six, stockily built – or so they say. It fits his usual pattern.'

'That's the trouble,' reflected Shand. 'That's all they ever manage to say about him. There isn't even a picture of him in existence.'

'There is now, I understand. The Madrid police wired one to Central Records earlier this morning. Take a copy along to that woman who peered through the curtains and see if she recognises him as one of the men who hustled Carlo into the house. Have another word with Greek Street station. See if they've located anyone who noticed them switching cars.'

'Looks like another busy day for me,' said Shand, and rang off.

Events of the morning – with their disappointment and nervous strain – called for an early lunch. Afterwards, feeling somewhat restored, Shand took Sammy in the car for an afternoon check-up of the general situation.

Martin told them Margo Corranzi had not yet returned to the flat.

'Nobody else called?' inquired Shand sarcastically. 'No gentlemen wanting to read the gas meter or cut the canary's claws?'

Flushing, Martin said, 'No, sir. I checked up, as you told me to. It's quite true about her and the uncle being – well, hard up. And about her job in that department store – only she left without notice a fortnight ago and hasn't been seen there since.'

Shand frowned. So something had been brewing with Carlo Corranzi and his niece for quite a time! Else why give up her job? And what about the money they needed?

He got in the car again, and Sammy drove to Greek Street. Passing through the charge-office, he asked the desk-sergeant, 'Remember that Corranzi girl who came in yesterday to report her uncle's disappearance?'

The officer nodded. 'Yes, sir. She came in again today.'

Shand waved him down. 'I know. I know. If the Operations Room rings through could you give a description?'

'Yes, sir.'

'Brown hair, hazel eyes, and all the rest of it?'

'That's right, sir. About five foot four, medium oval face, pale complexion.'

Shand nodded again and walked on.

In the Operations Room he shook hands with a round-faced mournful-looking Irishman. 'Hello, Mulvaney. Anything new?'

Mulvaney sighed. 'There's always something new, worse luck. How nice it would be, now, if for once we didn't have anything new – just a quiet, peaceful hour when we could relax and . . .'

'You'd only start thinking about pigs and potatoes and peat-bogs. Tell me – how's the big chase coming along?'

'You mean your own particular big chase, I suppose. We've one or two others on hand, of course, but they wouldn't mean much.'

Shand said, 'Never mind the delicate sarcasm.'

'Well, we've put the routine on. Extra watch at all ports, airfields, railway stations, and bus depots. Afternoon police patrols will have the descriptions as far as a hundred miles north and west. We're concentrating on the areas mentioned to find anyone who saw those cars.'

'Fine,' said Shand. 'Now I want another call to go out. Margo Corranzi. Your own desk sergeant can give the details. He's seen her twice.'

'I wouldn't do it for anybody but you,' said Mulvaney. Then his expression hardened. 'Don't know what this is all about, Terry, my boy,' he said gruffly. 'But it's – serious?'

Shand nodded.

'Something, maybe, to do with this?' He thrust a hand into a recess of his desk and dropped a folder within Shand's reach. 'Madrid wired this in about ten o'clock this morning.'

Several sheets of typewritten paper inside the folder listed crimes – actual and suspected – committed over the years by one Lorne Masters. Two older folios contained rather sketchy biographical material. Shand shoved them aside. He knew them almost by heart. An envelope containing the newly wired photograph interested him much more.

'They tell me,' said Mulvaney, 'that the name of Von Grinling has cropped up again.'

'Who told you?' demanded Shand sharply.

'A little bird. Can't give you a photograph of *him*, I'm afraid.

That's a thing nobody owns in the wide, wide world.' He sighed again. 'You'll have to content your heart with what we've got for you there.'

Shand opened the envelope and drew out the clear, keen-focussed picture of a man's likeness. He didn't normally show much emotion, but what he saw before him made him gasp with surprise.

'The Madrid people guarantee this is a photograph of Lorne Masters?'

Mulvaney nodded. 'Cross their hearts.'

'How did they get it?'

'A misguided Spaniard named Manuel Lollobroso exchanged shots with the Civil Guard when they caught him breaking into a jeweller's shop. They fired straighter than he did. At his home they found papers showing him to be an old associate – in a quite minor way – of Masters.' He shrugged. 'He probably kept the papers in the hope of blackmail – I don't know. Anyway, that photo was among them, pinned to a piece of writing that identified it. Good enough?'

Shand stared down at the small square picture lying on the desk. From it there looked up at him an excellent likeness – although obviously taken quite a number of years previously – of the man he had met as Zorrio Corranzi.

A Sudden Journey

Little more than an hour later Shand opened his apartment door and halted upon the threshold. The living-room was in hopeless disorder, almost ankle-deep in papers, clothes, and assorted articles flung from drawers. His glance swung from left to right, taking in the writing-bureau ruthlessly hurled on its side, the carpet folded back, the slashed upholstery and torn chair-seats. Then he saw the cold, dark eye of an automatic pistol looking unwaveringly at his midriff – and the skinny, ferret-faced man holding the gun.

'Step right inside,' said the man. 'Don't be bashful. It's your apartment. Only move slow, an' don't try any tricks.'

Someone else closed the door behind him. Shand, trying to see who it was, raised hands and eyebrows simultaneously. 'Looks as though I came back too early.'

'Shut your trap and get across to that chair.'

Shand stared into the mean eyes and decided to obey. He wasn't anxious for any scared, vindictive little rat to pull the trigger through sheer nervousness.

The other man came into his line of vision – a thick-set individual, fairly tall and with a coarse red face.

Shand knew them both. They were two of the three who had taken Carlo Corranzi from Sylvia's Pantry the previous afternoon.

'I can't congratulate your lot on the way they search places. Do you always make a mess like this?' He spoke coolly enough; inside he was seething.

'It don't signify,' said the ferret-faced man with the gun. 'We got what we wanted.' His lips drew back in an unpleasant grin. 'Show him, Jules.'

Stubby fingers were thrust into a jacket pocket. Coming out again, they dangled a fine chain from which was suspended a shining medallion.

'You shouldn't have come back so soon,' said the little man. 'You really shouldn't have.' Shand said nothing. He must not let these two know that he associated them with Carlo's last moments – that they were probably identifiable by the curtain-peeping neighbour.

Jules wriggled powerful shoulders uneasily beneath his padded jacket and muttered something in Parisian slum-argot.

'Speak English, you silly frog!' said the one with the gun. 'What's the matter?'

Jules wiped his mouth. 'Come,' he said thickly. 'I do not care for – what do you say? – cat and mouse.'

'Nor me,' said Shand. 'You've got the trinket. Why don't you clear off? My assistant's putting the car away. He'll be here in a minute.'

The little man cackled. 'Oh, no 'e won't! We know you've come back alone. An' if you didn't you wouldn't be such a fool as to tell us! Think we're barmy? Sit down in that chair, Shand – before I slap you down with this gun!'

Shand sat. Jules, fastening blind-cord round his ankles and wrists with cruel efficiency, said, 'I tie 'im good. Now we go quick? Yes?'

'All right, all right.' The gun was put away. 'I'll help you finish the job. There ain't that hurry, though. We'll be back in the old Pigalle quick enough.'

They stuffed cotton-wool into Shand's mouth and wrenched tightly across his face a length of broad adhesive tape. Then they carried the chair and its occupant to the bathroom, stumbling twice over scattered debris, dumped him down and locked the door from the outside.

Able to move only his eyelids, he stared for a long time at the tiled wall. He tried hopping along, dragging the chair with him. Craning his neck painfully, he looked round the place. Nothing that might be flipped by fingers through the window lay within reach. Perhaps if he drummed his heels against the door long enough someone might hear. But by the time he had covered the short distance he was exhausted and bathed in sweat.

He tried to hop round, so that the chair came nearer the white-enamelled woodwork. Suddenly, he fell sideways. His shoulder struck the floor painfully. The wad of cotton-wool was pushed to the back of his throat, and he started to choke.

Sammy pushed his hat to the back of his head and leaned against the coolness of the wall, pulling thoughtfully at his underlip. From time to time he shook his head and muttered, 'I dunno. I just dunno.'

The Greek Street desk-sergeant eyed him speculatively. 'Don't know what?'

'What to do next. And don't you dare tell me, either.'

'Only in a helpful way,' said the sergeant. 'For my own benefit, as well as yours. It's bad for young constables' morale having you sighing and grunting in the corner.'

'So you've got something to suggest?'

'Come off it,' said the sergeant. 'It just struck me how this lot you're looking for are foreigners. Why don't you trot along and look at the pictures in the Aliens Department.'

Sammy raised his eyebrows. 'That's not a bad idea.' He flipped the brim of his hat in farewell. 'Thanks.'

'Don't mention it,' said the sergeant. 'You were making the place look untidy, anyway.'

Sammy knew from experience that any departments owning picture records are as happy to display them to authorised visitors as holiday-makers with snapshot albums. 'Saves dusting the covers, don't it?' he said to the officer on duty in the Aliens Department. Unfortunately, they had no photographs of naturalised subjects, sch as Carlo Corranzi and his niece. 'Perhaps the Passport Section at the Foreign Office might help,' the officer suggested, with an amiable smile.

'Too hot to walk all the way,' said Sammy. 'Let's try one of the others.'

'Which one had you in mind?'

'I'll make it difficult.'

The officer gave a stiff smile. 'Our customers are filed and cross-indexed.'

Sammy leaned back and closed his eyes. Four or five assorted faces passed across his mind's eye. 'Let's say a thick-set, red-faced man with heavy eyebrows.'

'Nationality?'

He shook his head.

'Fair-haired?'

'No – dark.'

'High cheek-bones?'

'Not particularly.'

The questions went on. Suddenly Sammy opened his eyes. 'You know something? You're getting close!'

The officer smiled. 'Ethnological deduction. Might mean anything or nothing.'

'Big words mean nothing to me,' said Sammy. 'All I know is we're getting warm. Do we start looking yet?'

The big books were produced and duly turned over. Fat-faced men, heavily-moustached and clean-shaven, stared at Sammy from every page. He had seen none before.

'Don't give up,' urged the officer. 'There's another couple of hundred.' He broke off. 'Found something?'

'You know,' said Sammy slowly, 'I owe you an apology.' He prodded one particular portrait with a podgy finger. 'I never dreamt for a moment – to be honest, it was just a try-on.' He grabbed a proffered envelope. 'This his record?' He started to read:

> 'JULES DELFONT, alias Marcus de Froileux, alias Jacques Marcand. Born Laurette-en-Seine, 21st January 1912.
> Height 5 ft 10 in; weight 12 st 12 lb. Hair dark brown, eyes brown, complexion fresh to ruddy, no visible distinguishing marks.'

'Jules Delfont,' murmured the officer. 'He was over here, living in London until May 1948. He has not landed since.'

'That's what you think!' said Sammy. 'He was here yesterday! He's one of the crowd who grabbed Carlo Corranzi! I'll have to tell Shand. He's my boss.'

'Use the 'phone with pleasure.'

'No, I'll pop round to his flat. Maybe he'll stand me a drink on the strength of the good news.'

When a purple-faced Shand had the sticking-plaster ripped off his face and got back sufficient breath to speak, Sammy was heartily invited to take the entire bottleful. 'If I ever accuse you again of sponging on me for drinks,' he croaked from a rasped and painful throat, 'just remind me about this.'

'Don't worry,' said Sammy. 'I will.' He stared at the chaos surrounding them. 'What were they after? The little medal?'

Shand, moving groggily towards the kitchen, nodded. 'They got it, too.'

He returned with Sammy's reward. 'Confound it! You'll have to pour your own.' He massaged wrists still numbed by viciously tied cords.

'You'd know 'em again?' asked Sammy.

'I know them now!' snarled Shand. 'They were two of the so-and-so's we saw take Corranzi.'

Sammy suddenly choked.

'What's the matter?'

'Don't tell me one of 'em was a big, red-faced Frenchman named Jules . . .'

Shand stared. 'Why – that's what the little rat called him. How'd you find out?'

'Jules Delfont – comes from Paris.'

'That's right! I heard him speak – genuine Parisian slang, or I never heard it! Let me tell Trensham.'

Trensham listened, as usual in silence. Sometimes he listened so patiently and quietly it was difficult to believe he had not already hung up. At the end he said, 'That's as good an excuse for spending a week-end in Paris as I've ever heard. Won't work though, I'm afraid. They'll be very clever to get out of the country with the net we've spread. Even more so now there's a name to add to the descriptions.'

'You think they'll try to get out?'

'The medallion – if it really means anything – won't be much use to them here, will it?' He paused. 'Better get some sleep.'

Early to bed, early to rise. Trensham telephoned again at 4.30 a.m. 'They were clever, after all,' he admitted. 'They took a privately chartered ocean-going launch across to Calais. Our agents spotted them in the harbour area. They're being shadowed, of course, but we may not be able to follow them all the way. They took a train to Paris.'

Shand looked at his watch to find that he and Sammy had three-quarters of an hour to reach the airport and occupy the seats Trensham had reserved for them aboard the plane.

Sentenced to Death

The plane descended through thin, summery clouds at Le Bourget into the pearly air of a Paris morning. Shand waved a badge at the customs officials that sped Sammy and himself through the *douane* to an accompaniment of salutes and stiff little bows.

A big man, dressed in black and wearing a bowler hat, fell into step beside them. 'M'sieu Shand? My name is Laudaire. May I speak with you, please?'

Even in Paris you could recognise a plain-clothes man, thought Sammy. Why was it?

'Police Judiciaire Centrale?' inquired Shand.

The officer shook his head. 'No – Préfecture.'

'Ah. Then we have to thank you, M'sieu Laudaire. Our arrangements are in hand with Inspector Faugeront of the Centrale. It is, however, most kind of you.'

'I am happy that all is in order for your visit.'

'Our regrets that we have not been able to avail ourselves of your generously offered help.'

'Allow me, at least to call a taxi.'

'Delighted, M'sieu Laudaire.'

In the cab Sammy said, 'Nice chap.'

Shand looked at him narrowly. 'Laudaire? Don't let him fool you. He was curious, that's all. They're wondering what we're up to. One vague hint, and we'll have them on the trail, too. As if we didn't have enough competition.'

'So we aren't really going to this Centrale place?'

'Certainly we are! Don't get the idea the French are dumb. Two to one in cognacs that chap Laudaire's checking with Faugeront right now. And that this taxi-driver's under orders to report back where he takes us.'

Sammy shook his head solemnly. 'Makes you lose faith in the *entente cordiale*.'

More time had to be wasted exchanging pleasantries with Inspector Faugeront, who had been suitably softened up with a telephone story from Scotland Yard concerning British tourists' lack of conscience about foreign exchange.

'At this disgracefully early hour, my dear inspector,' said Shand, spreading his hands ruefully, 'I must disturb you with business in which, logically, you cannot be greatly interested.'

There was coffee and much mutual politeness. Sammy, whose knowledge of French was rudimentary, kept stifling yawns. The place smelt odd, he thought. Perhaps it was the coarse black tobacco of the cigarettes; or maybe the pomade on Inspector Faugeront's thinning hair.

'The estimable M'sieu Foster,' said Faugeront. 'I have not seen him for some time.'

'I will be sure to convey your felicitations,' promised Shand. 'We are meeting him.' He looked at his watch. 'Dear me, in less than half-an-hour! Forgive us if we leave in haste, my dear inspector.'

While being buffeted in another taxi, Sammy asked suspiciously, 'Who's this Foster chap you spoke of?'

'Joe Foster's the Treasury agent in this part of the world. He keeps an eye on British tourists and businessmen – seeing they don't spend more francs than they should.'

'So what?'

'Use your brains. The French police are watching us. We've given them a yarn about checking sterling allocations and travellers' cheques. If we didn't have a word with Foster they'd think it rather peculiar.'

Sammy brooded on this for a moment. 'Was Foster watching the station here for that lot coming through from Calais?'

'Right first time.' Shand smiled and gazed out at the chestnut trees along the Bois de Boulogne.

Joe Foster (the Hon. Joseph Delaney Vere Foster) was an elegant young man who greeted Shand with a glad cry. 'Well, hello! Old Trensham 'phoned me you were on the way. What's the good news?'

They slapped each other on the back and gripped hands so vigorously that Sammy expected to hear bone splinter.

'Have a drink,' said Joe hospitably. 'How long are you here for?'

'That's up to you,' said Shand. 'What have our criminal friends been doing since you laid eyes on them earlier this morning?' Again he gazed out at the trees.

'Lying doggo. They took rooms at a small hotel not far from here. Two of my men are in a café across the street waiting for 'em to come out when they've caught up with some sleep.' He cocked an expectant eyebrow. 'Can I know what it's all in aid of?'

'Sorry. Very hush-hush.'

Joe nodded. He didn't seem particularly disappointed. 'I'll take you out soon for an early lunch and buy you a drink. Maybe that'll loosen you up. Or dare you be seen out with me?'

Shand looked at Sammy and winked. 'We'll lower our dignity for the sake of a lunch in Paris.'

Then the telephone rang. Joe Foster listened, carefully, making notes on a small memo pad.

'Very well. Don't let 'em out of your sight. I'll want a full report.'

He dropped back the receiver and passed the slip of notes to Shand. 'They've booked seats on the Paris-Milan express. It leaves at four o'clock.'

Milan? Sammy wanted to yell out with excitement, but managed to control himself. He noticed that not a muscle of Shand's face moved.

'Here are their reservation numbers,' said Foster. 'Want us to book you on the same train?'

'Yes, please – in the next coach, if you can.'

Sammy suddenly felt disappointed. 'Ain't we having even one night in Paris?'

Joe Foster drummed fingers ruminatively on the desk. 'Ought to be a nice trip this time of year – once you reach the mountains. Bit cooler than it is here. Don't know much about Milan, though. July's usually a stinker there.'

'The lunch,' said Shand, firmly. 'Remember your duties as a host and stop babbling.'

Later in the afternoon Shand and Sammy found themselves occupying opposite seats at one side of a saloon coach. Between them rested a small table bearing a pink-shaded lamp, an ash-tray, a bell push to summon the steward, and two long, cool drinks.

'This is the life,' said Sammy contentedly. 'This is how an investigation ought to be done – me sitting here letting other people do the legwork.'

Shand looked at his watch. 'Five minutes to four. Joe said he'd look in to give a final report – oh, there he is!'

The Hon. Joseph Delaney Vere Foster moved along the centre gangway with the unmistakable dignity of an Englishman abroad, taking no notice of fat passengers who puffed in the wake of overburdened porters.

'Got what you need?' he asked brightly. 'Luggage all right? How about some magazines?' Then, changing neither tone nor expression: 'One of my chaps on the platform says those seats in the next coach have been taken. Two green trunks have been put in the luggage van.' He prepared to move off. 'Have a nice time. Good hunting. Don't forget the old signal.'

'So long, Joe,' said Shand. 'And thanks.'

The train started to move and Shand looked back at the people left standing on the platform. At the far end, by the barrier, stood Joe Foster, smiling and waving his hand.

Shand sighed with satisfaction and leaned back in his seat.

'Was that,' inquired Sammy, 'anything to do with "the old signal"?'

'If there'd been any slip-up, Joe would have waved his handkerchief instead of his hand. Those two could have been trying it on, you know. They might have slipped away from the train just before it started.'

'Would that have been bad?'

'It would,' said Shand curtly. 'This train doesn't stop till Dijon.' Suddenly, he began to think about his stomach.

'Ah . . .'

'What d'you mean – "Ah"?'

'I've just remembered,' said Sammy. 'They start serving dinner when we leave Dijon.'

'Pooh!' said Shand in disgust. 'That lunch you put away ought to last you till tomorrow night.' He made himself more comfortable and drew the blind to shut out the bright afternoon sunshine. 'I'm going to take a nap. Trot along through the next coach some time and locate our two birds. You've got their seat numbers – and they don't know you. Wake me in about an hour.'

Shand's thoughts carried him farther than Dijon and dinner. They were on the way to Milan. In turn, Milan – in the sunny south beyond the Alps – provided a key centre for reaching the Dolomites, that toothy ridge of mountains extending across north-east Italy. The Children of the Dolomites . . . the little gold medallion now held by Jules Delfont and Ferret-face . . . the Dolomites . . . Dolomites . . . Dolomites . . .

Gradually the rhythm of train wheels took up the syllables, and he slept.

But not for long. Fingers shook him by the shoulders, bringing him to instant, guarded wakefulness. Something was wrong. He could read that much in Sammy's expression. Sammy gulped. 'Those two fellows.'

'Well?'

'They ain't on the train!'

Shand said, 'But Foster's men checked the seats!'

'Oh, somebody's sitting in 'em all right – only it ain't who we expected!'

Shand glanced round quickly. Other passengers seemed to be minding their own business.

'Who?' he demanded.

'Well,' admitted Sammy, 'I don't know their real names – but the last time we saw 'em they were Zorrio and Margo Corranzi!'

He looked across Shand's shoulder along the gangway. His jaw dropped, and for once a flicker of expression showed in his eyes. 'Here's one of 'em now!'

It was 'Margo'. She wore a simple, short-sleeved dress of

deep, rich blue, which even Shand could recognise as hideously expensive, with a little white hat to set off her black hair, elbow-length white doeskin gloves, and a white silk scarf.

She held out one of the gloved hands with perfect self-possession and her pale face lit up with a dazzling smile. 'Why, Mr Shand! How nice! And Sammy too!'

Shand smiled. 'Well, hello! Move out, Sammy, and let the lady sit down.'

'Oh, what a shame! Poor Sammy! Look, this bigger table isn't occupied – let's all sit here. You shall order me a drink.'

This wasn't Margo Corranzi, the bewildered shop-girl, short of money and grieving about her vanished uncle. Shand began to wonder whether the real Margo existed.

'This drink,' said Shand. 'Give me one good reason why I should.'

'Margo' didn't bat an eyelid. 'Because one good turn deserves another.'

Shand rang for the steward and gave the order.

'Judging by what happened last time,' said Sammy glowering, 'it's you who ought to be buying the drinks.'

'Poor Sammy,' she said again. 'Is your head still hurting?'

'The refreshment's on its way,' said Shand. 'It's as good as in your pretty gullet. What's this good turn you spoke of?'

Her expression froze. 'Advice,' she said in a low tone. 'First-rate advice.'

'Which is?'

The silent steward solemnly set out three frosted glasses.

She waited until he had gone, then flourished her drink in a mock toast. 'To you – and your solid English commonsense.'

Sammy imitated the gesture. 'To your alleged uncle – and I've a good mind to pop along and chuck it in his eye!'

'Let's cut out the trimmings,' suggested Shand. 'What's this advice?'

The girl leaned forward slightly, dropping her voice even more confidentially. 'Get off this train at Dijon. Get away while you're safe. Keep away from the man you know as Zorrio.'

Shand raised his eyebrows. 'Without our dinner?'

'You can find plenty of good dinners in Dijon.'

'I like eating on trains. Besides, we've bought our tickets as far as Milan.'

The violet eyes looked steadily into his own. 'It's not a matter of joking. You may not reach Milan.'

'These continental trains,' sighed Shand. 'Unreliable, aren't they?'

She finished her drink and stood up. She did not hold out the white-gloved hand this time. 'Good-bye, Shand. It's been nice knowing you.'

'We'll be seeing each other again,' he said easily. 'I've been threatened by better men than Lorne Masters.'

Her poise was shaken, but she recovered instantly. 'Good-bye, Terry Shand. And I mean – good-bye!'

His eyes followed her along the gangway. Sammy unashamedly craned his neck round the seat-back to do likewise.

After a while Shand asked. 'What d'you make of it?'

'Only that everybody on this train seems to know everybody else's business.'

'Hm.' He thought again. 'We still don't know that girl's real name, do we?'

'Who cares?' asked Sammy, whose attention was attracted by another woman coming down the corridor. She was very good-looking and expensively dressed. To his surprise she paused at their table.

'Excuse me – it's Mr Shand, isn't it?'

He stood up. 'That's right.'

'I'm Ella Findlay. We met once at the Clarence Club in London. There was quite a crowd of us – remember?'

'How could I ever forget,' Shand replied gallantly.

'By the way,' she went on, 'this is John – my brother.'

A tall, equally elegant man came forward. He shook Shand by the hand, and laughed. 'You're a diplomat, making an answer like that! I'm sorry about Ella – she's an inveterate meeter.'

'A what?'

'She likes to meet people, you know. Hoards up names in her memory like a squirrel hoards nuts. Then she expects them to remember her years afterwards.'

'Really, John! It's nothing of the kind. Only we had such a cheerful party that night.'

Shand asked: 'Was I – let's say, a little too cheerful, maybe?'

'Of course not. You were grand company.'

'We'll retire with apologies,' said John Findlay and grinned again. 'No, don't be embarrassed. I'm not. I told you, it's happening all the time.'

There was only one thing to say. Shand said it. 'Since we've gone to all the trouble of introductions, could I interest you in a drink?'

They moved across the gangway to the table where he and Sammy had sat with 'Margo'.

'Travelling far?' asked Shand.

'Lausanne,' said John Findlay. 'Spot of climbing in view.'

'Don't look at me!' said Ella hurriedly. 'I only tag along for the parties in the evenings. I'm useless at climbing.'

'Not a bit of it. For a girl – especially a chap's sister – she crawls up cliffs quite well.'

After a time Findlay glanced at his watch. 'We won't impose ourselves on you any longer. Been nice meeting you.'

Shand smiled in return, looking at Ella, who fluttered her eyelashes. 'The pleasure's ours.'

He watched them depart along the gangway.

Sammy said, 'Smart as a pin, eh?' His round face depicted

admiring approval. 'I'd never miss picking that one among a crowd.'

'Nor would I,' said Shand shortly, 'if I'd ever seen her before.' He paused thoughtfully. 'I wonder what their little game is.'

'Something to do with the other business?'

He shook his head. 'Don't see how it can be. Look here – this coach lies between where Masters is sitting and the luggage van. Let's go along and see what we can find.'

They strolled down the rocking corridors and gangways of the train, seeing as they went how the flat countryside of the Paris region had begun to give way to gentle, wooded slopes. They were approaching Burgundy.

The corridor ended at a small door which resisted pressure.

Shand grunted. 'Good! If it's locked, there's not so much chance of a guard sitting inside. Get busy.'

It was a scene reminiscent of what had happened in the doorway of a dark house on the outskirts of London. Only now, broad daylight bathed the setting, and danger of discovery was more imminent as Shand once more covered Sammy's manipulation of the lock.

A click went unheard above the thunder of express wheels.

'Get inside! Snap the bolt behind us.'

They found themselves alone amid heaps of assorted heavy travelling-cases, steamer trunks, and valises.

'Green ones,' said Shand, by way of reminder. 'You take that stack, I'll see to this one. Don't waste time.'

It needed less than half a minute to locate a couple of likely looking pieces. Shand examined the labels. One read: 'G. Tortelli. Milano via Lausanne.' The other, affixed to the larger and more ornate wardrobe trunk read: 'Mlle M. Tortelli.'

Sammy produced his neat little bunch of small-sized skeleton keys. 'Hard lines on the Tortelli girl – whoever she is – and her old man if these aren't the right cases.'

'Open them up,' ordered Shand. 'And don't hesitate to slit the linings if we seem to be on the right track. Look specially for documents – papers, letters, tickets.'

'And that medallion gadget, I suppose?!'

'If Masters has got any sense he won't have packed it here.'

Both trunks were filled with clothes and toilet articles. Lorne Masters' ideas of values, however, remained debatable. The little medallion winked back at Shand when he opened a jeweller's box containing an assortment of gold studs and cuff-links. He caught his breath.

Sammy caught his too. A face had appeared at one of the windows of the luggage van. The owner of the face clung to the outside of the coach with one hand, while in the other he levelled a gun at the two British agents. They recognised the man instantly as Lorne Masters.

'Duck!' yelled Shand. He dived behind the stack of trunks simultaneously with Sammy, yet Masters withheld his fire. Perhaps he feared discovery, but with the great clatter and roar of the speeding express a gunshot would certainly attract less attention than a man clinging to the outside of a moving train.

'What the hell's he doing out there?' demanded Sammy in a hoarse whisper.

'Probably found the door locked. He could have tried it, and we wouldn't have heard him. So he went round to see if everything was all right.'

'I said he was a fool. He should have kept that little trinket in his waistcoat pocket.'

Shand wasn't so sure. 'Suppose he thought we – or somebody else – might try a spot of kidnapping? Or flourish a gun and search him?'

He risked a cautious peep round the edge of a stout, brass-bound box. Lorne Masters no longer stared through the dusty glass.

'Come on,' said Shand. 'Quickly! If he fetches the conductor we're sunk!'

With Sammy at his heels he rushed for the door, disregarding the litter of clothing from the trunks spread over the floor of the coach. He flipped back the small brass bolt and prepare to hare along the corridor.

Then he stopped dead in his tracks – as though struck by a bullet from the revolver still gripped in Masters' hand.

'Back in there!' snapped Masters. 'Quick! And keep your hands where I can see 'em!'

Still facing him, Shand and Sammy retreated. He shoved the door closed.

'You're looking a bit paler than when I saw you last,' said Shand. 'Could it be annoyance – or have you actually washed and got rid of the walnut juice?'

The eyes were still the same, though. Queer, light-brown, staring eyes – now without the fake twinkle assumed for the role of Zorrio. Except for those eyes, he would have struck a ridiculous figure – a short, stocky man with grey, balding head, training a revolver upon two others amid the clutter of a moving luggage van. But in their bright, unwinking, menacing gaze they resembled the eyes of a snake.

'You thought I'd fetch the conductor, didn't you?' said Masters. 'Only I didn't.' His small hands began to sweat.

He was smart all right. He knew very well that if he reported the matter officially the medallion would be hidden long before he could arrange for Shand to be searched, even though criminal charges might be brought later. Shand, on the other hand, could not afford to waste time straightening matters out with the French police. So neither side wanted detectives around, and if necessary all knowledge of the ransacked trunks must be disclaimed. Yet Shand could not be allowed to get away with the little gold trinket.

'I'll have my property, if you don't mind,' said Masters. 'The item you stole from my trunk.'

Shand laughed, although he did not feel very happy or amused. 'You'll have to come over here and fetch it.'

'Listen! We'll be pulling into Dijon soon. I'm not fooling. I can easily shoot you both – nobody'd hear the noise over the row this train's making – and chuck your bodies through that door on to the line!' Masters wasn't bluffing, either. 'You'd better be sensible.'

Sammy spoke up. 'We're not dumb enough to fall for that one! What guarantee have we got you won't shoot us anyway?'

Masters was frank about it. 'None. That's why tricks won't do you any good.'

Shand had a suggestion. 'We'll feel safer when this train pulls into Dijon. You won't dare shoot then.'

'I dare now,' said Masters between his teeth. 'And I will, unless . . .' The glazed, fixed eyes were those of a killer. 'Drop that medallion on the floor – and move your hand slowly. Shove more than one finger and thumb in your pockets, and you get it regardless!'

Shand's heart sank into the cold, heavy void where his stomach used to be. He could not see any way out of it. There wasn't the slightest doubt that Masters intended to shoot both himself and Sammy, whether the trinket was surrendered willingly or otherwise. His heart pumped madly.

'Shoot and get it over. Go on,' he said bitterly.

Masters braced himself against the swaying wood floor. 'All right! You asked for it.'

Shand saw the plump finger tighten on the trigger. He wanted to close his eyes but could not. A roaring in his ears wasn't entirely due to the hurtling express. He waited for the paralysing blow of a bullet.

Shand had only a fleeting recollection of what happened next. Events followed too fast to become firmly imprinted on his memory.

He became suddenly aware of a stout walking-stick poised in the air beyond Lorne Masters' head. A surprised flicker of his eyes – or perhaps something in Sammy's expression – betrayed the fact. Masters could not be certain whether the pair of them were practising the old try-on game, yet, in that split-second needed to make up his mind, the damage was done.

It might have been the way he half-turned, the swaying of the train, or an imperfection of aim that caused the walking-stick to miss Masters' head and smack down upon his shoulder.

The gun went off simultaneously. The bullet buried itself in the door, spraying splinters that Shand found later embedded in his trouser-legs.

An instant after the gun fired, Shand dived for Masters' ankles, Sammy hurled his powerful, stocky form into the mêlée regardless, while on top of the three – evidently thoroughly at home in a football scrimmage – came John Finlay.

They picked themselves up, leaving Masters glaring and groaning on the floor. The tables had been turned . . .

'Stop that horrible noise,' said Findlay. 'I didn't hit you very hard.' He turned to the others. 'What the devil did he think he was doing?'

Shand picked up the fallen gun. 'He pinched something belonging to us. When we got it back just now he pulled his revolver on us.'

Findlay looked at the trunks with their contents scattered over the floor. 'Bit of a mess you made,' he said. 'Not that I blame you for that. Not when you've got to deal with a shifty character like this one.' He prodded Masters with his stick. 'Saw him earlier, talking to two other very unsavoury types.'

'You'll suffer for this!' Masters heaved himself upright, and stood snarling, clutching his bruised shoulder.

'Watch him!' said Shand. 'Amongst other things he's probably a murderer.'

The snake-eyes sparkled with malevolence. 'You're insane! You can't prove a thing! But I can – I can prove robbery and assault! When you're rotting a couple of years in some filthy French prison I'll come and laugh at you through the bars.'

Findlay raised his eyebrows and looked at Shand. His mood remained one of casual charm, mingled with hostility towards Masters, yet there was the faintest hint of reproach. 'I imagine you've left rather a lot of finger-prints on those trunks, old boy.'

'I'm not bothered so much about that as his two stooges. Tell me – was one a big red-faced thug? The other a little ferret-faced man?'

Findlay seemed amused. 'Obviously you've met 'em.' He rubbed his chin thoughtfully. 'Only one thing for it, you know.'

Shand, too, could think of only one solution. He nodded. 'All right. He was going to do it to us. Poetic justice, they call it.'

Masters read their intentions and backed away. 'You wouldn't dare!' he breathed. 'You wouldn't dare – not in broad daylight.'

'We're as devil-may-care as you are,' said Sammy. 'Be thankful we don't put a bullet in you as well!' He went across and unbarred the double-doors, sliding them a couple of feet apart. A thunder of wheels roared into the van.

'No!' yelled Masters. 'No – I'll be killed.'

'The train isn't going very fast,' said Findlay, comfortingly. 'Bit of gravel-rash, maybe.'

Shand grabbed Masters by the lapels. 'It's not half as bad as the way you treated Carlo! So you're lucky! We're throwing you off because you're a dangerous nuisance. And there's three of us. You try telephoning ahead from Dijon and telling tales to the police – and we'll all swear blind you dreamt the whole thing!'

He stared again into the beady brown eyes and knew from their expression that he had won. Temporarily, at any rate.

Then, still with a grip upon Masters' jacket, he hurled him sideways and outwards.

Clutching vainly at the door as he passed, Masters yelled again. Flailing arms snatching at air, he struck the side of a low, grassy embankment and rolled to the bottom.

Shand and Findlay leaned out of the van to catch a last glimpse of Masters, before a curve in the track removed him from their line of vision.

'Hope nobody saw him,' muttered Sammy apprehensively. 'This van being in the middle of the train, someone might have spotted him from one of the rear coaches.'

'He went out on the sunny side,' said Shand. 'Most of the passengers would have the blinds drawn. Anyway, we'd better get busy clearing up this mess.'

Working quickly, half-expecting at any moment to feel the jar and shudder of hurriedly applied brakes as a result of some observant passenger pulling the communication cord, they used one of Masters' own shirts to scrub fingerprints from the trunks, afterwards re-locking both cases and the door to the van.

At the end of the corridor they met Ella Findlay. She smiled quietly. 'Everything go off all right?'

Shand grinned back at the question. Her brother laughed aloud. 'That chap Masters did, anyway!'

'Oh, good.' Apparently she did not know exactly what had happened, and Shand had no intention of telling her.

'I think,' said Findlay, 'we've earned ourselves another drink.

He hurled Masters sideways and outwards.

I'll buy you one.'

Shand smiled. 'After the way you socked Masters the debt's on our side. Still, we'll join you in a couple of minutes, when we've tidied ourselves up – on condition you have dinner with us when we leave Dijon.'

'Yes, rather. Glad to have been useful, you know.'

While they washed, Shand said, 'We'd be better off with a little privacy. See about renting a sleeper. Tonight may bring fresh trouble.'

'You mean Jules and Ferret-face? Why don't we pop along and settle their hash? Findlay might like to help us. He seems an enthusiastic chap for a rough house.'

Busy with the towel, Shand said, 'I rather like him. I don't know why.'

'Probably because he stopped Masters bumping you off.'

'Funny about that sister of his, though. I'm certain I've never laid eyes on her before.' He shrugged. 'Never mind. Let's go and buy them that thanksgiving dinner.'

The express roared on through a quiet evening towards the Swiss frontier, and one particular party of four in the restaurant car were digging into chicken when two uniformed train officials halted beside the table. Accompanying them was 'Margo Corranzi'. She did not smile now, nor was she particularly self-possessed. In fact, she looked the way Shand and Sammy had first seen her in the role of Carlo's bereaved niece.

One of the officials indicated Shand, and looked at her questioningly. She nodded.

He bowed politely and said to Shand, 'M'sieu – I have the honour to be the senior official on this train. Is it possible for me to speak to you privately?'

Shand decided to play it tough. The situation might well develop awkwardly. 'Anything to be said can be said here.'

The official coughed. 'It is a matter of some delicacy.' When Shand did not answer, he went on. 'Very well, m'sieu. One of the passengers has disappeared. This young lady, Mlle Tortelli, thinks you may have spoken to the gentleman in question and can help our inquiries. It is her uncle, m'sieu.'

'Disappeared? He has gone from the train?'

'That is so, m'sieu.'

'Perhaps he got off at Dijon.' From the corner of his eyes he saw Findlay's faint, mocking grin.

'Mlle Tortelli thinks not, m'sieu.'

Shand threw his napkin on the table and stood up. 'Since Mlle Tortelli has such decided views, how does she believe I know anything?'

The official seemed vaguely shocked. He glanced uneasily at 'Margo'. She stood there looking as though she might burst into tears at any moment.

Shand purred. 'Mlle Tortelli has a habit of mislaying uncles?'

'Really, m'sieu! It is no matter for joking!'

'What's it all about, then?'

'It would be better to speak in private, m'sieu.'

Shand shook his head. He had to seem casual about it.

'*Alors!*' The guard straightened himself and drew a deep breath. 'The lady says that you and the gentleman here' – he indicated Sammy – 'were seen in conversation with M'sieu Tortelli near the luggage compartment. After that conversation, he never returned to his seat. The train has been searched.' He spread his hands. 'M'sieu Tortelli is no longer aboard.'

'But I told you. He must have alighted at Dijon.'

'The train, m'sieu, was searched before it reached Dijon.'

'Why weren't the Dijon police told then?'

'Unfortunately, m'sieu, this express must maintain its schedule. Also, our full preliminary inquiries were not complete. The matter will be reported at the next stop, however.'

Worse and worse. Moreover, Shand became uncomfortably aware of flapping ears in nearby seats. He wished now he had taken the guard's opening advice. 'Where is the next stop?'

'The frontier, m'sieu.'

Shand envisaged the possibility of himself and Sammy being hauled off the train and subjected to a French third-degree – an examination not only unpleasant but also long drawn out. There wasn't any Trensham to work miracles at this end. The difficulty lay in the fact that this hunt for the treasure of Monte Ragazzo had developed into a race. Any competitor stumbling over unexpected hurdles – such as police interrogation – might find himself fatally delayed. Lorne Masters was still alive – possibly active, too. Also, somewhere the vulture-faced Von Grinling was undoubtedly up to something.

Suddenly John Findlay spoke up. 'Tortelli? Is he an elderly gent? Short – sort of well-built. Grey hair, slightly balding.'

'Margo' spoke for the first time. 'You have seen him?'

'Oh, yes. Matter of fact I was with my friends' – he waved a languid hand towards Shand and Sammy – 'when he came up to us. Something about wanting to get into the luggage van. Said it was locked.'

'That is correct, m'sieu,' said the guard. 'The luggage van is always locked until Customs officials enter for examinations.'

'So we told him to look for you. He thanked us and went away.' He spread his long, sensitive fingers helplessly. 'That was all. We were together for the rest of the time, and never saw him again. Sorry we can't be of more help.'

The guard seemed relieved. 'These are the facts? You all agree, messieurs?'

Shand and Sammy nodded.

'It's not true!' Margo's eyes flashed with anger. 'You lying devils!' she shouted.

The guard had had enough. He pursed his lips and said,

'Please, mademoiselle.'

'You have killed him maybe? You are his enemies – all of you! Where is my uncle?'

'Mademoiselle! There is nothing we can do now! Come away, if you please. I will escort you.' He bowed again. 'My apologies, messieurs. And madame, too. Anxiety has made this poor young lady nervous and overwrought.'

'Pray, don't mention it,' said Shand politely.

The 'poor young lady' looked back at him – just once. What he saw in her face did not leave him much appetite for the rest of the chicken.

In any case, he had other matters on his mind. He eyed Findlay speculatively. 'Debt Number Two, John,' he said. 'I won't ask why you did it – but thanks again, anyway.'

'Well, you know, I don't like to stick my nose into other people's business –'

'It's long and rather pointed,' said Ella with a sister's brutal frankness. 'He finds it difficult.'

'– but when I saw what's-his-name – Tortelli – in a huddle with those two thugs farther along the train I got suspicious right-away. I don't know if you're aware of it, but Tortelli and his raven-haired niece – if that's what she really is – had been watching you like hawks ever since we left Paris. There was a lot of urgent whispering and nudging when they found you'd left your seat, and Tortelli passed us with blood in his eye. For all I knew he might have collected his thugs on the way. Pity he didn't – pity for him, that is.' He laughed and drank a little wine. 'Excuse me – I talk too much.'

'What time does this train get into Lausanne?' asked Shand.

'About eleven. Why?'

Shand paused, then made up his mind. 'You know, it wouldn't surprise me if those two stooges of Tortelli's don't try some dirty work when it grows dark.'

Ella nodded vigorously. 'Probably put up to it by that awful, black-haired creature. I don't trust her.'

'What girl ever did trust another?' Her brother grinned, then grew serious again. 'I see. If you need help, count me in.'

'Thanks,' said Shand. 'That's what I had in mind.'

There was a moment's speculative silence.

'Eleven o'clock,' said Findlay reflectively. 'Time for a lot more dirty work before dawn.'

'We'll look after ourselves later on. Only if you wouldn't mind keeping an eye open while we catch a few hours' sleep between here and Lausanne . . .'

'Remember what I said just now about poking my nose into other people's business?' asked Findlay. 'Don't hesitate to choke me off if necessary, but you're going through to Milan, aren't you? Would it help if we came all the way with you instead of dropping off at Lausanne?'

'To be quite frank,' said Shand, 'it would. But I can't spoil your holiday.'

Findlay laughed. 'I believe they've got mountains in Italy. I can climb up them just as well as the old Swiss variety.'

'No, no,' said Shand. 'It's awfully good of you – but quite out of the question.'

'Never mind, then. Consider it unsaid. Have a spot more wine. Pity to leave the rest of this bottle for the waiter.'

'You're a brute!' said Ella. 'An utter brute!'

'Who?' said Shand, in surprise. 'Me?'

'You didn't behave like this that night at the Clarence Club. Here's a chance for me to see Milan for the first time – instead of waiting at the bottom of some lonely mountain ready to catch John if he slips – and you won't let me take it! You're mean – really mean!'

Her brother grinned and stood up. 'Come along – before I put you over my knee! Thanks for the grub, you two.'

'Just a minute,' said Shand thoughtfully. 'You're quite sure you don't mind?'

'Mind?' John Findlay's eyes were lively with anticipation. 'I'll tell you something! If we don't have any trouble from those two thugs I'll be horribly disappointed.'

He was disappointed.

Shand did not get much sleep. He woke once during the night to find the train running alongside the waters of Lake Geneva. By breakfast time they were following the shore-line of an incredibly blue Lake Maggiore, with white buildings, red-roofed, glowing in sunshine against green-wooded hills. Jules Delfont and Ferret-face had still put in no further appearance; nor had 'Margo'.

Then at last the smoky outline of Italy's great northern city appeared on the horizon, and shortly afterwards they were stepping down on to the platform of Milan's main railway station.

They competed with early business travellers for a taxi.

'Come along to the hotel with us,' suggested Findlay. 'We can all get a clean-up there. Will you be too busy for lunch?'

Ella leaned back and looked through the cab windows. 'Shops and hotels!' she said with a sigh of satisfaction. 'Dresses, hats, and stockings! Dinners and dances! Oh, I'm glad we came to Milan!'

'Lunch would be fine,' said Shand. 'We've just one or two things to fix first. Say about twelve?'

An hour later, refreshed and changed, he and Sammy visited the main poste restante. A telegram awaited them. It read:

'Mining engineer Shand and assistant proceed immediately Rossanata. Pay Mayor Perera official visit.'

It was signed 'Trensham'.

Shand made noises of disgust. 'Mining engineer? What next?'

Sammy had something else on his mind. 'Wonder where that

lot went off the train.' He chewed over matters a little longer. 'I don't like it. Besides, what's happened to Masters?'

'I couldn't care less,' said Shand. He waited for a moment, then snorted. 'Mining engineer, indeed!'

'When you come to think of it,' said Sammy, 'we are digging for gold – in a manner of speaking!'

It was decided over lunch that suitable mountains for John Findlay to climb could be found in the area to which Shand and Sammy were travelling. This meant, moreover, that they journeyed in some degree of style and luxury, since Findlay drove from the hotel in a large car lent to him by a Swiss business friend whom he had met previously in Milan.

The car nosed out of the city with Findlay at the wheel and the luggage-boot crammed with suit-cases and climbing gear. Within half an hour they reached the great autostrada, heading east towards Venice. For mile upon mile it stretched in a straight, undeviating line, like an asphalt ribbon monotonously unwinding itself before their eyes. The surrounding countryside was almost as flat and was very uninteresting.

The effect on Findlay's passengers proved soporific. Nobody spoke much, and Shand, sitting in the back with Ella, once or twice felt his head nod.

They woke up fairly quickly, though, when John Findlay said, in a quiet voice, 'Hope nobody's going to get over-excited – but there's a hefty, fast-looking car behind us. He's been on our tail ever since we left Milan.'

'Might mean anything – or nothing,' Shand said. 'You haven't given him much of a chance to pass.'

Findlay grinned. 'Two ways to tell – either speed this crate up a bit more, or slow down and wait for him.'

'Don't let's waste time,' suggested Ella, brightly. 'Speed it up!'

John Findlay depressed the accelerator pedal to its full extent. Shand, judging progress keenly, saw distance between the two cars widen. 'Don't turn round,' he warned Ella. 'They'll see you in the window. Watch that driving-mirror.'

The needle crept to eighty-five . . . ninety . . . ninety-five. That seemed the engine's natural limit, although speed rose to a hundred-and-three when the road made a slight descent. Sammy said, 'Not much chance of catching us – even if he wants to.'

'Don't be so sure,' Findlay replied calmly. 'I know the type of car they've got. It could give us a good ten miles an hour.'

Sammy looked into the mirror, seeing the other vehicle now roaring down the slope in their wake.

Findlay said, 'A lot depends on the driving.'

'And other things,' said Sammy grimly. He pulled out his big automatic. 'I'll have a go at their tyres if they try to pass.' Shand thought they might be merely shadowed. 'So long as they keep us in sight – making sure we don't turn off anywhere – perhaps they'll be happy.'

Eyes on the road, fingers steady on the wheel, Findlay said, 'If they raced us to San Sagrado it could only be by about thirty minutes. Is half an hour all that vital?'

Shand shook his head. 'I wonder if they know we're bound for Rossanata.'

'Maybe,' said Ella, 'they'll try to stop us getting there at all.'

Findlay's longish face grew serious. 'You could be right.' He eased his foot on the accelerator. 'If they're ready for rough stuff I'd rather not have it happen at ninety miles an hour.' His lips clamped together purposefully. 'I'm slowing down to see their reaction. That all right with you, Shand?'

'Good idea.' He saw the image of the pursuing car grow larger in the mirror.

'I know this road,' said Findlay. 'About four miles ahead there's a stretch highly suitable for skullduggery – deserted, no side-entrances or nearby villages. If anything's going to happen it'll be there.'

'I'm all for a show-down. Let's switch the proceedings. Pull into the side. Either they'll stop, too, or they'll push on ahead and we can chase them for a change.'

Findlay slowed to a mere fifty miles an hour.

The other car approached rapidly.

Shand said, 'Delfont – I can see him next to the driver. Keep as you're going – they'll have to pass.'

For a long moment the vehicles dropped into slow motion, crawling past each other like ships manoeuvring for position. Eight pairs of eyes stared from behind windows closed to keep out the rush of air. Four pairs in the pursuing car belonged to Lorne Masters, Jules Delfont, Ferret-face and an unknown, beetle-browed driver.

Then another eye looked out, peering between glass partitions which suddenly moved a scant inch apart – the single eye of a machine-carbine muzzle. The other end was pressed against Delfont's chest.

In a split second the drama switched to fast tempo.

'Brake!' yelled Shand. 'And duck!'

Findlay stamped on the pedal and dived down as far as he could beneath the steering-wheel rim. Beside him farthest from the menacing muzzle – Sammy bent double. In the rear seat Ella Findlay's mouth formed a round 'O' of astonished disbelief. Shand dragged her unceremoniously from the upholstery and followed her to the carpeted floor, helped by momentum as squealing brake-linings bit into the drums.

Next instant the tommy-gun chattered.

Findlay's prompt braking saved them. The first bullets whipped head-high past the windscreen to bury themselves in the grassy bank. Then, as Delfont tried to correct his aim, others ricochetted off the front bumper and radiator covering.

Shand's car jerked to a standstill. Raising his head, he saw the other vehicle slowing and pulling into the side of the road a hundred yards distant.

'Outside, everybody!' he snapped, 'Behind the car!'

He did not add that the men in the overtaking vehicle had halted with the full intention of committing cold-blooded massacre before further traffic approached.

They saw Delfont jump out, holding the tommy-gun ready to sweep the space between bank and cars with bullets.

More by luck than judgment in view of the range, Sammy shot him through the chest with the big automatic. The sound of the shot slammed into Shand's ears like a cannon.

'More like level terms now,' said Findlay calmly, moving behind cover. 'That's something he didn't expect. I thought he'd got us then.'

Shand said he wasn't the only one. 'You got a gun?'

Findlay shook his head and grinned faintly. 'Not much needed in mountain-climbing.'

'Well I have – and so has Sammy.'

'I heard Sammy's,' said Findlay.

They heard it again next second when Ferret-face tried to scoop up the tommy-gun from where it lay in the drainage channel at the side of the road near their car, crawling behind Delfont's body for cover. The heavy bullet cracked past his hand like a steel whiplash, causing fingers to be hurriedly withdrawn.

Masters then tried to provide covering fire while sheltering behind the front wheels of his car, shooting parallel with the banks so that Sammy had to pull in with the others crouched behind their vehicle's luggage-boot.

'If they get that tommy-gun, it'll be all up with us,' said

Shand. He fired three times along the road beneath the axles, so that Masters did a quick double-shuffle as slugs snapped and whined about his ankles.

'Why doesn't some traffic come along?' fretted Ella.

'It's stalemate,' said Shand. 'Unless . . .'

'Yes?'

'Unless I slipped along on the offside, got in the driving seat, and used our car like a tank. You two could creep along behind it with the guns. I'd be safe because there's protection from the engine.'

Findlay jumped. 'Like a tank? Of course! Why, it's a perfect Panzer text-book manoeuvre! The lines of fire . . .'

'If I ease her along slowly.'

'One gun could enfilade there – see? Now, if Sammy . . .'

Shand, still crouching, nipped into the driver's seat. He reached up for the starter button on the dashboard, yanked the steering-wheel gear-lever into its notch, and worked the control pedals with the flat of his palms. The car moved jerkily into motion. The pedals seemed stiffer than usual.

He knew that, apart from any other advantages of the plan, the powerful engine might actually succeed, in low gear, in pushing the other vehicle along the road. Once that happened, an incautious antagonist could find himself spreadeagled over the bonnet or even under the wheels. Moreover, by the time that car had been shifted seven or eight yards, his own friends could safely acquire the tommy-gun – key to victory in any battle against opponents armed with revolvers.

Whether Lorne Masters was also something of a tank expert or merely a swift seizer of opportunities, they were not to know. He tried one or two ineffectual shots, then, seeing the way matters were developing, he yelled staccato instructions in Italian. With Ferret-face and the driver, he suddenly scrambled into the car and the vehicle roared away.

'The tyres!' yelled Shand, bobbing up to see what was happening. 'Rip his tyres!'

Sammy stood in the middle of the road emptying his automatic at the disappearing car. John Findlay grabbed the tommy-gun and, after a single trial shot, moved into position beside them to blast the remainder of the magazine along the autostrada. Except for causing spectacular avoiding action by the driver, none of the bullets seemed to take any effect.

'No luck!' said Shand, walking back slowly to where Delfont lay. The Frenchman was dead.

Findlay looked down at the corpse and shrugged. 'Better leave him here and press on, eh? You're in a hurry, anyway, and don't want to start making long-winded statements to excitable Italian police. Likewise, I'm not anxious to spoil my holiday.'

'If it were me,' said Ella, 'I'd count it spoiled anyway. What's poor George going to say when he sees his car?'

Her brother studied a row of slug holes through the side of the bonnet, with here and there bright splashes of lead where bullets had flattened themselves. He smiled ruefully. 'Perhaps he'll expect me to buy him another.'

'If the thing'll still go,' said Sammy, 'let's get out of here before anybody comes along.'

They left the autostrada at Brescia, skirting the town as far as possible by means of side roads in the hope of avoiding police, who might be curious about the damage.

Now they saw ahead of them, ghostly through the late afternoon haze, great humps of mountain ranges shining purple and white along the horizon. The road at first moved gradually upwards, then began to wind continually at a steeper angle. They reached a ridge and plunged into another broad valley, and thus they came in the early evening to San Sagrado – a town that Sammy described as 'clinging by its teeth to the hillside'.

A signpost read 'Albergo Vittorio'. Findlay swung the wheel in the direction of the arrow. 'One hotel's as good as another in these parts, I suppose. You staying the night here, Shand, or is it just a meal and drink before you press on?'

'Another seventy miles yet. Might as well finish the trip tomorrow.'

Ella sighed. 'I've had enough excitement for one day. If we're enjoying a few hours of civilisation before John takes me among the wild rocks, I'll treat you to a view of the dinner dress I picked up in Milan.'

Shand grinned. It was so long since he had smiled that his face seemed to crack. 'I'd stop for that, if nothing else.'

An hour later found him bathed, changed, and drinking whisky with Sammy and Findlay in the hotel bar. There were no other customers.

'I've had a word with the hall porter,' he said. 'He's putting out a few discreet inquiries about Masters. Handy to know if he's in town.'

John Findlay thought it unlikely. 'That is, unless he deliberately followed you here. This isn't the easiest or the most direct way to that village of yours, only it's a handy parting of the ways. I can shove off to my climbing and you can press on to – where is it? Rossanata?'

At that moment Ella came in, wearing her new evening gown. 'Like it?' she asked.

'Like it?' echoed Shand. 'Why – it's breath-taking!'

John Findlay picked up his glass. 'Not bad. How much have you got left of your travel allowance after buying the thing?'

Ella pulled a face at him and said, 'Brothers! Why, they don't even ask what a girl's drinking!'

Shand remedied the omission on Findlay's behalf, and a little later they went into the small restaurant, causing no uncertain stir among the other diners.

'My treat this time,' said Findlay when they had ended the meal.

No less a person than the manager approached while he was in the act of paying the waiter.

The manager had a scared, anxious look that he tried hard to hide, and gave quick, nodding bows all the time in an embarrassed sort of way. *'Scusi, signori* – and the *signorina,* also. But – please – would you have the goodness to visit my office? It is *importanta – molto importanta* – I am sorry to intrude – but you understand?'

'Important?' asked Shand watchfully. 'What is it? A message?'

'*Si, si* – a message, most important.'

'Who's the message for ? Need we all come?'

'All of you, please! Please – this way.'

They followed along a narrow corridor leading from the vestibule, the hall porter lurking watchfully in his glassfronted cubby-hole. The manager stopped and flung open the door.

'If you please.'

Shand paused a moment, then went in, very puzzled.

Beside the manager's desk stood two dark-complexioned Italian police officials. The senior of this pair said harshly, 'You will all come right into the room. Ciocco – guard the door!'

'The manager . . .'

'We do not require his presence. He may go. We have the hotel register here.'

He read off their names. 'Do any of you speak Italian?'

'I do,' said Shand.

'Tell your companions that I can identify all of you from these names and descriptions we have received. Charges have been laid that must be investigated.'

Shand thought fast. Charges? Throwing Lorne Masters off the train? But surely the French police could not have traced them so quickly. Was it, perhaps, a move by the still-hidden Von Grinling, seeking to delay their arrival at Rossanata by trumped-up accusations?

Yet it was neither. 'I intend to question all of you,' announced the official pompously, 'concerning the discovery of a man's body on the Milan-Brescia autostrada this afternoon. You will be well advised to tell the truth – especially as a great number of shots were fired and there are bullet-holes in your car.'

Findlay's eyebrows went up. 'Bullet-holes?'

'So you, also, speak Italian, eh? Yes, bullet-holes. The car has been brought outside this hotel. You will be shown these bullet-holes. Denial is useless. I will take preliminary statements in the presence of you all, so that any recriminations developing between yourselves may be thrashed out.' He sat down at the desk, pulled a sheaf of paper towards him, and pointed the end of his pen at Shand. 'I shall take your particulars first.'

Now the hand of Lorne Masters could be clearly seen. Shand was not prepared to admit such fast work by the Italian police. Somebody had deliberately tipped them off. And who better than one of his rivals in the race? Even if he got away with his neck, the treasure of Monte Ragazzo might be whipped away almost from beneath his nose.

There was only one thing to do. Moving to the desk, he gripped the edge and tipped it over, following the action with a headlong dive right on top of the astonished and already-winded official.

Ciocco, near the door, drew his revolver and tried to intervene. 'Do not move!' he shouted. 'Surrender, Englishman, or I will shoot!'

Then Sammy smacked him across the back of his neck with an edgewise palm, and he folded from the knees. Out came the big automatic again. 'Will you watch the door, Mr. Findlay? I'll get these two untangled.'

Shand lifted himself off the other policeman and stood up.

'Chuck across a couple of those small chairs. And find me something to tie with.' He knew from experience just how it ought to be done. He remembered the little precautionary tricks of Jules Delfont – an expert in such matters. He didn't like tying policemen up, but in the present circumstances there was no alternative. When the two of them were firmly secured he made for the door. 'Follow me,' he said. 'Try not to seem excited.'

The corridor was deserted. In the vestibule the manager conversed in whispers with the hall porter. When he saw them coming he broke off and forced a smile. 'Everything is settled satisfactorily, signor? All is well, is it not? I assured the gentlemen of the police that some dreadful mistake had occurred, but naturally it is their duty to investigate.'

'They wish to remain in your office a little longer,' said Shand. 'They ask not to be disturbed. Their work is important and complicated, you understand. There are many papers.'

'Of course, of course,' said the manager. 'How excellent that you may now continue to enjoy your holiday. A glass of wine perhaps, to restore you?'

Shand yawned. 'It is a warm and pleasant evening. We will take the air for a while.'

'But of course. *Buona sera, signorina. Buona sera, signori.*'

'I'll get my wrap,' said Ella.

They strolled past the potted palms and through the small revolving door that was the hotel's particular pride.

'There's the car,' said Findlay. 'Nobody guarding it. Where the devil's Ella got to?'

Shand shrugged. 'If we're making a break for it – as I imagine we are – she'll need something more than the outfit she's wearing now.'

Findlay fidgeted uneasily. 'So long as she doesn't stop for a complete change.'

It was a nerve-racking few minutes for them, standing there waiting for Ella, and every moment half expecting to hear cries for help coming fom the manager's office.

Sammy asked: 'How long do you get in jail for socking an Italian cop?'

Then, at last, the door whirled again, and Ella came towards them, still wearing her evening dress but with a fringed shawl across her shoulders.

'All right?' breathed Shand.

None among the passers-by took much notice of the party entering the car. It seemed quite normal.

'Round the corner to the right,' said Ella. 'There's a back way to the hotel along an alley. I've put our suitcases there. Yours, too, Shand; I hope you don't mind.'

Findlay beamed. 'First sensible thing I've known you do.'

Within five minutes they had collected their luggage and were almost out of the town. They did not rush, though, in case it drew attention to themselves. As Shand said, it was an occasion for making haste slowly. Shand was always right.

'I'll need some more petrol soon,' said Findlay. 'Garages on the main road may have been warned.'

Their map showed a lane leading to a couple of villages and by-passing the highway. Once beyond San Sagrado, the car speeded up, its headlights cutting a tunnel through the darkness.

Then they came to a village and Shand spotted a notice: *Benzine. Essenza.* They pulled up outside a tiny garage and a big, unshaven man came out to ask what they wanted. He spoke in German.

Shand realised then with something of a shock how far they had travelled. Here, this side of San Sagrado, the local populace were bi-lingual, having German as a mother tongue from the years when the area formed part of the Austro-Hungarian Empire. He realised, too, that because French, Italian and German were the three other languages he spoke, this was probably why Trensham had selected him for the assignment in the first place.

'Petrol,' he said. 'How much can you let us have?' He peered around in vain for sight of a pump.

'Enough to get you over the border,' grunted the man. He paused significantly. 'If you get that far.'

He hauled out some cans, motioning Shand to give him a hand.

While the petrol was being poured, the man said. 'Getting cold – especially in the mountains.'

'Oh?'

'I can let you have a bonnet-cover cheap. One in the shed will fit this car nicely. Keep the engine warm' – his eyes sought Shand's in the dim light – 'and prevent people seeing bullet-holes.'

Shand straightened up and looked at the man with some suspicion. 'Why are you offering to help, instead of 'phoning for the police?' Shand was doubtful of the man's intentions.

The man spat. 'We're supposed to be Italians – only we don't admit it to ourselves. I'm no friend of the Italian police.' He spat again and went to fetch the bonnet-cover.

'Take the Migado road,' he said coming back. 'You'll find it on your map. Once you hit that you'll be safe. They won't have the barriers out so far away.'

'Thanks,' said Shand.

'Don't mention it.' He spat for the third time. 'These Italians . . .'

Shand got into the seat beside Findlay. 'You know what's happened?'

The car moved off. 'Found a friend in need, I imagine.'

'The Migado road runs the other side of Rossanata from the way we intended to go in.'

Findlay nodded. 'Good enough.'

During the next hour of strenuous driving over narrow roads winding through the mountains they met only two other cars. Now the night air had a bite in it. Wind laden with frost funnelled into the valleys, and they were all glad of extra clothing from the valises Ella had hurriedly assembled.

'Look here,' said Shand, 'we owe you quite a debt already – we mustn't ask too much. What are you going to do? Try to make Austria before dawn? Don't get into any more trouble on our account.'

Findlay's eyes followed the row of small white posts marking a sheer drop. The lights obediently followed his swing of the wheel to light up a horizontal cliff on the offside. 'We'll take you to Rossanata, anyway.'

Shand saw Ella Findlay's frightened expression. Probably her nerve was giving way. Most other girls would have cracked up already.

During the next hour they gradually traversed a huge shoulder of mountain clad in gloomy pine forests. When Findlay brought the car round the last winding hairpin of road which never ran straight for more than fifty yards, they found themselves looking down upon a long narrow valley. A river running the length of it reflected the moonlight like a silvery thread. And at the far end could be seen the dim, dominating outline of the Monte Ragazzo.

A thick drizzle started to come down, and the monotonous tick-tock of the windscreen wipers made them feel drowsy, despite the cold. Only John Findlay remained alert at the wheel, as the car continued along the narrow, slippery road.

Then, at last, the drizzle cleared and they came in sight of the village of Rossanata, nestling at the foot of Monte Ragazzo.

From the driving-seat, Findlay called, 'Wake up, one and all! Journey's end in sight – for Shand and Sammy, anyhow.'

'We – we're not going down there with them?' Ella Findlay's voice held unmistakable tones of relief.

'Better not,' said Shand. 'The local police might happen to know about us.'

'Poor look-out for you if they do, isn't it?'

'We'll manage somehow. We can walk from here.' He grinned ruefully. 'Not much luggage to carry.'

Findlay rustled the map under the dashboard light. He stabbed a forefinger. 'There's a village along this side road about twelve miles north-east. I'll test the atmosphere there. If nothing's been heard about us we'll carry on normally into Austria.'

'And if it has?'

He grinned. 'We'll leave George's car for someone to pick up and go over the mountain frontier in the dark. Nice to have known you, Shand. Best of luck.'

The words were echoed by Ella from the lowered window as the two agents walked away. 'Good luck.'

It wasn't difficult to locate the mayor's office. A small electric lantern, held in a bow-shaped iron frame, burned at the foot of a small flight of steps and lit up a brass plate which announced the mayor's name as Ettore Perera.

'Wonder if he's still expecting us, or if he's in bed?' said Shand. He prodded the bell-push.

After a moment or two a light went on somewhere in the house, and through the glass panels a figure could be seen approaching. A key was turned, a bolt withdrawn, and a chain unhitched.

The man who opened the door was very large, and sported a correspondingly large moustache. He also wore his tunic of office, which was decorated with various insignia. He spoke in Italian. 'Signor Shand?' They could interpret nothing from the tone of the voice. 'Please to come in. We have been expecting you.'

Confronting them stood a policeman with a levelled revolver.

They climbed the steps, moved along the passage, and entered the room which was obviously the mayor's office. There was a desk of oak blackened by incredible age, covered with papers. On the side table stood a carafe and glasses.

And immediately confronting them stood a policeman with levelled revolver, who said, 'Raise your hands. You are under arrest for the murder of Jules Delfont on the autostrada between Milan and Brescia. There will also be charges concerning violence towards the police at San Sagrado, where you are to be taken immediately!'

The Face of Blood

Shand felt slightly sick, yet the sharp edge of disappointment was missing. Ever since San Sagrado he had known inwardly that the chances of success were small. Two men – minus friends and with all the resources of law enforcement squads against them – could not hope to hold out. And while he rotted in some stinking cell, either Lorne Masters or Von Grinling might locate the golden hoard which lay somewhere in the black mass of mountain they had reached after so desperate and uncertain a journey.

He stared at the revolver and slowly raised his hands. Sammy did the same.

The gigantic figure of the mayor stumped across to his desk. He never once went anywhere near the watchful carabiniere's line of fire. He regarded them sorrowfully from bleary grey eyes.

His voice was gruff and booming. 'Sit down, gentlemen. Then you will be less tempted to make a rush for Giuglielmo's revolver. I wish to speak to you informally for a moment. Do you understand German?'

'I do,' said Shand, 'and my friend knows a little.'

'Good. Italian is our official language, but among ourselves we use German.' He extended a huge hand for the carafe. 'A little wine?' He filled generous glasses. 'And now, Herr Shand, may I express regret at the manner of our reception. Nevertheless, orders are orders. Was it really necessary to employ violence against the police at San Sagrado?'

Shand wondered for a moment whether this might be a clever means of extorting a confession. Not that there was much purpose in denial. 'Yes,' he admitted. 'It was.'

The mayor nodded slowly. 'A pity.' He sighed noisily through the moustache. 'Your work here would have been a boon to us. This mining concession might have meant great things.' He noted Shand's expression. 'You seem surprised. I was given to understand you were a mining engineer.'

An inner voice told Shand, 'Go carefully. This big man's no fool.' Aloud he said, 'Moves have been taking place behind my back. All I know is that I came here to see you on orders from my superiors.'

The mayor nodded and heaved himself to his feet. From a locked iron box that served as a safe for official documents he withdrew a long parchment bearing elaborate seals. 'Here is a concession granted to your company for mineral exploration over a wide area of Monte Ragazzo. The cases of machinery have preceded your arrival. They are quite heavy, weighing several tons. They are in store at a suitable place outside the village. Now, alas, there will be delays. We will have to wait for our new prosperity – and we are a poor community.'

What the devil was Trensham's idea? Concessions? Mining machinery?

'Still,' continued the mayor, 'duty is duty. The law must take its course.' He came round the desk towards them. 'No, do not get up until I give you permission. Keep your revolver ready Giuglielmo. I shall have to search you, gentlemen, in the prescribed manner.'

Shand stood and held up his arms. Only then did he realise how little he had slept in the past forty-eight hours. He was glad when the big man had taken all papers and belongings from his inside pockets so that he might let his arms and shoulders sag once more.

The contents made quite a miscellaneous heap on the desk. After sorting through them with quick fingers, the mayor produced a linen-reinforced envelope into which he placed the items one by one. 'These shall be listed and returned to you later. We are honest folk in Rossanata. You need have no fear on that score.' He shook out Shand's wallet. 'Except, possibly, for the excellent automatic pistol.'

Then he found the little gold medallion. He stared at it silently for one long moment.

'Where did you get this?' he demanded hoarsely. 'Who are you?' His discovery of the talisman had clearly altered the situation for him. He sat down again at his desk and seemed to deflate.

There was a full half-minute of bewildered silence.

At length the mayor said quietly, 'Put that pistol away, Giuglielmo. These gentlemen are our guests. You have never seen them. Understand?'

He left the room and they heard his great voice bawling somewhere at the rear of the building. 'Gerda! Get out of bed and prepare some food!'

The mayor returned. 'Come this way, gentlemen. Everything in my house is at your disposal. A meal will be ready soon. After that you might like to rest a while.'

Shand never believed in questioning good fortune. He looked at his watch. It was 1.35 a.m. With luck he might get his head down by two o'clock.

They were ushered into a room crammed with enormous

items of furniture, all highly polished. The mayor set down more wine on the spotless tablecloth. 'Please – allow me to help you. The food is coming. Only simple fare, I'm afraid.' He made no further mention of the little gold medallion.

The simple fare turned out to be an assortment of olives, cold sausage, smoked fish, an enormous ham, a large dish of sizzling eggs, and a bowl of fruit. There was also brandy and coffee.

Afterwards, they were escorted to an upstairs room containing two deep, bolstered feather-beds. Shand's head touched the pillow and – instantly – he knew no more.

It was broad daylight when he woke. Little bright splinters of sunshine found their way between shutters over the window, and when he got out of bed to throw them open the brilliance of the afternoon sun struck him almost like a physical blow. Rolling fields on the outskirts of Rossanata lay heavy beneath the heat, giving way in the distance to wooded hills, and there – like a vast painted backcloth occupying fully half the view – stood the mass of snow-topped Monte Ragazzo.

Sammy stirred in the light, sat up and rubbed his eyes.

There was a knock on the door, bringing momentary alarm.

'Who's there?'

A girl outside said, 'Breakfast, *meine Herren*.' She came in, bearing a heavy tray. 'Please to meet the Herr Burgomeister when you are ready.'

They found the mayor in the room where they had eaten the night before. The inevitable tray bearing carafe and glasses decorated the broad table.

'We shall be more comfortable here, gentlemen, than in my office,' said Perera. 'And more private.' He stroked the ends of his moustache with a flourish. 'Now tell me what I can do for you.'

'We're looking for a man who is well known in Rossanata.

His name is Corranzi – Zorrio Corranzi.'

'Ah!' Perera's huge head nodded knowingly. 'Of course, of course.'

'Where can we find him?'

Two large hands spread themselves. 'He left the village towards the end of April. People believe he headed for the mountain. No one has seen him since.'

Shand moistened his lips. He had to pick his way carefully once more. Any mention of treasure – hidden somewhere in this neighbourhood in circumstances well known to all inhabitants – would undoubtedly bring further competitors into the field. Including, maybe, the dreaded, mysterious Children of the Dolomites.

'Could he be living somewhere on the mountain?'

The mayor nodded again. 'Some believe that to be so.' A peculiar look came into his eye. 'Including a stranger who entered the village soon after dawn with a similar inquiry. He and his companions bought ropes, boots, and blankets. They left three hours ago, also taking food with them.'

Shand sprang to his feet. 'This man – what did he look like? Please try and describe him to me in exact detail.'

Before the mayor had uttered more than two or three sentences, Shand knew the stranger to be Masters. 'Does anyone live on the mountain who might have seen Zorrio?'

'There is, of course, the Mad Hermit.' He raised a soothing palm. 'He is not really mad, of course – merely eccentric. I believe his real name is Maccario. Our people have seen him in the distance occasionally. Frankly, gentlemen, he is something of a mystery. Our policeman, Giuglielmo, wonders from time to time where his food comes from. Also, there is the question of his survival during severe weather. Yet he does not bother us, so we do not bother him.' He shrugged. 'In any case, it is doubtful whether Giuglielmo could catch him. Maccario knows Monte

Ragazzo better than any living soul. You would indeed have a valuable ally if you could persuade him to help in your search for the silver ore.'

Sammy looked at Shand with his customary blankness, yet his cold eye spoke volumes.

'This stranger,' continued the mayor. 'He has no right whatever to attempt prospecting work. Your concession provides exclusive privileges.'

'Where can we get ropes, boots, and blankets?' demanded Shand.

'I have sufficient here. May I ask whether it is your intention to pursue the intruder? I can supply guides and other helpers. There is also Giuglielmo.'

'Thank you – but we had better go alone, I think.'

Perera shrugged. 'As you wish, gentlemen. At least let me drive you as far as the mountain.'

Perera's car was old and noisy, but it moved swiftly enough with the mayor at the wheel. He had changed his tunic for more serviceable dress.

Once they had left Rossanata, Shand began to survey the landscape. High on the first slopes of the mountain rested a tiny hamlet where the partisans had planned their ambush; beyond that a narrow road along which the gold convoy must have escaped after hiding the treasure. Somewhere in this region they would have to seek any trails leading into wilder territory towards the snowline. He craned his neck still more. Through the hot, clear air the eternal ice looked surprisingly near.

Perera drove along the track across a wider road, always onwards and upwards. He half-turned in the driving-seat as they passed the broader thoroughfare. 'This is an extension of the Migado road. It leads eventually to the frontier – to Switzerland.' He shrugged his shoulders. 'It may be of no particular importance, of course – but I mention it.'

'Thanks,' said Shand, understanding very well.

When they had got through the hamlet the track petered out altogether, and the mayor brought his car to a halt. 'From here on, gentlemen, you must proceed on foot. The packs contain all you require for two days. It will be cold when the sun goes down, but there is a small alcohol stove, and you have good blankets.' He shook hands solemnly. 'Beyond that first spur lies a cabin for climbers, where anyone on the mountain may shelter. You will reach it well before dusk. Good luck.'

He stood looking after them for several minutes, until they disappeared into the undergrowth.

Climbing proved to be warm work, even though Shand and Sammy took matters gently. In the early stages they had no need to do more than walk. Without much difficulty they found ways which led them upwards, constantly upwards, towards the great, overhanging shoulder of rock. They paused for half an hour to open one of the mayor's parcels – cold chicken, ham, cheese, a bottle of wine and peaches – before pressing on.

By eight o'clock they heaved weary bodies over a rocky ridge to find themselves gazing into a shallow depression some quarter of a mile across, at the far side of which the ascent proper of Monte Ragazzo began. The hut of which Perera had spoken lay in the middle of the grassy basin, beside a mountain stream. Inside, the wooden building provided a single room, with half a dozen bunks.

'Lay out the blankets,' said Shand. 'This is as far as we go tonight.'

They awoke to another blue sky, with clouds to the south as hard and white as cauliflowers. The air was chilly from a frosty dawn, and the stream in which they washed, fed by melting snow, set them shivering.

Sammy made coffee on the little spirit stove, and then they went inside the hut to pack.

Coming out, loaded with rucksacks and blankets, they found visitors. A young peasant in ragged clothes had brought a herd of about fifteen goats and a couple of mules to crop the rough grass near by. He stood looking at them until they passed within a few yards.

'*Buon giorno*,' said Shand.

The youth did not reply, but touched his cap in half-hearted salute.

He tried another language. '*Grüss Gott*. A fine morning.'

The answer came in slurred dialect. 'You're late to make Matzenhof Ledge before nightfall, gentlemen.'

'Matzenhof? Where's that?'

'Just above the snow-line. Some of it is sliding, they say.'

Shand went up to him.

'We're strangers. Is the mountain difficult to climb?'

'All depends,' was the reply. 'Maybe 'tis and maybe 'tisn't. All depends.'

'What if anybody isn't used to climbing?'

'Still depends – depends whether they can go where a mule can go. That's good enough – unless you want the very top – above Matzenhof. Then it is more difficult climbing.'

Sammy fidgeted impatiently. 'What's he talking about? I can't follow these dialects.'

'Matzenhof Ledge will do us,' said Shand. 'Thank you.'

'Them others'll get there first.'

Shand looked at him sharply. 'Others? What others?'

'I see 'em on the South Face nearly two hours ago. Four of 'em there were – going strong.'

Masters! It couldn't be anyone else! Had he found some clue? Otherwise, why should his party be climbing so purposefully?

'Did you know these men? Had you seen them before?'

The youth shook his head from side to side. 'Too far away.'

Shand tried another tack. 'Do you know Zorrio Corranzi? From Rossanata?'

'Oh, yes. 'Tweren't him.'

'Have you seen Zorrio lately?'

A pause. Then slowly, 'No. Not since last summer.' The crafty, half-scared look in his eyes showed that he lied.

'There's someone else on this mountain – an old man named Maccario. They call him the Mad Hermit. Ever heard of him?'

The eyes went blank. The head shook again from side to side. 'No.'

Shand persisted, 'Other people in Rossanata have heard about him. Why not you?'

The young peasant began to back away.

'Come here!' cried Shand. 'Ever seen one of these before?' He let the gold medallion dangle from his forefinger on its fine chain.

The goatherd's jaw dropped. Then he fell to his knees. 'I didn't know who you were!' he babbled. 'I didn't know, I tell you! Have mercy, gracious sir! Please – I didn't know.'

'Get up!' said Shand. 'Stop that nonsense! We won't hurt you. Tell us what we want – and you can shove off back to your goats.'

'Maccario's got a hut in a cleft near the South Face. Every summer he goes up into the mountain when the snow melts. It's three weeks since he was down here last. That's the truth, noble sir! I swear it. Zorrio I saw two days ago.'

Shand's heart leapt. 'Two days? Where?'

'On the South Face. He'd got ropes and blankets – please may I go now?'

'Yes, you can go now,' said Shand. 'If you see Zorrio, tell the mayor at Rossanata. Apart from Herr Perera, none must know we passed this way. Understand?'

'Yes, gracious Herr.'

They set off again. 'He's not so dumb as he looks,' said Sammy.

Shand's lips formed themselves into a tight grin. 'He's been well brought up – by the Children of the Dolomites!'

After that they saved their breath for climbing. Despite one or two false moves, they found the goatherd's words to be true – always a route existed which they could take without actual climbing, although one particular stretch of the way towards the South Face was no more than a narrow ledge of rock above a breath-taking precipice into which, after a first apprehensive glance, they dared not look. Spread beyond them, thousands of feet below, was the pine-filled valley down which they had travelled with John and Ella Findlay in the car, the winding river still shining as a silver thread.

'You could sit down,' said Sammy, his round face shining with sweat, 'and think you were in an aeroplane.'

'Don't use too much imagination,' grunted Shand, 'or you'll begin wanting to go into a power-dive.'

Despite frequent pauses for observation, they saw no other climbers, either above or below them. Still the trail wound onwards and upwards. The grass became thinner and sparser, while above them now loomed great, bare rocks – and, higher still, the snow which marked the Matzenhof Ledge.

Every time they reached a sizable ridge, outcrop, or spur, the two men paused to survey the scene. Suddenly Shand pointed.

'Down there!' he whispered. 'Inside that cleft! It's a hut of some kind. Looks like odd bits of crates and a few petrol tins.'

Nothing stirred in the crisp, silent air.

'Stay here,' he said. 'I'm going down.'

Shand slithered as silently as possible into the cleft, pausing every few yards to look and listen. Sammy, lying with his head over the edge, watched him reach the bottom and creep cautiously towards the hut.

A pause. Then Shand went inside.

He was gone so long that Sammy decided to follow. At the open door he met Shand coming out. Shand looked white and shaken.

Inside the rough hut, Sammy could see a man lying upon a heap of rags that apparently served for a bed. A certain amount of light entered through a displaced board high in the wall, enough to show that he was dead.

'Who is he? Maccario?'

Shand shook his head. 'He's not wearing the right sort of clothes for a mad hermit. Besides, I took this off his wrist.' He held up a metal identification bracelet, either of silver or some nickel-plated metal. 'The name's Zorrio Corranzi!'

'I suppose Masters' lot killed him?'

'They did something of the kind to his brother, Carlo, didn't they?' said Shand. What really worried him was whether Zorrio had talked before he died.

If he did talk, thought Shand, other people were probably speeding now towards the hidden treasure . . .

The Marksman Hits the Target

Screwing up his eyes against the glare, Shand looked across the mountain. No tiny figures were visible toiling towards the Matzenhof Ledge. Nevertheless, somewhere along there lay the goal – a cleft, a cave, or even a mere hollow in the rocks where lay eight million pounds in gold.

He looked back the way they had come. The base of Monte Ragazzo hid both Rossanata and the nearer hamlet from view, but far beneath he could just see the hut, set in a speck of green, where they had spent the night. Where, too, the emblem belonging to the Children of the Dolomites had for a second time demonstrated its peculiar power. He recollected how the young peasant had reacted when he was shown the medallion.

What was it the lad had said? 'Depends whether you can go where mules can go . . .' One part of the puzzle was as good as solved. At some point between the scene of the intended ambush and one of those tracks leading up the mountainside the cases of gold must have been unloaded and transported by mulepack!

The major point remaining was this – did the gold still lie there? He wondered whether Maccario's hut might be made from the wooden casing of the boxes holding the bullion. In which case, where was the treasure now?

Sammy seemed to be thinking along the same lines. 'Is it any good going on with the search?' he asked. 'Zorrio was our only hope.'

Shand paused and scratched his chin thoughtfully. 'We can stick on Masters' trail. He and his crowd know something. They aren't going to all the trouble of climbing to the Matzenhof Ledge for the fun of it.'

'Ah, well,' said Sammy philosophically, 'press on, then.'

Clouds now descended from the rugged mountain-top, and the sun disappeared. Soon they were moving through a thick mist, and within the hour Shand was forced to admit that nothing more could be done until the weather cleared.

'It's turning to rain,' said Sammy, and shivered.

'Maybe there's an overhanging rock somewhere that'll keep us dry.'

For thirty minutes they squatted within a rocky little cell they discovered, talking seldom and staring into the cold grey curtain hanging a few yards distant.

'Listen?' said Sammy suddenly. 'Hear that?'

'Hear what?'

'Boots – on the stones – coming nearer.'

Their ears, straining against the damp, shivery silence, heard a scrape and slither of pebbles.

Shand held his revolver at the ready.

'Two of 'em!' whispered Sammy. 'I'm sure of it.'

Feet crunched nearer. A dim figure, magnified by the mist, loomed up outside their hiding-place.

'Well, well!' said John Findlay, staring with amusement at the gun. 'What a reception!' Rucksack and rope were on his shoulders, together with expertly folded blanket roll.

'You!' said Shand. 'You!'

'That's right – me and Ella.'

'Hello,' she said brightly, emerging from the outer fog. 'Phew! Closed down a bit, hasn't it!' She wore some kind of ski-ing outfit, with dark-blue slacks tucked into heavy boots, a windproof jacket, and little woolly hat.

'But,' said Shand, 'we thought you were in Austria.'

Findlay grinned. 'As a matter of fact, we got rather cut off from the frontier post we were aiming at. Italian police telephones are more efficient than you'd think.'

'I know,' said Shand grimly.

'We were in quite a tight spot for a time.' He slipped the pack from his shoulders. 'Still, I said I wouldn't go back without a spot of climbing – and here we are!' He laughed rather ruefully. 'Matter of fact, after driving round and round the district it got quite obvious it was the only place we could go.'

'Lucky to find us,' said Shand, 'in this mist.'

'Not luck – we saw you from lower down. I'd picked this place out in case of a rainstorm, and wondered if you'd have sense enough to make for it when the cloud dropped.'

'Seen anything of Lorne Masters?'

Findlay's eyebrows went up. 'Is he here, too?'

Shand nodded. 'Three others with him – somewhere higher up on a piece of mountain they call the Matzenhof Ledge.'

'Seeing that we're here,' said Ella, 'and likely to be for another hour if I'm any judge, how about trying to get a fire going for some coffee. Can we find some dry wood?'

With a wink at Sammy, Shand opened another of the mayor's parcels. 'No need for a fire. We've got a spirit stove. And a little food.'

He set out thick slices of roast pork, olives, smoked salmon, frankfurter sausages and potato salad, pears, and grapes. There was also the inevitable bottle of wine.

'Well!' said Findlay admiringly. 'You been burgling a hotel party?' He moistened his lips. 'I don't mind admitting we haven't eaten very well in the last twenty-four hours.'

By the time the meal was finished the mist had begun to lighten. Through gaps in the grey, swirling vapour dark glimpses of the distant valley appeared momentarily.

'This is a bit of luck for us as well as you,' said Shand. 'You're at home on mountains. Will you help us catch Masters?'

Findlay sighed gently. 'After a meal like that I'll run him right up to the top and throw him off if you say so.'

'Last we heard of him and his companions they were climbing the South Face; but the mist must have stopped them, too.'

'Climbing?' Findlay looked surprised. 'Why, I had a look at the place through my glasses, and anybody except a cripple could walk it easily.'

Mentally, Shand cursed himself for failing to foresee the need for binoculars.

'I'll probably call it climbing,' said Sammy plaintively.

Ella laughed. 'You can hold my hand.'

They set off through the last wraiths of disappearing mist. The blue-grey slopes of Monte Ragazzo were bathed in sunshine again.

'Careful on the damp places,' said Findlay. 'Easy to slip.'

The snow-line now seemed very near. From time to time, in suitably sheltered spots, they paused to scan the rocky shoulders and clefts for signs of movement. 'The Matzenhof Ledge is round the other side,' Findlay explained. 'See the big circular shelf with all the snow? That's the way in.'

'Good!' puffed Sammy. 'I don't think I can keep up this pace much longer.'

Findlay grinned again. 'We won't make it tonight! It's a lot farther off than you'd think. There ought to be a chalet somewhere around – except that Masters' crowd are probably in possession.' He cocked an eyebrow. 'Want to fight 'em for it?'

More and more Shand began to thank his lucky stars that Findlay had caught up with them. 'We shall freeze solid if we stay in the open,' he said.

'Not with experienced mountaineers like us to arrange matters,' Ella replied briskly. 'It's happened before – and it's not as though we were up here in mid-winter.'

Half an hour later Findlay spotted a suitably sheltered corner, where he and Ella quickly roped into place an assortment of waterproof sheets and blankets for an efficient tent.

With everyone inside and the spirit stove boiling water for coffee, it soon grew warm enough to throw off the heavier clothing that had protected them from the chill of the fog.

'Nice piece of sheepskin,' said Findlay, fingering Shand's borrowed jacket. 'Natty colour, too. You certainly did all right for yourself in Rossanata.'

Shand laughed. 'We found some more friends, all right.'

'To tell you the truth,' said Findlay rubbing his hands expectantly, 'I wouldn't mind another bite of their grub and a mouthful of their brandy.'

Supper over, they rinsed the plates in a pool fed by a stream some thirty yards away, while a brilliant red sunset spread across the sky.

Shand woke suddenly while it was still quite dark. Within

the tent someone moved, making slight, furtive sounds and breathing audibly. He remained still, collecting his senses.

The blanket flap was raised, providing a momentary glimpse of a frozen sky studded with a million hard, glittering stars. Against their faintly glowing, haphazard pattern a form became silhouetted. Then the flap dropped noiselessly into place and the tent was plunged into darkness again.

He wondered who it might be. Sammy, perhaps? Or Findlay?

Unable to settle, Shand wriggled from beneath the covers and slipped outside.

He kept low to the ground, hoping for a sight of any moving shape against the dim skyline. He saw someone passing near the little pool and followed silently. The form appeared again for a second, then was gone.

He crept to the pool. The silence was broken only by the sound of the stream.

Then a soft slithering noise on the rock behind – like the sinister rustling of a snake – brought him wheeling round in sudden alarm. The blow meant for the back of his head glanced across his jaw. It was followed by the impact of a hurtling body that sent him stumbling.

He saw the black water before him, and thought with his last shreds of consciousness, 'If I go in, you go in, too!'

Together they plunged into the icy water.

The man who answered the description of Ferret-face flapped his arms trying to flog a little warmth into his skinny, trembling frame. Between chattering teeth, he said 'Blimey! I wouldn't go through another blasted night like that for all the gold in South Africa.'

'Stop squealing,' said Lorne Masters. 'At least you had a roof over your head.'

'Not most of the night, I didn't. You had me outside the hut with a gun in case that so-and-so Shand came along.'

The girl who had once been known as Margo Corranzi looked round at him. 'Shut up! What's a little snow matter?'

Where they crouched in the early morning light on the Matzenhof Ledge the snow lay thick, wet, and heavy. Immediately below them was the bare side of the mountain – a steep slope broken only by a rough gully zigzagging across the South Face, and after that another almost perpendicular drop into the pine-filled valley far, far below. Above their heads the rock rose at a less acute angle towards the summit of Monte Ragazzo, forming a great snow-laden escarpment which merged another five or six hundred feet higher with the eternal ice.

'Get that shiver-and-shake out of your system,' said Masters, 'else you won't be able to hold the gun steady. Macarrio's told you where to wait. It's the only way he can reach here.' He turned to a patient figure, huddled in ragged blankets, which squatted nearby. 'Isn't that right, Maccario?'

The man's face, burnt almost black by fierce mountain sunshine, split across in a white-toothed grin. '*Si, si,* that's right.' He held out a hand. 'And afterwards, signor, you will give me a share of the gold?'

Masters slapped him on the back and guffawed. 'You can fill your hat with it!'

Ferret-face sneered. 'I thought it was silver – thirty pieces.'

'Get that rifle!' snapped Masters. 'If it wasn't for this old man we'd never find the gold at all. He's told you what Shand looks like. Get down there and wait. Don't let him get nearer than four hundred yards, or he'll be able to take cover in the rocks. There'll only be time for one shot as it is.' He looked menacingly at Ferret-face. 'One shot – you won't miss, will you?'

Ferret-face didn't like it when Masters stared at him like that. 'No – no,' he muttered. 'I won't miss.'

Master straightened up and dismissed the matter. 'Meanwhile, the rest of us can try digging through to this cave. Come on.'

Maccario, the girl, and the beetle-browed car-driver last seen on the Milan-Brescia autostrada all picked up small axes and spades before they followed him.

For no apparent reason, Sammy jerked into wakefulness. Where the outer blanket had hung there was a gap through which the stars could be seen. Their dim light ought to have shown vague, dark humps of three people sleeping; instead a curious flatness met his straining gaze. He was alone, shivering, in the little makeshift tent.

He threw off the covers and ventured into the open. To his right the moon was about to rise over the rugged slopes of Monte Ragazzo. Uneasiness gripped him. He hauled out the automatic and, gun in hand, began to creep silently round the rocks, the night air damp and icy on his face.

Nothing moved in that stillness before the dawn. The only sound was the trickling of the tiny stream.

Sammy went cautiously around, methodically, quartering the area and keeping careful watch on the gradually lightening sky but seeing nothing.

It seemed to grow colder. Within a matter of minutes the moon-glow brightened, reflecting his breath as wisps of vapour. Then he saw Shand lying at the water's edge – a black blur against the dark ground.

There was only one way to get the soaked, chilled body back to shelter. Sammy just grabbed Shand under the armpits and dragged.

Once inside the tent, he stripped off waterlogged clothing, poured nearly a tumblerful of brandy between lips blue with cold, and scrubbed vigorously with a rough towel.

Then he wrapped Shand in several thicknesses of blanket and

lit the stove.

The first sign of returning life came with the third sip of bitter, steaming coffee. Shand shivered violently and choked. Then he opened his eyes and said ungratefully, 'What are you trying to do? Scald me to death?'

'Which way would you like it?' retorted Sammy. 'Frozen or boiled?'

Shand sat up and the blankets fell away. 'Hey – how did I get like this?'

'Don't be bashful. I dragged you in from beside the pond and gave you a rub down.'

Shand touched his sore skin gingerly. 'What did you use? Wire wool? Thanks, anyway. More to the point – who chucked me in?'

'Didn't you get a look at him?'

Shand shook his head.

Thoughtfully, Sammy said, 'Might have been the same lot who've kidnapped the Findlays.'

Shand jumped up.

'Lie back,' said Sammy, shoving him down again. 'Ask me, you're in for a dose of pneumonia. Anyway, pneumonia or not, you can't do anything till it gets light. Might as well take a nap.'

Shand grimaced at him through the gloom. 'How did they get the Findlays without waking you?'

'I dunno. Quite a lot seems to have been going on.'

'How long before the sun gets up?'

'About three hours. Here – get some more hot coffee inside you and have a spot of shut-eye.'

Sammy piled all the spare blankets on him, and Shand lay back, secretly thankful, knowing that the coming day would need all his strength.

Ferret-face lay in a crevice of wet rock looking down on

the approach to Matzenhof Ledge. There was a stretch of about twenty yards without cover – a spot where a man approaching in the normal way would have to remain in full view for more than a quarter of a minute. The rifle was sighted at five hundred yards. It was going to be a piece of cake. Lucky there weren't any bushes or grass to speak of – otherwise Shand's sage-green sheepskin jacket might not show up clearly. But there was a gap – half against grey rock, half against plain sky. He couldn't miss.

Ferret-face caught his breath. He jammed the binoculars once more to pink-rimmed eyes. He could have sworn something moved beyond the outlying spur of rock.

He set down the glasses, and snuggled the rifle butt into his shoulder, fixing the sights on the spot where a man might first expect to appear.

With feet moving methodically over loose stones, Shand came into view toiling up the slope.

Ferret-face lowered the sights slightly and took first pressure on the trigger. He was sweating now. He held his breath, aiming an inch in front of the green jacket's right shoulder.

Something like a gigantic steel whip slashed across the mountainside. Shand stumbled and fell on his face.

Ferret-face rose with that feeling of certainty which comes to all experienced marksmen when a good shot has been fired.

'Got the so-and-so!' he said triumphantly.

Cave of Coins

Lorne Masters moved cautiously forward with Maccario. Facing the ledge along which they made their way, the mountainside rose steeply to the summit. Here and there falls of snow blocked the stony path, so that often they had to dig before climbing over icy debris.

Maccario suddenly halted and sniffed the air like an animal.

He looked around him. 'Here – I think it is near here.'

'Better be sure,' Masters said. 'We don't want a lot of work for nothing.'

But the hermit nodded his head. 'It is here – yes. I am sure.'

'You'd better be. All right, the rest of you grab the axes.'

Bright blades and spikes dug into the frozen wall, dislodging first snow, then flakes of slatey stone. But by the time they had cleared ten yards or so it was obvious that they had come up against solid rock.

Breathing hard, Masters signalled for work to stop. 'What's the idea, you old fool?' he shouted at Maccario.

'Signore! Please! It – it must be here. I saw them at this very spot – with these eyes!'

'We've only your word for it. How do we know you're not playing some deep game?'

'I do not deceive you, signore.' Maccario turned to the girl. 'Signorina! I would not deceive anyone.'

'All right then,' said Masters. 'We'll try a bit further on. If there's no result there, we'll give this scruffy old fool a spot of treatment. That'll make him liven his wits up.'

At that moment there was the sharp sound of a single rifle shot from further down the mountain.

'That's it!' Masters exclaimed. 'He's done it. He's got Shand!'

Only seconds after came the rumble of falling stones and rock a little way along the ledge, followed by excited shouts. Masters and the girl ran back towards the other. Loose boulders and gravel littered the snow, while a dark hole had appeared in the side of the rock.

'So this is the place!' cried Masters. The girl stepped forward in her excitement. 'Wait!' he continued. 'I'm the one who's going in first! But before any of us do anything, let's take a few sensible precautions. Bring a candle for me to light. If it goes out when I hold it by the entrance, we'll know there's bad air in there.'

While they were lighting a candle, Ferret-face returned. The first few moments of excitement he had felt after shooting Shand had given way to apprehension, even fear. He was now a murderer – and the rest of the gang all knew it. A man as unscrupulous as Lorne Masters wouldn't hesitate to hold that fact against him if it suited his purposes.

'You got him, then,' said Masters. It was a statement rather than a question.

Ferret-face nodded in a subdued way. 'Aye, I got 'im.'

'You don't seem so pleased about it, though,' commented Masters. 'Afraid his partner might catch up with you one day?'

'I ain't afraid of nothing,' snarled Ferret-face. 'Nor nobody – not even you!' Then his jaw dropped as he saw the gap in the mountainside. 'You found it? Is the gold there?'

'We're just going to have a look.'

Masters squeezed into the tunnel. The air inside smelt musty, cold and damp. Moving cautiously, he found that the way widened abruptly, so that after a few steps he could walk in a crouching fashion.

After eight or nine yards the tunnel floor dropped abruptly by fully two feet. Masters rocked on his heels, trying to maintain his balance. He kept upright and took a few more awkward steps. His boots made a slippery, sliding sound upon the loose shale shining faintly in the candle-light.

'Bring the torch!' he called. He was panting now. Not so much with excitement but for lack of oxygen.

He snapped on the beam, while those behind – staring breathlessly over his shoulder – screwed up their eyes, dazzled after the dimness of the candlelight. They were dazzled by something else as well – by the golden shimmering light that came up at them from the floor of the cave.

Lorne Masters took three more steps – walking on a deep

carpet of gold sovereigns – and stood there, looking around.

The girl gripped his arm tightly. 'Oh, Lorne!' she said. 'Oh, Lorne!' Golden reflections struck from where the torch-beam fell, and brought a strange glint to her eyes.

Maccario had gone down on his knees, muttering, *'Mama mia! O mama mia!'*

The beetle-browed driver clawed at handfuls of the coins, cramming them into sagging pockets.

Ferret-face, completely losing his head, kept scooping up money in cupped palms and letting it gently trickle over his shoulders and arms like water.

Thus it was that Shand came upon them, gun in hand.

He stood watching. He saw the rough walls of the cave – some eight yards across – and its thick, glittering carpet of gold. And he saw them standing round it.

Then they saw him.

Instantly, after that one shattering split-second of recognition, Masters doused his torch.

Shand, ready, switched on his own. 'Over there to the left – all of you!'

Masters, groggy from shock, muttered disbelievingly, 'You're – you're dead!'

Shand showed his teeth. 'Want to bet? Over to the left – all of you!'

Ferret-face, the colour of dirty paper, kept staring. His jaw worked up and down, but no sound came.

'You so-and-so!' said Masters. 'You told me you shot him!'

'I – I – ' Ferret-face choked. 'I did! I couldn't have missed.'

'We aren't making much progress,' said Shand. 'Move over! I'm coming in. Then you'll file out, one by one. Sammy's outside, waiting. He's got a gun, too!'

He stepped forward across the loose, tinkling floor. 'Hands over your heads – all of you. Masters – take a last look at

Ali Baba's cave and lead the way.'

He called to Sammy along the tunnel, 'First man coming! Watch out for tricks!'

Lorne Masters said hoarsely, 'Look here, Shand! There's all this gold – plenty for everybody. How about a deal?'

He stood for a moment longer, trying to read Shand's face, then hunched his stocky shoulders in despair. He seemed suddenly to shrink, so that the clothes hung upon him in loose folds. He ducked his head and re-entered the tunnel.

Ferret-face was shivering so violently that he could scarcely walk. He followed on Masters' heels muttering, 'I didn't miss! I couldn't have.'

The girl stopped and looked up with glowing eyes narrowed to mere slits. 'Fool!' she said huskily. 'What a fool you are, Shand!'

The beetle-browed driver gave one malevolent glance and departed without a word.

Maccario came past, cringing. 'Kind signore – I am a poor man. They call me the Mad Hermit. I did not mean any harm.'

Shand motioned with the gun and said, 'You're no more mad than I am. Nor any hermit, either.'

He allowed the group time to clear the tunnel, then crouched to follow.

He came out again into blinding daylight to find them grouped round the entrance. Masters was standing behind Sammy, with an arm-lock round his neck and Sammy's own big automatic pressing into its owner's ribs. Nearby was Ferret-face, covering him with the rifle held at the hip. The Italian driver had also found a pistol from somewhere. The girl waited about ten yards distant, just looking on.

'Drop that gun, Shand!' rapped Masters. 'Or your fat pal gets it!'

Shand's revolver fell into the snow.

'Now,' said Ferret-face, 'I'm ready to bet I don't miss this time!'

Masters said, 'Hold it! Wait till Maccario comes back. I've worked it all out – I want Shand to hear this.'

The hermit came staggering and panting across snow-covered rocks. '*Si, signore!* He lies there – in the green jacket.'

Who was the man Ferret-face had shot farther along the approaches to the Matzenhof Ledge?

'I'm good at mind-reading,' said Masters. 'You're wondering who it is. Well, I can tell you – it's Von Grinling!'

Shand's hard, hostile stare didn't soften. 'Expect me to believe that?'

'Somebody raided your tent in the night, didn't they? Smacked you on the head and pinched food and clothes? Didn't they take a sheepskin jacket, dyed green?'

'So what?'

'Who else knew about the treasure? Who else was after it, even though he'd been keeping under cover?' Master threw back his head and laughed. 'You dragged him into the pool with you, and he pinched your dry clothes, including the green jacket. And got a bullet through the heart because we thought it was you.' His expression changed. 'Now there's nobody left to try to get this gold away from me. Except you – and you won't be around for very much longer!'

'Have a good gloat,' said Sammy, 'while you can!'

Masters stepped to the front and smacked him across the face.

'Leave him alone,' said Shand, 'or I'll chuck you over the edge – gun or no gun!'

Masters grinned again. 'Don't worry – that's where *you're* going! Like to stick your head over and have a look?'

'Use a bit of sense, man! Somebody else is on this mountain.'

'You mean Findlay?' asked Masters softly. 'Your "friend" – John Findlay?' He laughed again. 'He was Von Grinling, you fool!'

The interval that followed was brief, but long enough for the whole picture to become clear in Shand's mind. John Findlay – with his command of English and his easy manner – didn't seem anything like photographs and descriptions of the evil, stiff-necked Von Grinling. But plastic surgery could work wonders these days, and on reflection Shand could see that there were some similarities between 'John Findlay' and the pictures he had seen of the German.

Shand cast his mind back to the incident on the train and the way Findlay had stuck his nose into the affair. He, too, must have been trailing Masters. He had thrown in his lot with the side which seemed most likely to locate the treasure first – ready to show his true colours as soon as the gold lay within his grasp.

Then there was the battle along the autostrada. Significant facts clicked together in his brain, like Findlay's unguarded, enthusiastic reference to 'Panzer text-book manoeuvres' with the two cars. What should an Englishman know about Panzer text-books? And there was the single 'trial' shot with the captured tommy-gun which ended the life of Jules Delfont. Was this because the Frenchman knew Findlay's true identity and might have squealed?

Moreover, there was that nonsense about being unable to sneak across the Austrian frontier. He had never intended to – he was far too anxious to keep an eye on Shand's activities. And during that drive towards Rossanata, had not his knowledge of roads and mountain routes been just a little too good for one who had never dreamed of visiting the district until a few hours earlier?

'Thought it all out?' taunted Masters. 'Bit slow, aren't you? Just about as slow as your pal was just now when he had us with our hands up. We'd got a fistful of coins each,' he went on, 'and we let him have 'em.' Masters' eyes glittered. 'Ever been hit with a handful of sovereigns, Shand? It's apt to take your mind off your business.' The brown eyes hardened. 'S'long, Shand. Been nice knowing you – most of the time, anyway.'

'Don't do it,' said Shand quickly. 'People in Rossanata know we've come up the mountain. They know you're here, too. Bodies with bullets in them cause comment.'

Masters' mouth twitched slightly.

'Anybody who comes near enough to chuck me over,' grated Shand, 'I'll take him with me! Just like I did Von Grinling into the pond. Like to try, Masters?'

Take no notice!' the girl said in a low voice. 'Shoot them.'

Masters waited a moment longer. 'I've changed my mind. We'll knock 'em off inside the cave.' He gave a sinister chuckle. 'They'll stay hidden there all right – especially after we've taken the gold away and blocked the entrance again.' He gestured with his gun. 'In you go – now!'

Slowly, hands still raised, Shand and Sammy shuffled towards the black hole gaping in the cliff face. Neither of them could think of any way out – except, maybe, a dash in the opposite direction and a flying suicide leap into space to rob Masters of personal satisfaction.

'You, too,' said Masters, in a hard voice.

Risking a backward glance, Shand saw Maccario begin to tremble violently inside his tattered clothes. 'Me? Signore – you joke! There is some mistake.'

'No mistake – get in there!'

A wail of mortal fear rose upon the cold air of Monte Ragazzo. 'You would not shoot me, signore? Me – Maccario? Did I not show you where the treasure was hidden? Is this gratitude? I implore you, signore.'

Masters made no answer save for a menacing jerk of the gun. A reply of a different sort, however, came from Monte Ragazzo itself – until now passive spectator in the fatal game of hide-and-seek played by those puny humans clambering

A vast section of snow had broken loose.

among its giant rocks.

Rumbling sounds issued from somewhere above the Matzenhof Ledge. Ferret-face looked up automatically and froze in his tracks at what he saw. A vast section of snow had broken loose along the upper slope, and was sliding towards them. The thunderous sound of its approach reached them in a five-second crescendo of death.

In the valley near Rossanata watchers saw a tiny wisp of cloud materialise on the bare mountain-side and drift lazily outwards and downwards, fading as it spread. To those on the rocky shelf near the treasure cave that wispy cloud represented thousands of tons of ice, snow, and boulders, roaring and bouncing in an irresistible avalanche upon them.

Shand, crouched in the tunnel and expecting every moment a bullet in his back, heard a sound like a dozen express trains booming overhead. There was a great rush of air and something cannoned painfully into his back. It was Maccario.

The hermit picked himself up and beckoned to Shand and Sammy. 'Quick! Into the cave! The tunnel may collapse!' They heard the detonation of great stones and blocks of ice shattering themselves upon the ledge, while they stood alone amid the terrifying noise and darkness.

Outside, the last of the avalanche threw itself into space from the Matzenhof Ledge. All gradually grew quiet again.

'Come,' said Maccario, 'we must dig our way out – maybe a little, maybe much. We shall not know until we try. Also, we must be careful not to dig our way over the edge.' He shrugged. 'However, there is but room for one man at a time to work, so you, Signor Shand, shall say who is to take the first turn.'

Shand, shining a torch on him and raising an eyebrow, said, 'This is a change, isn't it? I thought you were the original wild boy of the woods.'

Maccario grinned. In fluent English he said, 'So you guessed I wasn't a hermit, eh?'

Shand shook his head slowly. 'I didn't guess – I knew.' He turned to Sammy. 'Take the first turn. I've got to listen to explanations.'

They heard him hauling and rattling loose stones for a moment, then Maccario said, 'Where did I make my mistake?'

'When they killed the real Maccario. It was all very well putting your clothes and identity bracelet on him – but I had a look at the man's body. He hadn't had a bath for years. He was filthy and crawling – yet the clothes weren't at all bad.'

The other nodded regretfully. 'It wasn't pleasant. I didn't have much time, either.' He grinned again. 'So I have to confess I'm Zorrio Corranzi, eh?'

'I knew that,' said Shand. 'There's a lot of other things I don't know, though. If Masters' lot were watching as closely as they said, why didn't they know it was Von Grinling – not me – who wore that green jacket?'

'Because,' said Zorrio calmly, 'I told them. I saw how Findlay left you in the pool and set off with your dry clothes. I got you out of the water, but had to leave you on the edge because one of Masters' men started prowling round. I hope you suffer no ill-effects?'

'To tell you the truth, I haven't had time to find out.'

Sammy returned, sweating. 'A lot of stuff's blocking the entrance. Nothing particularly big, but it's awkward digging with your hands. Cold, too,' he added as an afterthought. 'Besides, it's going to be tricky if any of that lot outside escaped. They could be waiting for us with a gun.'

'They won't be waiting,' said Zorrio confidently. 'If any did escape the avalanche there's somebody to deal with them.'

'I'll take my turn at digging,' said Shand.

Zorrio chuckled. 'There may be more hard work for us later.'

He pointed downwards at the gold coins. 'These will have to be moved somehow.'

'Downhill, anyway,' said Sammy.

Zorrio looked up at him. 'Do you know, my friends, how much eight million pounds' worth of gold weighs?'

'Never gave it a thought.'

'Neither did the others. Nor did I till the matter was raised by your very resourceful Signor Trensham. He calculates it at something in excess of nine tons.'

'Trensham? You know him?'

'Not yet – but I certainly admire him.' He chuckled. 'Mining machinery.'

Sammy gulped. 'You mean those cases down at Rossanata don't carry machinery?'

'Oh, yes, Signor Trensham is far too clever for that. The machinery is very new and very good, I believe. Worth at least five thousand pounds.' He sighed. 'But the expert investigation will report it to be useless for work on silver ore in these mountains, and it will have to be sent back to England. The Italian customs seals will be intact – so that the cases can be shipped back without much trouble, probably from Genoa.'

Sammy clicked his tongue. 'That's smuggling! And a waste of good machinery.'

Zorrio laughed. 'Is it a fair exchange – five thousand pounds for eight million?'

Sammy flapped his arms, trying to restore circulation in numbed fingers. 'Will it be as easy as all that? What about the Children of the Dolomites? Won't they claim a share?'

'Most likely – if they hear about it. But the gold is not theirs, and these days their numbers are few.'

'They've got influence, though.'

Zorrio smiled mischievously. 'I don't think you need worry about the police at San Sagrado. Enough influence remains for them to deal with that little affair.'

Sammy said Zorrio knew an awful lot about what had been going on.

'And why not? Poor Carlo and I worked for years to solve the mystery of Monte Ragazzo – even before Lorne Masters and Von Grinling came on the scene. And because we have a debt of gratitude to your country – and because we think it is the rightful property of Great Britain – we resolved to hand over the gold to the British government, if possible. The unfortunate Maccario kept the secret all these years. He didn't bother about money himself, and long ago he vowed he would never speak of it. But he spoke to Von Grinling before he died his very unpleasant death. And I – coming upon them and overhearing when it was too late to help the poor, crazy man – decided to play off Von Grinling and Masters against one another for the last time.'

'Even to the extent of giving Masters the trouble of digging out the entrance to the cave, and finding all the treasure?'

Zorrio laughed. 'Even that.'

Silence fell. At the far end of the tunnel they could hear Shand's heavy breathing and the scrape of stones.

'Better take some of these back into the cave,' he called. 'No room for them here.'

'Nearly through?' asked Sammy.

'Hard to tell.'

While they passed lumps of debris from hand to hand, Sammy said, 'I never thought I was particularly lucky, but that avalanche certainly came at the right moment.'

'You think that was luck?' asked Zorrio, dumping a large rock on the gold-strewn floor. 'You had better think again, my friend.'

'What's that?' asked Shand. 'How could it be anything else but luck?' He thought for a moment. 'You did say you'd got somebody outside ready to deal with Masters, didn't you?'

Zorrio nodded.

A great lump of snow fell from the top of their excavation, and the light of day flooded in. Silhouetted against the brilliant sky was a head crowned with a little woolly hat.

'Ella! Ella Findlay!'

'Not Ella,' said Zorrio gently. 'That's not her name. She was waiting a couple of hundred feet above the ledge in case of difficulties. If I called.'

They climbed from their temporary prison into the cold, clear air. Shand, looking across the noble prospect of wide valleys below, remembered that peculiarly penetrating wail for mercy from 'Maccario' before he dived after them into the protecting tunnel.

She was to make a diversion by knocking a boulder down.

Another blinding light dawned – a light of understanding. 'Margo!' said Shand. 'You're the real Margo Corranzi!'

'I hung on a spur,' said Margo, 'and pushed a fair-sized loose stone with my foot. Uncle said it was something that might gain time in a tight corner.' Her pert, cheerful face lacked its usual smile. 'I was never so frightened in my life as when I saw that avalanche starting. I thought I'd killed all of you.'

'She is a very brave girl,' said Zorrio proudly, 'and only those who deserved to die have done so. She has done much to bring Masters and Von Grinling to the point where they destroyed themselves. It needed no little nerve to guide that German on the proper trail.'

'You're not telling me,' protested Sammy, 'anybody with Von Grinling's experience was taken in as simply as that!'

'It wasn't simple at all, my friend. The safest and most foolproof way was to admit her identity to Von Grinling, once an acquaintanceship had been scraped. Then she asked him very prettily to help her find the treasure for her family.'

Margo laughed and pulled off the woolly cap, shaking her soft brown hair loose in the sunshine. 'He was only too glad – having been looking for it himself all along.'

She looked at Shand. 'There's a reward, you know. What's two per cent of eight million?'

'I'm never any good at arithmetic,' said Shand slowly, 'but it should be enough to buy us all a good meal or two.'

'I'm hungry,' said Zorrio, 'perhaps there's some of Mayor Perera's very appetising lunch basket left.'

'Not much. Not enough to make a square meal for all of us.' Zorrio glanced at his watch.

'Never mind,' he said. 'It's still quite early. We should all be able to get back to civilisation in time for a good dinner. It's my belief that the local cuisine in this part of the country is the best in Italy.'

Alpine Assignment

It was an easy enough game to play with unsuspecting tourists – if you were Hans Schaefer, that is. You kept watch in the lower terminal of the *Luftseilbahn* – the mountain suspension railway, which was unmanned, all the working being done from the top end of the line. You waited until some harassed-looking foreigner came along. English and Americans paid best.

The tourist would peer anxiously around, walk across to the waiting empty car, walk away again, consult a wrist-watch for about the fiftieth time, and almost explode with vexation.

With luck, no one else would be at the terminal, and you would then politely offer your help.

The *Luftseilbahn* telephone and directions for use you would previously have hidden behind a carefully hung jacket or knapsack.

You would assume an expression at least as worried as the tourist's and, after some aimless searching, finally discover the telephone.

You would shout excitedly into it, then quickly skip back again. 'Hurrah!' you would cry. 'I have done it! I have been able to arrange your journey for you. Come this way – I have obtained special permission for you to proceed immediately, without any delay, to the top station!'

The tourist would follow you into the empty car. You pressed a little bell, jumped back on to the platform, closed the doors and, in a moment or two, the car would glide away upwards on its long span of cable. You saluted, and your face showed pleasure that your intervention had enabled this tourist to travel on his way. A silver coin lay in your hand, its size varying according to the generosity and nationality of the tourist.

You were happy. The tourist was happy. If it was discovered later that the normal procedure was for intending passengers automatically to telephone the other terminal – well, you weren't there when the tourist returned, and that was that.

Gregory Bradshaw stepped on to the little lake steamer and looked around him at his fellow passengers. Serge Fedroff wasn't there, and Gregory Bradshaw's information was that he should have been.

The steamer's telegraph bell sounded shrilly. The vessel backed away from the landing stage and Lucerne soon fell astern.

Without feeling really worried, Bradshaw was annoyed at this hitch in the scheme of things. He hoped his search would prove more fruitful when he reached Stansstad.

He breathed in great gulps of the invigorating air. What a holiday all this would make!

But he wasn't on holiday. This was his work – dangerous work. His briefing for this assignment came from the Foreign Office in London. For all he knew, any one of the small band of tourists sharing the lake steamer with him might be an enemy, a member of Fedroff's international gang. Bradshaw glanced around warily again.

Since it was obvious that Fedroff wasn't aboard, this meant that he must already have reached Stansstad. Bradshaw had learned, only just before he left Lucerne, that Fedroff intended catching the ten o'clock train from Stansstad to Engelberg.

Possibly he would then be travelling up into the mountains, first by *Luftseilbahn*, then by chair-lift.

On arrival in Stansstad, Bradshaw lost no time in boarding the two-coach electric train by the steamer pier. The journey was definitely an experience. Much of the way the train had to be assisted by a rack-and-pinion locomotive. In that way, the final one-in-four grade was mounted, giving a breath-taking view of the mountains behind Engelberg. Bradshaw, however, paid scant attention to the scenery. He was rather more interested in one of the passengers from the other carriage, who carried an attaché-case. He was a dark, bearded individual, and when they reached Engelberg he passed quickly out of the terminus. Bradshaw followed, but not too closely.

Fedroff turned to the right, then to the right again. He made off across some fields, and soon led Bradshaw close to the station for the funicular railway which ascends still higher to Grünlialp.

Bradshaw waited behind the cover of a clump of firs, then stepped out to investigate further. Something caught him a heavy blow over the head. He collapsed in a heap and lay still.

Fedroff, having thus satisfactorily concluded his own stalking, smiled grimly to himself and walked quickly into the station. When, about ten minutes later, Bradshaw recovered his senses and, somewhat unsteadily, picked himself up, there was no sign of Fedroff. He had well and truly given him the slip, and made him feel very sore into the bargain.

Bradshaw shook his head to clear it from the effects of the blow, thanked his lucky stars that he had such a thick skull, and ruefully inspected the funicular station. Then he bought a ticket for Grünlialp, nearly a thousand feet above him. It seemed the only sensible thing to do, assuming the rest of his information to be correct.

From Grünlialp the little box cars of the *Luftseilbahn* were hauled up as far as Brütsee – one car down balancing one car up.

'Try removing that jacket,' he suggested.

From Brütsee a chairlift carried on the good work as far as the Wildische Pass, over ten thousand feet above sea level. And on the morrow certain statemen, who had been attending a Heads of Government meeting at Geneva, would be visiting the Wildische Pass – ostensibly as part of a tour of Switzerland arranged for their benefit, but in actual fact to try to reach agreement on matters affecting the peace of the whole world.

Bradshaw arrived at Grünlialp and at once entered the lower station of the *Luftseilbahn*. A tall, athletic-looking lad regarded him somewhat anxiously from farther along the platform. No one else was about.

Bradshaw went over to the waiting car and inspected it. It was empty. He wandered back to the barrier.

'If the Herr pleases . . .' said a young, courteous voice behind him.

Bradshaw turned and raised his eyebrows at the lad who had wandered up.

'The Herr wishes to travel up to Brütsee?'

Bradshaw nodded.

Hans Schaefer looked somewhat helplessly around him. It was beautifully acted.

'I – I should like to help the Herr if it is possible. I – allow me to investigate on the Herr's behalf.' He wandered off, peering into various places.

Bradshaw, amused, watched him for a minute. Then he called out to him in a tone offering no alternative.

'Try removing that jacket from the station telephone,' he suggested. 'Then I can tell the Upper Terminal to expect me.'

Hans flushed. He had never been caught out like this before.

'Why, yes – good gracious! How discerning of the Herr! I will remove the jacket instantly. One wonders how it could have come to be left there.'

'Come off it!' said Bradshaw.

Hans flushed a deeper shade of red; then bit his lip and shrugged his shoulders. This friendly-looking Englishman was no fool. Hans put on his jacket and just stood there, saying nothing.

'Has anyone else been here recently?' asked Bradshaw. 'A tallish man, for instance, with a thick black beard and a somewhat impulsive nature?'

Hans nodded vigorously.

'Indeed, *ja, mein Herr*. He was not, perhaps, the Herr's friend?'

'No!' said Bradshaw shortly.

'Ah – that is good – I hoped he would not be. I did not get on well with him, as I do with the Herr. I tried to help the black-bearded one as I try to help all strangers in difficulty,' continued Hans virtuously. 'He was unfriendly. I approached him while he was inspecting the *Luftseilbahn* car, and he showed anger.'

Bradshaw looked puzzled.

'He struck me,' explained Hans, rubbing his left ear tenderly.

'You should have dodged,' said Bradshaw grinning.

'One does not expect to be treated thus by helpless-looking bearded gentlemen whom one sees crawling about on the floor of empty *Luftseilbahn* cars,' replied Hans, with dignity.

'What do you mean – crawling?' queried Bradshaw, instantly alert, with a serious look on his face.

'He opened the door of the car, entered, and, when I went over to offer my help a little later, he was on his hands and knees inspecting a piece of floorboard which seemed to have come loose. He had, in fact, just replaced it as I entered the car. You can imagine my astonishment on finding him like that.'

'Then what? Speed it up, my lad. This is important!'

Hans shrugged his shoulders. 'Then he shouted at me to get out, attacked me in a most ill-mannered fashion, and I – er – left the car. That is all. The Herr will understand that I had no wish to linger any longer than necessary in the presence of one so ill-bred.'

'You acted more wisely than you knew, actually. Tell me – have there been other passengers since?'

'*Nein, mein Herr*. And the bearded one has not returned.'

'Good! And now, what is your name?'

'Hans – Hans Schaefer.'

'Right, Hans! Now listen. There is a police bureau in Grünlialp, is there not?'

'*Ja, mein Herr.*'

'Go there instantly with this note. It is urgent.' Bradshaw hastily scribbled in a notebook, tore out the sheet, folded it, and gave it to Hans. 'When you have handed it over to the policeman, come back here.'

Off Hans dashed. In less than five minutes he was back, breathing heavily and flushed with excitement.

'The policeman, Duckelheimer, almost leapt through the ceiling when he read your note,' said Hans happily.

Bradshaw patted Hans on the shoulder and went over to the station telephone. He held a long and earnest conversation. Afterwards he returned to Hans.

'You are going up in the car to Brütsee,' he said.

'As the Herr wishes,' Hans gleefully replied.

'It may well be that our bearded friend will be travelling down in the other car alone – for it seems there are no passengers waiting to descend from Brütsee. If you were to gesticulate somewhat rudely as you pass, it would undoubtedly annoy him, but it would also set his mind at rest. He would suspect you of travelling upwards on purpose to bring him down. Perhaps by the time he reaches here, he will have finished whatever it is he is doing to the floorboards.'

'*Ja, mein Herr,*' said Hans, puzzled.

'Yes. One hopes so, anyway, because by then your policeman friend will be awaiting him here. But for the time being Black Beauty must not get suspicious or he may react violently.'

'Ah, yes – how I know that!' agreed Hans, ruefully.

The *Luftseilbahn* car came slowly to a stop at Grünlialp, and its solitary passenger stepped out. He had scarcely covered half a dozen yards when a burly uniformed figure grasped him firmly by the arm.

'Monsieur Fedroff, I believe? You will please come with me.'

Fedroff, taken completely by surprise, spluttered indignantly. Struggling violently for a few seconds, he looked almost as if he might break away. Then the policeman's grip tightened perceptibly, and Fedroff tried to bluff it out instead. He turned a scowling face towards his captor.

'Let me go!' he hissed. 'This is an outrage! What are you holding me for?'

The policeman motioned grimly to a colleague who disappeared into the rail car. A minute later he reappeared, holding a small box at arm's length. He glanced stonily towards the prisoner.

'It was there, all right, just as we were warned, under the floorboards,' he muttered.

Fedroff paled. He suddenly realised the game was up. He shrugged his shoulders, smiled a little bitterly, and was led away unresisting.

The contents of the box were later examined by experts. They discovered a twenty-four hour timing device attached to a bomb powerful enough to wreck the whole *Luftseilbahn* car, with fatal results to anyone travelling inside it.

'Your government, then, instructed you that such a thing might happen?' asked Hans later, as he lunched with Bradshaw.

He didn't wait for the reply before making inroads into a large *apfelstrudel*.

'Not exactly. They instructed me to keep an eye on Black Beauty in case it did,' replied Bradshaw with a smile. 'Now that he's out of the way, an important meeting will be able to take place near here tomorrow, without any fireworks.'

'Fireworks, *mein Herr?* I am afraid I do not understand this talk of fireworks. Were there some fireworks there then?'

'Yes – beneath the floorboards of the *Luftseilbahn* car, in which certain Foreign Secretaries may be travelling. They will be able to enjoy the scenery and, we hope, to talk to some purpose without any interruption. In other words, my hungry young friend,' said Bradshaw genially, 'you may have helped to save the peace of the world by your acute observations. Doesn't that give you a sense of responsibility? I think you can be quite proud of this day's work!'

Hans nodded his understanding and looked suitably awed, despite the fact that, in his excitement, he had rather over-estimated the capacity of his mouth and his stomach.

'Yes, I see it all clearly,' he said presently as he sighed and pushed away his plate. 'I am indeed grateful to the Herr. And these – these Foreign Secretaries you mention, they will be travelling alone, or in separate little groups, yes? Perhaps it will be that I can assist them also if they arrive at the *Luftseilbahn* terminal and are puzzled by the empty car and station!'

Contact Zodiac!

by Justin Long

'S-someone's climbing in the kitchen window, Pete!'

Pete Williams hurriedly joined his pal, Midge, at the attic window of the derelict old house. Suddenly tense, the two boys stared down through the gathering dusk into the backyard.

A burly figure, hardly visible in the gloom, was easing himself over the kitchen window-sill. Then he must have unlocked the back door from the inside, because next moment a second sinister figure, crouching and silent as a cat, crossed the yard in the wake of the first and disappeared through the kitchen doorway.

Now the boys, no longer alone in the creepy old house, could hear the creak of footsteps on the bare boards downstairs.

'Gosh, Pete,' Midge Morris whispered, 'they're coming up the stairs!'

Finger to lips, Pete warned Midge to silence. The footsteps had reached the landing, one short flight of steps below the attic where the boys crouched. One of the strangers down there in the darkness seemed to be exploring each empty room in turn.

Pete fought his panic and wished he had never thought of coming to the eerie, broken-windowed house, waiting to be demolished. In daylight it had seemed a marvellous idea to him and to Midge. The back of the house overlooked the Portdown football ground next to the harbour, and the attic window had given them a free grandstand view of the home team playing a visiting Navy Eleven of soccer celebrities.

Again the sinister creaking sounded, now on the landing below, and Pete knew their big mistake had been to stay on after the match was over in a vain effort to rescue a penny which Midge had dropped through the loose floorboards.

Already dusk was turning to darkness – the menacing darkness of the black-out in wartime Britain, when no friendly town lights were permitted. And the creeping footsteps had reached the flight of steps to the attic.

'In the cupboard!' Pete breathed in Midge's ear.

Midge fumbled forward in the gloom, glad for once that Pete was a year the elder and knew the best thing to do in a jam.

The cupboard door was ajar, and step by cautious step they squeezed inside the narrow recess. Heart thudding, Pete inched the door almost shut behind them just as a shadowy form appeared in the attic doorway.

A pencil-thin beam of light from a torch flickered over the walls and floor. Then the mystery visitor's companion called softly to him from the stairs.

'What's keeping you, Ernst? Have you seen something else?'

'No but I had to make sure that whoever came to this house today had gone!' The light snapped off and quiet footfalls told that the man called Ernst was retracing his steps to the landing. 'That schoolboy's cap I found in the kitchen alters everything!'

In the darkness of the attic cupboard Pete heard Midge's indrawn breath. It was Midge's cap that had fallen off when they had scrambled through the kitchen window three hours before. And it was just like Midge to leave his cap where it had fallen. They listened, tensed, to the whispers of the two intruders on the landing.

'We can no longer operate from this place,' said Ernst. 'Whoever came today may return – and bring others!'

The voices faded as the men went downstairs, and Pete eased open the cupboard door, keeping a warning grip on Midge's arm. It was safer for the time being to stay in their dusty hiding place.

For ten minutes they heard movements in the depths of the house. Then there was silence. At last Pete stirred. In slow motion he left the cupboard. Midge followed him cautiously and they listened.

'I reckon they've gone!' Pete breathed. 'But we mustn't take any chances. We'll creep down the stairs. Don't make a sound till we're clear of this place – they might still be somewhere around!'

One step at a time they felt their way out of the attic and down the top flight of stairs.

'Pete, I'm going to sneeze!' Midge whispered, on the landing. 'I can feel it coming on!'

'You mustn't!' Pete strained his ears for any suspicious movements downstairs. 'Hold your nose – keep it pinched!'

Not a sound came from the depths of the house. Gripping Midge's arm, Pete crept slowly down to the next landing.

'Cad I leggo by dose?' Midge asked.

'No, keep it pinched till we're sure they've gone!'

Followed by Midge, Pete crept down the remaining stairs to the ground floor.

'The back way – same way we came in!' he whispered.

They had almost reached the old kitchen when suddenly a door opened and a shaft of light froze them where they stood. From the angle in the passage they saw a man in a belted mack at the top of the cellar steps, a suitcase in his hand. His back was turned to them as he spoke to someone below him in the cellar. The boys prayed he wouldn't turn and see them.

'How long will you be, Ernst?' he asked. 'Does this mean you are leaving Portdown?'

'No, I stay in Portdown until our operation is over!' the cold, hard voice of Ernst answered from the cellar. 'But from now on we must separate. Don't waste time – get going! Carl is due here any moment. Stop him and tell him this house is no longer safe for us! In another ten minutes I shall have hidden the traces of our occupation here and I, too, shall go!'

'But Carl and the others will want to know how to contact you!'

'Tell them to contact Zodiac! It is all they need to know!' Ernst snapped. 'Now get going – I do not wish our loyal but impatient gunman, Carl, to come blundering in here!'

'I'll meet him and turn him back!' muttered the man with the suitcase, and without another word he made off into the gloom of the hall. The crouching boys heard a door creak on rusty hinges. One, at least, of the men had gone.

But next moment Pete's heart bumped as he peeped round the angle of the wall and Ernst loomed into view at the top of the cellar steps. A pair of radio headphones in his hand, he stared round suspiciously – a powerful man in a roll-neck jersey and slacks. With pebble-hard eyes and close-cropped dark hair he looked a dangerous type to cross.

The boys shrank into the shadows and held their breath. The sudden pounce they feared did not come. Ernst, evidently satisfied he was alone, merely wanted to finish his work in the cellar with the door closed. It clicked shut and the boys heard him go back down the cellar steps.

Midge tugged at Pete's sleeve and then pointed at the open kitchen door with his free hand – the other hand was still pinching his nose.

Pete nodded for Midge to lead the way. But before he followed he tip-toed three paces to the cellar door. Quietly he turned the key in the lock.

Then he was outside, thrusting the key in his mack pocket and hurrying after Midge over the cracked cement of the back-yard, through a broken-down gate into the alley-way that skirted the side of the house. Midge, his eyes watering, let go his nose and fumbled for a handkerchief.

'No time for that!' Pete whispered. 'We've got to get away from here!'

'It's no good, Pete, I – AHH-TISHOO!' Midge's violent sneeze, echoing down the alley, shocked even Midge with the row it made.

Pete dragged him down behind the cover of a dustbin.

'I – I'm going to do it again, Pete!'

'Grab your nose! Stuff your hanky in your mouth!' Pete whispered. 'One of the gang that have been using this house might be around – oh heck, someone's arrived!'

A boot crunched on the gravel of the front path and a man's shadow in the rising moon slid along the moonlit alley. The boys, not daring to move behind the dustbin, saw him coming at a cat-like crouching lope. Now they saw a craggy-jawed, long-nosed man, pistol in hand, coming along the alley towards them. This must be Carl, the gunman, Pete thought in chill dismay. The other man must have failed to meet him and turn him back.

But an instant later he had passed the two boys and they breathed again, knowing that they had not been seen. They heard the gunman prowling through the back-yard towards the lane bordering the football ground.

Without a word they were running full pelt out of the alley-way across the overgrown front garden, through the gateway into the road.

They ran for three minutes non-stop, faster than they had ever run before. By the time they reached the High Street and slowed down they were breathing in great gulps of air.

'There won't half – be a scare at home!' Midge gasped. 'Us out as late as this – and nearly shot by gangsters – and my cap gone!'

'We're not going home yet! There's a policeman, Midge!'

Pete hurried across the deserted road, followed more slowly by Midge. The policeman turned round and stared at them.

'What are you youngsters doing out after dark? There might be an air raid warning any moment!'

'We've caught a spy!' Pete panted.

'That's it!' Midge exclaimed in delighted surprise. 'That's what they were – spies! And they've captured my school cap!'

'Pinched your cap, eh? Terrible thing, total war!' The policeman patted Midge on the shoulder. 'Now you'd better run along home before your folks get worried!'

'But it's true! They *were* spies!' Pete produced the key from his pocket. 'I locked one of them in the cellar of the old house in Marsden Road!'

'The derelict house – is *that* where you boys have been?' The policeman's voice was suddenly grim as he took the key. 'I think you'd both better come with mc to the station. I don't know what you've been up to, but if I'm right you two have butted in on a big spy-catching operation!'

'Think we'll get medals?' Midge broke into a trot to keep up with the striding constable.

'Medals? Crikey!' The policeman whistled. 'My guess is that you two boys have gummed up plans so special that Scotland Yard will be gibbering with rage before the night's out!'

'We've notified the parents of the two boys . . . No sir, the boys are still here . . . Yes, we have questioned them and it's quite clear they saw the spies . . . Very good, sir!' The police sergeant put down the telephone and scowled at Pete and Midge.

'Was that the Chief Constable?' asked a plain-clothes detective.

'Yes, and he blames us for tonight's shambles – reckons we

should have stopped the boys going anywhere near that house!' the sergeant grunted.

Midge and Pete wriggled uncomfortably on the hard bench in the interview room of the police-station. For half-an-hour they had answered questions, while an emergency patrol of policemen were assembled, briefed and sent out into the night. Plain-clothes detectives hurried in to make reports and every few minutes the telephone was ringing.

'No luck, Sarge!' Another detective who had just come in made his report. 'The cellar door had been locked all right. But it was broken open from the inside. All the birds have flown – and they haven't left so much as a finger-print!'

'That's the last straw!' The sergeant glared at Pete. 'You know what that means?'

'All the spies have got away?' Pete whispered in dismay, knowing that somehow he and Midge were responsible for all this. The sergeant did not deign to answer. The telephone was ringing again.

'I'm hungry!' Midge muttered.

'Take the little blighters down to the canteen till their parents arrive!' snapped the sergeant.

'Mind if I take them, Sarge? I'm Joe Manders from headquarters. I'd like to have a talk with them!' A newcomer wearing an officer's mack over civilian clothes showed his identity card.

'Lieutenant Manders?' The sergeant looked respectfully at the broad-shouldered young officer. 'Yes, of course, Mr Manders!'

The lieutenant in 'civvies' turned and beckoned to Pete and Midge, and, for the first time since they had left the old house, they saw a friendly smile.

They jumped up from their bench and followed Joe Manders from the interview room along a stone paved corridor to a warmly lit canteen.

Two minutes later, the boys had introduced themselves, and

the three of them were sitting at a little table in the corner with mugs of steaming cocoa and platefuls of sandwiches in front of them. Pete and Midge relaxed and their host told them to call him Joe.

'I know you boys have had to put up with a lot of questions,' he said. 'Your answers have been typewritten – I have 'em here! But there's another way you could be a great help in this case!'

'We've said all we know!' Pete assured him. 'I'm sorry if we've messed everything up!'

'You did the best you could, Pete. And you were right when you guessed they were spies you saw. I can't tell you much because it's all top secret. But I believe you chaps might still be able to do something for us in this case!'

Midge stared over the rim of his cocoa mug at Joe Manders' grey eyes and square-cut face, and decided he was all right.

'We'll help *you*,' Midge told him. 'But I'm not going to help that police sergeant any more – not if he begs me to! He's had it!'

'You mustn't blame the police for feeling sore about tonight!' Joe put down his cup. 'We knew a part of what was going on in that old house. We had a plain-clothes man from headquarters keeping an eye on it. But policemen in uniform were told to keep away from the place till we could trap the ringleaders we wanted in a sudden raid. That raid was timed for next week!'

'And we spoiled it! Gosh, I wish we'd never gone there!' Pete was filled with remorse.

'But you two are the only ones who have had a close-up view of some of the spy ring,' continued Joe Manders. 'If you saw Ernst again would you know him?'

Pete nodded vigorously.

'And the man with the gun – the one you reckon must be Carl?'

'I'd know that big, ugly gorilla anywhere!' Midge exclaimed. 'Ugh, he was horrible! Frankenstein wasn't in it!'

'A giant of a man with staring eyes and matted hair!' Joe read through the description the boys had given the police. 'Well, you've added a new one to our list and the hunt for him is under way. But it's Ernst, the leader, I want you chaps to help me catch!'

He drew his chair closer and lowered his voice.

'Your parents are on the way here and I'll have to get their permission. They'll probably be worried about all this. But I'm going to have you two tailed by our people for the next few days . . .'

'You mean we'll be shadowed?' Pete breathed.

'Everywhere you go!' Joe nodded. 'You won't see the one who's shadowing you. Our people are experts. Now, we know Ernst is still somewhere here in Portdown, and I'll give you a list of places in the town that I'd like you to visit – places where we reckon Ernst is most likely to show up.'

'And if we see him?' Pete put in.

'We'll fix up a special signal. The moment you spot Ernst or Carl you give the signal. Our people will take over and you two must beat it as fast as you can go. It's our one chance of getting Ernst back in our sights, so that we can round up a ring that is deadly dangerous to Britain! Are you on?'

'You bet!' Pete and Midge exclaimed in one voice.

'All right, we'll fix up a signal! Something nobody else will notice except our man following you – and tomorrow it will be me.'

'I could give my Indian bird call – like this!' Midge opened his mouth and proudly demonstrated the echoing call it had taken him weeks of practice to perfect. 'WHA-WHA-WHA-OOOOOH!' he wailed.

The man behind the canteen counter dropped a coffee cup and two off-duty policemen waiting to be served swung round to stare at Midge.

'It must be the grub they dish up here!' exclaimed one of them. 'The poor kid's got tummy-ache!'

'No, Midge! The Indian call won't do!' Joe said firmly. 'It's got to be something that won't attract general attention. Dropping a handkerchief will be signal enough. And we'll have a codeword which only you two and our man following you will know. So even if our man is a complete stranger to you the codeword will identify him. Now what codeword would you like?'

'Kippers,' said Midge. 'I like kippers.'

'All right! Kippers it is! And the answering codeword can be custard!'

The swing doors opened and a policeman came towards them.

'The boys' parents are outside, Mr Manders!' he said. 'They are a bit anxious!'

'I'll see them!' Joe got up. 'Come on, you two! I want to talk to your folks. And then I'll drive you all home!'

'Now the High Street!' said Pete.

'But we've been along the High Street about ten times since yesterday!' Midge protested. 'I'm getting tired of all this tramping about and not getting anywhere!'

'Come on, Midge! Joe had a hard enough job persuading our folks to let us in on the spy hunt – we can't let him down now! Besides, it's got us off school since Monday, hasn't it!'

Midge heaved a sigh and followed Pete on their eleventh trip down the High Street since they had made their pact to help Joe three days before.

As well as patrolling the High Street and visiting each of its shops in turn, they had toured the harbour approaches as near as war-time regulations and barbed wire fences would permit. They had visited the post office, the local sports clubs, the railway station half-a-dozen times, and loitered near factories at the hours of clocking-on and clocking-off.

Only once had they caught sight of their 'shadow' – and that was on the previous afternoon when they had glimpsed Joe Manders, twenty yards behind them, buying a newspaper and giving no sign that he had ever met them.

'Here's a shop we haven't been in yet!' Pete halted outside the ironmongery stores.

'That's another thing!' Midge said. 'I'm running out of excuses for looking in shops where I don't want to buy anything. That man in the shoe shop thought we were nuts when we asked him if he sold lollies!'

'That was *you* – blurting out the first thing you thought of. From now on leave *me* to do the talking, Midge!'

Pete turned towards the ironmonger's, but even as he did so, Midge grabbed his arm.

'Look, Pete, over there – that man looking in the bookshop window! *It's Carl, the gunman!*'

There was no doubt about it. The man outside the bookshop was the man they had last seen sneaking along the dark alley, pistol in hand. He was not as huge, or as shock-haired as he had seemed in the moonlight. But he was the same man all right.

'Bags I give the handkerchief signal!' Midge dived his hands into his mack pockets. 'Oh gosh, I've got no hanky!'

But Pete's handkerchief was already in his hand. He dropped it carefully in the middle of the pavement and a burly cyclist pulled up.

'You just dropped it, son!' The cyclist pointed at the handkerchief.

'Are you kippers?' Pete asked eagerly.

'There's no need to be rude!' The cyclist scowled and rode on.

'Oh crumbs, that zombie Carl is coming this way!' Midge tugged at Pete's sleeve. 'He looks as if he suspects something!

The cyclist scowled and rode on.

He's staring at us, Pete. I reckon it's time we beat it!'

'But where's Joe or whoever is tailing us today?' Pete looked round in dismay. The gunman was coming on – and he was gazing fixedly at them.

'I'm off!' Midge turned and darted round the corner.

The gunman, grim-faced and only twenty yards away, quickened his pace, shouldering people out of the way. Pete gaped up and down the street. Even now he felt sure that Joe or one of his men would appear. Joe would not let them down.

But among all the people in the street only the on-coming, purposeful gunman gave Pete so much as a glance.

His mouth suddenly dry, Pete backed off and then turned and bolted after Midge. Dodging and weaving among the shoppers, he realised Midge was taking the short cut home down Fairfield Gardens. Midge slowed to a trot as Pete caught up with him.

'Speed up!' Pete panted. 'He's still after us! Cut down the back of the flats!'

At the back of the flats was a concrete-paved approach with an exit to the next side-road. They scooted round a row of lock-up garages for cars belonging to the people who lived in the tall block.

'Carl's followed us!' Midge gasped, peering round the garages.

'He's making for the exit – quick, Midge, up that stairway! Wiley Watkins lives at Number Thirty-Six! His Mum will let us in and they can send for the police straight away!'

They rushed up the fire-escape stairway on the rear outer wall of the block. Wiley lived on the second floor. But when they reached the veranda outside his back door and rang the bell there was no answer.

Pete rang again, desperately, and Midge peered over the balcony wall between a window box and a tub with snowdrops in it.

'I reckon we've fooled that zombie,' he whispered. He craned further to look directly below them. 'Oh my gosh, he wasn't fooled – he's down there right underneath us!'

'It's all right, we're saved, Midge! I can hear Wiley's Mum coming to the door!'

Midge turned thankfully, and as he did so his elbow caught the tub with snowdrops in it. It tilted and fell. At the very moment that Mrs Watkins opened the back door to them they heard a thud and a gasping cry from below.

They peeped over the balcony to see the gunman sprawled face downwards on the concrete pavement with broken bits of the flower-tub and snowdrops scattered around him.

'Crikey, he's knocked out!' Pete gasped.

'Oh my goodness, what have you done!' Mrs Watkins, leaning over the narrow parapet, looked most upset.

'He's a spy!' Pete exclaimed. 'We've got to call the police before he comes round and escapes!'

Other back doors were opening. People called out to know what was happening and two tenants hurried across the courtyard to the fallen man.

'*Police!*' Midge was jumping up and down and shouting at the top of his voice. 'Watch out! He's sitting up! Don't let him get away – he's a gunman!'

A police car appeared and two policemen jumped out.

'Thank goodness for that!' Pete said. 'They've got him – they're taking him away! We'd better go down, Mrs Watkins! The police will want to thank us for catching a spy!'

A policeman met them on the stairway.

'I'm taking you two to the police station,' he said curtly.

'That's all right,' Pete told him. It was one of the unfriendly policemen. But all that would be changed from now on, Pete thought cheerfully. From now on, the police were going to be very pleased with him and Midge.

Ten minutes later they were at the station, and almost the first person they saw in the interview room was Joe Manders talking to the police sergeant.

'That man you two boys beaned with the flower pot – who did you think he was?' Joe asked.

'Why, it was the spy called Carl – the one with the gun!' Pete exclaimed, mystified at Joe's serious look.

The sergeant snorted.

'But you said Carl was a hairy, ugly giant of a chap – quite different from the fellow you bowled over!' Joe stared at them.

'That's how he seemed when we saw him that night in the alley.' Pete was suddenly uneasy at the grim faces staring at him and Midge. 'But he's the same man all right. He's the one we saw outside the derelict house, isn't he, Midge?'

'Same one!' Midge nodded vigorously.

Joe rubbed his chin thoughtfully.

'It's all my fault,' he said at last to the sergeant. 'From their lurid description of the zombie they reckoned they saw in the alley – the chap they took to be Carl – I never thought for a moment it could possibly be Ted Stringer they were describing.'

The sergeant snorted again – a snort of deep disgust for all boys and particularly the two who were gaping across the table.

'You – you mean the man we saw in the alley wasn't a spy?' Pete tried to keep his dismay out of his voice.

'If he wasn't a spy why did he chase us this afternoon?' Midge demanded.

'Because he's one of our special duty men – the one who was keeping an eye on the derelict house the night you saw him, and today he happened to be taking a turn at shadowing you!'

'Oh no!' Pete swallowed hard. 'So *that's* why he came after us when we dropped the handkerchief! Is – is he badly hurt?'

'A bit sore, that's all!' said a voice from the doorway, and Ted Stringer, special duties man, with a piece of sticking-plaster on his forehead, came into the interview room. 'Sore at being mistaken for a zombie and then getting knocked out by a bouquet of snowdrops!'

The boys saw with relief the glint of humour in their victim's eyes, and as they looked at Ted Stringer's rugged, likeable face they wondered how, even in fitful moonlight, they could have believed he was a ruthless killer-spy.

'Phew, I'm glad everything's all right after all!' Pete breathed a sigh of relief. 'We'll get right back on the job, Joe. We've pretty nearly finished combing the High Street. And the fairground is the next place you wanted us to search for Ernst.'

'We'll spend the whole day at the fair – we don't mind hard work!' Midge said keenly.

'You can go home and stay home!' the sergeant snapped. 'At least one good thing has come out of your nearly braining Mr Stringer. The powers that be have decided to keep you two menaces out of any further part in this business!'

'B-but they wouldn't do that – just because we made a little mistake!' Pete stared pleadingly at Joe.

'Sorry, boys!' Joe's voice was sympathetic. 'I'm afraid it's true. The authorities, whose orders the police have to take and I have to take, say that from now on you boys must be kept out of this job. They don't need your help any more!'

It was no good arguing. Five minutes later Midge and Pete had said their glum farewells and were outside the police station.

'Well, that's that!' said Midge.

'No, it's not!' Pete's voice was grim. 'We're on our own now, that's all! And tomorrow we're going to search that fairground, Midge!'

'That's a good idea!' said Midge. 'If you hadn't thought of it first I was just going to think of it myself!'

'Let's have one more go on the scenic railway!' Midge tugged at Pete's arm. 'I reckon Ernst might be on it next time round!'

'No, I've almost run out of money, and anyway we didn't come here just to have fun!' Pete stared across the fairground, past the roundabouts and swings towards the sideshows the two boys had so far not explored.

It was the day following their dismissal from the police station, and for an hour they had toured the fair, trying to catch a glimpse of everybody there – the fairground operators as well as the pleasure-seekers.

Once they had caught a glimpse of Joe Manders at the roadside bordering the fair, and then he had disappeared in the crowd, evidently pursuing a search of his own.

It was Midge who first noticed the gipsy fortune-teller's tent, pitched between the coconut shy and a roll-the-pennies stall.

'The name – look at the name on the tent, Midge!' Suddenly tense, Pete pointed at the sign board.

FOR TODAY ONLY
ZODIAC, FAMOUS MYSTIC OF THE ORIENT
WILL READ YOUR FUTURE!
£1 TO LEARN WHAT THE STARS FORETELL!

For a long moment they gaped at the signboard.

'That's new,' said Midge. 'I don't remember a tent for telling fortunes the last time I was here!'

'What was it Ernst said about Zodiac?' Pete asked.

'I dunno; *you* were the one who heard him! Orient sounds like a football club. Is that a clue, Pete?'

'Don't be an idiot, Midge! Orient means the East. But that isn't the important bit. It's Zodiac that's important. Ernst said his spy-ring had to contact Zodiac!'

'That's it!' Midge almost leaped in his excitement. 'We might have guessed what it meant – I practically *did* guess it actually, well almost, anyway!'

'Come on, we've got to find Joe and the police!'

They raced through the fair. Already people were beginning to drift away. The black-out regulations after dusk prevented gaily lit evening amusements, and soon the pleasure park would have to close down.

'There's a policeman!' Midge panted in Pete's wake.

The policeman halted as they rushed out of the strolling crowd towards him.

'The spies you want to capture!' Pete gasped. 'We've found their new hiding-place!'

'Not you two again!' the policeman stared sternly down at them.

'You don't understand!' Pete exclaimed. 'We've found Zodiac – he's the eastern fortune-teller!'

'You boys have caused enough trouble!' The policeman frowned. 'I don't know what fortune-tellers have got to do with this. But I do know the sergeant told you to stay out of what doesn't concern you any more! You take my tip and hop it!'

'But the fair's beginning to close down – Zodiac will escape!' Pete cried.

'I said hop it! Clear off, both of you!' The policeman gave them a shove hard enough to show that he meant what he said, and then resumed his measured march through the fair – away from the amusement booths.

'Oh gosh, Pete, now what do we do? D'you think we could get Joe if we went to the police station?'

'They'd never even let us past the door! Besides, all the fairground people are leaving for the night – and Zodiac will pack up and go and he won't be back tomorrow either!'

They retraced their steps to the fortune-teller's booth. A shifty-looking man in the pay-box at the entrance to the tent was already beginning to dismantle the flimsy wooden structure.

'If only Joe was here,' Pete groaned. 'If only we could start something that would bring the police running!'

'Like burning down old Zodiac's tent?' Midge followed Pete in an anxious circle of the fortune-teller's booth.

'I've got it!' Pete grabbed Midge's arm and pointed. 'See that truck with the tow-rope fixed to the back? We'll tie the tow-rope to the corner-pole of Zodiac's tent! That truck is going to move off at any moment!'

'Crikey! You mean, bring the whole tent down with a wham!' Midge chuckled. 'That's a great idea, Pete! But *you* can do it. I don't want mystic old Zodiac catching *me* tying ropes to his tent!'

'I'm going to do it! Your job, Midge, is to get that policeman here!'

'How?'

'Pull faces at him – *anything!* Make him chase you and lead him back here!'

Midge gaped in admiration at Pete's daring as his friend crept up to the truck parked nearby and took the loose end of the tow-rope.

Dusk was coming on, but it seemed impossible for Pete not to be noticed on his hands and knees by the corner pole at the rear of the fortune-teller's tent, close to the truck.

Open-mouthed, Midge forgot his own part in the operation till Pete had knotted the rope at the base of the pole. It was just as Pete was turning to crawl past the back wall of the tent that an angry bellow turned Midge's blood cold.

He saw Pete yanked to his feet by the shifty-looking man who had finished dismantling the pay-box.

'What's the big idea, snooping round this tent?' the man hissed as he frog-marched Pete towards the entrance. 'We'll see what Zodiac has to say about this!'

Pulling himself out of his horrified trance, Midge turned and ran at breakneck speed through the home-going groups of people.

'Save Pete!' he bawled. 'They've got Pete!'

'Little hooligan!' gasped an elderly man as Midge, changing direction, bounced off his waistcoat.

Midge had seen a distant, blue-uniformed figure.

'Spies!' Midge shouted. 'Zodiac's mob have captured Pete!'

The policeman paused in his ponderous march and waited for Midge to reach him.

'I'm not telling you again! Clear off!' said the policeman coldly.

'Please, you've *got* to come at once!' Midge begged.

'Hop it before I get mad with you!' The policeman turned away. 'You boys are more trouble than you're worth!'

Midge cast around, desperate to know what to do. He did the first thing that came into his mind. Stooping, he scooped up a handful of mud. Running near enough to feel sure he would not miss the departing policeman, he flung his sticky handful. But he did miss.

The mud hurtled through the air homed with a dull thud on an immaculate white shirt-front. The wearer of the shirt, a dignified and respected citizen, stared down in pop-eyed disbelief at the gooey mess which hid his tie.

'Mud!' he spluttered angrily. 'That boy threw mud at me!'

'Sorry!' Midge gasped. But his stuttering apology was cut short. The man with the mud-spattered shirt suddenly let out an angry yell and sprang at him.

Midge dodged. Then the policeman lunged and Midge had to dodge again. He bolted, weaving and swerving with the policeman and the man thudding after him. Others joined in the chase and Midge knew then what it was like to be a hare with the hounds in full cry.

All at once he saw Joe opening the door of a car at the roadside beyond the sideshows.

'Joe, help!' Midge managed a husky cry.

The tent collapsed in a tangle of heaving canvas.

But the car was starting up and taking Joe away and Midge knew with sinking heart that his anguished call had been lost on the wind. The policeman's hand fell on his shoulder and he was jerked to a stop.

At that moment new chaos hit the fair. Over by the showmen's booths, the truck with the tow-rope attached was beginning to move off. There was a rending crash as the fortune-teller's tent swayed and collapsed in a tangle of heaving canvas, to be dragged in the wake of the departing truck.

Rolling on the ground, tangled in the guy ropes with a crystal ball nearby, and playing cards scattered around him, was the mystic Zodiac in eastern robes and turban. His furtive partner, still gripping Pete, sprawled in the canvas folds.

'Help!' Pete shouted, struggling to free himself. 'Zodiac is Ernst!'

In the mounting bedlam his yell was meaningless to the fairground people who rushed to the scene. But it was not meaningless to Zodiac. Wrenching himself clear of the guy ropes, he went at a staggering run towards the fairground exit, pulling off his robes as he went.

A car swung across his path and a broad-shouldered, grim-faced young man leaped out.

'It's Joe!' Midge's voice squeaked.

Too late, Zodiac saw his danger. Joe was on him in a flying tackle and the fortune-teller thudded to the ground, a dazed and winded captive.

For Pete and Midge, that instant changed everything. At a shout from Joe, the policeman collared the rat-faced man who had looked after the pay-box. Plain-clothes detectives from the car ordered the crowd back. One of them shepherded Pete and Midge out of the throng – it was Ted Stringer, beaming and congratulating the boys, as he made sure they were unharmed. Another detective was gathering papers from the debris of the tent.

The man who had called himself Zodiac and his furtive-looking companion were handcuffed and taken away. And at last Joe Manders had time to turn to Pete and Midge.

'Well, it's thanks to you chaps that we've captured Zodiac – or Ernst, to give him his real name!' Joe said. 'Our people searched these sideshows yesterday and there was no sign of him then! This afternoon we were combing the main amusement park and Ernst would have got clean away if you two hadn't spotted the Zodiac clue in time! As it is, we've nabbed him and another gang member and also got the very revealing messages his agents have given him today – no doubt when they came along pretending to get their fortunes told! So you've done your share, Pete and Midge! And just in time! I was on the point of leaving when you started up that chaos! Now our people and the police are going to finish it off!'

Pete was still in a daze. 'I've lost my cap!' he said. 'First Midge and now me! Ernst recognised that cap when the pay-box man marched me into the tent. I thought I was done for!'

'We'll think about caps later. I want you two to come back to the station with me!' Joe told them, grinning broadly.

'Not the station!' Midge backed off. 'The sergeant doesn't like us!'

'Don't worry, he will!' Joe grinned. 'After what you've done this afternoon, you'll be friends for life!'

In the next two hectic hours at the police station the boys were told enough to know they had helped to bring off the biggest spy-catching operation of the year.

It put behind bars the entire ring of six English-speaking enemy agents, led by Ernst, all of whom had forged or stolen identity papers, and were working in Portdown on jobs that allowed them to filch vital information about troop and shipping movements from the harbour.

The spies were rounded up and brought in one by one, while Pete and Midge were looked after by the sergeant.

'Great work, lads!' he kept saying.

They could hardly believe he was the same sergeant. He ordered mugs of tea and the best cakes from the station canteen, and beamed at them like a kindly uncle.

'I was wrong about you two!' he said. 'Your folks are going to be proud of you! We've sent round to tell 'em you're here. You'll be the heroes of the hour when your part in this story is released to the papers!'

'You've probably helped to save the lives of hundreds of British seamen from enemy submarine operations!' Joe put in. 'The information leaking out of Portdown to the submarines has been cut off for good and all!'

'Well, I don't mind so much now that the spies got our school caps!' Midge bit happily into his third cream cake.

'The secret service have authorised me to say you two will be presented with special caps of your own choice in honour of what you've done!' Joe beamed. 'In fact, you could say you've been awarded England caps!'

The Battle of Wits

by Tom Stirling

It was the noise of an aeroplane engine directly overhead that woke Richard. The sound had come suddenly, and increased with a deafening roar as if the aeroplane were only just above his own bed. The sound came and went very quickly; and then it seemed that every anti-aircraft gun in the area opened up. He sat up in bed as a searchlight beam flashed across the sky, filling the room with light, even though the curtains were drawn.

Hurling back the bedclothes, Richard leaped out of bed and rushed to the window, pulling back the heavy curtains with the lithe agility of a fourteen-year-old. Tense and eager with excitement, he stared out at the night sky – black, except where it was stabbed by the raking beams of searchlights, and lit now and again by the sparkle of bursting shells, winking and darting like shooting stars.

'*Bonne chance!*' he breathed to the unknown pilot; for the mere fact that the German searchlights were seeking him and all the guns shooting at him was proof that he was either British or American – an Allied airman who intended no good to the German occupiers of Richard's island. For it was as 'his' island that Richard thought of it, just as all Channel Islanders thought of the islands as their own, although still oppressed by the occupying forces. The Islanders were in a tight grip, but now it was being slackened; for it was 1944 – the year of the Allied invasion of Europe, in northern France.

Richard pulled on socks and stepped into trouser legs without removing his pyjamas. He hauled on a thick sweater, for the island nights could be chilly, even in August; then he knelt to find his rubber boots, and made sure that he had his secret pocket-torch tied to his leg below the knee. It was no night for an active boy to remain in bed when, outside, guns were firing again and again, and a German night fighter had become air-borne – or so he judged by the familiar engine sound. It seemed that all hell was let loose.

Although the Channel Islands were not attacked by Allied aeroplanes, it did sometimes happen that mines were laid in the sea lanes to trap E-Boats that took shelter in the harbour. Moreover, by means of his own private 'grapevine', Richard had learned that there was now an even bigger and more important fish in the harbour – a U-Boat. Doubtless some loyal Channel Islander had somehow managed to get that information through to London. If so, it was likely that bombers, escorted by fighters, might fly over to destroy it or else to lay mines to the same end.

A hundred thoughts chased through Richard's head as he finished dressing by wrapping a thick scarf round his neck. Would the Allied aircraft, he wondered, attack the harbour? Even at risk of Channel Islanders' lives? Would the pilots machine-gun the quays and jetties to keep away the German defenders? He was a long way from the harbour – too far to be able to reach it before all the excitement was over; he was, indeed, on the opposite side of the island. But he could have some idea of what was going on by climbing a nearby tall tree that stood on rising ground. It would give him a view, if, alas, a little remote, of the action around the harbour: at least he would see the gun flashes and the general fireworks display which he associated with military action.

Almost all the Channel Island children had been evacuated to the English mainland just before the German invasion; but because of his widowed mother's illness at the time, which had proved fatal, Richard had stayed on to comfort her. He was ten years old when his mother died, and he went to live with his grandfather, who also lived on the Island, and was too old for military service or arduous work. Then ran a small-holding together, and grew tomatoes.

Since then, life seemed to Richard to have been a long period of virtual imprisonment; but now the Islanders hoped that the Day – the Day of Freedom – was not far away. The Allied armies had already invaded the mainland of Europe, and he was sure they were winning, and that the Islands would soon be free again. Uncles, aunts, cousins and friends would come home to the Island – how he longed for that day!

According to German reports, the Allied forces, far from being victorious, were being driven back to the coast. However, such reports did not depress Richard, for he did not believe them. In secret, he and his grandfather listened in to the B.B.C. news on their well hidden radio.

It was at times such as this night, when the action of war almost involved him, that Richard suffered most from intense frustration. The strict curfew imposed by the Germans forbade everyone to be out of doors at night without special authorisation – and Richard, at fourteen, had no such indulgence, nor any excuse for asking for it. If, nevertheless, he chose to go out at night, and was spotted by a member of the invading force, then he would most certainly be shot at, or arrested and taken before the German commander who would show him little lenience.

But this situation did not daunt Richard. Out he went, as he had often gone before. Having learned from previous escapades how to dodge, and how to creep silently through undergrowth at night, he had become quite confident. He was proud of his skill in evading sentries who, it had to be admitted, were not always as alert as they should have been. So, taut with excitement, he set out. When by ill chance he made a noise by treading on a stone that slipped or that he unwarily kicked, he halted, and stood as still as a statue. Sometimes, hearing a German gutteral voice alarmingly close, he lay down, and stayed flat and motionless, like a frightened mouse.

But there was too much noise everywhere tonight, with guns firing from all directions, for any sound he made to be heard. Now and then, he suddenly became the anxious listener, when a red hot piece of burst flak shell came whistling dangerously near, making its characteristic whining sound, before thudding with grim finality into the singed earth.

Tonight, Richard was not just an observer. When he had climbed his tree, and watched whatever there was to see, he had a most important mission to carry out. There was something he most particularly wanted to look at – indeed had to look at – only a few hundred yards away. This 'thing' was a structure being built by German sappers, in great secrecy. This cloak of secrecy only emphasised how important it was; but no one who had seen it had any idea what it was, except that it seemed to be directional, and to point to the English coast – perhaps Southampton? Only Russian prisoners of war, who spoke no English, were allowed to work on it: Islanders were driven off, at the point of a bayonet if necessary.

Yet Richard had got within yards of it, and had even made a sketch of it. The guard dogs – usually Alsatians – which were supposed to snout out any spies, did not give him away. If they did nose him out, it was only in order to enjoy any snack he had taken for them. And they were even clever enough to know that what they were doing was wrong: for they greeted him with discretion, and, he swore, wagged their tails only very gently, making hardly any movement.

So there it was: he was a spy, perhaps the youngest spy in the war, drawing sketch maps of secret enemy installations. He might even have been regarded as a member of a spy ring, for he did not work quite alone. Somewhere in the darkness was his secret ally, a Russian prisoner of war who spoke a little English – a fact not known by the Germans.

There was no signal tonight from Serge, as he was called, and Richard prayed that he was still safe. Without attracting enemy attention, he safely reached the tree, and climbed it quickly and easily, even in darkness – for the searchlights had suddenly gone out. When that happened, it meant that an order to do so had been given. Some trap was being set for an enemy aircraft – an Allied aircraft, which meant a friend to Richard. Sure enough, he heard an aero engine. It was misfiring, chattering and banging, and obviously in trouble.

Suddenly the searchlights blazed on again, focused in a cone forming an apex on the cloud base, bringing out of the darkness a lone Spitfire – in trouble. It was coming down. Richard watched, spellbound, and came near to yelling a warning when, behind the Spitfire, seen against the gleaming background of clouds, came a lone Messerschmidt fighter, spitting flame and bullets. With anguished scream of expiring engine, the Spitfire dived. Again the searchlights went off – so that the German pilot would not be blinded, Richard guessed.

A minute passed; then a glow and a blaze of fire showed in the darkness. To his amazement he saw, by the light of its own fire, that the victim was not, as he had supposed, the Spitfire, but the Messerschmidt. Flames engulfed it as it came down, trailing a long tail of thick black smoke, thundering over the headland, down and down to the quenching sea.

But Richard was still staring where the Spitfire had been, at a strange object which the trailing glow from the burning Messerschmidt had shown him – a parachute. But distracting him, the doomed Spitfire suddenly reappeared from over the sea, flying crazily at a very low altitude, spluttering, banging, and spraying glycol from a punctured radiator, glowing bright cherry-red, and creating a fearful, scorching hurricane of hot air that almost blew him from the tree as it sped past at some four hundred miles an hour. It went on and away, avoiding trees as if by a miracle, over the headland, then down, out of his sight to the sea. The glimpse he had of it was brief, yet it was enough to convince him that it was indeed the Spitfire – pilotless. Without doubt he knew then that it was its pilot whom he had seen making a 'brolly hop', going down by parachute towards the dark, deep sea. He could no longer see anything at all in the night sky where the combat had been, so the pilot might still be there, drifting down, as invisible to the Germans as to himself. The searchlights had been dowsed and the only remaining light came from the burning aeroplane, which gave off a distant, fading glow, unpleasantly red, with the thickening column of black smoke clouding it completely now and then.

Shivering with the thrill of the air battle, Richard slipped down from the tree and turned towards the narrow path that led to the only route down to the beach. It was narrow and treacherous, but he knew every inch of the way, although the darkness now was pitch black. From the distance he heard the sound of guttural voices shouting and the eerie foreboding siren of the ambulance, its note rising and falling monotonously.

He had a new mission. He was at last really taking part in the war. If the British pilot ditched safely, he would still have to swim ashore. It would be no mean feat in the darkness, and he might be handicapped by a wound. Even when he did reach the shore, he would need help. He would need to be hidden from the enemy. Moreover his parachute, a giveaway, had to be destroyed. One way and another, there was quite a lot of organisation to be done by someone – and that someone evidently had to be Richard. The story of another British pilot who had been saved and hidden on the Islands, to be smuggled back to England, came to his mind. He had been told the details, so he thought he knew the drill.

Richard had never felt so excited in his life before.

On top of the headland he paused, looking down towards the restless sea thundering against the rock a hundred feet below – all the more awesome because it could not be seen. Nothing could be seen: not the jagged path, nor the treacherous slippery places where footholds were tricky, nor the rocks on which an unlucky climber would fall far below. It was not the moment for hesitation. Slithering, stumbling, sometimes crawling warily on all fours, making the descent from memory, Richard Baptiste went down into the darkness which he hoped he shared with the parachuted Spitfire pilot, somewhere out there.

At nineteen, Flight-Lieutenant Jim Brady had learned not to believe all he was told. And he was glad he had not believed that joining the Caterpillar Club was fun. He was a potential member now of that exclusive club, membership of which was open only to those who had saved their lives by parachuting from a doomed aeroplane in the face of the enemy. He felt that now he really knew what hard water was – the substance there had been so much talk about. It took him some minutes to recover, and then he realised that he had to start work again; he had to rid himself of the parachute which was adrift on the water, catching the wind now and then, as ready to sink as to save him, and a sure clue to the enemy. He had to shed it; and as he trod water he was glad that his life jacket was keeping him up, giving support.

But he had no clue as to direction. Somewhere in his flying suit was a home-made compass – a brass cap, as from a bottle in the middle of which was a point on which a magnetised needle, if he could find it, would swing, seek, and find the north. It was there in case he evaded the enemy and had to find his way around.

It was cold in the water, or seemed so, yet it was August, and he should be able to swim without clothes. As far as he could remember, Bunnyface, the Intelligence Officer, had told them all quite a lot about what to do in just this situation, but it all escaped him at that moment. There was a list of Do's and Don't's stacked away neatly somewhere in his memory, no doubt in the wrong place.

Not a light came from the Island; no searchlights shone, and the glow of the burning aeroplane was no more. In one direction he could reach the coast of America – a few thousand miles west, according to cynical Bunnyface. But which direction *was* west? And in which the Island that now had vanished into darkness? And how far out to sea was he? One mile? Five? He had no dinghy – only the suit. He could not survive long, even on his sodden emergency rations.

The outlook was indeed grim. It might be better to be picked up by the enemy than to drift into the Atlantic. There was no hope even of locating the direction in which he had seen the glow of the burning aeroplane.

And then from somewhere came a winking light. Faint, but in the pitch darkness unmistakable. He watched it. It flickered; it stopped; it flickered again. He was certain that it was a signal. A signal to someone . . . to a ship? From a ship? It must be Morse! He watched, straining his eyes as he bobbed up and down in the water, feeling horribly seasick and lonely. Morse . . . dot dot dash . . . dot dash dot . . . It was coming back to him and finally made sense. 'Friend!' he shouted, startled by his own voice. He shouted again but broke off half way as something large pushed against his legs. A porpoise? Or what had Bunnyface of Intelligence told them about sharks? Sharks . . . He kicked out vaguely, and tried to work himself forward. FRIEND. That's what the signal said. And then . . . COME HERE. It took him a little time to understand, and the message was repeated patiently half a dozen times before he really grasped it. But the light seemed to be getting brighter and nearer – and suddenly the thought came to him that he was being carried in on a flood tide. He was being swept forward. He had undone the parachute but had not been able to gather it in and fold it, and it was obviously unwilling to sink at his whim. So he let go, muttering, 'Fool! It'll come in on the tide, anyway.'

Jim wriggled and struggled, treading water. He would strip to his pants and vest, so as to swim ashore more easily, and then hope that his parachute and gear would follow him. There was nothing of use to the enemy in his pockets – only Jenny's photograph, and she was safely far away for either that or her telephone number to help them.

On the shore Richard waited, patient, alert and resolute. He had signalled the message over and over again because he remembered being told that crashed pilots would be dazed, and were often only casually acquainted with Morse code.

He had fitted over the torch head a piece of paper with a small hole in it, tinted light green with water-colour, and he wasn't sure of the distance from which it could be seen and read. He had never had a chance to test it with Serge, and there was no one else he could trust except his grandfather, who might have seized the torch and hidden it, or even destroyed it: for Richard had stolen it from a German corporal.

Richard waited and signalled until a sudden splashing from close at hand alerted him. He wished he dared shine the torch.

'Pwht!' came a soft whistle call; and Richard, shaking a little with excitement, dabbed the torch button. Out of the water, quite suddenly, came a dimly visible figure.

'British?' breathed Richard.

'Yes . . . And you?'

'Channel Islander.'

'You sound young. Anyone else with you?'

'No. Want to go back?' It was a silly question that Richard had not meant, but he was just a little hurt. Did he sound such a kid then?

Jim Brady splashed ashore.

'What goes on?' he asked hoarsely. 'Thanks for the reception. Saved my life, I can tell you. Lost at sea. Can't see you . . .' Neither could see the other yet.

'Follow me when I flick the torch. Careful of large loose stones.' It was to the cave that Richard went, and the going was far from easy, as the occasional gasp of pain from Jim, who had found some of the loose stones with a bare foot, indicated. The journey was short, fortunately, and the cave had a turn in it, although Richard warned Jim too late to duck once or twice.

'I can put the light on now,' said Richard.

All the same he shone it at the rocky wall so that only the reflection fell upon Jim, and little light could shine out to sea – especially round the bend. But he could not be too careful, as he explained, for the Germans had watch-towers along the coast, and used especially powerful periscopic binoculars with which they ranged the sea ceaselessly. Sometimes boats were on the prowl, just off shore, watching the coast.

'You'll be taken to the mainland . . . to England.'

'Oh yes . . . not at once . . . I hope.' And Jim, teeth chattering, sat down on a large stone. He was dressed only in pants and vest, soaked to the skin, and chilling rapidly.

'Here! Take my scarf,' urged Richard. 'I'll get you some clothes later. I should have brought a towel, but I didn't know . . . Gosh! How marvellous that you shot down that Messer! I thought *he* had got *you*!'

'Exactly the same thought crossed my mind. What's

your name?'

'Richard.'

'I'm Jim Brady.' He held out his hand. 'Now, where was I before I started on formalities . . . ? Ah, yes – going down in flames, out of control. Not quite out of control. Not quite in flames, only red-hot. Radiator holed, glycol pouring out. Hun on tail. Nasty. No time to call Flight Leader on blower to ask what to do. He'd gone for a Burton. So I just dove . . .'

'Dove?'

'Dived . . . down . . . Saw Messer passing aloft . . . in sights, pressed buttons. Lucky eight machine guns fired as one . . . engine stinking hot, almost seized solid . . . Messer took fire and blazed off . . . down in drink. Hatch opened O.K. . . . chute opened . . . Sea was there on time, waiting – or what I took to be a concrete floor when it hit me! And here I am, and here you are . . .' He stared at Richard intently. 'Are all Channel Islanders as brave as you? You deserve my D.F.C. more than I do. And all I've got with me is the ribbon . . .'

Richard had wrapped his long scarf round Jim's throat, and now he peeled off his sweater, revealing only his pyjamas underneath.

'Oh, no! That's too much,' protested Jim.

'Dry yourself with the ends of the scarf; then put the sweater on. It'll mop up the water well.' It did, and Jim was grateful. While he dried himself, he persuaded Richard to give him a few facts. To explain why he had stayed on the island took only a few words; but Richard had something of greater interest to impart.

'Actually I'm a spy,' he said, fearing that Jim would laugh.

'Is that so? Are you spying on the Germans?'

'Yes. My grandfather doesn't know, so please, if you meet him, don't mention it. You see, although he is loyal, and hates the Germans, he is old, and doesn't want to run foul of them, he says. He may be an old man, but they might still take him – if they caught him helping the other side . . .'

Jim, feeling a little warmer, looked at his rescuer thoughtfully and with real admiration.

'You are helping me at risk of your life? I don't think I should let you. I'll fend for myself rather than involve you, Richard, grateful though I am.'

'It isn't just that. There's something else. I said I am a spy, and it's true.' His voice almost rose above the guarded whisper they had been using. 'You see, I am making sketches of a secret new fortification. Serge says it's a new kind of war weapon – a rocket.'

'A rocket? Against aeroplanes?'

'No, no. A big rocket – big enough to reach England.'

Jim understood.

'The V1 and the V2, we call them. You mean there's a launching site here? On the French mainland we've been bombing them, pouring down thousands of tons on those in the Pas de Calais area. But here? Do they think we couldn't or wouldn't bomb here? They could hit the invasion ports with rockets, of course.' It was pretty obvious that they might get the range, Jim thought; but there was the problem of supply.

'Serge isn't quite sure what they are for.'

'Isn't he? So who is this Serge?'

Richard hesitated before replying.

'He's a friend of mine. He's a Russian prisoner of war, and used to be in tanks before he was taken prisoner. He speaks a little English, which the Germans don't realise. We meet secretly. And he actually works on this thing! Sometimes, the officers speak in English when there are no Islanders around, so that neither the Russians nor Germans will understand them – or so they hope. But Serge is crafty. He remembers not to understand English, even if a sentry says "Have a drink?" suddenly; or "Like a brandy?" or "Got a light?" They're all trick questions because, without thinking, anyone knowing English and seeing a man with a cigarette, might move his hand to get matches or a lighter.'

'They are clever,' admitted Jim. 'I couldn't cope at that level.'

'Oh, it isn't difficult. Grandfather warned me to pretend to be simple and stupid. They think I'm a bit weak in the head! They often call me *Dummkopf* – stupid, you know. They teach me the wrong German words for things, and I make them laugh by saying *'Gute Nacht'* first thing in the morning when I see them. Also . . .' He stopped in mid-sentence as Jim suddenly stood up, and breathed 'Quiet!'

They both listened. The restless sea still fought its ceaseless battle with the rocks, a sound so continuous that it was no longer noticed. But Jim had heard another, different sound. It came again. Then, from the mouth of the tunnel, came a shout in German.

Richard quaked. Jim drew back, thinking quickly. To save Richard he would give himself up. At the same moment, Richard had decided that he would willingly be captured and even tortured rather than betray the Spitfire pilot.

'Ssh . . . I know what to do . . . Stay here,' said Richard; but as he moved off, Jim seized his shoulder.

'No, Richard,' Jim whispered. 'You mustn't endanger your life.'

'Go further into the cave. There's a small alcove at the end. Go on! Please! They suspect nothing or someone would have shone one of their brilliant thousand-yard torch beams . . . I know! In pyjamas only, would I be out helping the enemy? No! I am sleep walking . . .' He put his hands out at arms length and walked towards the cave mouth.

Uncertain, yet filled with admiration for the boy's quick thinking, Jim stayed where he was. His military duty was to evade capture unless doing so meant sacrifice of his life without any hope of saving it when, if taken prisoner, there might be at least some hope of escape. His life was not threatened yet . . . so he went to the end of the cave.

At the mouth, Richard halted. Two Germans were outside and they were shouting to another who suddenly flashed on a torch, beam shining upwards. At once, Richard dropped to the ground, so that when the German with the torch arrived, he was lying at the entrance to the cave, curled up, wearing only his pyjamas with a large stone as a pillow.

'Wake!' shouted a German corporal, shining the torch full into his face, and then stirring him with a jack-boot.

Richard 'awoke' suddenly, looked about him widly, caught sight of the Germans, sprang up, stumbled, and fell to his knees.

'No, no! Don't shoot!' he yelled. *'Guten nacht! Ein gut gebratene Ganz ist guten Gabe Gottes . . . ja, ja!'* He had been told it means that a well-cooked goose was a good gift from God. But an under-officer had said it meant 'Please be kind and I will sing for you.' He started to sing a tuneless, wordless song.

'Enough,' pleaded the Corporal, putting a hand to his ear.

'He is stupid,' said another soldier, touching his head with a finger, and winking.

The Corporal took Richard by the shoulder as he rose, and shook him gently.

'Why are you here?' he demanded. 'Why not wearing more clothes; nought but pyjammies, eh?'

'Because,' Richard explained, pointing to the sky, 'the shells and bombs. If in cottage, could be killed. Better in open. Cottage fall down sometime from bomb.' He pretended to cry. 'We get buried inside under lots of bricks. Not nice.' He shuddered and pulled a face as if scared.

'Idiot boy. If fright, why not go inside cave, eh? Better nor outside ain't it?' He exchanged a look with the soldier, and they both laughed derisively.

Richard moved a step towards the cave, and stared briefly into its darkness, beyond the glow of the shielded torch rays. With an expression of extreme dread, he pulled a horrible face, drew back and shuddered. Then, lowering his voice, he spoke confidentially and very secretly behind his hand, looking back towards the cave, as if fearful of being overheard.

'Octopus . . . eight legs in dark hiding place.' All the Islanders had told the Germans gruesome stories of what an octopus can do, so the soldiers were prepared. 'It lives in there.' He then put his hands together, and moved all eight fingers, imitating the supposed movements of the octopus's tentacles, on the assumption that being foreigners they could not otherwise understand. 'German soldier ate piece of octopus, then he died. Ugh!' He pulled a horrible face, and wriggled and twisted, miming the contortions of someone dying with a horrific painful certainty. 'Sometimes octopus put tentacles round neck. So . . .' And he wrapped an arm round his own neck to make certain that they understood the risk of going into the cave.

Watching him, pained and silent, the soldiers were troubled in their minds. They peered uneasily towards the dark mouth of the cave on which the torch-holder momentarily flashed his beam. Then the Corporal told them that he had read of such creatures living in the sea round the Channel Islands. These young soldiers were all farmer boys from the dark forests of Germany, and the sea was something of a mystery to them. The Corporal had himself read a story by a famous writer, describing how a man had been strangled by an octopus in the sea, and crushed to death. Richard could follow the gist of what the man was describing, though he spoke little German; for he, too, gave a dumb show performance.

'It has a secret home in the cave,' Richard added when the curtain fell, as it were, on the Corporal's dramatic recital.

The Corporal nodded, and then told Richard curtly that he

would be escorted back to the cottage at once, and must stay there. So, at his command, the soldier with the powerful torch led the way. Although the beam of light had to be shaded, it still made the journey as easy by night as it would have been in daylight.

They reached Richard's cottage without difficulty, finding it silent and in pitch darkness – evidence that the old man had neither been roused, nor was aware of Richard's absence. From the doorway Richard looked back, and saw them – still, shadowy figures. He waved, and the Corporal called softly, 'Sleep well, *Dummkopf*. Try putting your feet on the pillow, and your head where foots should was. Sleep thus better sometimes!' And they departed, laughing.

Richard had no intention of sleeping that way or any other – yet. There was too much to be done. He had to get clothes for Jim. Fortunately, there were some of his father's still in the wardrobe. And food . . .! That, too, was essential. Food was in short supply on the Island, but there was a secret, well-hidden supply of tinned food he had stolen from the Germans. To Richard, robbing them was a patriotic triumph, not a crime. There was milk; and some eggs.

As to other necessities, he suddenly thought of a bath towel, and swimming trunks; for it would help Jim during the day if he could pretend to be a casual bather or sunbather. People who are bold and move unwarily in the open do not arouse suspicion, he thought. And because of the cliffs he would be seen only from a distance – except through binoculars, which would have to be brought specially.

Still thinking primarily of Jim's safety, Richard made his final choice: some horse-hair stuffing from an old mattress in the loft. It might serve as the foundation for a false beard, he thought. He had seen Serge use something similar, with a thread woven artfully through it, and then tied over the head in some way to keep the beard in position. As a temporary beard that could be whipped off in a moment, and stuffed inside the shirt, it was marvellous. From a little distance, a beard like that would help to make Jim look older.

As to the means of getting all these things to him, Richard could think of nothing better than making a bundle wrapped up in a blanket, or perhaps a tarpaulin, and roping it. It could be bounced down the path, and he could follow, and find it. For fear of waking his grandfather, or drawing the attention of soldiers who might still be near the cottage, he had to work silently as well as swiftly, and almost in the dark. But he finished the job.

Two hours later, when all was quiet, he went to the cliff head, and rolled the bundle down. The sounds it made were hardly audible, and brought no lights. And when he did reach the cave, Jim was asleep.

But what an awakening! Jim could hardly believe his eyes. He kept patting Richard's head and slapping him on the back.

'You've done marvels!' he told Richard. 'We'll solve the riddle of that "Thing", get full details, and perhaps even blow it up ourselves. Who knows? With a chap like you around, anything's possible.'

They chatted for a while, then Richard made his way home.

General Von Streimer was an officer of great importance who was visiting the Island on a mission, the nature of which was known only to himself, his aide, and his Führer. He had arrived unexpectedly by aeroplane, and had commandeered the Commandant's Mercedes and chauffeur. His immediate destination did not surprise the Commandant; it was the secret structure that was well-hidden in a hollow, and covered with bushes which were fitted into an all-covering light mesh net.

The General was a man in his middle fifties, portly but

upright, with clear, cold grey eyes, a hawk nose, and thin, tight lips. His manner was decisive, and his reputation surrounded him like an aura. When he entered a military office, everyone immediately sprang to attention, aware of his presence even when there had been no warning of his approach. In front of him, no one spoke an unnecessary word. Indeed, no one spoke at all without either being spoken to or given permission to speak. Even the Commander himself, awe inspiring though he was to his own garrison troops, seemed, by comparison, like a junior officer, so humble and placatory was his manner when confronting the General.

It was on the fourth morning after Jim's arrival that the General's Mercedes came in sight on the road near the 'Thing'. It was immediately parked under trees and netting, so that Allied reconnaissance aeroplanes should not be intrigued by its presence. If they did see it, they would photograph it. Its presence in a photograph would arouse suspicion and young WAAF officers of the Photographic Interpretation Unit, using stereo lenses, would study it with great interest, and also the surrounding area. The camouflage netting thus closely scrutinised would be recognised for what it was. Within a day or so, it would be bombed!

The General's arrival in the underground working area was the signal for an under-officer to yell an order, bringing work to a halt. A dozen Russian prisoners were there, stripped to the waist; they were enormous men, powerful, and yet generally docile; although, if roused by anger or drink or cruelty, they were capable, it was said, of splintering a human head with one swipe of a spade. By order, therefore, they were disciplined – but not too heavily. When they saw the General, they only stared in sullen resentment at him, apart from one or two who spat on the ground with contempt. But he ignored them all as if they were wooden posts.

'None of the men speak English?' the General asked a sapper officer, softly in an aside.

'No, sir. Not one.'

'Then speak English – but softly. The work must be speeded up. It is of much importance . . . vital . . .' He broke off because a powerful Russian prisoner had started hammering. It was Serge, and the officer wheeled on him and yelled.

'It is a prisoner who is deaf, General. He did not know you were speaking.'

'Very well. Speed up. Redouble effort. Overtime if need be. Understood?'

'Understood, my General.'

'Good. It is this secret weapon that may yet settle the issue. There is now available by the Führer's command a secret explosive more powerful than any hitherto known – atomic, if you know what that means – made in our secret works, away from the enemy's bombing. It can blow a whole town up. It comes like forked lighting, without warning. It will be the first and the last; for one will be enough to destroy any town. It is terrible, unimaginable; but it will be used as retribution. By the order of our Führer, it will be used first on Southampton – then on London.'

The German sapper officer remained silent, deeply impressed.

'I am telling you this,' the General continued, 'for the sake of morale, and so that you shall all work the harder. It will bring an end to the war. To site it in France would be to risk attack on it. Here, unsuspected, away from spies, it is safe . . . and safe it *must* be. Where is the security officer?'

A young Gestapo colonel stepped into view from the shadows.

'Sir!' he cried, saluting in great style.

'See to it that no one loiters near. There shall be no mercy for

Richard was lying in the long grass.

spies. Arrest . . . trial, perhaps . . . and death, without fear, favour or mercy. If any spies are found by someone other than you, you shall be blamed, Colonel, and charged with negligence. Understood?'

It was understood; and the General continued his inspection. He studied the drawings, examined the work, made comments and sharp criticisms, and then went up to the open air and bright sunshine.

Richard saw him clearly, for he was only twenty yards away, lying in the long grass under a mat of woven grasses. A German police-dog friend of his lay beside him, dozing after a meal of the Gestapo colonel's lunch which Serge had stolen and given it.

'I will stroll down to the sea,' he heard the General say. 'I wish to be alone. See that I am not followed, Colonel, and call off those dogs.'

The General, tempted by the weather, was obviously going down to the beach to swim, or to sunbathe; and there, of course, was Jim – perhaps on view, perhaps not. Richard was thoroughly alarmed. But to go to that path now was certainly not safe, even though the German soldiers paid little attention to the movements of *Dummkopf* – stupid head. The general might be more alertly suspicious of his movements, or even turn nasty.

Moreover, Richard had an appointment with Serge, who was to tell him what the General had said, if it was significant. The arrangement made between them was that Serge, with the connivance of the under-officer, would sneak away from the other workers on the pretext of robbing Richard's cottage of eggs that the hens laid away somewhere in a secret spot known to Serge.

Meanwhile, Richard had returned to his cottage, and waited in the garden with three eggs, to keep the under-officer appeased. Presently, Serge came crawling through the grass towards him. He spoke in a tense undertone and told Richard all that he had heard about the fearful threat to Southampton and

London. It might indeed be a war-winning weapon. Whether it was or not, it must be destroyed; the bombers must know where to find it.

'The General,' whispered Serge, 'has the plans in the top left pocket of his tunic. You must get them. He is going down to the beach. It is now or never.'

Richard stared at him in wonder.

'I? But how?'

'Shsh . . . you and the British pilot. He must use his brains. He must get them! Tonight there is to be a British submarine lying off . . . a rubber dinghy will come ashore here. The underground has planned it. So tonight those plans must be sent, even if it means killing the General . . .'

But he fell silent. There were voices not far away and one belonged to the Gestapo colonel, who suddenly yelled, 'Who is there?' in German, in French, and then in English.

Richard and Serge lay motionless. All was silent – until a burst of machine gun fire broke the stillness, bringing the whine of bullets close to them. Bullets streaked through the grass; one went *thud!* into a tree. Looking towards Serge, his feet icy cold, Richard saw that he now had a hand grenade ready for action.

'Go to the beach,' mouthed Serge. 'Not by the path . . . by rope, near tree . . . when I have gone . . .' His arm moved and there was a flash and a bang, after which a thick yellow cloud of smoke rose. Serge, on all fours, crawled away. Again bullets whistled through the smoke, and it seemed certain to Richard that Serge must have been hit; but he did not know whether he was or not. Serge was lost in the smoke.

Suddenly he realised that he, too, must move. He could not, like a coward, lie there until he was found. But his legs had turned to lead; his heart thumped, and his feet felt like blocks of ice.

It was minutes later that, by a great effort of will power, he moved his reluctant limbs, and crawled forward. He crouched and ran when he heard shouting that came from further away. Above the scream of gulls rose the wail of the ambulance siren. He ran, not thinking at all; his mind was paralysed. Only when he was a hundred yards or more away did he slow down to a saunter. He was wearing the red jersey which everyone knew, so that they would recognise him at once, and not pay too much attention to him. He strolled along, pausing now and then to watch the crying gulls, until he reached the tree. There, fastened to an iron staple and dangling over the cliff edge, was a strong, thin rope. It was double, entwined rope, and at intervals of a yard there were cross pegs fixed as footholds.

Nevertheless, it needed nerve and courage to use it as the means of going down the cliff face to the beach a hundred feet below. But down he went, to be swooped and pecked at every now and then by angry gulls. Swinging and turning on the rope, he felt with his feet for each foothold and could hardly believe his fortune when at last he did reach the beach.

Even then, he had some hazardous rock-climbing to do before reaching Jim's beach; but it came into view suddenly . . . and there he saw General Von Streimer seated on the sand, jacket open and unbelted, his back to the rocks, sunbathing with his eyes closed.

Richard, fingers in mouth, whistled his imitation sea-bird's call that was his signal to Jim; and within a minute or two Jim was peering round the cave mouth, stripped for sunbathing himself. Richard put a warning finger to his lips and decided what to do.

In order to avoid awakening the General, he waded quietly through the sea. It might have seemed to an onlooker that he was only concerned for the General's personal comfort; but he was well aware that there might be a German sniper watching, and if he made a false, threatening move, the sniper might focus him in telescopic sights and fire. A kill at five hundred yards was an average routine performance for a sniper. Trying to appear casual, once he had passed the General – not hurrying, and even pausing to inspect an anemone left in a pool by the retreating tide – he reached the cave.

In a few words he told Jim the whole situation. They thought swiftly and desperately; and then, suddenly, Jim hit on an idea. It was risky, but there was hope of success. Eagerly adopting it, Richard returned to the General. He coughed and woke him.

'Highness,' piped Richard nervously, 'are you a general?'

'Eh? Yes, boy. What are you doing here?'

'I live here. They call me *Dummkopf* because I'm a bit simple. I came to tell you there's another like you in the cave.'

'Another like me?' scowled the General.

'In *that* uniform. Only he's dead. He was washed up by the sea, and I dragged him in there.'

The General stared at him intently. It sounded the kind of thing a *Dummkopf* would do. Had the boy told anyone? No. He did not think it mattered. They would miss the General and look for him . . . Naturally, Von Streimer was intrigued, and alarmed. But before warning the Commander or Gestapo colonel, he wanted to be sure of his facts. He would look a fool if the boy was lying; and as the cave was only a short distance away the only intelligent course to take was to go there, and see for himself. He went, leaving his belt unbuckled and his jacket unfastened.

'At the end,' said Richard beckoning him into the darkness.

It was the General's own end – for the time being. He went down like a felled ox, as Jim, lurking in wait in the darkness, struck him down.

Methodically, they went to work. They took the package from the pocket, and, at Jim's advice, slit the envelope with a razor blade, removed the contents, and then refilled it with folded newspaper so that it looked the same. Back it went into the pocket. After discussion, they stripped the General, bound his feet and wrists, gagged him, and dragged him far up into the cave round the bend. That done, it was Richard's task to put the clothes in a neat pile as if the General had gone for a swim. As sometimes happens in such waters, it would be assumed that he had not returned. There would be no reason to suspect foul play.

Sub-Lieutenant Bryan Jones, R.N., paddled the rubber dinghy through the inky darkness of night to the shore. It was a triumph of navigation, although his last few yards were made easier by the flicker of a very small green light.

'Wizard of Oz?' asked a soft voice.

'Mickey Mouse,' came the Sub-Lieutenant's reassuring reply.

The rubber dinghy was pulled in, and Jim climbed aboard, giving his rank and name. Then he helped Richard to climb in.

'This is the real hero of the operation,' he whispered. 'The super-spy. He has special information for Winston Churchill; after H.M. the King, of course!'

'Ssssh!' warned the Sub-Lieutenant. 'They're about!'

But it was only when they were within yards of the submarine that the searchlights went on. None could be got down to sea level. When Richard and Jim were aboard and below, the deck gun fired, and the one groping searchlight went out. As the submarine dived, everything opened up from the Island; but by then they were going down.

It is recorded history that the launching site was obliterated; that the secret weapon was never used; and that the German atomic bomb was never brought to full development. But the information contained in that document carried by Richard was of such vital importance that it remained Top Secret in the archives. The King knew of it, for he mentioned it when he presented a proud, excited Richard with the George Cross.

Later, after the Liberation, when Richard returned to his Island, he found to his joy that his grandfather was still alive, and that Serge, recovering from two bullet wounds, was well enough to be sent to his home.

As for General Von Streimer, he had escaped from his bonds, and walked naked back to camp, putting on to the Gestapo colonel all the blame for his being attacked and overpowered by five enormous Russian prisoners . . .

But the story that Jim and Richard told was different, and never failed to delight their audience – especially Richard's fellow Islanders!

Ghost Planes

by Lee Mayne

The jeep rocked and lurched over the rough jungle track, finally emerging into the glaring sunshine that beat down on to the primitive airstrip. Here the driver was able to put his foot down and, with a surge of power, the vehicle roared across the runway and skidded to a halt beside the small charter plane.

'Pop' Williams heaved his burly frame out from behind the wheel and stood for a moment letting the slight breeze ruffle through his thinning grey hair. It felt good after the steamy heat along the jungle track. He turned to his companion, who was dragging a small tin box from the jeep.

'Take care of it, Jim,' he said. 'It's worth nearly £10,000.'

Jim Langly grinned, confidently. 'Don't worry, Pop – five hours from now, it'll be in the bank . . .' He heaved the box aboard the plane and climbed up after it. 'And I'll be having the coldest drink in Hong Kong!'

Pop flipped a hand in cheerful acknowledgment. 'Keep radio contact with us until you pick up the airport!' he called.

Langly waved back. 'Check!' he shouted.

A few moments later, the little plane was skimming down the runway. Pop stopped the jeep on the edge of the jungle and gave a brief nod of satisfaction, as he watched the aircraft lift over the tops of the trees. Within seconds, it had gone from sight.

Jim Langly levelled off at four thousand feet and settled himself more comfortably in his seat. He flipped the radio button.

'GHK2 calling PMC – GHK2 calling PMC! Are you receiving me? Over . . .'

In the tiny radio-hut attached to the Paitok Mining Company, Pete Roper pressed down his 'talk' switch.

'Hullo, GHK2 – PMC answering! Receiving you strength five – over . . .'

Langly's voice came back over the speaker. 'Strength five – check. You know something, Pete – you never appreciate just how much jungle there is in Burma, until you sit up here and look at it.'

Roper stared out at the towering trees crowding in on the mining compound. He flipped the switch.

'Do *you* know something, Jim? he grinned. 'I just don't appreciate the Burmese jungle – period! Check again in fifteen minutes. PMC over and out!'

The speaker crackled. 'O.K., Pete – GHK2 over and out!'

Forty-five minutes later, Roper made his fourth entry in the log-book: '11.15 hours. GHK2 check – O.K.' He looked up as Pop Williams entered the hut.

'Everything all right, son?' asked the mine-owner.

'Sure thing, Mr Williams,' Roper nodded. 'Jim's just checked in.'

'Good . . .' Pop let out a long breath. 'Phew! This hut gets like an oven.' He smiled kindly at the radio man. 'Best take a break, son – before you get over-done.' Roper hesitated. 'It's O.K. – I'll stand watch for half an hour.'

For a while after the operator had gone, the old man stood in the hut doorway, staring at the activity in the compound. 'A ruby mine,' he thought. 'Sounds like something out of the Arabian Nights.' He laughed cynically to himself as he thought of the slow, grinding, physical effort that had to be poured in, month after month. 'And for what?' he grunted.

Suddenly, the radio crackled into life. 'GHK2 calling PMC – GHK2 calling PMC!' Langly's voice was urgent.

Pop dived for the switch. 'PMC answering! What's wrong, Jim?'

In the plane, Jim Langly was working feverishly to coax his spluttering engine back into full life. 'A fuel blockage!' he reported, tersely. The engine gave one last kick-back – then died. Langly's jaw tightened grimly as he put the aircraft into a long, shallow glide. 'Now it's quit for good!' He stared ahead at the limitless expanse of jungle. No man could take a plane down into that – and live!

Inspector Jean Collet leant back in the comfortable cane chair and stared at the ceiling. He appeared to be watching the broad-bladed fan than spun lazily overhead, but his keen brain was concentrating on each detail of the facts which the Burmese Police Captain was recounting. The Hawk had flown into Rangoon that morning, at the request of the Burma Government.

'So, in a nutshell, it amounts to this,' he said, when the Captain had finished. 'Two charter planes have disappeared on the flight from the Paitok Mine to Hong Kong. Each carried a cargo of rough rubies valued at £10,000. A full-scale air search has failed to reveal any sign of wreckage.'

Captain U Min nodded, gloomily. 'The question is – which country is responsible for the investigation? Look at the map, and you'll see the problem.'

In one swift, easy movement, the Interpol ace came out of his chair and joined the little Captain by the wall-map.

U Min pointed to a spot about 20° 30′ N, 100° 15′ E. 'The borders of three countries meet at this point . . .' he said. 'Burma, Laos, Thailand.' His finger made a quick circle. 'Almost exactly the centre of the area in which the planes disappeared.'

He looked at The Hawk. 'So,' he shrugged, 'as the Americans say – whose baby is it?'

The Hawk grinned. 'You've missed one out,' he said. 'The British Police in Hong Kong are also interested. It's one of their companies losing the planes – and one of their insurance companies standing to lose a lot of money!'

U Min pulled a wry face. 'So?'

'So it's Interpol's baby – that way, we can work on behalf of all four countries.' The Hawk smiled broadly as he saw the look of relief in the Burmese policeman's eyes. Then he turned to the map again. 'How do we get to the Paitok mine?'

'By air,' answered U Min. 'They have a small landing strip.' His manner became brisk and efficient. 'I'll fix a plane.'

Pop Williams paced the low veranda of his bungalow like a caged tiger. He swung round to confront The Hawk, who was sitting relaxed, in a long chair.

'Insurance company – huh!' growled the old man, angrily. 'Worrying about their money! What about the two pilots?'

'Maybe they're all right – they might have baled out,' said The Hawk quietly.

Pop gave him a withering glance. 'Where they came down is the most rugged country in the East. They wouldn't have a hope!'

The Hawk stood up. 'Coincidence, isn't it?' he said. 'Two planes – both carrying a small fortune in rough rubies – and both disappear in the same area.'

Pop's eyes narrowed. 'I know what you're thinking, Inspector. Plenty of men would risk their necks for that money.'

'Including the pilots,' said The Hawk.

The old man shook his head wearily. 'I've thought of that too. I just can't believe it – I've known them for years.'

The sound of a plane warming up on the airstrip made The

Hawk turn quickly towards the sound. 'What's that?'

Pop moved to the veranda steps. 'Come and see,' he said. The two men climbed into the waiting jeep. 'It's what you might call old Pop Williams's last chance!'

Al Jones stood beside his aircraft and grinned broadly.

'You can relax this trip, Pop,' he said. 'There won't be any trouble!' He nodded towards the plane. 'Listen to that motor – sweet music.'

'It ought to be,' returned the mine-owner, tersely. 'I spent half the night checking every nut and bolt on her personally!'

The Hawk stared at the pilot. 'Why don't you take a different course,' he said. 'Avoid the trouble area.'

'That's what I keep telling him,' snapped Williams. 'But he's as obstinate as a mule!'

Jones's expression was hard and determined, as he faced the Interpol man. 'Inspector,' he said, 'two good pilots have disappeared on this run. Whatever has happened to them can happen to me, too. I want to know about it.'

Ten minutes later, The Hawk and Williams watched the plane take off. 'Well,' said the old man, as they made their way back to the mine compound, 'Jones is the best pilot Avron have got.'

Jean Collet looked at him quickly. 'Avron,' he said. 'That's the same company as the other two.'

For the next half hour, The Hawk strolled casually around the mine area. One by one, he questioned the workers and overseers. He knew that, if the loss of the planes – and the rubies – was not due to accident, then he was dealing with one of the most cleverly planned crimes he had ever come across. Was an employee of the mine supplying inside information?

But The Hawk got nowhere. Nobody had left the place for several weeks, and most of them had been working for Pop Williams for years. They were all solidly behind the old man, and seemed to have a genuine affection for him. He turned back thoughtfully towards the bungalow. As he did so, Jean saw the mine-owner come to the door of the radio-hut, his face lined with fear. Even before he shouted, The Hawk was sprinting flat out to join him.

'What is it?' jerked the Inspector, as he reached the hut.

Pop stared at him. 'I can't raise Jones!' he said. 'His radio's gone dead – just like the other two!'

'Where did you lose him this time?' The Hawk's voice was sharp and commanding.

'Same place,' answered Pop Williams, tersely. He pointed out the area on the wall map which covered most of one side of the tiny radio hut.

'When?' snapped The Hawk.

'About three minutes ago.' Pop's face was drawn and worried. He turned as Roper, the radio operator, burst into the hut. 'It's Jones,' he said, briefly. 'We've lost contact – like the others. Take over, Pete – and keep trying!'

The Hawk turned to face the owner of the Paitok Mine. 'What exactly happened?' he asked.

'We'd just agreed to keep a constant check while he was over the danger area.' Pop drew a circle on the map round a point about 20° 30′ N, 100° 15′ E. 'One minute the pilot was talking to me, next minute – nothing!'

'Right!' said The Hawk, incisively. 'Contact Police H.Q. at Rangoon. Tell them to request co-operation from the police in Laos and Thailand. I want a full-scale air search over the area as soon as they can get the planes off the ground.' He turned to the door.

Pop moved with him. 'Where are you going?' he asked anxiously.

The Hawk stared at the old man. His face was set and determined. 'This time, Mr Williams,' he said, 'the plane is going to be found!'

Captain U Min sat perched on the corner of his desk watching The Hawk, who was staring at a large-scale map with deep concentration. The Interpol man had arrived back at Rangoon Police Headquarters an hour before, but, apart from sketching in brief details of the situation at the Paitok Mine, he had said very little. Suddenly, he straightened up and looked across at U Min.

'Have you got a trained jungle scout?' he asked. 'A man who is familiar with this area?' He pointed to the map.

The little Burmese Captain looked at him, quizzically. 'What's on your mind?' he asked.

The Hawk again gestured to the map. 'Look at this.' U Min bent forward to watch as the Interpol agent explained.

'According to the Paitok Mine people, the three planes broke radio contact here . . . here . . . and here.' The Hawk made three little pencil crosses on the line of flight between Paitok and Honk Kong. 'Almost exactly the same place on each occasion – right?'

U Min nodded.

The Hawk drew a circle to enclose an area just forward of the crosses. 'This area is being swept now.'

Again U Min nodded. 'There are a dozen aircraft searching,' he said.

The Interpol man held his pencil poised over the map. 'All right,' he said. 'But supposing the plane didn't go *on* when it lost contact. Supposing it turned *back?*'

The Captain looked at him with sudden understanding. 'Then it would have come down somewhere – here.' His finger stabbed at the map.

The Hawk's pencil drew a second circle, this time behind the little cluster of crosses. 'Between the danger point and the Paitok Mine,' he said. He straightened up. 'And that's where I'm going to look.' He smiled. 'If you can supply a scout.'

Captain U Min shook his head doubtfully. 'That's no problem,' he said. 'Sergeant Cheing is one of the best in Burma. But it'll take weeks to cover even a small part of that area on foot. It's some of the toughest jungle country in the East.' He reached for the telephone. 'Let me switch the air search.'

'Do that,' said The Hawk. 'But I'm still going to take a look at ground level. Once an aircraft dives into those trees, it's completely swallowed up. It must be nearly impossible to spot any trace of it from the air.'

The little Burmese looked at him steadily. 'And on the ground,' he said, 'it will be like finding a grain of rice in a wheat field.'

The jeep churned its way through the muddy clearing and stopped on the river bank. The Hawk and Sergeant Cheing climbed out and stood for a moment easing their cramped limbs. The stockily built, brown-skinned Burmese showed his fine white teeth in a broad grin that seemed to be his permanent expression.

'Now we must go left or right, sir,' he said, in a sing-song voice. 'Impossible to go ahead, sir. Jeep cannot swim.' He beamed at The Hawk, happily.

The Hawk grinned. In the three days they had been together, he had developed a high regard for this tough little sergeant. Despite his happy, carefree manner and his quaint use of English, The Hawk recognised that he was a shrewd, resourceful and loyal partner.

The Interpol man reached into the jeep for his map.

'It's all right, Cheing,' he said, as he spread the map on the bonnet. 'We don't want to go ahead.'

He plotted their position. 'This river is a small tributary of the Salween.' He straightened up. 'For about ten miles it follows the direct line of flight taken by the three missing planes. We're going to follow it, too, along the banks.'

'That is a very clever thinking, sir,' beamed Chein. 'The plane breaking his engine sees river and prefers bath to meat skewer.' He pointed significantly to the towering jungle trees.

'It's worth taking a look,' nodded the Interpol detective.

'Then the look must be with our feet, sir.' Cheing started to get their rifles and trail packs out of the jeep. 'There is no track that we can follow.'

Hours later, the two men reached a point about three miles up-stream from where they had left the jeep. The Hawk slipped off his pack and eased his aching shoulders. More than ever now, he appreciated the worth of Sergeant Cheing. Without the jungle scout's uncanny flair for picking a trail where none, in fact, existed, their progress would have been reduced to a snail's pace.

He stared at the river. It was fast flowing, but not too deep. He felt reasonably confident that plenty of evidence would remain if a plane *had* crash-landed in it.

Suddenly, he tensed and swung round. Cutting through the incessant cacophony of jungle noises he heard a scream of terror. Unslinging his rifle, he plunged into the undergrowth and began forcing his way through in the direction of the cry.

'Take care, sir!' Cheing shouted a warning. For once, the Sergeant was left behind. In trying to slip out of his heavy pack, a buckle had snarled up in his cross belt. He struggled frantically to wrench it free.

The Hawk burst through the bushes on to a narrow trail. Like a photographic plate, his brain registered the scene in front of him. A small native boy crouched, terror stricken, a snarling leopard inching its way along the tree branch above. In that same fleeting instant, the leopard sprang – launching its body towards the boy with all the power in its powerful hindquarters!

With split-second reaction, The Hawk fired from the hip.

The bullet caught the big cat fair and square while it was still in

The bullet caught the big cat fair and square.

mid-air. It landed in a twisting, snarling heap not two yards from where the terrified boy was crouching.

Taking quick aim, The Hawk pumped two more bullets into the wounded animal, then rapidly jumped forward to drag the boy out of reach of the murderous, razor-sharp talons.

The leopard gave one last convulsive twitch – then lay limp and lifeless.

For the first time, The Hawk realised that the native boy was a dead weight against him. He eased the youngster to the ground and rolled him on to his back. His heart missed a beat – blood was pouring from a wound in the boy's head.

He looked up to find Sergeant Cheing standing beside him. For once, the little man was not smiling.

'The cat didn't touch him,' said The Hawk. 'One of the bullets must have ricochetted. Go and get the First Aid kit – quickly!'

Cheing did not move. 'Sorry, sir,' he said, still without smiling. 'It is an impossibility order, sir.'

The Hawk sprang to his feet, angrily. 'What d'you mean?'

Cheing shrugged his shoulders. 'I mean nothing, sir.' He turned and gestured towards the surrounding jungle. 'But I think, sir – they mean troubles!'

The Hawk looked round, quickly. As he did so, it seemed as if the undergrowth suddenly became alive. Armed tribesmen leapt from behind every tree and bush and closed in on the two police officers! Very soon, a menacing ring of angry faces surrounded them.

'They think you shot the boy also, as well as the leopard, sir.' Cheing translated the growls of the tribesmen.

The Hawk stared grimly at the blood oozing from the wound in the unconscious boy's head. 'Tell them they've got to let us get the First Aid kit,' he snapped. 'Before he bleeds to death!'

The Sergeant rapped out a stream of dialect, but his words seemed to have no effect on the grim-faced men. The Hawk's mouth tightened – whatever happened, he had to try to help the wounded youngster. Calmly and deliberately, he moved forward and knelt beside the prostrate body. Padding his handkerchief, he started to work on the ugly wound.

'*Sir!*' Cheing's warning shout was enough for the Interpol man. Without even turning his head, he threw himself sideways. *Thud!* The razor-sharp jungle knife buried itself in the soft ground within inches of his twisting shoulders.

The Hawk was on his feet like a cat and, in the same movement, he flung himself at Cheing. The tough little sergeant had snatched up his companion's rifle and was in the act of taking a snap shot at thc man who had thrown the knife. *Crack!* The bullet whistled harmlessly over the tribesmen's heads as The Hawk knocked the gun barrel up.

'No killing, Sergeant!' he rapped out. The fighting gleam slowly faded from Cheing's eyes.

'No, sir,' he said. He bent and pulled the jungle knife out of the ground, then turned to face its owner. With utter contempt in his voice, he spat out a stream of dialect. When he had finished, he sliced the blade of the knife hard across the steel rifle barrel, blunting the edge irretrievably. Then, with an almost casual gesture, he sent the useless weapon spinning in a gleaming arc to thud into the earth an inch from the man's foot.

Cheing's habitual broad grin had returned to his face as he turned back to The Hawk. 'Sir, I tell him he is a child, sir,' he beamed. 'And for a child to have a sharp knife is bad. Danger of finger chopping, sir.'

The Hawk smiled appreciatively. The quick succession of events had happened in a matter of moments, but he sensed that they had made the tribesmen hesitant and uncertain.

Deliberately, he turned back to the inert figure of the native boy. Again a shout made him spin round, but this time it was no warning.

'*Taung!*' The tribesmen were greeting a tall, dignified figure and moving respectfully aside as he came forward to face The Hawk. It was their headman. 'I am Taung.' He raised his hand in salutation. 'You tell me, please, what had happened here.'

The Hawk was unable to conceal a quick look of surprise at the man's knowledge of English. Taung eyed him gravely. 'Many time I work with the British soldiers in the war,' he said.

In a few crisp sentences, the Interpol man explained the situation. 'But how the boy was hurt, and how badly,' he finished, 'we have not had a chance to discover.' He gestured towards the encircling tribesmen.

'Sir!' Before the headman could speak, Sergeant Cheing's voice cut in. He was kneeling beside the wounded youngster, attempting some rough First Aid. He looked up, excitedly. 'Sir – he is waking up, sir!' The Hawk and Taung moved quickly to join him.

'It is Awa,' said Taung, as he recognised the limp form.

The boy's eyes flickered open. For a moment, he stared up at the three anxious faces bent over him; then he fixed his gaze on The Hawk and smiled. He whispered something which Cheing's keen ears were able to catch.

'He's thanking you for shooting the leopard, sir,' said the Sergeant.

The Hawk gave a short, humourless laugh. 'Tell him I'm sorry about shooting him, too!' As Cheing translated, the boy looked puzzled then anxious. He half sat up and directed a stream of chattering dialect at Taung. When he had finished, the headman turned to The Hawk with a broad smile.

'He says you did not shoot him. When you dragged him out of the way of the leopard's claws, he hit his head on something. He thinks it may have been a spiked branch amongst the bushes.'

From that moment, The Hawk and Sergeant Cheing were treated as honoured guests. Taung insisted that they return with him to the nearby jungle village to be present at the celebrations that would take place to mark the death of the leopard. From him, The Hawk learned that the beast had been terrorising the area for some weeks, and had claimed several victims.

The following morning found Cheing beaming happily. 'Sir,' he said eagerly. 'I think maybe perhaps we have very good time, sir!'

Sergeant Cheing groaned slightly as he struggled with his pack. The Hawk looked across at him and grinned.

'Maybe perhaps you had a too good very good time, Sergeant,' he said, imitating the little man's quaint English.

Cheing rubbed his stomach, ruefully. 'Sir – eating too much is beautiful when one eats. But it is very painfully after!'

The two men were preparing to leave Taung's village. The leopard-killing celebration had been well up to the Sergeant's expectations, and he had joined in enthusiastically – *too* enthusiastically!

The Hawk turned to greet Taung as he approached in company with a group of elders.

'It is agreed between us,' smiled the headman. 'We are happy to help you.'

Sergeant Cheing looked at The Hawk with a puzzled frown.

'I asked Taung if his young men would help us look for the missing plane,' explained The Hawk. 'A hundred pairs of eyes are better than two.'

'And five hundred are better still,' added Taung. 'I have sent runners to all the other villages along the river. They will help; I have told them exactly what to look for.'

The Hawk spread his map for Taung to see. 'This is the area I want searched.' His fingers described a circle on the map.

Taung nodded, gravely. 'If the plane is in the jungle – we will find it.' He looked at The Hawk. 'Our people are happy to show their thanks for killing the leopard.'

Two days later, a helicopter grounded gently in a small jungle clearing close by Taung's village. As Captain U Min got out, he was met by The Hawk and Sergeant Cheing. For a moment, the three men stood hunched against the blasting gusts of wind from the idling rotor blades.

'Urgent request helicopter – found plane!' U Min quoted The Hawk's radio message back at him. 'I thought I'd better come, too.' He glanced around the clearing. 'Where is it?'

'About eight miles south-west of here, according to Taung's men. Get in – we'll take a look.' The Hawk gestured towards the helicopter, and together the three men piled in.

Within ten minutes, they were hovering over the area which the headman had pin-pointed on The Hawk's map.

'*There!*' shouted The Hawk suddenly, pointing off to the right. The pilot swung the aircraft towards the long, irregular gap in the tree-tops which indicated the clearing they had been searching for.

As soon as the helicopter touched down, The Hawk was out, ducking under the rotor blades. He signalled the pilot to cut his engine, then sood surveying the long, narrow stretch of open ground.

'A good man could bring a small aircraft down here,' he said, as the others joined him.

'He could – but *did* he?' answered U Min, staring around the deserted area.

It was Sergeant Cheing's keen, jungle-wise eyes that spotted the irregularity in the thick, tangled brush along the edge of the clearing.

'Sir,' he said, pointing. 'There is something that is not what it is!'

He ran towards the spot, The Hawk and Captain U Min hard on his heels.

'Camouflage netting!' gasped U Min.

'Right!' snapped The Hawk grimly. He started ripping the stuff away. Suddenly he stopped, and glanced at the little Burmese Captain. 'You know something else?' he said. 'Taung's men can't count!' He swung all his strength on the curtain of netting. 'They said they'd found *one* plane . . .' With a crackling of twigs and branches, the camouflage collapsed. The Hawk stood back. Lined up in a neat row under the overhanging trees were all *three* of the missing planes – and they were completely undamaged.

The Hawk finished his examination of the three planes and walked over to join Captain U Min.

'All undamaged – all controls working – all petrol gauges registering three-quarters full,' he said, staring thoughtfully at the little Burmese. 'So what made them come down? All in the same spot?'

'Ten thousand pounds' worth of rough rubies!' The Captain's voice was hard.

'Yes,' nodded The Hawk. 'Which points to the pilots themselves.' His forehead creased in a puzzled frown. 'But why pick a spot like this? There must be a hundred better places where they could make a clean getaway!'

A rustle in the bushes caused both men to turn. Sergeant Cheing's beaming face confronted them; he had the carcass of a small water buck slung over his shoulder. 'While you are doing thinkings, sir, I am doing huntings,' he grinned. 'Lake Ko is very near. Very good for supplies, sir.'

'Food for thought, eh?' The Hawk smiled. 'No, thanks, Cheing.' He gazed reflectively at the three aircraft. 'Right now, the only thing I'm hungry for is important information.'

He turned briskly to U Min. 'I'd like Cheing to stay here and guard the planes. I want to go back to Rangoon and check on the Avron Charter Company!'

The Captain nodded. 'I'll have kit and supplies dropped here for you, Sergeant.'

Once again, in Captain U Min's office, The Hawk lounged back in his chair, staring through half-closed eyes at the slow, spinning blades of the fan overhead. His check on the Avron Company had proved negative. All the missing pilots had first-class references and records, so had the Company itself.

His keen brain went over the facts for the hundredth time. Again he came to the same conclusion – the three planes couldn't have landed in exactly the same spot by accident. Therefore, they must have been directed there. How? The only possible answer was – radio!

The Hawk came out of his chair fast. 'Come on!' he said, brusquely.

U Min grabbed his hat. 'Where now?' he asked.

'The Paitok Mine,' answered the Interpol man. 'I want a word with that radio operator!'

Peter Roper faced the two policemen across the tiny radio hut. 'The pilots made contact every fifteen minutes from the time they were airborne,' he said. 'It was regular routine.'

'Sure that's all?' queried The Hawk.

Roper shifted, uncertainly. 'Well – yes. Unless there was something special to report.' He looked slightly guilty. 'Or maybe they'd come through for a chat – it gets pretty dull up there at times.'

'Did that happen on the last three flights?' Captain U Min snapped.

'It might have,' said Roper, defensively. 'I don't remember.'

'Then you'd better start trying!' The Hawk's voice was hard. 'I want to know every last word those three pilots said in the fifteen minutes before they finally broke contact!'

'Hold it!' The three men turned to find Pop Williams standing in the doorway. He glared angrily at The Hawk. 'I'm not having

Pete browbeaten by you or anyone else!' He paused. 'Besides, he can't tell you what he doesn't know. During the times the planes broke contact. I was on the set myself. There wasn't a word from any of them, I can assure you!'

'Thank you, Mr Williams.' The Hawk spoke in an easy voice, but his eyes held a gleam of understanding. 'Just two more questions. Why have you been shipping such valuable payloads recently?'

Pop shrugged. 'To keep this mine going, I need new plant. All our present machinery is out of date. I was going to re-equip completely – that takes a lot of money, you know.'

The Hawk nodded. 'I see,' he said. 'And why did you keep all those valuable stones here on the site? Why not in the bank?'

'Just habit, I guess.' Williams grinned suddenly. 'Old-timers like Frank and me never got used to banks.'

'Frank?' queried The Hawk.

Pop pointed to a small snapshot hanging on the wall by the transmitter. 'Frank Porter,' he said. 'He was my partner for twenty years.' He sighed. 'He died four months ago.'

The Hawk studied the photograph. It showed a grizzled-looking man holding a fishing rod in one hand and a sizeable string of fish in the other. There was a hastily scribbled place-name and date across one corner, in faded ink.

'Taken five years ago,' said Pop Williams reminiscently.

'Seems like a keen fisherman,' nodded the Interpol ace. He turned towards the door. 'Well, thanks again, Mr Williams. I think you've told me everything that I wanted to know.'

Outside the hut, The Hawk grabbed U Min's arm and hustled him out of earshot of the others. 'Captain!' His voice was urgent. 'Don't let Williams out of your sight and above all, don't let him know we've found the planes!'

The bewildered little Burmese nodded. 'Are you sure you know what you are doing?' he queried.

'Almost,' rapped The Hawk. 'I'll be certain when I find them!'
'Find who?' U Min stared at him.
'A dead man!' grinned The Hawk. 'And three live ones– I hope!' He turned and headed for the Paitok jeep. He wanted to reach the landing strip and the helicopter in a hurry.

Sergeant Cheing was bursting with curiosity as he watched The Hawk. The Interpol man had cut himself a long stick and was carrying out a dipstick test on the petrol tanks of the three planes.
'Sir!' The Sergeant could restrain himself no longer. 'I am not understandable. What for do you make a test?'
'For this, Cheing,' smiled The Hawk. He held out the stick for the Sergeant to see. It was bone dry.
'The reason the planes came down – no petrol!' He continued talking, but it was half to himself. 'The petrol gauges were fixed – they still read three-quarters full. This is the only possible landing place for miles. He must have known exactly how much petrol to put in so that their engines would cut out within easy gliding distance. Then he'd talk them on to it by means of the radio.'
Cheing had followed his reasoning. 'But who would be doing this, sir?' he asked.
'The owner of the Paitok Mine,' said The Hawk. 'And a dead man.' He slapped Cheing on the shoulder. 'Let's go,' he said cheerfully. 'It's the dead man I want to find first, and I know where to look – somewhere along the shores of Lake Ko!'
The two men had covered nearly three miles, following the perimeter of the lake, when Sergeant Cheing, in the lead, suddenly held up his hand. The Hawk eased up alongside him.
'You were rightfully thinking, sir,' muttered the Sergeant. He pointed ahead to where a small hut had been built beneath two huge, jungle trees. With the undergrowth crowding in on three

sides, it must have been practically invisible from every angle except directly across the lake.

Crack! The sound sent both men diving for cover as a bullet ricochetted off a tree close to The Hawk's head.

The Hawk acted. 'Fire at the hut!' he rapped. 'Keep him busy until you see I'm in position, then try and get him to come to the door.' Then, as silently as any jungle creature, he turned and disappeared.

For a while, the little Sergeant enjoyed himself, slipping from cover to cover as he exchanged shots with the man in the hut. Then a slight movement in one of the trees overhanging the building caught his eye. Easing his way along a branch, ten feet above the doorway, was The Hawk. The Interpol man lifted his hand in a signal. Cheing raised his bush hat on the muzzle of his rifle to invite another shot. When it came, he let out a realistic shout of pain and immediately rolled to another position some yards away. In almost the same movement, he was on his feet, breaking cover and running towards the hut.

'Don't shoot! Don't shoot!' he yelled. He threw his rifle away and stood stock still, facing the hut.

A grey-haired, tough-looking man came out. He covered Cheing with his rifle. 'Who are you?' he shouted.

Cheing moved forward with his hands up. 'Sir – I am Police Sergeant Cheing, please, sir.' He sounded scared.

The man gave an ugly grin. 'Police,' he growled. 'That's all I wanted to know!' He raised the rifle . . .

Thud! The Hawk plummeted out of the tree like a stone, landing fair and square on the shoulders of the would-be killer! With all the breath knocked out of his body, the man collapsed on the ground and lay gasping for air.

'Well done, Cheing,' smiled The Hawk, picking up the rifle. 'But you shouldn't have taken such a risk.'

'It was the best way, sir, to attract his attention,' beamed

Cheing. He looked at the gasping man. 'Is this the ghost, sir?'

The Hawk nodded. 'He died four months ago – officially,' he said. 'It's Frank Porter! Now, let's find the others.'

Standing guard over Porter, Cheing watched tensely as the Hawk disappeared into the hut. Minutes later, he showed his white teeth in the biggest grin even he was capable of . . .

Stumbling out into the open, blinking their eyes against the sunlight, came the three pilots of the missing planes!

Pop Williams stared morosely at The Hawk. 'What gave us away?' he asked.

Captain U Min had formally arrested the two owners of the Paitok Mine, and now the four men were crowded into the tiny radio hut, waiting for a plane that would take them back to Rangoon.

The Hawk pointed to Porter's photograph. 'The inscription clinched it,' he said. 'Ko Lake – 1955.'

Pop gave a sour grin. 'We might have got away with it,' he growled. 'Twenty years hard sweat Frank and I put into this mine, and all we'd got at the end of it was a measly £10,000 between us. By claiming insurance on three phoney shipments, we could have trebled it inside a couple of months.'

'By fraud!' snapped U Min.

The sound of a plane landing on the airstrip took Captain U Min to the window. 'That's it,' he said. 'Let's go!'

The Hawk looked at Williams, and grinned. 'And *this* trip, Pop,' he said, 'I'm going to check the refuelling myself!'